SEEDS OF EARTH

SEEDS OF EARTH

BOOK 1 OF
HUMANITY'S FIRE

MICHAEL COBLEY

www.orbitbooks.net

ORBIT

First published in Great Britain in 2009 by Orbit

A CIP catalogue record for this book is
available from the British Library.

ISBN 978-1-84149-632-0

Typeset in Sabon by M Rules
Printed and bound in Great Britain by
Clays Ltd, St Ives plc

Papers used by Orbit are natural, renewable and recyclable
products made from wood grown in sustainable forest and certified
in accordance with the rules of the Forest Stewardship Council.

Mixed Sources
Product group from well-managed
forests and other controlled sources
www.fsc.org Cert no. SGS-COC-004081
© 1996 Forest Stewardship Council
FSC

Orbit
An imprint of
Little, Brown Book Group
100 Victoria Embankment
London EC4Y 0DY

An Hachette Livre UK Company
www.hachettelivre.co.uk

www.orbitbooks.net

For Susan

Who brought the sun into my life

PROLOGUE

DARIEN INSTITUTE: HYPERION DATA
RECOVERY PROJECT

Cluster Location – Subsidiary Hardmem Substrate (Deck 9 quarters)
Tranche – 298
Decryption Status – 9th pass, 26 video files recovered

File 15 – The Battle of Mars (Swarm War)
Veracity – Virtual Re-enactment
Original Time Log – 16:09:24, 23 November 2126

>>>>>>   <<<<<<

FADE IN:
CAPTION:

MARS
THE CRATER PLAIN: OLYMPUS MONS
19 MARCH 2126

The Sergeant was on the carrier's command deck, checking and rechecking the engineering console's modifications, when voices began clamouring over his helmet comm.

'Marine force stragglers incoming with enemy units in pursuit . . .'

'. . . eight, nine Swarmers, maybe ten . . .'

The Sergeant cursed, grabbed his heavy carbine and left the command deck as quickly as his combat armour would allow.

The clatter of his boots echoed down the vessel's spinal corridor while he issued a string of terse orders. By the time he reached the wrecked and gaping doors of the rear deployment hold, the stragglers had arrived. Five wounded and unconscious, all from the Indonesia regiment, going by their helmet flashes. As the last was being carried up the ramp, the leading Swarmers came into view over the brow of a rocky ridge about 80 metres away.

A first glimpse revealed a nightmare jumble of claws, spikes and gleaming black eye-clusters. Swarm biology had many reptilian similarities yet their appearance was unavoidably insectoid. With six, eight, ten or more limbs, they could be as small as a pony or as big as a whale, depending on their specialisation. These were bull-sized skirmishers, eleven black-and-green monsters that were unlimbering tine-snouted weapons as they rushed down towards the crippled carrier.

'Hold your fire,' the Sergeant said, glancing at the six marines crouched behind the improvised barricade of ammo cases and deck plating. These were all that were left to him after the Colonel and the rest had left in the hovermags a few hours ago, heading for the caldera and the Swarm's main hive. One of them hunched his shoulders a little, head tilting to aim down his carbine's sights . . .

'I said wait,' said the Sergeant, gauging the diminishing distance. 'Ready aft turrets . . . acquire targets . . . fire!'

Streams of heavy-calibre shells converged on the leading Swarmers, knocking them off their spidery legs. Then the Sergeant cursed when he saw them right themselves, protected by the bio-armour which had confounded Earth's military ever since the beginning of the invasion two years ago.

'Pulse rounds,' the Sergeant shouted. 'Now!'

Bright bolts began to pound the Swarmers, dense knots of energised matter designed to simultaneously heat and corrode their armour. The enemy returned fire, their weapons delivering repeating arcs of long, thin black rounds, but as the turret jockeys focused their targeting the Swarmers broke off and scattered. The Sergeant then ordered his men to open up, joining in with his own carbine, and the withering crossfire tore into the weakened, confused enemies. In less than a minute, nothing was left alive or in one piece out on the rocky slope.

The defending marines exchanged laughs and grins, and knocked gauntleted knuckles together. The Sergeant barely had time to draw breath and reload his carbine when the consoleman's urgent voice came over the comm:

'Sergeant! – airborne contact, three klicks and closing!'

Immediately, he swung round and made for the starboard companionway, shouldering his carbine as he climbed. 'What's their profile, soldier?'

'Hard to tell – half the sensor suite is junk . . .'

'Get me something and quick!'

He then ordered all four turrets to target the approaching craft and was clambering out of the carrier's topside hatch when the consoleman came back to him.

'IFF confirms it's a friendly, Sergeant – it's a vortiwing, and the pilot is asking for you.'

'Patch him through.'

One of his helmet's miniscreens blinked suddenly and showed the vortiwing pilot. He was possibly German, going by the instructions on the bulkhead behind him.

'Sergeant, I've not much time,' the pilot said in accented English. 'I'm to evacuate you and your men up to orbit . . .'

'Sorry, Lieutenant, but . . . my commanding officer is down in that caldera, engaging in combat! Look, the brink of the caldera is less than half a klick away – you could airlift me and my men over there before returning to—'

'Request denied. My orders are specific. Besides, every unit that made it down there has been overwhelmed and destroyed, whole regiments and brigades, Sergeant. I'm sorry . . .' The pilot reached up to adjust controls. 'ETD in less than five minutes, Sergeant. Please have your men ready.'

The miniscreen went dead. The Sergeant leaned on the topside rail and stared bitterly at the kilometre-long furrow which the carrier had gouged in the sloping flank of Olympus Mons. Then he gave the order to abandon ship.

In the shroud-like Martian sky overhead, the vortiwing transport grew from a speck to a broad-built craft descending on four
gimbal-mounted spinjets. Landing struts found purchase on the
carrier's upper hull, and amid the howling blast of the engines the
walking wounded and the stretcher cases were lifted into the
transport's belly hold. The turret jockeys, the consoleman and
his half-dozen marines were following suit when the German
pilot's voice spoke suddenly.

'Large number of flying Swarmers heading our way, Sergeant.
Suggest you get aboard fast.'

As the last of his men climbed up into the vortiwing, the
Sergeant turned to face the caldera of Olympus Mons. Through a
haze of windblown dust and the thin black fumes of battle, he
saw a dense cloud of dark motes rising just a few klicks away. It
took only a moment to realise how quickly they would be here,
and for him to decide what to do.

'Best you button up and get going, Lieutenant,' he said as he
leaped back into the carrier and sealed the hatch behind him. 'I
can keep them busy with our turrets, give you time to make orbit.'

'*Nein*! Sergeant, I order you—'

'Apologies, sir, but you'd never get away otherwise, so my task
is clear.'

He cut the link as he rushed back along to the command deck,
closing hatches as he went. True, the Colonel's science officer had
slaved all four of the turrets to the engineering console, but that
wasn't the only modification he had carried out . . .

The roar of the vortiwing's spinjets grew to a shriek, landing
struts loosened their grip and the transport lurched free.
Moments later, the fourfold angled thrust was driving it upwards
on a steep trajectory. Some of the Swarm outriders were already
leading the flying host on an intercept course, until the carrier's
turrets opened fire upon them. Yet they would still have kept on
after the ascending prey, had not the carrier itself now shifted like
a great wounded beast and risen slowly from the long gouge it
had made in the ground. Curtains of dust and grit fell from its
underside, along with shattered fragments of hull plating and

exterior sensors, and when the carrier turned its battered prow towards the centre of the caldera the Swarm host altered its course.

On the command deck, the Sergeant sweated and swore as he struggled to coax every last erg from protesting engines. Damage sustained during the atmospheric descent had left the carrier unable to make a safe landing on the caldera floor, hence the Colonel's decision to continue in the hovermags. However, a safe landing was not what the Sergeant had in mind.

As the ship headed into the caldera, steadily gaining height, the groan of overloaded substructures came up through the deck. Even as he glanced at the glowing panels, red telltales started to flicker, warnings that some of the port suspensors were close to operational tolerance. But most of his attention was focused on the host of Swarmers now converging on the Earth vessel.

Suddenly the carrier was enfolded in a swirling cloud of the creatures, some of which landed on the hull, scrabbling for hold points, seeking entrance. Almost at the same time, two suspensors failed and the ship listed to port. The Sergeant boosted power to the port burners, ignoring the beeping alarms and the crashing, hammering sounds coming from somewhere amidships. The carrier straightened up as it reached the zenith of its trajectory, a huge missile that the Sergeant was aiming directly at the Swarm Hive.

Ten seconds into the dive the clangorous hammering came nearer, perhaps a hatch or two away from the command deck.

Twenty seconds into the dive, with the pitted, grey-brown spires of the Hive looming in the louvred viewport, the starboard aft burner blew. The Sergeant cut power to the port aft engine and boosted the starboard for'ard into the red.

Thirty seconds into the dive, amid the deafening cacophony of metallic hammering and the roar of the engines, the hatch to the command deck finally burst open. A grotesque creature that was half-wasp, half-alligator, struggled to squeeze through the gap. It froze for a second when it saw the structures of the Hive rushing up to meet the carrier head-on, then frantically reversed direction and was gone. The Sergeant tossed a thermite grenade after it and turned to face the viewport, arms spread wide, laughing . . .

CUT TO:

VIEW OF OLYMPUS MONS FROM ORBIT

Visible within its attendant cloud of Swarmers, the brigade carrier leaves a trail of leaking gases and fluids in its wake as it plummets towards the Hive complex. The perspective suddenly zooms out, showing much of the wreckage-strewn, battle-scarred caldera as the carrier impacts. For a moment there is only an outburst of debris from the collision, then three bright explosions in quick succession obscure the outlines of the hive . . .

VOICE OVER:
In the first phase of the Battle of Mars, a number of purpose-built heavy boosters were used to send a flotilla of asteroids against the Swarm Armada, thus drawing key vessels away from Mars orbit. The main battle, and ground offensive, cost Earth over 400,000 dead and the loss of seventy-nine major warships as well as scores of support craft. This act of sacrifice did not destroy all the Overminds of the Swarm or deter them from their purpose. Yet vast stores of bioweapons, like the missiles that devastated cities in China, Europe and America, were destroyed along with several hatching chambers, thus halting the production of fresh Swarm warriors and delaying the expected assault on Earth.

That battle brought grief and sorrow to all of Humanity, yet it also bought us a breathing space, five crucial months during which the construction of three interstellar colony ships was completed, three out of the original fifteen. The last of them, the *Tenebrosa*, was launched from the high-orbit Poseidon Docks just four days ago, following its sister ships, the *Hyperion* and the *Forrestal*, on a trajectory away from the enemy's main forces. All three vessels are fitted with a revolutionary new translight drive, allowing them to cross vast distances via the strange subreality of hyperspace. First to make the translight jump was the *Hyperion*, then two days later the *Forrestal*, and the *Tenebrosa* will be the last. Their journeys will be determined by custodian AIs programmed to evade pursuit with random course changes, and thereafter to search for Earthlike worlds suitable for colonisation.

And so they depart, three arks bearing Humanity's hope for survival, three seeds of Earth flying out into the vast and starry night. Now we must turn our attention and all our strength to the onslaught that will soon be upon us. In twelve days, spearhead formations of the Swarm will land on the Moon and at once attack our civilian and military outposts there. We know what to expect. The Swarm's strategy of slaughter and obliterate has never wavered, so we know that there will be no pity, no mercy and no quarter when, at last, they enter the skies above Earth.

Yet for all that the Swarm soldiers are regimented drones, their leaders, the Overminds, must themselves be sentient and able to learn, otherwise they would not have developed space travel. So if the Overminds can learn, let us be their teachers – let us teach them what it means to attack the cradle of Humanity . . .

>>>>>>   <<<<<<

END OF FILE . . .

PART ONE

1

GREG

Dusk was creeping in over the sea from the east as Greg Cameron walked Chel down to the zep station. The great mass of Giant's Shoulder loomed on the right side of the path, its shadowy darkness speckled with the tiny blue glows of *ineka* beetles, while a fenced-off sheer drop fell away to the left. The sky was cloudless, laying bare the starmist which swirled for ever through the upper atmosphere of Darien. Tonight it was a soft purple tinged with threads of roseate, a restful, slow-shifting ghost sky.

But Greg knew that his companion was anything but restful. In the light of the pathway lamps, the Uvovo stalked along with head down and bony, four-fingered hands gripping the chest straps of his harness. They were a slender, diminutive race with a bony frame, and large amber eyes set in a small face. Glancing at him, Greg smiled.

'Chel, don't worry – you'll be fine.'

The Uvovo looked up and seemed to think for a moment before his finely furred features broke into a wide smile.

'Friend-Gregori,' came his hollow, fluty voice. 'Whether I ride in a dirigible or make the shuttle journey to our blessed Segrana, I am always amazed to discover myself alive at the end!'

They laughed together as they continued down the side of Giant's Shoulder. It was a cool, clammy night and Greg wished he had worn something heavier than just a work shirt.

'And you've still no idea why they're holding this *zinsilu* at Ibsenskog?' Greg said. For the Uvovo, a *zinsilu* was part life evaluation, part meditation. 'I mean, the Listeners do have access to the government comnet if they need to contact any of the seeders and scholars . . .' Then something occurred to him. 'Here, they're not going to reassign ye, are they? Chel, I won't be able to manage both the dig and the daughter-forest reports on my own! – I really need your help.'

'Do not worry, friend-Gregori,' said the Uvovo. 'Listener Weynl has always let it be known that my role here is considered very important. Once this *zinsilu* is concluded, I am sure that I will be returning without delay.'

I hope you're right, Greg thought. *The Institute isna very forgiving when it comes to shortcomings and unachieved goals.*

'After all,' Chel went on, 'Your Founders' Victory celebrations are only a few days away and I want to be here to observe all your ceremonies and rituals.'

Greg gave a wry half-grin. 'Aye . . . well, some of our "rituals" can get a bit boisterous . . .'

By now the gravel path was levelling off as they approached the zep station and overhead Greg could hear the faint peeps of *umisk* lizards calling to each other from their little lairs scattered across the sheer face of Giant's Shoulder. The station was little more than a buttressed platform with a couple of buildings and a five-yard-long covered gantry jutting straight out. A government dirigible was moored there, a gently swaying 50-footer consisting of two cylindrical gasbags lashed together with taut webbing and an enclosed gondola hanging beneath. The skin of the inflatable sections was made from a tough composite fabric, but exposure to the elements and a number of patch repairs gave it a ramshackle appearance, in common with most of the workaday government zeplins. A light glowed in the cockpit of the boatlike gondola, and the rear-facing, three-bladed propeller turned lazily in the steady breeze coming in from the sea.

Fredriksen, the station manager, waved from the waiting-room door while a man in a green and grey jumpsuit emerged from the gantry to meet them.

'Good day, good day,' he said, regarding first Greg then the

Uvovo. 'I am Pilot Yakov. If either of you is Scholar Cheluvahar, I am ready to depart.'

'I am Scholar Cheluvahar,' Chel said.

'Most excellent. I shall start the engine.' He nodded at Greg then went back to the gantry, ducking as he entered.

'Mind to send a message when you reach Ibsenskog,' Greg told Chel. 'And don't worry about the flight – it'll be over before you know it . . .'

'Ah, friend-Gregori – I am of the Warrior Uvovo. Such tests are breath and life itself!'

Then with a smile he turned and hurried after the pilot. A pure electric whine came from the gondola's aft section, rising in pitch as the prop spun faster. Greg heard the solid knock of wooden gears as the station manager cranked in the gantry then triggered the mooring cable releases. Suddenly free upon the air, the dirigible swayed as it began drifting away, picking up speed and banking away from the sheer face of Giant's Shoulder. The trip down to Port Gagarin was only a half-hour hop, after which Chel would catch a commercial lifter bound for the Eastern Towns and the daughter-forest Ibsenskog. Greg could not see his friend at any of the gondola's opaque portholes but he waved anyway for about a minute, then just stood watching the zeplin's descent into the deepening dusk. Feeling a chill in the air, he fastened some of his shirt buttons while continuing to enjoy the peace. The zep station was nearly 50 feet below the main dig site but it was still some 300 feet above sea level. Giant's Shoulder itself was an imposing spur jutting eastwards from a towering massif known as the Kentigern Mountains, a raw wilderness largely avoided by trappers and hunters, although the Uvovo claimed to have explored a good deal of it.

As the zeplin's running lamps receded, Greg took in the panorama before him, the coastal plain stretching several miles east to the darkening expanse of the Korzybski Sea and the lights of towns scattered all around its long western shore. Far off to the south was the bright glitterglow of Hammergard, sitting astride a land bridge separating Loch Morwen from the sea; beyond the city, hidden by the misty murk of evening, was a ragged coastline of sealochs and fjords where the Eastern Towns nestled. South of them were hills and a high valley cloaked by the daughter-forest Ibsenskog. Before his standpoint were the jewelled clusters of Port Gagarin, slightly to the south, High Lochiel a few miles northwest, and Landfall, where the cannibalised hulk of the old colonyship, the *Hyperion*, lay in the sad tranquillity of Membrance Vale. Then further north were New Kelso, Engerhold, Laika, and the logging and farmer settlements scattering north and west, while off past the northeast horizon was Trond.

His mood darkened. Trond was the city he had left just two short months ago, fleeing the trap of his disastrous cohabitance with Inga, a mistake whose wounds were still raw. But before his thoughts could begin circling the pain of it, he stood straighter and breathed in the cold air, determined not to dwell on bitterness and regret. Instead, he turned his gaze southwards to see the moonrise.

A curve of blue-green was gradually emerging from behind the jagged peaks of the Hrothgar Range which lined the horizon: Nivyesta, Darien's lush arboreal moon, brimming with life and mystery, and home to the Uvovo, wardens of the girdling forest they called Segrana. Once, millennia ago, the greater part of their arboreal civilisation had inhabited Darien, which they called Umara, but some indeterminate catastrophe had wiped out the planetary population, leaving those on the moon alive but stranded.

On a clear night like this, the starmist in Darien's upper atmosphere wreathed Nivyesta in a gauzy halo of mingling colours like some fabulous eye staring down on the little niche that humans had made for themselves on this alien world. It was a sight that never failed to raise his spirits. But the night was growing chilly now, so he buttoned his shirt to the neck and began retracing his steps. He was halfway up the path when his comm chimed. Digging it out of his shirt pocket he saw that it was his elder brother and decided to answer.

'Hi, Ian – how're ye doing?' he said, walking on.

'Not so bad. Just back from manoeuvres and looking forward to FV Day, chance to get a wee bit of R&R. Yourself?'

Greg smiled. Ian was a part-time soldier with the Darien Volunteer Corps and was never happier than when he was marching across miles of sodden bog or scaling basalt cliffs in the Hrothgars, apart from when he was home with his wife and daughter.

'I'm settling in pretty well,' he said. 'Getting to grips with all the details of the job, making sure that the various teams file their reports on something like a regular schedule, that sort of thing.'

'But are you happy staying at the temple site, Greg? – because you know that we've plenty of room here and I know that you loved living in Hammergard, before the whole Inga episode . . .'

Greg grinned.

'Honest, Ian, I'm fine right here. I love my work, the surroundings are peaceful and the view is fantastic! I appreciate the offer, big brother, but I'm where I want to be.'

'S'okay, laddie, just making sure. Have you heard from Ned since you got back, by the way?'

'Just a brief letter, which is okay. He's a busy doctor these days . . .'

Ned, the third and youngest brother, was very poor at keeping in touch, much to Ian's annoyance, which often prompted Greg to defend him.

'Aye, right, busy. So – when are we likely to see ye next? Can ye not come down for the celebrations?'

'Sorry, Ian, I'm needed here, but I do have a meeting scheduled at the Uminsky Institute in a fortnight – shall we get together then?'

'That sounds great. Let me know nearer the time and I'll make arrangements.'

They both said farewell and hung up. Greg strolled leisurely on, smiling expectantly, keeping the comm in his hand. As he walked he thought about the dig site up on Giant's Shoulder, the many hours he'd spent painstakingly uncovering this carven stela

or that section of intricately tiled floor, not to mention the countless days devoted to cataloguing, dating, sample analysis and
correlation matching. Sometimes – well, a lot of the time – it was
a frustrating process, as there was nothing to guide them in com-
prehending the meaning of the site's layout and function. Even the
Uvovo scholars were at a loss, explaining that the working of
stone was a skill lost at the time of the War of the Long Night,
one of the darker episodes in Uvovo folklore.

Ten minutes later he was near the top of the path when his
comm chimed again, and without looking at the display he
brought it up and said:

'Hi, Mum.'

'*Gregory, son, are you well?*'

'Mum, I'm fine, feeling okay and happy too, really . . .'

'*Yes, now that you're out of her clutches! But are you not
lonely up there amongst those cold stones and only the little
Uvovo to talk to?*'

Greg held back the urge to sigh. In a way, she was right – it was
a secluded existence, living pretty much on his own in one of the
site cabins. There was a three-man team of researchers from the
university working on the site's carvings, but they were all
Russian and mostly kept to themselves, as did the Uvovo teams
who came in from the outlying stations now and then. Some of
the Uvovo scholars he knew by name but only Chel had become
a friend.

'A bit of solitude is just what I need right now, Mum. Beside,
there's always people coming and going up here.'

'*Mm-hmm. There were always people coming and going here
at the house when your father was a councilman, but most of
them I did not care for, as you might recall.*'

'Oh, I remember, all right.'

Greg also remembered which ones stayed loyal when his father
fell ill with the tumour that eventually killed him.

'*As a matter of fact, I was discussing both you and your father
with your Uncle Theodor, who came by this afternoon.*'

Greg raised his eyebrows. Theodor Karlsson was his mother's

oldest brother and had earned himself a certain notoriety and the nickname 'Black Theo' for his role in the abortive Winter Coup twenty years ago. As a punishment he had been kept under house arrest on New Kelso for twelve years, during which he fished, studied military history and wrote, although on his release the Hammergard government informed him that he was forbidden to publish anything, fact or fiction, on pain of bail suspension. For the last eight years he had tried his hand at a variety of jobs, while keeping in occasional contact with his sister, and Greg vaguely recalled that he had somehow got involved with the Hyperion Data Project . . .

'So what's Uncle Theo been saying?'

'*Well, he has heard some news that will amaze you – I can still scarcely believe it myself. It is going to change everyone's life.*'

'Don't tell me that he wants to overthrow the government again.'

'*Please, Gregori, that is not even slightly funny . . .*'

'Sorry, Mum, sorry. Please, what did he say?'

From where he stood at the head of the path he had a clear view of the dig, the square central building looking bleached and grey in the glare of the nightlamps. As Greg listened his expression went from puzzled to astonished, and he let out an elated laugh as he looked up at the stars. Then he got his mother to tell him again.

'Mum, you've got to be kidding me! . . .'

2

THEO

Theodor Karlsson had a spring in his step as he walked up a private footpath towards the presidential villa. Tall, thick bushes concealed it from inquisitive eyes, and waist-high lantern posts shed pools of subdued radiance all along its length. His long, heavy coat was three-quarters fastened and his custom-soled shoes made little noise on the tiled path. The villa grounds were dark and still in the cool of the evening but Karlsson could almost smell the weave of seamless security which enclosed the place. There was a visible perimeter of patrols and cameras down at the main wall and gate, and a pair of guards at the side-door up ahead, but Theo knew that the best security was seldom seen. The question that loomed large in his mind, however, was who was it all meant to keep out?

The guards, both wearing dark imager eye-pieces, were muttering into collar mikes as he approached.

'Good evening, Major,' said one. 'If you could look into the scanner with your right eye.'

He stepped up to the plain wooden door, followed instructions, and moments later he heard several muffled thuds. The door swung open. Inside he was met by a composed, middle-aged woman who took his coat then led him along a narrow, windowless corridor, past a number of bland, pastoral paintings, then up a poorly lit curve of steps to a landing with two doors. Without pause she continued through the left one and Karlsson found himself in a warm, carpeted study.

'Please make yourself comfortable, Major Karlsson. The president will see you shortly.'

'Thank you . . .' Theo began to say, but she was already leaving the room, closing the door behind her. He surveyed his surroundings, a medium-sized room with well-stocked bookshelves, a log fire burning in the hearth, and an ornate adjustable lamp hanging over a large desk. A ceiling-high rack of shelves partially concealed a second door in one corner and a hand-eye security lock.

The belly of the beast, he thought. *Or maybe the lion's den.*

It always felt like this whenever he had these meetings with Sundstrom, no matter where they took place. Which was why he had got into the habit of visiting his sister, Solvjeg, shortly beforehand, just to quietly let her know where he would be for the next few hours, with a veiled hint as to whom he was meeting. Today, though, she was full of eagerness to know if the rumours were true, that there had been a signal from Earth.

Theo grinned, recalling the moment. The message had apparently been received that morning, yet he had heard it sixth-hand from an old friend in the Corps by mid-afternoon, so it was no surprise that Solvjeg picked it up from the old girls' network. Now it was evening and the rumours were all over the colony. Even Kirkland, the leader of the opposition, had issued a statement, but so far there had been no official confirmation from either the council or the president's office.

A ship from Earth! he thought. *So now we know that the human race survived the Swarm War, but did we beat them or did other survivors flee from Earth? And what happened to the other two colonyships, the* Forrestal *and the* Tenebrosa?

His mind was a ferment of questions, the outcome of a year and a half of unpaid work at the Hyperion Data Project. It had been his own soldiering experience that had led to helping one of the supervisors with the transcription of a military treatise in Swedish. It turned out to be a Swedish translation of *On War* by the Prussian Von Clausewitz, a book that Theo had only ever read references to. Engrossed in the steady work of extracting it from the *Hyperion*'s reams of raw text, and having to guess where the paragraphs began, he had become fascinated with the *Hyperion* and her sister ships, including the ones that were never launched . . .

The door behind the shelves in the corner opened and the president entered, his wheelchair pushed by a young man in a brown and grey onepiece.

'Evening, Theodor,' Sundstrom said, dismissing the attendant then dextrously propelling himself across the room to stop behind his desk.

'Good evening, Holger,' Theo said. 'Interesting study you have, some nice books too.' He indicated a glass-fronted cabinet. 'Is that the Serov edition of *Nineteen Eighty-four* over there?'

'Yes, it is,' said Sundstrom. 'Collins's *Moonstone* is rarer, of course, but Orwell is much more of a politician's writer.'

Theo chuckled. Vasili Serov had been a systems tech on board the colonyship *Hyperion* and had played a decisive role in the deadly struggle against the ship's Command AI. In the Hardship Years that followed, Serov had cobbled together a crude manual printing press and painstakingly typeset those few novels sitting in datapods that had not been linked to the shipboard comnet. The huge memorybanks of the *Hyperion*, buried under layers of encryption by the ship AI, were to remain inaccessible for decades, so Serov's work had proved invaluable to the surviving colonists.

For a moment both men were thoughtfully silent, then Sundstrom spoke:

'I assume you've heard.'

'About two hours before I got your invitation,' Theo said, watching him. 'So it's true – Earth has sent a ship to find us, which means that the Swarm were defeated and all our troubles are over, yes?'

Sundstrom gave a thin smile.

'If only matters were that straightforward. Theo, the Swarm War lasted two and a half years before the Hegemony helped chase the last of the Swarm away, and that was a century and a

half ago, which is a long time in the history of a culture or a society. Just think about all the strife and upheavals that our little
enclave has been through – the Hyperion AI war, First Families
against the New Generation, the Consolidators versus the
Expansionists, the New Town Secession – and multiply that to a
planetary level.' He shook his head. 'I'm afraid that our lives are
about to become quite a bit more complicated, not to say uncomfortable.'

Frowning, Theo sat back, going over in his mind the dozen or
so meetings he'd had with Sundstrom in the last two years.

'You speak as if you know something I've not heard about . . .'
He leaned forward. 'When you first asked me to join your little
cabal, you said that we were preparing for the worst, like the possibility of occupation by an unfriendly species. Now it seems that
there's an Earth ship due in . . . how long?'

'Fourteen hours.'

'Less than a day, fine,' Theo said. 'Yet your demeanour is not
that of, shall we say, delighted anticipation.' Then he laughed
and snapped his fingers. 'Or has it been this contact with Earth
that we've been preparing for all along?'

Sundstrom leaned back in his wheelchair, gnarled hands loosely
clasping the handrests. 'Your intuition has always been sharp,
Theodor,' he said. 'If you had been the leader of the Winter Coup
rather than Viktor Ingram . . .'

'If I'd had that sharp an intuition back then, I would have shot
the bastard, not trusted him,' Theo said testily. 'But you're dodging the question, Holger.'

'I'm waiting for the others to join us first – ah, I think they're
here now.' He reached forward and fingered an angled display set
in the desktop.

The others, Theo thought. Sundstrom had occasionally hinted
at the existence of other cabal members, but in two years Theo
had met only one of them, a broad-shouldered, muscular Scot
who was introduced as Boris. He was not among the three who
now entered the study, two of whom – a man and a woman – he
had never seen before. The third he recognised immediately as

Vitaly Pyatkov, assistant director at the Office of Guidance, an intelligence organisation founded in the wake of the Winter Coup. Theo was amused by the look of aghast surprise that flashed across the man's features on seeing who was in the president's company, and also by the bland expression that slammed into place an instant later.

'Thank you all for coming here this evening,' said Sundstrom. 'You have all agreed to be part of my little advisory inner circle, but I intend to keep identities to a minimum for now.' He then introduced the man as Donny, and the woman as Tanya. Once everyone had settled, he began.

'First, as I'm sure you've all realised, the rumours are true. One of our comm satellites picked up a message claiming to be from the Earthsphere ship *Heracles*, offering friendly greetings and informing us that they will be entering Darien orbit at about ten tomorrow morning. Simurg 2, our satellite orbiting Nivyesta, is tracking an object on an intercept course with Darien; further communications have confirmed that the object is their source.'

'Further communications, sir?' said the woman Tanya. 'Has there been dialogue? Do we have any clues about what to expect?'

'There is a special ambassador on board, going by the name of Robert Horst, but thus far we have exchanged little more than diplomatic pleasantries.' Sundstrom's face grew serious. 'However, there are certain truths that I must make you all aware of from the outset.'

He raised a wire remote and clicked it. The screen at his back blinked on, showing a blue world from orbit, with a small green moon in attendance – Darien and Nivyesta. The perspective swung round gradually, bringing the sun, New Sol, into view, causing a lens flare before it slid out of the frame, leaving planet and moon against a hazy backdrop through which a few bright stars shone, diamond points suspended in misty veils.

'The tract of stellar dust and debris that surrounds us,' he went on, 'is rather larger than some observers had reckoned, nearly a thousand lightyears across at its widest, and our star system is located in one of the denser swirls. This tract is known as the Huvuun Deepzone and is one of several scattered around this part of the galaxy. It also happens to be the focus of a bitter border dispute between two regional civilisations, the Imisil and the Broltura.'

On the screen, Darien and its solar system dwindled into the mottled murk of interstellar dust clouds while strangely contoured walls emerged, stretching across lightyears, the three-dimensional boundaries between the deepzone and adjacent territories.

'The Brolturan Compact is closely allied to a huge interstellar empire called the Sendruka Hegemony, who also happen to be allies of Earthsphere. Unfortunately, the Solar System is nearly 15,000 lightyears away, which puts us well outside Earth's region of influence. The Imisil Mergence were once at war with the Hegemony, which adds a certain tension to the situation.'

Sundstrom paused, and there was an astonished silence. The others glanced at the screen and each other as the revelations sank in, and Theo's mind spun with the implications.

Complicated and uncomfortable? he thought. *That's an understatement.*

Pyatkov the intelligence officer spoke:

'Sir, respectfully – I know that your exchanges with the ambassador have not contained such information, so I must ask where it comes from.'

'I'm sorry, Vitaly, but I cannot reveal that at the moment.'

'Then how long have you known all this?' Theo said.

'Nearly two and a half years,' the president said. 'You will all find out the nature of this source in time, but they do not wish others to know straight away in fear of an inevitable political backlash.'

It's got to be the Enhanced, Theo thought. *They're involved in all the tech-heavy projects, and I'll bet that old Holger has a couple tucked away, translating signals trawled from the Great Beyond.*

'So who should we fear the most?'

Sundstrom smiled ruefully. 'Realpolitik being what it is, I feel that none of them are to be entirely trusted, but Earth's alliance with the Sendruka Hegemony is disturbing . . .'

As they listened, Sundstrom launched into an amazing disclosure, sketching the outlines of a topography of interstellar power, rivalry and conflict they had never dreamed existed. The Sendruka Hegemony was an authoritarian, militaristic empire which dominated this part of the galaxy: it employed a range of unprincipled tactics in order to get its way while laying claim to the most altruistic of motives and holding itself up as the example to which other civilisations should aspire. Unfortunately, close bonds of gratitude and trade existed between Earthsphere and the Hegemony, since the latter had been instrumental in defeating the Swarm invasion fleet which had nearly overwhelmed Earth and a dozen other civilisations 150 years ago. That was when the *Hyperion* and two other colonyships had departed the home solar system, after the beginning of the invasion but before the Hegemony's intervention.

As Sundstrom spoke, Theo glanced at the others. The woman Tanya was utterly engrossed, her gaze fixed on the president, while Pyatkov seemed more reserved, frowning slightly as he took it all in. The other man, Donny, seemed to be listening but had a relaxed alertness about him that Theo recognised.

Definitely special forces, he thought. *Plus an intelligence officer, a networker – maybe she's in government admin or communications – and a disgraced ex-major. There have to be others besides us.*

'So we're a human colony world very far from home,' Pyatkov said. 'We've appeared in the middle of contested territory, and Earth's allies are powerful and unsavoury. What of these Brolturans? Are they preferable to these others, the Imisil?'

'The Brolturans constitute a fanatical offshoot of mainstream Sendruka civilisation,' Sundstrom said. 'Their culture is centred on the precepts of a faith called Voloasti which elevates them to the status of God's paladins. The Imisil Mergence on the other hand—' He shrugged. 'They are a confederation of mainly non-humanoid races, non-expansionist, yet they're contesting ownership of this area we're in, the Huvuun Deepzone, purely to maintain some kind of buffer between themselves and the Brolturans.'

At this Donny smiled and sat straighter. 'So what do they look like, these Sendruka?'

'A lot like us,' Sundstrom said. 'They are very humanlike, except that they average about ten feet in height.'

Theo got a sudden flash of insight, imagining these tall humanoid aliens fighting shoulder-to-shoulder with humans to save Earth from the insectoid Swarm. *Yeah, that would generate a good deal of useful gratitude.* Tanya and Pyatkov were openly surprised at this piece of infomation, but Donny just smiled and nodded.

'They sound formidable,' Theo said. 'Anything else?'

The president gave one of his twinkly-eyed, mischievous smiles. 'Quite a lot else, actually, but there is one particular nugget which I think you'll all find interesting.' He looked at them. 'Since the Swarm War, and especially since Earth allied itself with the Hegemony, the development of artificial intelligence and awareness has moved ahead in leaps and bounds. AIs have spread to every level and sector of Earth culture, permeating the social fabric to the point where many people carry personalised ones around with them, sometimes as implants, and calling them "companions", never AIs. In the Hegemony, such entities are even more widespread, with the majority conferred autonomous rights by law. Several of the oldest and most complex even hold senior posts in government.'

There was a shocked pause, and a shared look of alarm as the meaning of his words dawned. One hundred and forty-eight years ago, soon after the detection of the world that was to become their new home, the crew and colonists of the *Hyperion* had fought a savage and desperate war against the ship's Command AI. From the point when the ship had dropped out of hyperspace, the onboard systems had begun to exhibit malfunctions which grew steadily more hazardous as the landing approached. By the time they made landfall they were actively struggling against the ship, whose AI had ceased to obey instructions. It took control of machinery, bots and various repair drones with which to sabotage the crew's efforts to get supplies out of locked storerooms or to directly attack them. Eventually it had begun waking other colonists from cryosleep, implanting them with neural devices to force them to carry out its instructions: 11 of the original crew of 46, plus 29 out of the cryosleep contingent of 1,200, had been killed by the time the survivors shut off power to the AI core. As to why it had turned against them, the weary victors could only speculate that the unknown stresses of hyperspace had corrupted its data or its cognitive substrate, turning it against them. The horrors of that struggle had echoed down the decades, becoming a potent symbol and a widely accepted justification for banning any research into AI, and commemorated in the annual Founders' Victory celebrations.

'I shall be making my widecast address to the colony in a couple of hours, after making a statement in the Assembly,' the president said. 'There will be no mention of anything that I've related here, of course, except for whatever generalities came in the ambassador's messages. But I wanted to tell you this in person now, since even our most secure communications may cease to be so in days to come.'

'Is it possible that the Earth ambassador will have one of these AIs with him?' asked Pyatkov.

'It might be wise to assume that he has,' Sundstrom said. 'Which may lead to umbrage on his part come FV Day, but we'll paper over that crack when we come to it.' He spread his hands. 'That is all for the time being, my friends. Continue with your preparations, maintain your colleagues lists, and expect new code-words by tomorrow night.'

As Theo rose with the others, Sundstrom beckoned him back. 'Theodor, if you could wait behind a moment.'

Once the rest had made their farewells and left, Pyatkov looking grim as he did so, the president manoeuvred his wheelchair out from behind the desk and over to a stolidly designed drinks cabinet. He poured himself a small glass of something dark red without offering one to Theo, knocked it back and gave a throaty sigh of satisfaction.

'I'm very glad that you agreed to join my little conspiracy, Theodor,' he said. 'Even though you still associate with various rogues and misfits, those Diehards of yours.'

'Ah, merely a group of friends from my army days, family friends . . .' He shrugged, smiling. 'Like-minded folk.'

Sundstrom's smile was knowing. 'In any case, I still value your experience and military insight, even your dissenter's viewpoint. But there's something else you bring to our clandestine scheming, something that could prove crucial.'

Theo laughed. 'Somehow I don't think you're referring to my charm and boyish good looks.'

Sundstrom gave him a sidelong look.

'I believe that you and your old friends from the Corps call it "the assets".'

Still standing, Theo almost froze but made himself relax. 'The assets?'

'A substantial quantity of arms and ammunition went missing after the Winter Coup, along with explosives, tech gear, and some vehicles. Now, assuming that this materiel has been stored at various locations in the vicinity of the colony townships, it's entirely possible that such hideaways may have come to the attention of some intel-gathering arm of government. In which case that data could be sitting in files that will shortly become, as I've already indicated, somewhat less than secure. Of course, if these stores turned out to be empty then such files could be closed and erased without delay.' He smiled. 'I don't know why you held on to it – perhaps you harboured long-term ambitions, or maybe you kept it so that it wouldn't fall into other hands. Either way, I'm glad that you did.'

Theo smiled blandly. 'Holger, I am at a loss to know how to reply to all that,' he said. 'But I shall give it careful consideration.'

'That's all I ask.'

'There is one small favour you might do for me,' he said.

'Which is?'

Theo smiled. 'From your communications with the Earth ship, were you told anything about the *Forrestal* and the *Tenebrosa*?'

'That was one of my first questions,' Sundstrom said. 'But it seems that they have not been found – the distinction of first contact is ours.'

'After which we will come under the microscope, no doubt.'

'Why is that?'

'To find out how our experiment in cultural admixture turned out,' Theo said. 'The original colonial project back on Earth computer-modelled a wide variety of national–cultural combinations, with the aim of finding those most likely to be able to survive conditions on alien worlds. And to build a worthwhile society.'

Sundstrom gave a rueful grin. 'Scandinavians, Russians and Scots – what were they thinking?'

A moment later the female assistant entered with Theo's overcoat. He donned it, shook the president's hand and moments later found himself outside the villa again. It was darker and colder now and he felt a distinct nip in the air as he left the villa grounds by a tree-shrouded pair of gates designed to look like the entrance of an adjacent property. The spinnercab he had ordered earlier was waiting at the side of the road, and took him downhill towards the city. Hammergard was spread along a narrow isthmus which separated Loch Morwen from the Korzybski Sea and the ocean beyond, both bodies of water glimmering with reflections of the night sky's starmist hues. But Theo was dwelling on Sundstrom's closing remarks about the Diehards, not to mention the assets, which was something of an unsettling surprise. And yet the president had decided to tell Theo that the assets were vulnerable, a revelation that could have only a limited number of implications, all of which spelled trouble.

He had the driver let him out on the Loch Morwen shore road in the city's Northvale district. With the hum of the spinnercab fading as it returned to the city centre, Theo took out his comm as he headed up the sideroad that led home. It was an older, larger model, its sangwood case scored and darkened from use, but the exterior belied its customised, upgraded components. A few thumbpresses later the blue oval screen read 'Welcome To The Crypt', and when he raised it to his ear he heard jaunty bagpipe music for a moment or two before someone answered.

'*Aye, whit is it now?*'

Theo cleared his throat. 'Rory, it's me.'

Silence for a moment. '*Ach, sorry about that, Major – I just had Stef on the line from Tangenberg bitching about the trainin' rota because he wants tae watch the Earth ambassador arriving on the vee and I thought that wiz him again—*'

'That's okay, never mind,' Theo said. Rory McGrain was his deputy, quartermaster and researcher all rolled into one. 'Listen, we'll need to roust out some loaders and crews tonight.'

'*Won't be easy, chief. What's it for?*'

'Sundstrom knows about the assets.'

'*Aw, naw . . .*'

'Or more accurately, he knows that government intel knows about them, so we have to move them all tonight.'

'*Hell's fire, chief – are we gonna have to shoot our way out?*'

Theo slowed as he reached the leaf-wreathed stairway leading up to his hab.

'That's the funny part, Rory – I don't think there'll be anyone watching the caches, never mind getting ready to jump us. Listen, I'm at my house right now. Have Ivanov or Janssen pick me up in fifteen. And one more thing – see what you can find out about a special forces guy called Donny.' He gave a brief description from memory.

'*That must have been some meeting ye had up at the palace,*' Rory said. '*Am I right in thinking that this ambassador's meet 'n' greet isna all it seems?*'

'Rory, you don't know the half of it.'

And as he hurried up the wooden steps, he thought – *And I don't think I do either.*

3

LEGION

It was a contract survey ship called *Segmenter* that found the planet Darien while studying the perilous gulfs of the Huvuun Deepzone.

Through tangled swirls and curtains of interstellar dust and debris, *Segmenter* had painstakingly (and clandestinely) plotted and scanned and measured for several long weeks before stumbling over an uncharted star system, complete with four planets, one of which was habitable. Since this part of the Huvuun was currently claimed by two antagonistic civilisations, the Brolturans and the Imisil, there then followed a tense hour or more during which the system was scanned for any other ships, beacons, probes or sensor nets. Once it was clear that there were no such hazards in the area, *Segmenter* moved in closer while its crew set to work.

Data soon began arriving: a variant-three habitable world, with a cluster of medium-tech-level settlements and also a large habitable moon. The planet's sentients were confirmed as Human, and their rudimentary information network revealed a population of approximately 2.75 million. The moon was inhabited by an indigenous biped sentient species called the Uvovo, who coexisted with an extensive forest ecology . . .

A full report was compiled by one of *Segmenter*'s scanners, then passed up to the captain. He saw at once that the Human element made it too important for his remit and had the report encrypted and dispatched via Tier 2 hyperspace comnet to the headquarters of the Suneye Combine, the huge interstellar corporation which had contracted *Segmenter*'s services. From there it flashed to the Office of External Measures on Iseri, the supreme homeworld of the Sendruka Hegemony. Six hours after leaving *Segmenter*, the report's contents were being discussed by the highest Hegemony figures and their AIs, and policy formulation was well under way.

But the *Segmenter*'s captain was not above trying to sell the same goods twice and had quickly found a customer at the rogue port of Blacknest. Pleased with his new acquisition, the datadealer deposited a tidy sum in a secure account, then streamed the data directly to a number of patrons with standing orders for information on new planets.

One patron was a Kiskashin line-pirate on Yndyeri Duvo, a 2nd-echelon world in the Erdindeso Autarky. His reputation for selling anything to anyone had gained him a string of customers for whom the word 'eccentric' was merely a starting point. And amongst the most taciturn was one he had named Lord Mysterious. Lord Mysterious had appeared nearly twenty years ago with a solid tap of Piraseri credit and a terse description of his information requirements tagged with a secure, localnet address on Duvo's sister world, Yndyeri Tetro. The Kiskashin was a phlegmatic merchant, and as long as a customer's credit held up he had no interest in finding out much more about them. So as soon as the Darien report blinked into his portable dataspace (while he was haggling with a tekmarker over the cost of band-depth for the coming hexad) he recognised this as the kind of thing Lord Mysterious had specified in his gatherer profile. But rather than sending it on immediately, he abstracted it and pondered the contents: a long-lost Human colony discovered in the middle of the Huvuun Deepzone with the Imisil in one corner, the Brolturans in the other, and the Hegemony looming over it all – hmm, a risky place to be, without a doubt, and fascinating. The Kiskashin did not know any Humans, but if any contacted him with a lucrative proposal in mind he would certainly be open-minded about it.

And just in case some of his other clients might be interested in this little morsel, he slotted the report into one of the slower outgoing queues. That would give him time to examine it later and assess its resale potential. After all, business is business.

4

CHEL

Every time he stepped aboard a Human vehicle, Chel found himself having to learn forbearance anew. They were hard, hollow things, completely lacking in the vitality of organic life yet endowed with cunning engines that drove them along their way. When the government zeplin set down at Port Gagarin, Chel breathed more easily as he hurried down the gantry to the hard ground of the sunken landing bay. It was difficult to trust to a thing that neither breathed nor had a beating heart, a thing that had no lifesong.

Yet we must have been very different in the long-distant past, he thought, gazing back up at the dirigible. *Once, the Uvovo worked with cold, dead stone and built places like the temple on Waonwir. What kind of people were we then?*

The short nightflight from Waonwir, which the Humans called Giant's Shoulder, to Port Gagarin was only the first stage of his journey. He was met at the landing bay exit by a breathless, harried-looking young Human female who introduced herself as Oxana as she quickly guided him along enclosed walkways to one of the big loading bays. There they boarded a large, ponderous freighter named *Skidhbladnir*, its appearance so battered and grimy as to make the government zeplin seem pristine by comparison.

Once inside, Oxana apologised for the rush, blaming incompetent couriers, and gave him his tickets for the rest of the journey.

'It should not take more than six or seven hours, and there are five stops along the way before you reach Invergault, where you will be met by someone from Ibsenskog. When you are ready to return, simply send us a message from the monitor office in the town.'

'I shall remember, Oxana,' Chel said. 'My thanks.'

'Think nothing of it, Scholar,' she said. 'Safe journey.'

After she was gone, Chel sought out the padded shelf that was his accommodation while the thuds and shouts of loading continued down in the main hold. A short while later the hold door was finally raised and the cargo zeplin lurched as its moorings were uncoupled. Engines droned and the shelf vibrated faintly beneath him, then a swaying sensation told him that they were aloft and under way.

However, Oxana's six or seven hours turned into nearly nine. As the freighter flew through the night and on into the morning, Chel managed to doze for a span, once he had grown accustomed to the dead hollowness of the Human craft. He almost grew used to the rattle of the hawser drums, the cries of the hefter crews, and the sounds of cargo being shifted. But by the time the *Skidhbladnir* arrived at Invergault it was an undeniable relief to clamber down to the zeplin station's small platform, with the cargo dirigible hanging overhead, creaking on taut cables.

Invergault was a small town sitting upslope from a pebbly cove near the end of a steep-sided sea loch. Like most of the Eastern Towns, it was a meeting point and marketplace for hunters, fishers and trappers. As he descended from the platform, he noticed that almost all roofs now carried windspinners, as well as large *affteg* roots affixed to their chimneys and flues, absorbing the ash and fumes from hearth and cooking fires, channelling heat into other uses rather than letting it escape. Chel knew from his teachers that, before the Humans sent their craft up to the home of Segrana, the colonists had been enthusiastic over-exploiters of natural resources and had scarcely practised any kind of wardenship. After the Accord of Friendship, the Uvovo were able to help the Humans to give up certain wasteful, destructive habits by showing them how to cultivate and use the many kinds of sifter root. This opened the way to the establishment of the seven daughter-forests, from which a change in cultural attitudes slowly percolated through the Humans' society. Wardenship of the natural world gradually became part of their custom and tradition.

On the pebbly slope near the zep station, Chel was met by a young female Uvovo dressed in plain green garments and wearing a Benevolent amulet. She looked anxious surrounded by the taller, bulkier Humans, but her face brightened when she spotted Chel. She introduced herself as Giseru and led him up to a *lohig* pen where an elderly Human stocksman tethered out a riding pair and lashed on the saddles with almost careless expertise. Moments later, Chel and his guide were heading out of town and along a broad, rutted track that led into a bushy gully and the wooded hills beyond.

Chel had to suppress the urge to laugh as he gripped the reining rod and followed Giseru through the trees. *Lohig* were six-legged creatures whose segmented bodies were protected by bony plates, and whose large dark eyes were veiled by flickering inner eyelids. Beneath the canopies of Segrana, they usually grew no larger than hand-size, but such marked divergence was found in several strains of plants and animals common to Umara and its forest moon. Chel had spoken with a few Human ecologists and heard them speak excitedly of this or that theory which tried to account for these differences. While they acknowledged that once the Uvovo had inhabited both planet and moon, they failed to understand that Segrana too had once held sway on both worlds and that the loss of that blessed presence was the root cause. The Humans spoke of 'die-back' and 'extinction events', but Uvovo legends told of a vast and terrible conflict, the War of the Long Night, a struggle between the Ghost Gods and the Dreamless which led to the burning of the world that Humans now called Darien. Human record-keepers and teachers knew of the Uvovo's legends but did not understand them, just as they came to visit the high homes of Segrana but did not hear her song.

He smiled ruefully, knowing that was not strictly true. There were a few whose perceptions ran a little deeper, like Lyssa Devlin or Pavel Ivanov, who might one day glimpse the outlines of the greatness of Segrana. Yet there was one Human, a female scientist called Catriona Macreadie, whose qualities of intellect might one day allow her to comprehend it.

The *lohig* he was riding ambled along with a steady, padding gait even as the track grew uneven and steep. The sun was high enough to be midday in a mainly cloudless sky, sending bright spears down through the layers of foliage. Insects buzzed and spun in the warm forest air, feathered *hizio* trilled in the high branches, and *ubakil* hooted mournfully to each other off in the distance. He smiled to hear these mingled sounds, the patchwork melody of the forest's denizens, while off at its edge he detected a calm, persevering voice, faint but unmistakable, the voice of Ibsenskog, Segrana's daughter-forest.

His guide, Giseru, said little as they wound their way through bushy undergrowth, ascending a trail that ran alongside a small stream. The trickling sounds of water over stones were a restful whisper merging with the susurrus of the wooded hills but the voice of the daughter-forest was strengthening with each passing moment. After a while Chel heard a hissing, splashing sound and before long the trail came out on a grassy bank near the foot of a waterfall. Narrow but smoothly made steps led up the sheer rock face, which the *lohig* managed without difficulty. Insects wove patterns in the warm air, and at the top a bushy slope led into a tree-shaded gully that tapered to a fissure full of the sound of rushing waters. But logs and shaped pieces of stone had been put in place as a rudimentary but solid walkway. It was dark in the fissure, its rough walls bearded with moss, beaded and glistening in a mist of water droplets descending from above. Then a notch appeared on the right and up they climbed, roughly hewn steps curving round to emerge on a grassy knoll with a large boulder at their backs. To one side, the ground dropped away to the rocky gully, the waterfall and the wooded hills, while on the other it dipped gently into a small, flowery dell beyond which lay Ibsenskog.

Segrana's daughter-forest stretched almost the entire length of a high mountain valley. Fifty years after the re-seeding, Ibsenskog and the others had become the lushest, most flourishing places on Umara yet were still only comparable to the sparser regions of Segrana, tracts where the medleys of living things were less numerous. Chel paused for a moment or two, letting the lifesong of the daughter-forest sink into him, feeding ears, taste and smell with its sweet richness, even as he knew it to be only an echo of Segrana's enfolding, never-ending song of celebration. Eyes closed for a moment, he smiled.

'Listener Faldri awaits us, Scholar,' came Giseru's voice.

In surprise he opened his eyes and saw the tall, cowled form of a Listener standing at the edge of the forest, near the path that led into its green embrace.

I knew that the Benevolent Uvovo were the wardens of Ibsenskog, he thought. *But I did not know that Faldri would be here.*

Giseru was already steering her *lohig* down into the dell, so Chel urged his mount into motion, his eagerness to enter the forest now tempered by reluctance.

The Listener was leaning on a long stave of red markwood and seemed not to acknowledge their arrival, even as they dismounted and tied the *lohigs* to a notched pole. Only when Giseru led Chel over to bow to his right side did the Listener respond – by turning away and striding unhurriedly towards the forest shade.

'Underscholars will attend to the creatures,' he said. 'Come.'

Giseru looked faintly embarrassed but Chel just smiled patiently and followed.

Faldri is testing me, he thought. *Whether he intends to or not.*

Curtains of fine-tendrilled *gumaus* hung from branches to either side, supporting a variety of other dependent plants and blooms from which fragrance drifted. As they walked, packs of small red-furred *igissa* scampered and leaped from tree to tree, making masses of foliage sway and rustle. Squeaks and drones, whistles and clatters, the exuberant sounds of Ibsenskog's wildlings over which the lifesong of the forest itself flowed, spilling through his thoughts. He was about to ask Giseru about the local water pattern but Faldri dismissed her, then wordlessly beckoned Chel to continue to follow. He thought that Faldri intended to avoid conversing with him entirely until, a short while later as they climbed a curve of bark steps, he spoke.

'You have made significant progress since attaining your scholarhood,' he said. 'Despite choosing to serve in the Warrior Uvovo.'

The Listener had pulled back a little and now the two walked side by side. Faldri had been Chel's teacher and their relationship had not been an amiable one.

'I chose to serve Segrana and the Great Purpose, Listener,' Chel said. 'I merely judged the Warrior clade to be more amenable to my temperament than the Benevolents.'

He was trying to sound conciliatory by downplaying his preference for the Warrior Uvovo. But instead his comments seemed to provoke anger.

'*Judged*?' the Listener said, slowing to look directly at him for the first time. Chel was taken aback by the changes wrought in his old teacher by the Listener husking: the lengthened features, the sunken eyes, the paring away of excess. 'Judgement is for Listeners, not Scholars!'

Then he was moving ahead, striding up to the top of the rise. 'Hurry – no dawdling! It will soon be time for the *zinsilu*.'

With his longer legs, Faldri was over the crest ahead of Chel, who had to break into a run to catch up. On the other side the path led down into a great dark mass of leafy undergrowth, bushes and small trees intertwined with climbing plants and borrower-weeds. Faldri ducked into a dark opening and Chel followed. A lumpy path wound down through mossy trees and came out at last in a clearing dominated by three big *vaskin* trees standing around a still pool. Listener Faldri was kneeling between two of the trees, eyes closed, wide, thin-lipped mouth murmuring, long-fingered hands held out, palms up. From some high opening in the canopy light filtered down and as he drew near Chel could see a fine mist of droplets falling between the three smooth, straight trunks.

Chel felt a growing quiver of uncertainty. This was utterly unlike his previous *zinsilu*, which had been fascinating discussions between himself and senior scholars on the direction of his learning, held in comfortable surroundings. This place reminded him of the few times he had taken the *vudron* vigil, except that the presence here was stern and brooding rather than tranquil and contemplative.

The fur on his scalp and neck prickled as he advanced. Faldri remained as he was, hands extended, lips muttering, his features just visible beneath the cowl. Chel halted at the edge of the pool, which he saw was not entirely still, its surface trembling very slightly now and then. Looking up he could see the falling mist and a shifting silvery radiance from above. Chel stood in silence for several moments before deciding to speak, but Faldri, eyes still closed, forestalled him with a fluid gesture. Wait.

Long moments passed. Chel inhaled and exhaled in a slow rhythm, calming himself, smelling and tasting the odours of wet wood and green leaves. Then Faldri ceased murmuring and drew an audible deep breath.

'The gate is now open, Great Elder. Your servants await.'

The Listener's voice seemed to resonate in Chel's ears. His senses hummed to the lifesong of the daughter-forest which gathered in strength, climbing up his body like a slow fountain of energy, rising through his limbs, his veins, his spine. And suddenly he knew that he was in the presence of sacred Segrana . . . and another. There, in the radiant mist above the pool, was a hulking, stooped form draped in long folds, an indistinct image.

Chel stared in awe and panic. Faldri had called out to the 'Great Elder', and Chel suddenly realised that he was looking at one of the legendary Pathmasters.

But the histories say that the last of them died after the War of the Long Night, he thought. *How could one still be alive after thousands of years?*

'There is no death,' came a sighing voice. 'Only a change in how the universe dreams about us . . .'

In reflex, Chel bowed his head, his thoughts in a whirl. The long-lived Pathmasters were the third huskings of the Uvovo, which only the wisest, most enlightened of Listeners could achieve. But the War of the Long Night had decimated the Uvovo and destroyed much of the ancient strength of Segrana, without which the third huskings could not be carried out. The surviving Uvovo had been confined to the forest moon, their history fraying and fading into legend after the Pathmasters were gone, their knowledge shrivelling into litany, their customs into ritual, until the Humans came.

'Dreams persist,' the Pathmaster sighed. 'The stronger the dreamer, the more resilient the dream. Some dream outward dreams, seeking unity with the eternal; others dream inwardly, dreams of hunger and conquest, of pain and the escape from pain. Some do not dream at all. Cheluvahar, do you dream?'

'Great Elder, I . . .' Panic seized him, mind suddenly blank. 'I have dreamed lately but the details escape me for now.'

'I know, I see them.' The voice faded to a whisper as the floating image of the Pathmaster tilted its hooded head to look upward, revealing a face far removed from Uvovo appearance, a cluster of bony ridges and two dark pits that might be eyes. Then the voice came back, stronger and sharper. 'A ship is coming to these worlds, a ship from the Humans' home stars. It bears a great evil, the eyes of a new breed of Dreamless who hunger for power and dominion as their abominable like did in the past.'

The Dreamless. The word sat in Chel's mind like a piece of ice, melting dread into his thoughts while his heart thudded in his chest.

'Great Elder,' he said. 'Will the War of the Long Night return?'

'No. This peril is more similar to the cause that led to the original Great Purpose, which is far more than that which you have been taught. Just as the Segrana you know is not the Segrana that once was. Nor do these Dreamless possess the shattering might of their long-vanished kin, yet it will be more than enough to turn the night sky into a vista of desolation. They secretly rule a vast empire and are as relentless as they are cruel and cunning.'

The peace of the tree-guarded pool and the rich lifesong that enlivened Chel's senses seemed in stark contrast to all that the Pathmaster was saying. Yet his thoughts circled back to why he was here, why he was being told these things . . .

'This is your *zinsilu*, Scholar,' said the Pathmaster, as if Chel's inner thoughts were clear as written words. 'A *zinsilu* such as has not been seen for a thousand generations. Scholar Cheluvahar – are you ready to serve the Great Purpose with all that is body and all that is mind? Are you ready to place your trust in a convoking of the Listeners and to obey their edicts?'

Chel felt swept up by the gravity of the Pathmaster's demand, but he breathed in deep, steadying himself.

'I am, Great Elder.'

'Good – I am pleased not to be disappointed. When we are done here, you will return to your work at Waonwir, which the Humans call Giant's Shoulder – do not concern yourself with events subsequent to the arrival of the Human ship. In two or three days you will be asked to leave for the daughter-forest to the north, where a secret husking chamber is being prepared . . .'

Suddenly he stopped, hooded head swinging towards Faldri. 'Ah, so you are shocked, Listener, outraged at our plan.'

Faldri stared up at the misty form. 'Only anxious for all our fates, Great Elder. This Scholar shows talent and promise, yet he is young and lacking in the experience required of a Listener . . .'

'This is not about husking forth more Listeners, Faldri,' the Pathmaster said. 'We are planning the creation of a new clade, the Artificer Uvovo. Once the Warriors and the Benevolents had artisans aplenty among their ranks, before the War of the Long Night took them all. The arrival of the Humans has led to a regeneration of such skills amongst the younger scholars, skills that will prove crucial in the times ahead. Those who might be considered Artificer Uvovo already exist, scattered around the Human towns and working in the daughter-forests and . . . other places. When Cheluvahar husks forth, it will be as a Listener of the Artificer Uvovo, nor will he be alone, since other scholars are undergoing similar examinations today.'

'I was not aware of this plan, Great Elder,' the Listener said, bowing his head. 'But I am confused as to the uses of such a new clade.'

A good question, Chel thought. *Are we expected to use Human weapons in battle?*

'There are a number of constructions on Umara, built in the time of our earliest forebears, built to merge with the powers of the ancient, greater Segrana and protect these worlds. It will be the task of the Artificer Uvovo to study them and bring them back to life in preparation for whatever we may face.'

'Are the Humans to be made aware of this approaching enemy, Great Elder?' said Faldri. 'Are we to cooperate with them?'

'There have been exchanges with their leadership,' the Pathmaster said. 'They already know about the Dreamless and are making their own arrangements. Cooperation may become inevitable, should events turn unfortunate.'

'Forgive me, Great Elder,' Chel said, 'but what is it that draws the Dreamless here? What do they want?'

The Pathmaster sighed. 'For long ages we guarded it, serving the Great Purpose, thinking that finally all knowledge and memory of it had passed irretrievably beyond the veil of the past. But some dreams persist longer than the lives of the stars and lurk and wait in hidden places for their time to come round again.' Dark eyeless hollows regarded him. 'The edifice atop that prow of rock, Waonwir, is not some old Uvovo temple of devotion as the Humans have surmised. Beneath its walls and foundations lies a gateway to the framework of the universe, a source of power once used to defeat the first enemy, the cause of the Great Purpose, a terrible adversary now long vanquished. If the Dreamless were to gain control of it, all thought in this galaxy and beyond would become enslaved to their will and life would have no song.'

He paused a moment. 'Now you know what you are meant to know. Go – return to Giant's Shoulder and wait for the command to travel northward.'

As the Pathmaster fell silent, his image blurred and dissolved into the pale, falling mist. With his vanishing, the light in the clearing dwindled suddenly, like a door closing, leaving Chel feeling adrift and burdened with portents.

War is coming, he thought, and *I am to become a Listener even though I have been a Scholar for only four hem-seasons* . . .

'I am not ready,' he muttered.

'On that I can only agree,' said Faldri, brushing off his long garments as he got to his feet. 'But higher counsel has determined the course of your doings – now we must wait to see if the meeting of fate and dream aids or hinders you.' He took his stave from where it leaned against one of the *vaskin* trees, and started up the slope. 'Come, Artificer, let me see you safely back to your *lohig*.'

5

CATRIONA

On the moon Nivyesta, beneath the lush, living canopy of the forest Segrana, it was forever dusk. Through humid green shadows a *trictra* swung, long hooked limbs finding purchase on branches, heavy vines and creeping webs, descending into the well of gloom. Catriona Macreadie clung to its dumbbell-shaped torso, strapped firmly into a woven harness and uncomfortably warm in a grey concealing robe, feeling slight waves of vertigo as the creature dipped and swooped in the moon's lower gravity. In front, Pgal the herder sat easily in the notch behind the *trictra*'s head, directing it with prods to either of its frontal joints or with single-syllable cries. Periodically, Pgal glanced back with his doleful eyes in a wordless query but Catriona, despite her discomfort, would shake her head and point onward and downward. The hunt was on and she was not for turning back.

Clouds of insects parted and swirled in their wake while innumerable creatures noticed the disturbance of their passing, mammalian *kizpi*, their large eyes staring from leafy niches, or *umisk* lizards startled and darting away. It was an exhilarating display of Segrana's biodiversity, which Catriona had charted and studied for nearly two years, filling scores of datacubes with profiles, reports and commentaries, as well as hundreds of images. She had seen how hexaformity was a trait common to different species, and how some subspecies exhibited tripartite or even quadripartite life cycles, changing their physical attributes as they aged, while others did not. She understood how the vast, continent-spanning biomass of Segrana shielded its multifarious denizens from the moon Nivyesta's weather patterns, regulating the many microclimates found beneath its canopy, while the lower gravity aided the growth of wider, taller trees and other plants.

She also knew that the map was not the territory and that Segrana hid many secrets. Satellite surveys confirmed that while Segrana's topmost extremities grew to nearly a mile above sea level, some of the unseen valleys fell to almost two miles below, which implied that the forest's roots went even deeper, an ancient and ubiquitous grasp. Almost half an hour after receiving the trip signal it was down there that Catriona was headed, seeking proof for a wild theory.

To either side massive trunks sloped up towards the light, some spiralling around each other for strength and support, others criss-crossing to form junctions where Uvovo villages nestled, glowing clusters of lamps and conical roofs, indistinct figures walking or climbing from dwelling to dwelling amid the entwining dimness. One such township lay directly below, but Catriona had given Pgal clear instructions earlier and he was swift to guide their *trictra* off to one side, behind a dense screen of cultivated symbiotic flora. She tugged on the cowl of her baggy robe, keeping her human features concealed from any chance Uvovo observer. Yet they were still taking risks, since only Listeners went about the underforest swathed in this manner.

Moments later the village was behind them as they plunged on into the depths. From beneath her robe she took a small direction-finder orb then tapped Pgal's shoulder.

'Leftward a little,' she said.

The Uvovo herder just nodded and guided the spidery *trictra* down one of several long, thick vines. Like the mooring hawsers of some immense ship they curved away into the gloom, bearded with lichenous webs. Others snaked up the gnarled, mossy sides of trunks and branches like veins, leaching away moisture and nutrients which in turn served to feed a further array of parasitic plantlife. As the *trictra* clambered down one of these great living towers, Catriona looked from side to side, smiling as she spotted a familiar beetle or reptiloid, reflexively matching them against the entries in her codex memory. Whenever she caught sight of something apparently new she stored it away in her reminder file for later reference.

All the memory advantages of Enhanced genes, she thought, *without the self-programming skills which would have earned me a well-paid, high-level research post. How tiresome would that have been . . .*

Catriona was a failed Enhanced. Her germ plasm came from the *Hyperion*'s cryostocks and had been genetically re-engineered to increase memory capacity and allow conscious, detailed control of information. The refined higher functions allowed an Enhanced to use their own cortex as a programmable computer, to run macros and test their own and others' theories; the best of them could illuminate solutions with their own flashes of insight. But Catriona had been part of the third and final generation, brought to term by surrogate mothers at a time when anomalies still emerged at unpredictable stages of development. She had begun to lose the ability to self-initiate neural pathways at fifteen years old, after which the pathway net she had already created in her head began to desync. By the time she was seventeen, her peers were strides ahead and she saw herself as being no better than an ordinary kid with an excellent memory.

And that just wasn't good enough for the martinets who ran Zhilinsky House, she thought bitterly.

Yet this, combined with her obsessive interest in the ecologies of Darien and Nivyesta, gave her something to hold on to after leaving the Enhanced programme. It led her along a career path that proved fruitful and satisfying, as well as aggravating when it came to putting in equipment requisitions.

Still, occasionally she yearned for that long-gone fledgling talent, especially when trying to get her head around the astonishing complexity of the forest Segrana and the Uvovo's place in it. There was an underlying story or relationship to it all which she had only caught glimpses of so far. Of course, deducing the Uvovo connection to the temple on Giant's Shoulder had opened entire new areas of possible inquiry, but it had also made the speculation wilder and more tantalising. If she had been a full Enhanced, rather than a cripple, she would have seen through to the truth by now, she was sure of it.

The descent to the deep valley floor took another half-hour, including pauses to rest the *trictra*. All the chirping, whirring sounds of the underforest, where most of the species lived, faded to a high, distant murmur. Down here the light was filtered and grainy, and the air was still, warm and very humid. *The Uvovo call it Segrana*, she thought, *the living forest. I can almost believe it – this forest moon is itself an anomaly and its all-encompassing ecology constitutes a strange, beautiful world. Sometimes, it's almost as if I can hear it singing, feel it watching . . .*

Following the glowing pointer in her direction-finder, they at last came to the base of one of the forest Segrana's oldest and biggest trees, a titan measuring almost 200 feet across. Massive knotted roots showed through the layer of decomposing foliage that blanketed the forest floor. Quiet streamlets trickled among some of the roots, pouring down towards a still deeper part of the valley. A family of dumpy six-legged *baro* grubbed for roots a short distance away, while ophidian *pasks* hunting bugs in the mat of decaying leaves made rustling sounds.

But Catriona's attention was fixed on a point about 20 feet up the side of the giant tree. She pointed across at it and the herder Pgal nodded, urging the *trictra* across the surrounding root tangle and up the tree's rough, dripping flank. Catriona could feel her heart beating as she spotted the cam's stalk lens protruding from the surrounding snarl of fibrous lichen, rootless and creepers, and once their mount was close enough she reached into the wet foliage and retrieved the device. She grinned as she studied it, blew away waterdrops and leaf fragments, then looked over her shoulder at what it had been observing.

Several yards away, six tall triangular stones stood in a circle on a flattened mound oddly free of saplings and bushes. Her first visit here had been brief and tense as her guide, an outcast Uvovo scholar called Amilo, had been terrified of being discovered by the

Listeners. He had been equally edgy on their second visit two days ago when she had secreted the cam on the tree, setting it to record anything over a certain size moving in or near the stone circle. When she called Amilo yesterday, though, he refused to help a third time but did put her in touch with Pgal, a young cladeless *trictra* herder who was unconcerned about anything as fanciful as Pathmasters.

She weighed the little cam in her hand for a moment, then pushed the lens stalk into its socket before tucking it away in a shoulder pouch. Yes, with any luck she might have something to prove that the Uvovo did indeed have a third stage in their life cycle after Scholars and Listeners, namely the Pathmasters, who were supposedly no more than folk tales. She turned to tell Pgal to head back to the canopy but paused when she saw him looking up, eyes wide. She followed his unblinking gaze to see a larger *trictra* hanging several yards overhead, clinging to the tree with a large garment-swathed figure perched on its back, one hand holding a herding stave.

'Ah, Mistress-Doctor Catriona,' said the newcomer. 'A pleasant surprise to meet you here in Segrana's field of birth and decay.' As he spoke he tugged aside his cowl to reveal the ageing, bony features of a male Uvovo she knew very well.

'Greetings, Listener Weynl,' she said. 'Seen any Pathmasters today?'

The Uvovo Listener's smile made his elongated face seem skull-like, but his demeanour was full of patient good humour.

'None yesterday, Mistress-Doctor, and none today. For they are only a *ssu-ne-ne*, a kind of myth or . . .' He frowned. 'There is another word in your Noranglic tongue – ah, yes, *fable*, an instructional tale, nothing more.'

'As I've heard before,' she said. 'Not least from yourself, and yet I have come across other tales that give different accounts.'

'Some of the handfolk of the Benevolent Uvovo have a more literal understanding of the *ssu-ne-ne*. They are often led astray by such things as that ruined stone ring, which was a very old but very ordinary meeting place and hub of a marketplace . . .'

As they conversed, the Listener urged his *trictra* down to

ground level. Catriona prompted Pgal to follow suit, and found that there were another three *trictra*-mounted Uvovo waiting below, all displaying on their beaded tunics the circular symbols of the Warrior Uvovo.

'. . . and so such imaginings should be considered with care. We of the Warrior Uvovo retain a more realist approach to these matters.' Then he indicated the others with his herding stave. 'Ah, these are my way-kin – we were returning from a *vudron* contemplation when we chanced upon you here.'

Catriona nodded, not believing him for a moment. 'So you feel that I am wasting my time chasing this . . . *arassu*?'

It was the Uvovo word for 'sad ghost', and as she said it astonishment flashed across the features of two of Weynl's companions. The Listener, however, only smiled.

'Just so,' he said. 'Now, since our destination is Starroof Upper-Way, we would be honoured to escort you back, Mistress-Doctor, if you wish.'

Part of her wanted to rebel and refuse, but common sense reminded her of the minicam in her shoulder pouch, so she graciously consented to the Listener's offer.

The journey back up the green canyons of Segrana seemed to take for ever. The weight and shape of the minicam teased her constantly as Pgal's *trictra* laboured from branch to vine-cluster to crossed-trunk. Listener Weynl stopped for a rest at a junction village that just happened to be the one that Catriona and Pgal had bypassed on the way down. As the Listener talked jovially with his way-kin she wondered if this was an example of Uvovo humour.

At last the light grew brighter as they neared the canopy, and when gantries, ladders and platform dwellings became frequent she knew that they were near the town of Starroof. Insects glittered in the shafts of sunlight that angled down through the foliage and wafts of cool, fresh air brought the fragrance of day-blooms.

'Our courses must part here, Mistress-Doctor Catriona,' Listener Weynl said. 'My *vudron* lies further above, in the Highsonglade. Please remember that if you wish to seek knowledge at the roots of Segrana, you should ask for guidance from myself or any Listener.'

'My apologies, Listener,' she said. 'I never intended to give offence.'

'It is more your safety that is of concern,' Weynl said. 'Some of the darker corners below harbour predators that could devour a Human in a bite or two.'

'I understand your concerns, Listener,' she said. 'I assure you that I will take them very seriously.'

The elderly Uvovo regarded her for a moment, his amiable smile never wavering, then he nodded.

'Seek with care, Doctor,' he said before tapping his *trictra*'s side carapace with his herding stave.

Even as the Listener and his companions continued up the braided cable-ladders, Catriona told Pgal to hurry. The herder guided the *trictra* up hanging nets and across leafy curtains, reaching the hammock platform nearest to the cluster of adapted native dwellings that constituted the enclave of Human scientists. Unstrapping herself from the saddle restraints, she climbed out onto the springy matting, stripped off the bulky robe and turned to Pgal. But he spoke first:

'I not carry you again.'

Astonished, she stared. 'Why, Pgal? Has someone threatened you?'

It was the herder's turn to be surprised. 'No! – I go to Highsong *vudron*. Rejoin Warrior clade.' He smiled. 'Very happy.'

Catriona nodded, understanding. *Vudrons* were large, spherical chambers fashioned from huge, empty seed husks which grew only at the highest places of Segrana. Bonded to a branch or trunk near a Uvovo town or village, they served as a Listener shrine, a refuge for private meditation, as well as the centrepiece of public ceremonies. An outcast like Pgal could become a full member of either Uvovo clade by taking a vigil in a *vudron*, but only if invited by a Listener. Like Weynl.

'I am happy for you, Pgal,' she said. 'Thank you for all your help, and go in peace.'

The herder smiled, bowed his head, then steered his *trictra* down from the platform and along the meshed vines.

And thank you, Weynl, she thought, watching him leave. *You really don't want me going near the forest floor, do you? Well, let's see what my wee camera spotted, shall we?*

She glanced around her to make sure she was alone, then took out the cam, fitted a viewing ocle to the output, pressed Play and held it up to her eye.

And saw . . . only flickering confusion. The timer readout was the same as when she got the trip signal, but the recording was a blurred, stuttering mess. She ran it again and again, trying to find more than just hints of a dark form that might have been a creature, or shaky stick-like things that might have been limbs . . .

She lowered the cam and sagged against one of the platform's heavy, woven hawsers. She suddenly felt weary, as if the recording had knocked the vitality out of her. It had been such a waste, scrounging the cam from Lyssa Devlin's team over at Skygarden, skulking down there to plant it then retrieving it, all a waste of time and effort. It might be possible to process and filter the image data, but only the Institute office at Viridian Station would have that kind of equipment and anyway, how could she explain how she obtained such a recording without admitting to multiple violations of the Respect Accords?

Disconsolate, she put the minicam away in her pouch, slung the baggy robe over one shoulder and climbed the branch stairway that led to the Human enclave. Halfway up, the stairs trembled a little underfoot as someone came hurrying across a flimsy-looking gantry from another platform. It was Tomas Villon, one of her team's tech assistants. His features were flushed and excited as he raised a hand in greeting and called out.

'Doctor Macreadie,' he said. 'Have you heard the news?'

'No – what news?'

He grinned. 'The president announced it in his widecast this morning, and the channel heads have been talking about nothing else . . .'

'Sorry, Tomas, but I've been working hard, and I've been away all morning. What's happened?'

Clearly delighted at being able to let her in on the story, he cleared his throat. 'Well, as I said, the president came on the vee this morning to tell us that the Hammergard government has been in contact with a ship from Earth!'

First she gasped in disbelief, then started talking, almost tripping over her own words.

'But that's . . . incredible! You're sure, Tomas, absolutely sure?'

'It's the honest truth, Catriona, I swear! The ship is called the *Heracles* and it's entering orbit around Darien right this moment. Look, there's a vee-panel up in the mess hut which is where the rest'll be, watching the live relay from Port Gagarin.'

A web-tethered flock of membrane insectoids drifted past on a warm updraught as they hastened up to the enclave buildings. Catriona grinned while trying to think through the giddy thrill she was feeling.

'It's unbelievable,' she said. 'I never thought I'd live to see this – I wonder what they'll be like? You remember that play by Fergus Brandon?'

'*The Lifeline*?' He chuckled. 'I doubt that any would-be colonists will be queueing to come out here. Said as much to Greg Cameron earlier.'

'Greg?' she said, trying to sound vaguely disinterested. 'What were you calling him about?'

'Neh, he called us to gossip about the announcement. We gabbed on about it and the Brandon play came up. Yah, he's just as excited about it as everyone.'

Of course, Catriona thought. *Those two were good friends at college, so it's no surprise that he would call.* She felt a small shiver go through her. *I wonder how he's been since he came back . . . but why should I wonder? He's just another man who's got better things to do than . . .*

She had only met him a few times, ever since she'd suggested the link between the proportions of the temple on Giant's Shoulder and the physique of the Uvovo, and she had hoped that their professional friendship might become something deeper. And then he gave up everything and moved away up north to Trond to get married, settle down and have kids, apparently – only to return several months later, alone. Hopes which had collapsed rose again, but tempered this time with a dash of realism and caution.

And now she was resolved not to let Greg Cameron or her failed minicam experiment dilute her excitement at Tomas's news.

'Right, Tomas,' she said with a determined laugh as they came up to the mess hut. 'Let's see if we can get a good seat!'

6

ROBERT

On board the Earthsphere cruiser *Heracles*, in the largest of its three staterooms, Ambassador Robert Horst was indulging in the archaic practice of packing luggage.

'I don't know why you don't ask the room to do it for you,' said Harry, his AI companion.

'But the room doesn't know what I need to take with me.'

'The room has access to your sartorial profile, as well as Darien's styles and customs, such as they are. So where's the problem?'

'The room can't know what I need,' Robert said, smiling as he placed a semi-formal tunic into his partitioned valise. 'Because I don't know myself. Or rather, when I see it I'll know that I need it.'

Harry smiled and shook his head. In Robert's field of vision, Harry seemed to be standing over by the stateroom's centrepiece, a sleek porcelain and perspex column with a holobase in each of its five faces. He resembled a young man dressed in an immaculate but outmoded black suit, his round features displaying a perpetual amusement and a hint of cynicism. Robert had chosen to model his companion upon the main character from an American black-and-white flat-movie from the mid-twentieth century, whose storyline dealt with postwar intrigue and betrayal. Orson Welles's portrayal of the mercurial Harry Lime had captivated the young Robert Horst, and after deciding on his companion's form he had also resolved that he would appear in monochrome. After all, he was the only one who would see it.

'I'm not sure that the personal touch will be helpful,' Harry said. 'After 150 years of isolation and resource scarcity, social fashions are bound to be a little rustic.'

'My God, Harry, you're a snob.'

'Not at all. I just feel sure that these poor, Earth-hungry colonists will want an ambassador from the auld country to look the part.'

Robert wagged a finger. 'What, play the lofty aristo come to dispense wisdom to the local yokels? Sorry, no – that's the Sendruka approach, not mine.'

'Shame on you, Robert, for denigrating the high ideals of our allies in the cause of peace and justice,' Harry said, adopting a stance of mock grandeur followed by a sly grin. 'Besides, your honoured Sendruka colleague Kuros and his Ezgara goons are just along the corridor. Who knows how many spymotes are drifting around the ship by now, listening to our every word?'

'Not with the new antisurveillance systems the Earthsphere Navy brought in after the *Freya* incident,' Robert said, selecting from a small open section of the storage wall a pair of Russian leather gloves, a couple of plaid kerchiefs and a carved wooden ring. 'I'm more concerned about why they're here at all.'

The *Heracles* had been en route to the Huvuun Deepzone when new orders came through to divert to Chasulon, the capital world of Broltur, and take on board the honoured High Monitor Utavess Kuros and his unspecified personal guard. Which turned out to be eight Ezgara commandos, four-armed biped soldiers with a fearsome reputation, who wore all-enclosing, steel-blue body-armour and never revealed their faces. But Kuros and his guards were to be accorded every courtesy, since they were there at the personal request of Earthsphere President Erica Castiglione, apparently in a dual capacity: as Alliance advisers, and as observers on behalf of the Brolturan government.

Personal request! he thought. *I bet it was more like a demand and Erica was on the receiving end of it.*

'I don't imagine that there's much to be anxious about,' Harry said, resting his foot on the edge of a low table. 'The Hegemony thinks that it has to keep tabs on every political event otherwise things might fall apart, the centre cannot hold and so on. Whereas things would probably proceed quite normally if Hegemony attention was elsewhere.'

'Harry, for you that's practically heresy.'

'I know. I blame it on prolonged exposure to the life and works of Robert Horst! Anyway, it'll be politics on a rather lesser scale for you in the weeks ahead.'

'True, but it could turn out to be quite productive. One of the files sent from President Sundstrom's office gave an interesting summary of their resource management and extraction policies . . .'

'Ah, you mean these sifter roots that they got from the Uvovo?' Harry chuckled. 'Ingenious way of getting hold of pure elements, for a pre-nanofac society. Properly adapted, they could be put to use in other contexts, like hardvac prospecting for example. Or even licensed out to cultures that prohibit nano applications.'

Robert shrugged. 'That sounds possible. I'm more interested in the relations between our people and the Uvovo, not to mention the colony's inner politics.'

'Well, for a small colony they've had a somewhat chequered history. Problems with a shipboard AI that went rogue, then a very tough first fifty years, expansion problems, lack of resources, then contact with these Uvovo sentients and an abortive civil war which exacerbated some already prickly divisions. But it's this AI taboo that could pose difficulties. You should read some of their novels and plays – artificial intelligences come across like the rampaging death machines of the Commodity Age. I find it positively insulting. What's more, every year they celebrate the trashing of that poor, dumb AI. Founders' Victory Day, they call it.'

'I agree, it's a problem, but I'm going to wait until I've experienced Darien culture first-hand before considering solutions.' Robert parted another tall section of the wall and touch-opened the units within. 'It's a matter of how to establish the notion of everyday, commonplace, benevolent AIs . . .'

As he reached in, almost absentmindedly, and pulled out one of the shallow drawers, he stopped and stared in dread at the palm-sized object it contained.

'Ah, so that's where the room put it,' Harry murmured. 'I can have it stored somewhere else if you like.'

'No, no, it's all right,' Robert said. 'I can't keep on avoiding it. . .'

It was an intersim, a flat octagonal pad, mainly pale blue in colour with ochre trim around the readout and fingertip controls on one of the sides. The projection plate on top was like dark, smoky glass within which clusters of faceted emitters were just visible. It had a certain solidity to it, like the weight of compacted technology, or the weight of memory.

It was now almost a year since his daughter Rosa had died while on board the *Pax Terra*, a refitted, unarmed scoutship owned by the protest group Life and Peace. The *Pax Terra* had been taking part in an attempted blockade of a wayport on the Metraj border from which Earthsphere and Sendruka Hegemony warships were leaving for the Yamanon Domain. The official version was that the protest boat was a suspected bombship pursuing a collision course with a Hegemony cruiser whose commander had no option but to open fire. Initially Earthsphere government had made mild objections, but soon dropped the matter.

Robert and his wife Giselle were distraught, and the Diplomatic Service was thankfully swift to offer him compassionate leave. But Robert was unable to stay at home in Bonn and mourn – he had to know the truth about Rosa's death.

Sitting at the end of a blue settle, he held the interactive sim in his hands and recalled the months spent tracking down witnesses to the blockade incident and speaking with her friends and colleagues at Life and Peace. What he learned utterly contradicted the official version of events, while confirming much of what he knew about his daughter, about her intellect and wit, and about her compassion and her willingness to put herself on the line for what she believed in. Millions had died when the Earthsphere–Hegemony coalition invaded the Yamanon Domain and bombarded the Dol-Das regime's key worlds. Rosa had called those deaths an atrocity, a judgement he could no longer disagree with.

'We taught her to love,' he once said in a message to his wife during his travels, 'and she did what she did out of love.'

He was on Xasome in the Kingdom of Metraj, trying to glean corroborating data from public archive reports, when he received a package via the local Earthsphere consulate. It was from Earth, from his wife, and accompanying it was a short note that read: 'Dearest, I have found a way to bring the light back into our lives, and now you have one too. With love and joy – Giselle.'

Thinking it to be some compendium of images and other recordings from the family archive, Robert had placed the inter-sim on a desk and switched it on. The device had emitted three flashes, mapping the room, and a moment later, abruptly, Rosa was standing there, dressed in one of her favourite outdoor rigs, smiling at him.

'Hi, Daddy!' she had said.

So brightly she spoke, so vibrant with that delighted alertness of hers, that he almost said, '*Rosa! – you're alive* . . .'

But the words had choked in his throat as reason took hold, and he had stared at the simulation of his daughter in a wordless horror.

'Daddy, how are you?'

Unable to speak or look away, still he had reached out deliberately, with all of his will, and switched the device off. Looking at it now, resting on his palm, he knew what had driven Giselle to have such a thing made. He had understood and let the anger fade, knowing that part of the anger had been directed at his own despairing need for Rosa not to be dead.

And yet . . . and yet he could not bring himself to destroy the sim, or at least have its memory wiped, not then and not now.

Then, reaching a decision, he slipped the intersim into his jacket pocket, stood and resumed packing.

'Are you sure that's wise?' said Harry.

Robert smiled as he tucked away the last items of clothing. 'You think I may be putting my negotiating temperament and thus this assignment at risk?'

Harry assumed a look of mock surprise.

'What a hurtful interpretation of my genuine concern. I merely suggest that leaving the damned thing here would help your peace of mind.' He paused, face becoming more serious. 'Robert, I think that you're hurting yourself by taking it with you.'

Robert sighed. 'I appreciate the concern, Harry, truly. But you worry too much. Unlike Giselle, I have come to terms with Rosa's death and I know that this simulation is not her but a made thing. Not a living, breathing person that I can touch.'

Harry gave him a considering look for a moment. 'Tell me – is that how you see me, as a made thing?'

'Well, yes. Made by experience and thought and accident, and by friendship!' Robert smiled. 'Whereas Giselle's device is a frozen vision, an exhibit that cannot learn or change. Satisfied?'

'Yes – my crippled self-esteem has been suitable bandaged.' Harry gestured towards the two fastened valises. 'Are you finished, because the people of Darien and their representatives await you, not to mention all those watching back home, in the Glow and elsewhere.'

Robert gave a groan. The Glow was the Solar System's virtual reality, where celebrity and excess reigned supreme. 'So the Office of Defence finally gave in to the media combines, did they?'

'Which means that we shall shortly be going live on Starstream,' Harry said with a wild grin. 'Since they were the only ones who would meet the OOD's asking price.'

'Starstream,' Robert said, activating the suspensors on his luggage. 'I can scarcely express my joy. Let's go.'

7

COLONISTS

West of Hammergard, across the two-mile width of Loch Morwen, a cluster of low buildings and two narrow towers sat on a headland overlooking the waters. Fenced off and patrolled, this was the main operational base for the Ranger division of the Darien Volunteer Corps. At that moment, almost six hours after the president's address to the colony, 185 of the division's 200 combat personnel were crammed into the base's small rec room, craning necks for a look at the sole v-screen.

'C'mon, get yer head down in front there!'

'Gonna no dae that?'

'Whit?'

'Shoutin' in my ear, ye howler!'

Donny Barbour grinned, listening to this and many other exchanges from the bench he had snagged at the front early on. At the moment, though, there was not much to see, just a pair of aycasters from Vizione, the main Darien channel, discussing background info that had already been well chewed over by the tabs and various radio pundits all day. Behind the sharp-dressed duo – Maggie and Lev – was a view of Port Gagarin's longest landing strip, seen from the main terminal. But when the shuttlecraft landed, Vizione would hand over to an Earthsphere media channel called Starstream, who had sent a coverage team on board the *Heracles*.

Now Maggie and Lev were offering their own tepid speculation on what the future would hold for Darien, based on the near-content-free summary documents released by the president's office that morning. Donny almost laughed out loud, recalling what he'd heard from Sundstrom's own lips the night before.

If only you knew the truth.

The two aycasters halted their feeble guesswork, announcing the approach of the shuttle before making the verbal handover to Starstream and their solo commentator, Lee Shan.

LEE SHAN: This is Lee Shan welcoming all our viewers and immersers across Earthsphere and beyond on this momentous day in the history of Humankind. I am speaking to you from the shuttlecraft *Achilles* as it descends through banks of cloud towards Darien Colony's largest landing zone, Port Gagarin, named, of course, after the Soviet-era astro-pioneer.

Video (low functionality) The shuttlecraft *Achilles* appears in the western sky, a distant speck that grows into a slender dart as it swoops down over the northern coast. Its flight-path then curves out over the sea before making the approach to Port Gagarin. The vessel's powered descent seems too swift and steep until it slows dramatically, braking on columns of force that ripple the air beneath its fuselage. Engines drone and moments later the *Achilles* settles down gently on its landing gear.

LEE SHAN: The *Achilles* is one of two fast picket boats that the cruiser *Heracles* possesses, both of which can be deployed for combat as well as peaceful purposes, as well as the ship's pinnace, the *Hermes*. The *Heracles*, of course, was recently on duty in the Yamanon Domain as part of Earthsphere's military commitment to the Hegemony-led Freedom Alliance, taking part in the overthrow of the brutal Dol-Das regime, and liberating scores of worlds. We at Starstream salute the bravery of all Earthsphere and Hegemony forces still engaged in pacification operations in the Yamanon.

In the kitchen of a farmhouse built into the side of a hill south-west of Hammergard, Theo Karlsson stared at the portable vee with a mixture of amusement and unease while Rory and the rest of the loader team guffawed.

'We salute the whit?'

'Ah, the brave troops, Rory, for whom we must be joyously united in support!' said Alexei Firmanov.

'*Da*, and not forgetting the songs,' said his brother, Nikolai. 'Heroic songs that we all sing while waving flags, lots of flags.'

Rory squinted at the two grinning Russians. He was a short wiry Scot with unkempt sandy hair and a pair of ice-blue eyes that were full of misgivings.

'You're yanking ma chain, the pair of ye.'

'They're not, Rory,' Theo said. 'All this saluting the troops, waving the flag and singing songs – it is common to authoritarian cultures, like Soviet-era Russia back on Earth.'

'Ah, right, ancient history, aye.' Rory sniffed. 'So is that how Earth is, the now, Major? I thought they've got elections and all that . . .'

'There were elections during the Soviet era, too,' said Alexei. 'But there were no alternatives to the Party's candidate and all the media were tightly controlled.' He glanced at Theo. 'Is it like that on Earth, Major?'

'I'm not entirely sure,' he said. 'But going by radio reports, the political mainstream across most of Earthsphere seems to be pro-Hegemony.'

Nikolai nodded vigorously. 'Is right – have they not elected a woman as interim president, and she's supposed to want to pursue more independent courses?'

Rory laughed. 'Aye, and then we pop up in the Hegemony's back yard, like helpless wee puppies! I bet they're using us tae make sure she toes the line!'

Theo grinned. *Rory, my boy*, he thought, *you're definitely one of the sharper tools in the box.*

Just then, Janssen and Ivanov entered by the kitchen's rear door, the former dumping a bag of tools noisily on the tiled floor, the latter handing Theo a large cluster of keys.

'That's the last of the false walls up,' Ivanov said, loosening his heavy work jacket. 'We restacked the crates and old Tove helped us dirty up his barn floor again.'

Theo laughed. 'Once he quarters his *baro* in there for a night or two it'll be more than filthy enough.' He looked at Janssen. 'Any news from the others?'

'Maclean and Bessonov finished up in the last half-hour,' Janssen said, tugging off his brown woollen hat and scratching his scalp through wild black hair. 'But Hansen's team was held up by a cracked loader axle. They're going to be another hour at least.'

Nikolai shook his head. 'What's that old saying? – "No plan survives contact with the enemy" . . .'

'Right, here we go!' said Rory loudly. 'That's him now, look . . .'

LEE SHAN: And now Ambassador Horst descends the gantry to meet the vice-president, John Balfour. They shake hands, then Vice-President Balfour introduces him to the president of Darien Colony, Holger Sundstrom, who is confined to a wheelchair due to a spinal injury considered untreatable by the colony's medical establishment until now.

Video (low functionality) The ambassador is a tall, grey-haired man with a straight-backed posture and lean but kind face. He smiles as he comes face to face with the president, who is accompanied by a flock of officials and guards, and the smile widens as he leans down slightly to shake the man's hand. After an exchange of pleasantries, the assembled party of dignitaries and their attendants head along a covered walkway towards the main terminal. Behind them, a handful of reporters hurries down from the shuttle, muttering into lip-bead mikes or fiddling with head-mounted cams.

LEE SHAN: Viewers and Glow immersers with holigital systems shall soon be receiving a higher-quality service now that myself and my, ah, assistant Tyberio have disembarked from the ambassador's shuttle. Other viewers, including the newest additions to the Starstream family right here on Darien, will be pleased to see a sharper, more vibrant picture.

'*So are you watching this?*'

'Well, we were, Tomas,' Greg said loudly into his comm above the babble of the score or more Uvovo crammed into the the dig site's meeting hut. 'But the picture just cut out – all we're getting now is intereference.'

'*Ah, no luck,*' said Tomas, his voice sounding thin and whistly. '*We got perfect reception up here, but then our signal is coming directly from Monitorsat.*'

'Aye – why doesna that surprise me?' Greg said, accepting a beaker of something pungent from the Russian researchers then toasting each other.

'*Nastrovya!*'

'*Slainte!*'

'*Hey, what is that you're drinking?*' Tomas said.

'I wish I knew,' Greg said in a hoarse voice, savouring the smoky aftertaste and the warmth in his throat. 'Tastes a bit like . . . grilled bark, or something. 'S no bad, though. So why are you calling me in the middle of this historical event?'

'*Just to let you know that Miss Macreadie is, as they say, carrying a torch for you.*'

'What?' Greg said, so surprised he almost spilled his refilled beaker. 'How d'ye know? – did she say so?'

'*Of course she didn't say so, but when I mentioned your name to her a short while ago she acted so disinterested it was like a sign saying "I want Greg" going on above her head.*'

Greg chuckled at the image. 'You know, your record in these matters isna exactly one hundred per cent.'

'*Maybe so, but I'm sure that she's thinking of you . . .*'

'Tomas, she's a former Enhanced,' he said. 'I don't really think that I'd measure up to her intellect, somehow . . . wait, hold on, our picture's back. I'll speak to you later, O great match-maker!'

'Okay, you're allowed to laugh now, but you'll see that I'm right, trust me. . .'

Video (mid-range functionality)   Together, the president, the ambassador and a senior officer inspect an honour guard of thirty soldiers from the Darien Volunteer Corps, drawn up in two ranks in front of the Port Gagarin terminal building. A small brass band is playing a march off to one side as the three men progress steadily along, pausing to speak with a couple of Corps troopers. The DVC dress uniform is a form-fitting two-piece in field green with dark brown trim, soft green cap with a red cockade, and brown gauntlets. Each soldier carries a sidearm and an autorifle, slug-thrower weapons based on proven twentieth-century designs, while a standard-bearer holds a ceremonial flag showing the DVC badge, crossed swords beneath a planetary globe.

LEE SHAN: The ambassador inspects the honour guard, pausing occasionally to ask a soldier's name or where they are from. Ambassador Robert Horst is a highly experienced diplomat who first came to prominence during the blockade and subsequent liberation of Prodas in 2259. He was involved in negotiations with Tyat terrorists during the Farplains hostage crisis in 2262, and later took up the post of Earthsphere delegate to the short-lived Convoke of Worlds. Most recently he played a key role in the concerted attempts to persuade the Dol-Das regime to give up its planetbreaker weapons. Since the toppling of the Dol-Das dictatorship, however, Robert Horst and his wife have suffered the loss of their only daughter Rosa, who died in a tragic accident while taking part in antiwar protests in the Kingdom of Metraj an e-year ago.

'Poor man,' murmured Svetlana.

Catriona nodded, privately wondering why a presenter would comment so publicly on such sensitive details. Wouldn't the ambassador and his wife be upset at the public discussion of their personal grief? But that was just one snippet in a flood of information which had no context or background for Darien viewers, bare facts merely stated, as if their importance were obvious.

As if we're expected to be impressed, she thought.

She glanced round the room at the rest of her team, or at least the nine who had been nearby and off-duty, and saw a few with perplexed expressions. Others, like Svetlana, were wide-eyed and engrossed in the unfolding ceremony.

Then Tomas sidled into the room and resumed his seat next to hers.

'You missed the ambassador shaking the president's hand,' she said sardonically. 'Where were you?'

He shrugged. 'I remembered that I had to call up Gunther's team to see if they have any spare sample cases – they said they'll send a box over tomorrow. So what's been happening?'

'I wish I could say it's been exciting, but . . .' She indicated the screen. 'It's all protocol and ceremony – the most interesting stuff so far has been this 'caster Lee Shan's side comments. There's been hardly any detail on recent history.'

'It seems that the daily sheets planetside have been running articles on the Swarm War and how Earth was saved from destruction by the brave and altruistic Sendruka Hegemony,' Tomas said, rolling his eyes.

'Aye, well, if that's what they did, then I'm glad,' Catriona said. 'I mean, we know how bad it was for the First Families when the Command AI turned on them – what must it have been like on Earth with the Swarm bombing cities and getting ready to invade?'

'I hope we'll be getting some reliable historical accounts from that period soon,' Tomas said. 'And maybe hear something about the other two colonyships . . . Hm, what's happening now?'

'They're about to hold a press conference,' Catriona said.

'Really?' Tomas said. 'I wonder if they'll take the risk of allowing questions?'

Video (variable functionality)   The terminal foyer is full of a noisy crowd of Dariens, some sitting in rows before a wide, green-draped platform while most of them stand to the rear and sides. Then they erupt into applause and cheering as President Sundstrom in his wheelchair and Ambassador Horst enter and approach the long ramp up to the platform. Once there, accompanied by the vice-president, the mayor of Port Gagarin and a dark-suited security detail, the president grins at the raucous welcome for a moment then raises his hands and makes hushing gestures.

PRESIDENT SUNDSTROM:
Thank you, thank you all for this rousing reception. Well, I can see how amazed and delighted you all are at this aston-ishing event, that 150 years after the *Hyperion* touched down we've re-established contact with Earth. To know that Earth survived the Swarm War and went on to become strong and influential is an incredible source of joy and pride. So before I become overwhelmed, let me just state that it gives me enormous pleasure to say on behalf of all our citizens – Ambassador Horst, welcome to Darien!

Video (variable functionality)   Even louder applause breaks out again and the president moves his wheelchair back a few feet. The ambassador smiles and as he steps forward the crowd quietens down to an expectant hush.

AMBASSADOR HORST:
From the bottom of my heart, I thank you for this warm and generous reception. It is a privilege and an honour to stand here before you as the personal representative of Erica Castiglione, president of Earthsphere, for the colony you have made here in the face of such hardship is proof of the indomitable spirit of Humanity!

[Applause]

The discovery of Darien Colony is of great importance to all the peoples of Earth, not least because the fate of the three colonyships has been an unresolved enigma since the defeat of the Swarm a century and a half ago. We know that each ship was under orders to flee the Solar System by taking random hyperspace jumps, which is why the destinations or whereabouts of the other two ships, the *Forrestal* and the *Tenebrosa*, remain a mystery.

Of course, the original colonisation plan consisted of fifteen ships, most of which were partially complete when the Swarm invaded the Solar System. Those first unprovoked attacks slaughtered millions across our world and destroyed many of those vessels, which is why your forebears became the first to depart Humanity's home on such a desperate mission.

It would be difficult to overstate the intensity of interest in Darien that is gripping Earth and all the Human communities across Earthsphere. Indeed, both the Migratory Service and the Diplomacy Office have been inundated with requests from Russia, Scotland and Scandinavia from those wishing to make contact with long-lost branches of their families. This will involve a considerable amount of work, matching records and DNA, but we'll begin this as soon as possible.

I feel I should at this point give you an outline of the wider interstellar situation and Darien's place in it. Your world is very far from Earth, almost 15,000 lightyears, and in your immediate vicinity are a host of civilisations with which Earthsphere has had little or no regular contact. Fortunately, the dominant power in the area is one of Earthsphere's allies, the Sendruka Hegemony, which has promised to maintain peace and stability in the region, thereby safeguarding Darien's independence and sovereignty. And in order to establish good relations without delay, a very senior representative of the Hegemony – High Monitor the Exalted Utavess Kuros – is on board the *Heracles* and will be coming down to meet you all tomorrow.

Yet despite the great distances involved, there will be many opportunities for aid and trade between Darien and Earthsphere, as well as other markets in the area. In addition, your contact with the Uvovo and the subsequent cooperation is bound to be a source of fascination for xeno-specialists and other scientists across civilised space. You may not be aware of it yet, but Human communities enjoy excellent relations with many different sentient races, an experience you will soon be able to share as friendly civilisations in the vicinity apply to open embassies here.

That is all that I have to say for now. I know many of you have hundreds of questions to put to me, but I intend to provide answers at a full press briefing to be held tomorrow afternoon in Hammergard. So let me once again thank you for your heartwarming welcome and I look forward to speaking with you tomorrow.

8

KUROS

High Monitor the Exalted Utavess Kuros watched as Horst and the Darien president left the platform to a chorus of futile shouted questions. There were others studying the screen in the *Heracles*'s lowlit lecture theatre, his personal bodyguard of eight Ezgara commandos. Quad-armed forms in dark blue body-armour, they sat in the front row, silent in close-fitting helmets, faceless, motionless.

And one other, visible only to Kuros.

'I mislike these Humans,' the General said. *'They are a disrespectful and undisciplined rabble riddled with dissidents who spread poisonous speculation through their media, which is lamentably unguided. Even after an alliance lasting nearly eighty velanns, they still have not learned their place, or shown any devotional progress, and these colonists are sure to be even worse!'*

Kuros smiled at his lifelong companion and AI mindbrother, General Gratach.

'Then you agree that they present something of a challenge?' he said in his thoughts.

The General folded his muscular arms and Kuros heard the metallic rustle of armour platelets. In keeping with the real, historical Gratach, the AI was attired in the battledress of a senior Abrogator officer of the Three Revolutions War, an ornate harness of gleaming gold and red, with powershield spikes studding his arms and shoulders, each one bearing a small votive pennon, silver lettering on black. His helmet had a bronze sheen and was plainer, its moulded circlet of *chusken* skulls offset by the tactical eyepieces that sat poised at eyebrow level, ready to swivel down.

'*Challenge*,' grunted Gratach. '*Only in terms of the Hegemony's immediate interests – militarily, the colony is insignificant.*'

Kuros nodded, thinking back to his audience with the Fifth Tri-Advocate just hours before leaving Iseri, the Sendrukan homeworld. Clad in austere grey, the Fifth had been sitting in a high-backed overpod, flanked by holograms of his mindbrother advocates, against a backdrop of translucent curtains. He had questioned Kuros on the Darien task dossier which he had received less than a day before. Satisfied with Kuros's grasp of the essentials, the Fifth had then offered his observations.

'We note that the bulk of your record is divided between Boundary Sector 12, where you held the post of Second Suppressor, and the Pothiwa Conformation, where you led several trade delegations. Hopefully, you will only need to draw upon the latter experience in this assignment. You will find that Humans are sentimental, especially about military events and achievements: helpfully, their governments routinely employ such sentimentality to mask historical details and to maintain doctrinal integrity as well as popular support.

'You should make frequent reference to the friendship between the Hegemony and Humans, mutual cooperation and shared values, even though these things are largely illusory. And be aware of media surveillance at all times: take no action and make no disclosure that may betray our interest in the ruins of the Ancients. Devise spectacles to divert the attention of both the media agents and the colonists . . .'

Then one of the AI advocates had turned in Kuros's direction – its image was that of the Avulser Hegemon Moardis, a gaunt, golden-eyed figure attired in a rich red robe whose collar supported an array of black vertical spikes that curved round the back of the head. Moardis was the Hegemon who, 400 years ago, had fought off the clandestine invasions of the Ghaw parasites and eventually eradicated them and the neighbouring civilisations that they had subverted. Only the most powerful of AIs were allowed to adopt the image of such an illustrious Hegemon.

'Much depends on this mission, Utavess Kuros. If you succeed, the future security and glory of the Hegemony will safeguarded in Voloasti's name for generations to come, such is the nature of the power that awaits us – do you know what it is called?'

'A warpwell, Your Immanence.'

'This is not the first we have investigated, but it may be the first to be found still functioning. If so, the Hegemony will have a gateway into the lower domains of hyperspace. When we control them, we can deny any foreseeable adversary the strategic scope to become a threat. Peace and glory shall be our legacy.'

The Fifth had spoken again. 'Prepare yourself thoroughly, Kuros. Pray to Voloasti for protection and guidance. Plan for all eventualities. Let nothing be a surprise to you. Use the media agents against your adversaries or even against themselves. Ensure a triumphant outcome, and fame, honour and riches will be your reward. The Hegemon himself has promised.'

And all through the audience, the second AI advocate had kept silent, its form that of a coiled, iron-scaled ocean mohoro, a mighty yet enigmatic creature from ancient Sendrukan mythology. While the other advocates had talked of glory and honour, the mohoro had simply stared at him, red-jewelled eyes fathomless, jaws parted to show triple rows of silver fangs.

Now, as he stood in the dimness of the lecture theatre, he reflected upon that encounter and knew that the mohoro's relentless gaze had spoken of the retribution he would suffer if he failed.

But there will be no humiliating blunders, he thought. *Nor any bitter bones of defeat. I shall steer events, rather than be steered by them.*

He considered the images on the screen, segments showing the Earth ambassador's answers to certain questions and switching back to the studio commentators, all sound muted. He smiled faintly as his purpose became a little clearer and glanced at the General.

'While the full glare of media interest is focused here, we cannot afford the luxury of deploying overt force to secure our objectives. We must apply a certain subtlety.'

General Gratach sneered. '*Subtlety! These media insects may buzz and chatter but their stings can still be a threat.*'

'Of course,' Kuros said. 'In every circle of life there are ruthless adepts, thus in our dealings with them it will pay to be subtle, especially since we Sendrukans have a reputation for directness.' He gazed thoughtfully at his Ezgara bodyguards. 'And if we steer the correct events, we shall gain indirect control by creating a situation in which our direct actions would appear normal. From there it is a short step to neutralising them altogether.'

'*So what is to be our strategy tomorrow?*' the General said. '*Sing the insects and the savages to sleep?*'

'Yes – flattery, charm, a dose of anti-Swarm flag-waving, an appropriate measure of self-deprecating humour to encourage trust, and after that normalisation.'

'*And if that fails to work in the short term?*'

Kuros smiled. 'Voloasti will guide us, old friend. Indirect control is still control.'

He turned to the Ezgara. Eight visored faces were looking his way, blue-armoured, still and waiting, all seemingly identical apart from the nearest, who wore an officer's flash on his temple, a small white triangle. Nothing about their posture betrayed any inner state of mind, but Kuros knew what lay hidden behind those masks.

'Captain,' he said. 'I have a lengthy and demanding assignment that will require two of your most adaptable warriors.'

'By your command, Exalted,' the Ezgara captain said in a flat voice, then pointed at two of the remaining seven; without a word they rose and moved out to stand before the High Monitor. They only came up to Kuros's shoulder, yet he knew that for ferocity and single-minded devotion to duty the Ezgara were unmatched. Then he began to explain the details of this special and undoubtedly dangerous assignment, while off to one side, General Gratach smiled his approval.

9

LEGION

On Yndyeri Duvo, the Kiskashin line-pirate was experiencing a glow of pride in his mercantile skills. He had managed to resell the Human colony report (tagged with some Human cultural profiles) to a wandering Vusarkan academic, a Piraseri market haruspex and a Makhori scholar with an obsession for all things Human-related. There had been other interested parties, but he decided against further delay in relaying it to Lord Mysterious. Besides, new merchandise was continually arriving: time might be a function of the space–entropy continuum but it was also money, thus money was intimately bound up with the structure of the universe. As he delighted in explaining to the clients and customers to whom he turned his attention as the Human colony report flashed away through the local systemnet to Duvo's sister planet.

Off the western coast of Yndyeri Tetro's single massive landmass, something stirred in the depths. The waters sparkled and teemed with life all the way from the shallow shoreline out to the continental shelf, until they plunged into descending gradations of shadow, increasingly turbid realms of oceanic gloom thinly populated by rare grotesque creatures. Only a meagre radiance reached the lower depths, reducing jutting features to vague, blurred outlines, yet a ragged trench gaped there, a sheer-sided fissure full of ancient, impenetrable night. And down, further down, where the last vestiges of surface light died in the intense darkness, where a cold, crushing pressure threatened obliteration, down there amongst unseen, undisturbed debris, an awareness stirred.

But it was an awareness without consciousness, an awareness of the environment: sea temperature, tides, currents and the presence of threat-level objects passing above or below sea-level. Awareness of the subjective physical, the balance of mechanical and organic, and the entropic state of both, which was not good. Objective assessment of repair and regulation systems, and of overall integrity, which was well below optimum. And awareness of the information that trickled in via its receptors from time to time, of the ancient biocrystalline matrices which deconstructed, analysed and searched for matches to an array of images in two, three and four dimensions as well as any linguistic equivalents. It was a search that the awareness had repeatedly and tirelessly undertaken for centuries upon centuries, without a single instance of success.

Until now, when the memory buffer received a data packet detailing the discovery of a lost Human colony world called Darien.

The awareness stripped the Darien report down to lists of phrases and words, and stacks of images: its analytic processes sorted them into levels of potential meaning, discarded the obviously trivial, then sorted through the visual data. When it came to the stills and motion images of some ruins which the Humans had uncovered near their settlements, additional processing capacity was quickly brought online as the images were examined down to extrapolated resolutions. The awareness devoted more resources to the analysis, and when it was finally certain it opened pathways in the biocrystalline matrices and let power from the duality core flood through them.

Tailored glands were stimulated, capillaries relaxed, and enzymes leaked into the heavily shielded organic cortex. Synaptic transfer spread through neural nets dormant for long ages, opening up level after level, augmenting the awareness, feeding a burgeoning brightness . . .

And he awoke to the steel pains of his aged, wounded body, lying on a cold seabed on an alien world in an alien universe. He knew that his aeons-old purpose and duty must have come round at last, otherwise he would still be sleeping, and that was a joy which in some ways helped him to endure the torment of old, old injuries. But when he reached for the memories of when and how he had been damaged, there was nothing, a gap where familiar recollection should have been waiting to be relived. He felt the panicky edge of fear and subdued it, focusing on discovering the reason.

What he found was a terrible swathe of decay which had eaten into one of the biocrystal chines of his cortical augmentation. His awareness function had failed to detect it as the sensor web had itself been affected, and the worst of it was that the rot was still advancing. If unchecked, it would in just a few years kill him.

His thoughts were wry with a black humour. <To have survived these limitless chasms of time and all the trials that came before is still a great achievement. And now I have the opportunity to deliver unto my brothers and sisters a final victory. I am of the Legion, and although individual knights may fall, the Legion must triumph. The laws of convergence must triumph.>

The analysis of the Darien report was before him, but he decided he would institute a final recovery trawl through the corroded biocrystal while he assessed the data.

He saw the world Darien, a place of lush vegetation and a living landscape of mountains and rivers; he saw the moon and recognised remnants of the enemy's defences with no sign of his presence . . .

With the powers of their machinemind planetoids, the Legion of Avatars cut through the extrinsic and intrinsic layers of material existence and opened an unstable fissure in the face of reality. In vast phalanxes they fled from a dying universe into this one, then used the planetoids to tunnel up through the hyperspace tiers of this one in search of a new home, a new dominion . . .

He saw the colonists, the Humans, saw all their weaknesses and saw how weak they were in the face of the political realities surrounding them . . .

There had been a battle, a gargantuan struggle spread across many thousands of star systems, a savage, resounding clash in

*which whole worlds and entire sentient species were eradicated as
a matter of course . . .*

He saw the visual data, the near-complete ruins amid the forest,
recognised more of the enemy's work and wondered if it held their
deadliest weapon, the one that had defeated the Legion even in the
full glory of its might. If so, it could be turned to their advantage . . .

*Fragmentary memories were being recovered . . . in hard vacuum,
a close-quarters grappling struggle with one of the enemy's sentient
machines, hooked and edged extensors searching for purchase on
each other, then one of his greater tentacles found the jutting edge of
a hull plate, wrenched it aside and thrust a high-energy lance into
the vitals . . . the knights of the Legion of Avatars gathered in a
council of war, their millions waiting in curved ranks and arrays
within the flickering gloom of a deep, desolate tier of hyperspace, all
intoning the catechisms of convergence . . . and an old, old memory
of his own cyborg-form not long after his transformation, the long,
armoured carapace patterned in dark reds and greens, the ten
greater, articulated tentacles and the six lesser ones tipped with every
kind of effector from tearing chainclaws to delicate manipulators, a
magnificent new body which had freed him from the pains of the
flesh . . . then a part of him realised that there was no memory of his
organic appearance from before his ascent to biomechanical immortality, nothing except the vague recollection that his chosen
cyborg-form was utterly different from his old body . . .*

He assessed the Darien situation and the strategic implications of
its location as well as the fact that the Humans were dispatching a
mission to their lost colony. Then he considered various possible
journey routes, but not for himself. With its battered substructures,
leaking carapace plates, stuttering main drives, and near-defunct
sensor array, his biomachine body might be able to drag itself into
orbit but the lengthy voyage to Darien would be too hazardous. He
would have to delegate that grave responsibility to lesser agents,
three Instruments to carry out the task, each one an abridged simulacrum of his own persona, each one created out of his own neural
substrate, each one a small loss, and a small addition to his freight
of pain.

10

THEO

Theo hated formal occasions, and since the ambassador's arrival three days ago he'd had to endure five of the damn things, at Sundstrom's insistence. Hammergard's main hospital, the McPhail Memorial, a zeplin yard, a root refinery, a church, and a distillery. Today, Ambassador Horst had been due to spend the morning at Pushkinskog, the Uvovo-tended daughter-forest south of Lake Morwen, but plans had changed overnight and now he was visiting Membrance Vale near Landfall Town, to see the hollow shell of the *Hyperion* and to pay his respects to the dead. And Sundstrom had asked Theo to attend, in an unofficial capacity. Tonight, a banquet in honour of the ambassadors was due to be held in the Assembly ballroom, followed by speeches and a ceilidh.

Theo was strolling along the westward road that led from Landfall to the vales of the Tuulikki Hills, which would take a good thirty minutes on foot. The morning sky was bright and clear, the air cold and laced with the odours of growth, ideal weather for walking. Besides, Theo had decided to walk so that he could meet someone on the way, and was pondering once more what Sundstrom had said yesterday. Holger was a few years older than Theo but he considered that they were essentially of the same generation; during the Winter Coup they had been on opposite sides, Sundstrom a Trond councilman who voted against supporting Viktor Ingram's insurrection then went underground to actively work against the coup. That and his political efforts at reconciliation while arguing forcibly for the new Accord policies had persuaded Theo that he was a man of integrity and substance. In addition, just as Theo had had his years in the wilderness after the failure of the coup, so too had Holger been forced to quit politics after the injury that led to his lower-body paralysis. Yet in later life, both found themselves back in the thick of it.

And Sundstrom's mysterious information source troubled Theo. The Enhanced were the living results of a short-sighted genetics programme shut down twenty years ago, most of whom worked on research programmes of one kind or another. Redesigned cortexes and synaptic connectivity had given them astonishing mental abilities, but they suffered from a corresponding lack of social intuition that made it hard for them to deal with ordinary people. Theo had only met a few in his time, but he knew from reliable contacts that the Enhanced were essentially looked upon by government departments not just as a kind of intellectual resource but as a badge of prestige which, once acquired, was retained for as long as possible. The president was supposed to be above this kind of bureaucratic jostling, which made Theo wonder how much political risk he might be taking if he was using Enhanced help.

Before long the road passed into the woods, their overarching branches interweaving to form a leafy tunnel through which spears of sunlight lanced to touch the road with gold. This was a sparsely populated area, and apart from the occasional spinner-bus taking visitors back and forth, Theo saw no one else. When he came to where the road crossed a steep-sided gully, he stepped off the verge and sat down on a weatherbeaten bench overlooking the crevice. Moments later heavy footsteps approached through the undergrowth and an overalled Rory sat down heavily beside him.

'You're not exactly a woodsman, Rory.'

'Aye, well, I was never any good at all that creepin' about and hidin', Major – canna stand the bugs.' As if to make his point he vigorously waved away a few hovering insects. Theo grinned.

'Let us hope we don't need to head off into the wilds,' he said. 'Anyway, what have you learned?'

'Right, Ah got tae the *Hyperion* early this morning and sure enough, more graffiti. The manager and his boss were practically tearing their hair out so when Ah turn up wi' my handy cleaning sprays and sponges they put me to work straight off.'

Theo frowned. Such vandalism was almost unheard of on Darien, yet since the arrival of the *Heracles* more and more had been cropping up, mainly in Hammergard and nearby towns. Then yesterday, the Knudson Ecumenical Church and the Chernov Brothers distillery had both been defaced shortly before Ambassador Horst was due to arrive, which was why Theo had sent Rory on ahead earlier, pre-equipped.

'What did it say? Any reference to these personal AIs?'

Rory's eyebrows went up. 'Oh aye! Stuff like "Machine-lovers leave Darien", "No AI-slaves here", "The only good AI is a deleted AI", that kinda thing, along with "Darien for Dariens" and FDF logos.'

FDF stood for 'Free Darien Faction', a previously unknown group clearly intent on stirring up resentment and unrest, neither of which Theo was strongly opposed to, provided it was for a good reason. But the FDF was appealing to the baser instincts of parochialism and prejudice, and with yesterday's breaking news about the use of AI implants by the Earthsphere ambassador and others, a dose of fear was stirred into the mix. No doubt Horst's visit to the site of the colonists' triumph over a deadly AI enemy was meant to counter such adverse popular opinion.

He'll never get that imp back in its bottle, he thought. *The only positive tack he could take is to meet the distrust head-on, but he doesn't seem to have the steel for it. Wonder what advice he's getting from this AI companion of his?*

'Okay, Rory,' he said, getting to his feet. 'I have to get along. You be on your way to the Pushkinskog daughter-forest – I've already told Listener Gansua to expect you.'

Rory stood, scratching his sandy hair. 'Whit d'ye think these FDF guys'll do there? – graffiti a tree?'

'God knows. For all we know they may not be willing to involve the Uvovo, but given their lack of respect for certain landmarks I wouldn't bet on it.'

Rory paused, a half-smile on his lips. 'I guess you'll have been asking about the ither colonyships, Major, aye? I heard that they've still no' been found.'

'Still missing, Rory, still a mystery.'

'Right, aye, but it makes ye wonder, ye know . . . I mean, there's the old *Hyperion* just up the road,' he said. 'What if the other ship AIs cracked up too, like a design flaw, maybe?'

Theo shrugged. 'I've heard that theory before, and if it is true then perhaps we are the lucky ones to have survived.'

'Call this luck, Major?'

Exchanging waves, they went their separate ways, Theo's smile fading a little, his thoughts growing sombre as he crossed the bridge that led to the outskirts of Membrance Vale.

11

GREG

The reporter Lee Shan scanned the ruins of the site through an opaque oval eyepiece attached to a sleek white headset, its flattened band encircling his bald head and anchored to a second around his neck. An equipment pannier floated quietly nearby on suspensors.

'Very nice, Doctor Cameron, very atmospheric, so what we would like to do is take lots of shots of the ruins – and some of you at work, obviously, especially at the sacrificial altar, then we embed simz of those Uvolos, but that'll be done Earthside, before tiercast . . .'

Greg stared at the reporter, Lee Shan, with a mixture of annoyance and intent curiosity, wondering who was speaking, the man or the AI implant. He then pointed to the grey stone bowl to which the reporter had been drawn.

'They're called the Uvovo, and that is not a sacrificial altar—'

'I see, I see, so do you know what it is, Doctor?'

'Mr Lee,' he said carefully, 'the Uvovo abandoned these ruins thousands of years ago, after which this entire promontory was covered with jungle. Where we are standing was the roof and this bowl was most probably used for ritual fires, perhaps even cooking.'

'So you're not completely certain what it is?'

'The Uvovo have affirmed that blood sacrifice never played any part in their culture.'

'A useful testimony, I am sure, Doctor, but after several millennia how can *they* be sure?'

Lee Shan smiled. In the background his aircams darted around just above head height, scanning everything in sight and unintentionally providing great amusement for the Uvovo scholars. The reporter's small, neat smile, however, served only to aggravate Greg beyond the already strained limits of his courtesy. He knew that he should ignore the man's arrogance, but the situation was like a door through which he could not help but walk.

He matched the reporter's smile with one of his own.

'You know, Mr Lee, perhaps you've got a point. Perhaps we're not being imaginative enough in our hypotheses. How about this – we could suggest that the ancient Uvovo sacrificed criminals and prisoners to, let's say, giant alligator creatures from the sea, and that these blood-soaked ceremonies took place at night because the alligator-things only came up to the beach after dark. It may be that those sea-borne predators who failed to consume any of the sacrificial carrion were themselves killed and eaten by the Uvovo ancestors . . .'

'Doctor, do you have any proof for any of this?'

'Not a scrap but it's such fun, don't you think? And – *and* to demonstrate these hypotheses I might be able to persuade our Uvovo scholars to dress up in furs and ritual paint then hold a re-enactment for you and the cameras after nightfall, complete with torches, drums and barefoot dancing. Perhaps some of my Norj and Dansk colleagues might come in horned helmets and I'll wear my kilt. What d'ye say?'

There was an awestruck silence, and the sense of breaths being held by the Uvovo scholars and Rus researchers, who had all paused to stare at the confrontation. Anger smouldered in the reporter's eyes, but his voice remained level and unhurried.

'I do not take kindly to those who impede my pursuit of the facts, Doctor.'

'Well, perhaps you made the mistake of ignoring the facts you didn't like and making up ones that you did.' He lowered his voice. 'You also made the mistake of thinking that we're all gullible yokels eager for your godlike wisdom. Or perhaps you were badly advised – I understand that these personal AIs aren't quite infallible.'

Lee Shan's gaze was all icy calm.

'So I am to be shown the way out?'

'Sadly no, Mr Lee, since you undoubtedly have written permission from the Institute to be here, which means that you are at liberty to record whatever you please. However, I insist that you do not interfere with any excavation or exposed relics, nor interrupt any of my staff while engaged in their work. As for background detail, you have a copy of the site's tourist dossier – I suggest that you read it.'

For a moment Lee Shan said nothing, then gave an acquiescing bow of the head and turned away to his pannier. Greg breathed in deeply and hurried back to the small hut where he had been categorising finds before the reporter's arrival. He knew that his treatment of the man had gone beyond rebuke into public humiliation, which a media celebrity like Lee Shan was not likely to forgive or forget. And yet it had been so satisfying, a guilty pleasure.

It took about fifteen minutes and a fresh cup of kaffe, but eventually he settled back into the familiar rhythm of his work, sorting, image-tabbing and storing. Before him was a shallow box full of cloth sample bags containing shards of pottery and other vessels removed from a recently discovered midden in the northern corner of the Giant's Shoulder site. Similar finds had been made ever since the colonists began building or tilling the land along the coast. Whatever the location, unearthed pottery fragments showed a fondness for bulbous, organic shapes fabulously adorned with flora and fauna. But those found on Giant's Shoulder were more plainly decorated with curious symbols like raindrops or stylised flames, usually drawn around small bumps and nubs in the glazed surface. Oddly, most Uvovo Greg spoke to expressed uncertainty about their meaning, claiming that such symbols were not used on Nivyesta, under the spreading canopies of Segrana.

So now the scholars and researchers had found a new source of remains, either a pile of discards or a store that had been wrecked in the cataclysm event that struck Darien ten millennia ago. Greg was just starting on the last bag of finds when there was a knock at the door. A glance at the clock on the shelf made him realise how long he had been working, and out loud he said, 'Come in.'

The door opened and a middle-aged man in an Earthsphere olive-and-maroon uniform entered.

'Doctor Cameron?'

'Indeed I am, and you must be Sub-Lieutenant Lavelle,' he said, rising to shake hands. 'Good to know that the *Heracles* can do without its junior officers – we must be living in a state of impeccable safety and security!'

'Certainly feels that way, sir,' said the officer with a smile. Then he saw what Greg was working on. 'If you're busy I can come back another time.'

'Just now is fine, Mr Lavelle,' he said. 'Since our exchange of messages yesterday, I've been looking forward to showing a real xeno-specialist round the place. I'm almost finished here anyway, so if you would follow me . . .'

'Please, call me Marcus.'

'Okay, you be Marcus and I'll be Greg,' he said as they stepped outside.

Despite his composed air, Greg was truly excited at being able to show off the site to a visitor from Earth. The vee and the papers were full of profiles of non-Human races, although the focus had settled on upright bipeds like the Sendruka, the Henkaya and the Gomedra. He was eager to find out how the temple site and other Uvovo remains rated in the Human experience of other worlds and civilisations.

Briskly, he led the xeno-specialist Lavelle across the flagstoned centre of the excavation, explaining on the way that this was the roof of a large central structure and that in all probability an ancient Uvovo complex lay directly beneath their feet.

'Houses, rooms, galleries, outbuildings,' Greg said. 'Who knows what might be down there, carved out of the rock? All we have to do is dig out ten thousand years' worth of compacted biomass soil and countless root networks. Just think of all the spades we'll go through.'

They came to a halt before a tall wooden scaffolding lashed here and there to a sheer stone wall covered with relief carvings. The action of rainwater and plant growth over the centuries had left veinlike grooves in the stone as well as cracked and blank areas, but what remained was breathtaking. An intricate inter-twining of images, trees, creatures and the Uvovo themselves filled the lower part of the wall, while above the carven jungle, hanging amid a starry sky, were several geometric shapes from which spine- and hook-like objects rained down. Yet from the jungle mass thin shafts lanced upwards, spearing through some of the invaders which were depicted in pieces. Greg pointed out the details as they climbed the scaffold.

'War in the heavens, Marcus,' he said. 'Uvovo legend calls it the War of the Long Night, an epic struggle between two groups of transcendent beings, the Dreamless, cold and pitiless, and the benevolent, compassionate Ghost Gods on whose side the Uvovo, or rather their protector Segrana, fought. Which is how their sagas tell it.'

Lavelle nodded. 'Segrana, the living forest – is it true that they believe it to be a conscious entity?'

'Yes, they do. Segrana is part of the web of life, opposed to an antilife principle occasionally referred to as the Unmaker . . . did you access the university files as I suggested?'

'Yes, I did – your notes on the Uvovo sites are quite extensive but I managed to pick up the main points before leaving for Darien.'

'I see,' Greg said, feeling slightly nonplussed. 'Well, I'll spare you the basic spiel then . . . oh, you know about Ferguson's maps of Nivyesta and the first shuttle missions?'

Lavelle nodded and took out a small flat grey unit and patted it. 'I went over a summary of the colony's history on my way down. You followed a very interesting path to get where you are today.'

Greg laughed. 'You mean we were a capricious, squabbling rabble!'

'Well, divergent and competitive,' Lavelle said with a half-smile.

'Wouldn't you say that Earth's history since the Swarm War has been at least as interesting?' Greg said. 'Explorers on other colony worlds must have uncovered the remains of vanished civilisations as well as discovering existing ones.'

'There are more historical parallels than you might think,' Lavelle said. 'About sixty years ago we and some of our allies joined the Sendruka Hegemony in their interdiction against the Jesme Aggregation because one of their planet-clans was supporting insurgents within Brolturan territory. Anyway, almost half of the Human colonies were so opposed to it that they resigned from the Earthplus Council, cut off all ties with the homeworld, and started calling themselves the Vox Humana League. When the campaign ended a few years later, some ties were restored but certain embargoes – on weapons for example – remain in force to this day.'

Greg nodded. 'We've had our schisms as well. During the New Town Secession, the Scots, Rus and Norj allies formed armed camps against one another which caused a lot of bitterness considering all the intermarriage and cross-community links.'

'Yes, and the bitterness still affects policy decisions decades later. The Vox Humana rebels continue to defy Earthsphere sovereignty and refuse to play their part in the Security Net, while malcontents on Earth and other worlds launch public attacks on our coalition with the Hegemony. But the fact is that it's a dangerous galaxy out there and we have to stand by our true friends in the face of the threat to our shared values. Anti-Sendrukans I've got no time for.'

Shared values? Greg thought. It seemed like a strange declaration to make, one he would normally have latched on to and probed until its meaning became clearer. But he decided to say nothing and let the man talk.

'As for remains of vanished cultures, some colony worlds have reported quite a few finds – habitable planets near the ancient centres and flows of galactic civilisation usually provide some evidence of previous occupation. As soon as major discoveries are made, however, the sites are supposed to be opened up for inspection by the Grand Commission for Antiquities unless a commission signatory files an objection. In the case of Darien, four have done so – four, which is almost unheard of. Earthsphere was first to file under rights of sovereignty and duty of care towards the Uvovo; the Brolturans then filed their objections with the Commission, claiming that the Darien system lies within a tract of space promised to them by their god, Voloasku, as explicitly written in the *Omgur*, their divine scripture . . .'

'Voloasku? So who's Voloasti? – I heard that mentioned by someone.'

'That's the supreme being of the Hegemony's orthodox creed,' Lavelle said. 'Also supported by their version of the *Omgur* which, for some reason, hasn't led to similar claims.'

'You cannot be serious,' Greg said, laughing.

'I'm afraid I am,' Lavelle said. 'The third to object was the Second Spiral Sage of Buranj, who claimed that your temple's position on a jutting promontory exactly matches the description of the tomb of the divine Father-Sage Arksasbe. He also insists that the defiling presence of non-believers ceases immediately.'

Greg stared at him for an astonished moment, then leaned forward to gaze out at the worn walls and columns, the Uvovo scholars working in a stepped trench near the northern barrier and the Rus researchers, who were patiently sifting dirt removed from the test ditches over to the south. Then he looked back at Lavelle, smiling.

'Unfortunately, Marcus, it doesn't look as though these non-believers are likely to drop what they are doing. And in fact, I think that my own non-devoutness has actually deepened since learning of the esteemed Second Spiral Sage's decree . . . by the way, is there a First Spiral Sage?'

'Oh yes, but he's far too devout to be sullied by temporal matters.'

'But of course. So who filed the fourth objection?'

'The Hegemony. They argued that the Grand Commission of Antiquities cannot carry out its work until the conflicting claims of sovereignty and title have been resolved. Accordingly, all four objectors have appointed adjudicators and the first hearings will take place soon.' Lavelle grinned. 'The whole process could take two or three years!'

Greg smiled uncertainly. 'You seem very pleased about all of this, Marcus, and I don't know why.'

'Well, if the Commission's inspectors had been empowered to oversee this site, you and your people would probably be prohib-ited from any excavation or artefact-handling, on grounds of inadequate training or the use of lo-tech instruments. But they haven't, which means you can continue working here . . .' He paused. '. . . and I can show you the location of the underground chambers and their hidden entrance.'

Greg's thoughts jolted to a halt, and he stared at the man. 'Wha . . . what did you say?'

Lavelle glanced out at the site then went on in quieter tones.

'Greg, the cornerstone of field archaeology is determining where the treasure is before you begin digging. A researcher from, say, Planitia University would have the equipment to make any number of subsurface scans before breaking ground, but you don't have that luxury. On the other hand, I have – I used *Heracles*'s sensor array to make focused scans of the interior of Giant's Shoulder.' From an inner pocket he took a folded sheaf of pages and gave them to Greg. 'These are copies made yester-day and the day before – there's not much fine detail but you can see the regular lines of the buried temple complex and beneath it . . .'

Greg stared at several views of Giant's Shoulder, digital sweeps showing a vaguely block-shaped recess extending about 60 metres down into the promontory, just as he had speculated. And there, not far below, was something circular – glancing between pages, contrasting different views, it really did look like a chamber of some kind, circular, perhaps 80 metres across . . .

He peered closer, sorted through the images, comparing two in particular, one of which seemed to show a thready, fragmentary straight line leaving the mysterious chamber and pointing south, while the other had a similar line leading inwards from the southern face of Giant's Shoulder, pointing north.

'It is what it looks like,' said Lavelle. 'It's an entranceway and a passage of some kind.'

Greg stared at the images with a burning intensity, thinking about the sheer sides of Giant's Shoulder, cracked and weathered rock faces veiled in tangles of vine and half-dead root. Only experienced climbers could safely traverse that kind of headwall, yet when he mentioned this to Lavelle he laughed and nodded.

'Well, fortunately I am a qualified climber, so if you need my help . . .'

Greg looked up. 'Is tomorrow too soon?'

'Hmm, I'm rostered on tomorrow morning – how about in the afternoon?'

'That would be . . . perfect. Marcus, forgive me for asking, but what do you have to gain out of this?'

Lavelle smiled thoughtfully, as if partly at his own thoughts. 'I guess I could say it's about fame and recognition – well, maybe that is part of it but mainly it's the chance to explore an ancient hidden mystery never before seen by Humans, to be the first to see it and touch it! It's the fourteen-year-old in me, I'm afraid.'

'In that case, my fourteen-year-old salutes yours – perhaps we should start a club.'

Laughing, the two men descended the scaffold ladders, arranged for tomorrow, said farewells and parted, Lavelle heading for the zeplin station, Greg hurrying back to the cataloguing hut. On entering he noticed a message tag on his workstation's screen, a black-and-yellow one signifying a locked priority, the kind that seldom contained good news. He keyed in his password, read it through, and groaned. Then reread it, just to be sure, and this time laughed drily. The message was from the office of V. Petrovich, the Director of the Darien Institute, informing Greg that tomorrow, at noon, High Monitor Kuros – and his extensive entourage – would be making a very official, very public visit to Giant's Shoulder. Several hours prior to this, an officer from the Office of Guidance and the commander of the High Monitor's bodyguard would arrive to inspect the site and ensure its security. Greg was to offer them complete cooperation and full access to all areas and to all personnel records. It ended with a pointed and direct instruction, essentially a prohibition on his 'indulging in any commentary or verbal wordplay that could be construed as antagonistic or insulting'.

Greg smiled, shook his head. The director was an old sparring partner and knew just what he was capable of, a state of being not unlike that of the reporter, Lee Shan ... who, he realised, would almost certainly be present tomorrow.

You wait and hope for a good audience to come along, he thought, *then suddenly it's there but you're not allowed to perform.*

Then he realised that he would have to postpone tomorrow's exploration with Lavelle so, with a sigh, he sat down at his desk and began composing a short message.

12

ROBERT

The Earthsphere embassy was a modest, two-storey townhouse near the centre of Hammergard, timber-framed and part of a short terrace of commercial properties and offices. Although the embassy staff had only had the keys for four days, Robert Horst had insisted that their public information desk was up and running from day one. This was in stark contrast to the Sendrukan Hegemony embassy, which was a villa in walled grounds in an affluent district, and which was reportedly refusing all requests and approaches.

Robert Horst was in a conference call with Deputy-President Jardine and the opposition Consolidation party's external affairs spokeswoman, Linn Kringen, and trying to explain why there was little or no openness from the Hegemony representative.

'. . . what you have to understand is that High Monitor Kuros is not an official Hegemony ambassador,' he said to the faces on his desk screen. 'Officially, Darien falls within the Brolturan sphere of influence, so Kuros has to wait for the Brolturans to appoint their own representative before taking on an ambassadorial rank and opening for business.'

Linn Kringen smiled blandly. She was a pale-blonde, middle-aged woman with a steely gaze. 'This is hardly a comforting situation, Ambassador, especially in the light of the recent revelation that the Brolturan Compact wants to assert sovereignty over us! You can surely see how troubling this would be to all Dariens.'

'Troubling' was putting it mildly. Someone in the Darien

Institute had leaked the Brolturans' faith-based territorial claim along with some choice excerpts from the less sympathetic chapters of the *Omgur*, and now all the media were in ferment.

'Legator Kringen, I don't think there's any genuine cause for concern, simply because much of this is no more than gesture politics,' Robert said. 'The Brolturans can be somewhat sensitive about their perceived status so this is a face-saving exercise.'

'Exactly, Ambassador,' said Deputy-President Jardine, a round-faced Scot with receding hair. 'The fact is that the Hegemony is the true power in the region and they're not going to let anything happen to one of their principal ally's colonies.' A calculating smile came to his lips. 'I fear that the real reason for Legator Kringen's visibility on this issue stems from the recent divisions within the Consolidation Alliance.'

'As ever, the honourable Deputy-President fails to comprehend the facts, even when they are plain to see.' Kringen shook her head. 'Ambassador Horst, as opposition spokesperson it is my duty to attend to the concerns and doubts of the people and to ensure that the government is doing its job. I thank you for your time and courtesy, sir, and I shall convey your estimation of this situation to the leader of my party. Mr Deputy-President . . .'

And with a smile that was as sharp as it was frosty, she broke the connection.

After that Robert was quick to bring the call with Jardine to a close, citing a pressing workload. Once the screen returned to the ready cycle, he heaved a sigh of relief, leaned back and turned his chair away from his desk.

'I quite liked Ms Kringen,' said Harry. He was sitting on the arm of a divan, shirtsleeves rolled up, and holding a sheaf of papers in one hand. The monochrome image of Robert's AI companion stood in stark contrast to the subdued browns and greens of the townhouse's drawing room. 'Under that prim exterior I bet there's a champion dancer and an amateur scrimshaw hobbyist.'

Robert gave him a mock-serious look. 'You were reading her file! – I wondered why you were so quiet.'

Harry shrugged. 'All colonial politics starts to look and sound the same after a while, Robert, and truthfully I didn't care too much for Sundstrom's deputy.'

'He was a trade-off placement, apparently,' Robert said. 'Sundstrom has his own coalition to keep in line too. But what is Kuros up to? – he's kept his doors closed, as we expected, yet he's off touring the colony, visiting landmarks, meeting local officials. We've already had to change my itinerary twice because he edged in before us. Then there's the presentation at that archaeological dig tomorrow, which I had planned to attend until one of Kuros's assisters told me, oh so politely, that the High Monitor wanted to be the sole dignitary, the "bearer of the Hegemony's friendship" to the Darien colony.'

'Why, Robert – you sound peeved,' Harry said with a wry smile.

Robert spread his hands. 'You'd think that I would be used to it by now, given our encounters with Hegemony functionaries down the years. Well, at least we'll be spared the joy of listening to one of these speeches he's been making.'

'Ah yes – I've seen the transcripts,' Harry said, shuffling through his papers then striking a theatrical pose. '"Across the galaxy's vast ocean of stars, and down through the river of ages, certain values of life and freedom have remained constant, changeless. As the willing inheritors of those cherished values, the Sendruka Hegemony bears the responsibility of promoting and sharing them amongst the many-formed family of sentient beings. We welcome you to our great family, as we welcomed your fellow Humans many years ago, and invite you to join with us in spreading the values and benefits of civilisation . . ."' Harry looked up, eyebrows arched. 'And on it goes.'

'What kind of reception is this bucket of platitudes getting?'

'Rapturous applause,' Harry said. 'But then, the colony's only source of offworld news is Starstream and they've always been most supportive of our Hegemonic allies.'

Robert nodded, feeling suddenly listless and tired, his neck and back full of aches, his mood growing despondent. It had been a long day and it wasn't over yet. He needed a short break from his cares and the chance to lift his spirits.

Looking out of the bay window at the even grey sky, he said, 'Harry, I need some time to myself, just to unwind before the reception this evening. Okay?'

'Of course, Robert. Say about an hour?'

'An hour would be fine.'

'See you later, then.'

When he looked round there was no sign of Harry and he got up and left the room. Along the polished wood corridor were his personal rooms, one of which he kept locked with an intricate old-fashioned key which came with the house sets. Once inside his bedroom he crossed to that door, unlocked it and stepped through.

'Hi, Daddy – glad you're back. Looks like it might rain.'

Rosa stood by the window, her faintly opaque form appearing oddly grainy in the natural light. Like an ancient, pre-digital photograph. Like a memory.

'It rains a lot in this part of Darien,' he said, settling into an armchair. 'So, what have you been doing today?'

'Oh, just reading my book and listening to the radio,' she said.

The ghostly shape of a book lay on the undisturbed bed, projected there by the intersim which sat on the shoulder-height mantelpiece. Two thin cables ran out from the small unit, one to a module that drew power from the house supply, the other to a pen-sized radio. The book, Robert knew, was most likely either Lewis Carroll's *Alice Through The Looking-Glass* or *The Empire of Propaganda* by Nolan Chilcott, her favourite dissident writer. Her grey cardigan and long blue woollen dress were from a family holiday six years ago, but her short hair and flower earrings were from the last time he saw her alive . . .

He knew what Harry would say, that he was being lulled and enervated by the holosim's verisimilitude, but he dismissed it. He was using this detailed imitation of his daughter to dull the grief that he still felt, to help him come to terms with the loss. Harry was mistaken – he knew what was real and what was not.

'If I look between those houses,' Rosa said. 'I can see a lake and a forest and mountains. So beautiful.' She turned to him. 'Daddy, on the radio I heard that the moon people, the Uvovo, have planted what they call daughter-forests, using seeds and saplings from their world. Have you seen one yet? I've heard that they glow at night.'

'Actually, I'm due to visit the one near Port Gagarin the day after tomorrow – would you like to come?'

'Oh, could I? That would be wonderful.'

'It's settled then – we'll go together.'

Rosa's face was bright with a smile free from the burden of care as she picked up the translucent book from the bed. 'I know you've not much time, Daddy,' she said. 'But would you like me to read some *Alice* to you?'

'I'd like that very much,' Robert said, smiling.

So he settled back in the armchair's comfort and listened to his daughter's precious voice tell the story of a little girl who passed through into a looking-glass world.

13

CATRIONA

As soon as the drinks waiter came up onto the temple rampart, she selected a glass of yellowbead and knocked it straight back. Ignoring the waiter's look of amusement, she took a second glass and went to stand next to the rampart's mossy, time-ruined wall, staring morosely down at the chattering knots of people. It was a cloudless day and not yet noon, and from where she stood she could see almost the entirety of the Giant's Shoulder dig site, from the sections of shattered wall that delineated the blunt point of the promontory to the grassy, hillocky expanse almost 300 metres to the rear, where steep, jagged rocks reared up to join the buttresses and crags that jutted from the densely forested ridge overseeing all. The bulk of the ruins were scattered around the area immediately behind the ramparts – fragments of walls, corners, tumbled heaps of masonry debris lying where they were discovered. Numerous ongoing excavations had been roped off, although some of the old ones, like the Stairwell or the Crypt, had been refurbished with benches and infopanels for sightseers. Areas of flagstones long since unearthed from the topsoil were now occupied by small tents within which cabinet displays depicted artefacts and an easy-to-digest potted history of the site. But it was the largely uninterrupted stretch directly below her vantage point where rows of seating had been laid out for the reception and presentation in honour of the Hegemony representative, High Monitor Kuros.

And part of that presentation was to be delivered by Catriona

Macreadie. It was a source of raw annoyance to her, knowing as she did that many of the Institute's Darien-based members were perfectly capable of giving a brief talk and answering the esteemed Sendrukan's questions. She had made this point bluntly to her superior, Professor Forbes, in his office at Pilipoint Station nearly fifteen hours ago, but to no avail.

'That may be so, Doctor Macreadie,' Forbes had said, wearing his habitual thin smile. 'But it seems that the Sendruka delegation has specifically requested that you be the one to assist Mr Cameron during their visit to the site.'

'Why me?'

'Sadly, I am not privy to these aliens' reasoning, nor did Director Petrovich indicate that he possessed such information. However, he was most insistent that you be on the next shuttle back to Darien which, . . .' he had paused to look round at the hideous ornamental clock on his wall '. . . leaves in less than an hour.'

Catriona had forced herself to be icy calm, determined not to lose her composure and tell him which species of forest-floor bug he most closely resembled. This time.

'Professor Forbes, that doesn't give me enough time to return to my quarters and prepare, not to mention the question of what to wear.'

'I'm sure that the Externals office at the Institute can provide suitable attire for you on your arrival,' he had said. 'And you may use the archive hub if you really feel the need to brush up on the Uvovo, but whatever you do please try not to embarrass us. Deliver a straight summary of our findings and restrict any spec-ulation to verified facts. That will be all . . .'

Now, standing on the temple rampart, she could still feel the anger and frustration simmering away inside, unquenched by the glass of yellowbead liqueur. Anger at Forbes, and frustration at being a world away while a certain package was probably sitting in the mail drawer in the enclave storage hut back at Starroof Town. She had persuaded Galyna, a researcher friend at Pilipoint Station, to process her forest-floor recording with a lab imager on the quiet, thus hopefully revealing just what had passed before the minicam. The processed file had been due to arrive in the daily drop several hours ago.

Instead here I am, getting ready to pose as a glorified tour-guide for some self-important alien bureaucrat. Yes, hand-holding offworlders through a pre-teen-level commentary seems to be all the Institute thinks I'm fit for . . .

She halted her spiralling bitterness, swallowed a mouthful of yellowbead, and sighed. Patience was a virtue she felt she was always having to learn anew, despite which she turned her thoughts to listing all the enigmas she had encountered, ranking the Pathmasters first . . .

Then music interrupted her musing, the sound of a lone piper, the high, pure tone of the chanter floating above the suddenly hushed crowd, picking out the notes of a stately, soulful pibroch. Then the deeper voices of the drones rose, a steady undercurrent for the deliberate pace of the melody. The piper, a young, dark-haired man decked out in the full regalia, walked in time through the ruins towards the attentive gathering.

Catriona loved pipe music in general, even the modernist tranzy dance fads, but it was the performance of a solo piper that truly moved her. To her it sounded lonely yet defiant, dignified but not pompous, and it spoke to her of faraway Earth and that small corner of it which only some of the First Families had known first-hand.

More than once during her years as an Enhanced, she had gone up onto the dormitory roof after dark to sit with pipe music playing quietly on her little radio as she looked up at the dust-hazed point of stars. With no way to know if Earth and Humanity had survived the Swarm invasion, she could only gaze and wonder and wish, thoughts and music spiralling up into the sky . . .

'He is a very good player, is he not?' said a female voice behind her.

She turned to see a tall, middle-aged woman dressed in a pale blue, ankle-length gown that was all elegant folds and embroidered hems and which stopped just short of ostentatious. A patterned grey shawl covered her shoulders and arms, and her silvery hair was braided and held back with a carved wood headband. She seemed vaguely familiar.

'Yes, he is,' she replied, smiling hesitantly. 'Very expressive.'

'When I was younger I saw his father win the Northern Towns Trophy three times,' the woman said in a Norj accent. 'I am Solvjeg Cameron.'

Recognition flooded Catriona's thoughts. 'Ah, you're Greg's mother . . . oh, I'm Catriona Macreadie.'

As they shook hands, Solvjeg Cameron smiled. 'So you are the Doctor Macreadie who worked with Greg before. Are you here today in an offical capacity?'

'Yes, I'm going to be giving a brief speech about the Uvovo, and answering questions.'

'Fascinating,' Solvjeg said, suddenly giving her a curious look. 'Macreadie . . . are you related to the New Kelso Macreadies, by any chance?'

Although outwardly calm and poised, Catriona's thoughts were scattering in panic, and the lie came to her lips seemingly of its own accord.

'No, my parents were both from Stranghold,' she said. 'They died when I was very young.'

'I am so sorry to hear that, my dear,' Greg's mother said, suddenly sympathetic. 'You must have had a difficult childhood . . .'

But before the next line of questioning could get under way, Solvjeg's gaze shifted to the side a little and she waved. Glancing round, Catriona saw an older man in hillwalker browns wave back briefly before heading along the grassy slope towards the steps that led up to the ramparts.

'My brother wants me to come down,' Solvjeg said. 'But no doubt we shall meet again. I hope the day goes well for you.'

Catriona smiled and gave a little wave goodbye while inside she was thinking, *Why did I say that? How could I be so stupid?* Greg's mother was one of those ultra-connected matriarch types – it would only take a couple of enquiries to find out that Catriona was a failed Enhanced. She knew she shouldn't be ashamed or embarrassed, but it was an undeniable fact that the Enhanced, failed or not, were treated differently and not especially positively, even though the programme ended years ago. And Solvjeg would then wonder why she had lied and might jump to conclusions about her and Greg . . .

Catriona gnawed her lip – and what if she asked Greg if they were involved? The embarrassment would be unbearable.

But before she could brood any further, her comm gave its cheery little call tune. Seeing it was Greg, she thumbed the accept and answered.

'Hello, Greg.'

'Cat, I thought you should know that our visiting VIP has just disembarked from his executive zeplin and will be here shortly. Can you meet me at the mural wall?'

'I'm on my way,' she said, heading for the stairs.

'Incidentally, will you be able to wait behind after this circus is over? There's some new findings I'd like your opinion on.'

'Sounds interesting,' she said. 'I'd like that.' *And hopefully I'll get up the courage to tell you what I said before you hear it from your mother.*

'Excellent,' he said. 'See you shortly.'

Finishing off the last of the yellowbead, she left the glass next to the waiter's table and hurried downstairs, wishing for the umpteenth time that she was back on Nivyesta.

14

CHEL

In an alcove at the top of a grassy slope, Cheluvahar sat with Listener Weynl and two other Uvovo scholars, watching the Human gathering. All had listened intently to the piper, who finished to an enthusiastic round of applause, and now another group of musicians was commencing on a variety of stringed and wind instruments.

'Humans are always making songs and stories,' Chel said. 'Interesting to discover that other races create similar things.'

'But not surprising,' said Listener Weynl. 'An existence divided always seeks attunement, ways to bridge the gap between the mind and the eternal. Songs and stories are expressions of the need for attunement, but when that becomes a yearning to hear the voice of the eternal it leads to gods and demons, holy books and such things as the Dreamless.'

Chel knew the principles of attunement well, as did every Uvovo – from birth the vital rhythms of Segrana were part of blood and breath and the daily pulse of living. But Humans had to imagine, *needed* to imagine the entirety of the world beyond their own poor senses, trying to bridge the gap with illusions.

Some distance away from where they sat, a solitary four-armed figure came into view, pacing deliberately along the perimeter of the temple site as it had done for well over an hour. It – there was no outward indication of gender – was a member of the Sendrukan envoy's bodyguard, a squad of Ezgara commandos. It wore some kind of close-fitting, full-body dull blue armour, with a near-black visor covering the face and no obvious sign of weapons.

On seeing the soldier making what had to be its fourth circuit, one of the scholars – a Meshtowner called Kolumivenur – turned to Weynl.

'Learned one,' he said. 'How can a race such as this one seek attunement while serving the Sendruka?'

'I know little about these Ezgara,' Weynl said. 'But it is clear that they have given themselves over to the needs and methods of military service, just as many Humans here do. I have heard it said, however, that Ezgara soldiers are fanatically loyal to their Sendruka masters, in which case I find myself wondering what kind of people require utter obedience from their servants. But then, we now know that all the worlds of the Sendruka, their society and culture and government, are permeated with the Dreamless. Machine minds are everywhere, spying, manipulating, and coordinating the resources of a vast empire, which clearly include these Ezgara. Perhaps they in turn extract a kind of obedience from the Sendruka.'

'What of the Humans from Earth,' said the other scholar, Tesobrenilor by name. 'Some of them have the Dreamless . . . tiny machines planted inside their heads, just like this High Monitor Kuros and his companions. Can they be trusted?'

'Everything they see and hear reaches the Dreamless,' Weynl said. 'At the time of the War of the Long Night, the Dreamless were joined to one another by a hidden web that reached into the underlayers of existence. We cannot know if these Dreamless have a similar . . . pattern but in caution we should assume so . . .'

The Listener suddenly stopped and looked round. Following his gaze, the rest saw that the Ezgara commando had paused at the foot of the grassy slope with the gleaming blackness of its visor angled up at them. For a moment or two no one moved, then the Ezgara began to ascend the slope.

'Remain seated,' Weynl said quietly. 'Be calm, there is nothing to fear.'

As the Listener got to his feet, Chel smiled reassuringly at the other two Uvovo, whose eyes were wide and bright with alarm.

'Greetings, offworlder,' Weynl said, hands clasped at his chest. 'I am Listener Weynl of the Warrior Uvovo and these three are my companions. Please be welcome.'

The Ezgara came to a halt and swept them all with an invisible gaze.

'Warriors?' The words were in Anglic, spoken in a flat, slightly buzzing voice. 'I see no weapons.'

'I likewise see none about your person, honoured guest, yet I am not sure I would recognise them if they were there.'

The Ezgara gave no reply for a moment, seeming to stare at Weynl as if studying him. The creature stood with its major arms hanging loosely at its sides while its lower, lesser arms were crooked back, hands resting in pockets. That dull blue armour, which covered every limb, on closer inspection appeared to consist of a worn, scored surface over a layer of thumbnail-sized platelets just discernible through the outer material.

'One amongst you spoke the name of my master, the High Monitor Utavess Kuros,' the commando said at last. 'Why?'

'We were only discussing . . .' began Tesobrenilor, abruptly falling silent when the Ezgara quickly turned on him.

'It is my duty to protect the High Monitor,' it said. 'Why were you discussing him?'

The Ezgara took a step towards Tesobrenilor, who backed away in fear. At the same time, Weynl moved in the commando's direction, one hand starting to reach out, and the moment he saw this Chel knew what was about to happen.

'Honoured guest,' the Listener said. 'There has been a misunderstanding . . .'

The commando reacted with a speed so blurring that afterwards Chel had difficulty recalling the exact sequence of movements. Listener Weynl had reached out to the soldier's lesser arm on the right side and an instant later he was hurtling backwards through the air. Chel caught a glimpse of the Ezgara's right-side arms and leg lowering but it was the Listener who drew every eye. In mid-flight he somehow twisted his body, robes fluttering, and flipped over to land on his feet, legs crouched.

Smiling, he straightened and calmly walked back to where the others stood, staring in astonishment.

'As I explained, honoured guest,' Weynl said, spreading his long-sleeved arms, with his bony hands open and empty. 'There has been a slight misunderstanding. My young companion was puzzled as to the meaning of your exalted superior's title and so, despite my scant knowledge, I attempted a doubtlessly inaccurate interpretation.'

Silence. For several seconds Uvovo stared at Ezgara, who seemed also to stare back, both perfectly immobile. Just when Chel thought he could no longer bear the tension, the Ezgara raised a hand to the side of its helmet as it looked downslope to where a second commando was standing. Then without a word it turned its back and retraced its steps to join the other one. Moments later both were moving away, patrolling the site perimeter along the foot of the western crags, as if nothing had happened. Glancing at Tesobrenilor and Kolumivenur, Chel saw his own puzzlement mirrored in their features, along with a certain relief.

Listener Weynl, on the other hand, seemed quite unperturbed, even as he guided Chel off to one side, a little way down the incline from the others.

'Once this ceremony is over,' Weynl said in low tones, 'you will be leaving for the Tapiola daughter-forest in the north. A floating craft shall be waiting for you at the zeplin station.'

Chel bobbed his head in respect, suddenly excited and apprehensive. 'I am prepared, Listener.'

Weynl smiled. 'Yes, I thought I was too, when my own time drew near. My advice would be to put aside all you have learned and read because your husking will be unique to you. Which is as it should be.' He breathed in deep and nodded. 'Now I must depart for Hammergard – I have an important meeting to attend.'

'But Listener Weynl – who will represent our people to the Sendrukans?'

'A straightforward task, Scholar, which I am confident you can undertake. Besides, you are far more knowledgeable about this delving site than I. A word of caution, however – should anything unforeseen take place here, resist any temptation to become involved.'

'Unforeseen?' Chel said. 'Is something bad going to happen?'

'I do not know,' Weynl said with a kind of sombre puzzlement. 'The event itself is provoking a sense of anticipation, but the instinctive violence of that Ezgara . . .' He surveyed the site's ruins with brooding eyes. 'Something else is approaching, something nascent . . . but whatever happens stay focused on your duty and the work to come. The first aspirants are already gathering down in the Glenkrylov daughter-forest, so when you return in a few days we will be ready to begin confirmations for the Artificer Uvovo.'

He gave Chel a fatherly pat on the shoulder and went to bid the other two goodbye. Chel thought about the many sheets of notes he had made on the ancient Uvovo ruins, the ones the Humans knew about as well as the ones they didn't, and wondered how much use they would be after he had gone through the husking.

Weynl waved to them all and Chel watched him hurry across the uneven floor of the site's western stretches. A little further on he paused to wave once more before disappearing behind one of the main walls. Chel already knew that the most obvious change wrought by the husking was the physical, a lengthening of certain bones, including the skull. Was he really ready for such an alteration? Those Listeners he had got to know seemed to be mostly sane most of the time, even Faldri, which was slightly reassuring.

Then these thoughts were chased away by a repetitive chiming sound coming from one of his waist pouches. It was the signal from Gregori that all senior duty staff were to meet outside the site office hut – Kuros was due soon. Moments later, the three Uvovo scholars were hastening back to the prepared gathering place, careful to avoid the Ezgara commandos, who were still doggedly patrolling the perimeter.

15

GREG

From the moment he got out of bed, nearly an hour before dawn, the whole day had just been one damned thing after another. Crates of seating and modular gazebos had been delivered overnight, and while he was organising the carriage and assembly teams, two grey-uniformed OG officers arrived with Institute authorisation countersigned by Petrovich himself. By the time he had given them a brief tour of the site and left them to their own devices, the caterers had turned up with a variety of containers and the need for somewhere reasonably clean to get ready. The only halfway suitable place was the recreation hut, so there they were sent, much to the annoyance of a group of Uvovo scholars who were just back from the mountains and enjoying a leisurely game of hexadominoes.

It was then that the Ezgara commandos had appeared, three quad-armed humanoids in worn, dull blue battledress, their heads enclosed by black-visored helmets. Trailing after them was one of the interns, a young Rus called Pyotr.

'So sorry for this, Mr Cameron,' he said, slightly out of breath. 'But these gentlemen. . .'

'That's all right, Pyotr – now that they're here, I'll see to them.'

Pyotr nodded, shot a glare at the oblivious newcomers and headed back to the site entrance. Greg smiled at the Ezgara, taking in the details of their armour, their identical stances and those extra arms.

'Well,' he said. 'You all look very intimidating, I must say. Are you here in advance of our honoured guest?'

He broke off as one suddenly stepped up close, bringing them face to face. Greg could see his own breath lightly fogging the commando's faceplate, but he neither flinched nor backed away.

'I am Juort,' the Ezgara said in a low, rasping voice that sounded synthetic. 'I command.'

The commandos all appeared of similar height, and up close Greg could see that he was a little taller than the one confronting him. If anything this made them more daunting, not less, but Greg was determined to hold his ground.

'By an amazing coincidence,' he said, smiling broadly, 'so do I. I command this site and its personnel – I am in command here, which means that I have the power to permit you to enter . . .'

'I command you . . .' began Juort.

'Ah, wait, I don't think ye've got it quite right. Y'see, you're supposed to ask me if you can . . .'

'Mr Cameron? A word, if you please.'

Greg turned to see Ingerson, one of the Office of Guidance men, giving him a look that said, *Are you completely out of your mind?* while beckoning to him.

'Mr Ingerson, how can I help you?'

'The Ezgara commandos are here to assist with the security arrangements, Mr Cameron,' he said. 'Their access is covered by our authorisation.'

'I see,' Greg said. 'If only I'd known earlier . . .' He turned to the Ezgara, but they were already following Ingerson in single file while ignoring Greg altogether. 'In that case, welcome to Giant's Shoulder! – enjoy your visit . . .'

Not a head turned in his direction, so he shrugged and went back to trying to cope with chaos.

The seating was done and three of the gazebos were up: he'd left the others in their packaging since the latest forecast was predicting dry, bright conditions for the rest of the day. The gazebos, however, were serving as shelters for three groups of exhibits – flora and fauna of Darien, ruins and remains, and ancient Uvovo culture. But the flora and fauna cases were empty since the ecologist and his materials (both on loan from the university) had so far failed to appear. Hastily, Greg persuaded one of the Russian researchers, Andrei, to assemble a small exhibit from the archive store – figurines, glyphs, decorated artefacts of any kind. It was going to cost half a bottle of Glenmarra single malt, but at least the cases would not be bare.

Then the first zeplin-load of guests arrived, bringing with them a clutch of reporters both local and offworld. With ruthless ease they bypassed the guides and attendants and tracked Greg down to the supply hut, where he was checking the water-tank level. Amid a barrage of brash, bizarre and often fantastical questioning he maintained a look of amused tolerance while giving vaguely surreal one- or two-word answers: it seemed that news of his encounter with Lee Shan had got around. Before long they realised that there would be no verbal fireworks, so off they wandered to hunt other quarry, and Greg headed for his quarters to shower and change.

But less than ten minutes later he was back outside, trying to calm down one of the Norj research teams, who had discovered an Earth reporter in their hut, opening drawers and recording everything in sight. In an effort to reach some kind of understanding, Greg gathered the senior reporters together with Olsen, Ingerson's colleague: the OG officer briefly outlined the case for security and propriety, and casually mentioned that the Ezgara commandos now patrolling the perimeter were very keen to ensure the Hegemony envoy's safety from any threat and were fully capable of doing so.

At the mention of the Ezgara, glances were exchanged and Greg noticed a certain shared nervousness. *Hmm, so they do have a reputation*, he thought. *Or should it be notoriety?*

After that it was a hectic rush to get ready for the presentation, to finalise the programme of events, negotiate a compromise between Andrei and the university ecologist who had turned up at the last minute, and arrange for some of the excavations to be roped off, since some reporters were still poking their noses where they shouldn't. In between all that he managed to meet some of the VIP guests, shaking hands and exchanging the usual pleasantries, and made sure that his mother and Uncle Theo knew where their seats were. At one point he caught sight of Catriona through the crowd, just after she had sent him a comm-note to let him know that she had arrived.

Then came news that High Monitor Kuros had disembarked from his official zeplin and was about to ascend the cliffside path in one of the electric visitor cars. Greg alerted Catriona and Chel with prearranged signals and hurried over to the central plaza area. Catriona appeared seconds after he got there, looking tense in a formal, high-collared kirtle suit made from some dark brown ridge-textured material. After an awkward, smiling pause they shook hands, a clasp which Catriona seemed to break first – or maybe it was because he was holding her hand for a moment too long.

'It's good to see you again, Catriona,' he said. 'I hope this PR exercise isn't interrupting your work the way it is mine, though I understand our guests specifically requested that you take part.'

She gave a wry half-smile, tucked a few stray dark hairs behind one ear, at which Greg felt a tiny thrill. He kept smiling.

'Well, I can't deny that there's other things I'd rather be doing,' she said. 'But they asked for me so here I am.'

A thought occurred to him. 'You don't think it's anything to do with your Enhanced past?'

'Why should it?'

He shrugged. 'Perhaps they're curious about why the Enhancement project came about.'

She regarded him. 'Hmm. Do you ever wonder why, Greg?'

Before he could answer, the Uvovo scholar Chel arrived. He had an anxious, slightly jittery air about him but he seemed otherwise alert and ready for the task ahead so Greg launched into a summary of the programme.

'Okay, this is the plan. The Underminister for Culture will give the official welcome to the Sendrukans and the other guests, then Catriona will deliver a short presentation on the early discoveries made here on Giant's Shoulder and later on Nivyesta. After that, I'll give an overview of the various archaeological sites and the main finds, and Chel will finish with the Uvovo perspective on themselves and Humans, past and future. How does that sound?'

Catriona nodded. 'I'm happy to lead off – gets it over with.'

'I too am satisfied,' said Chel. 'I shall learn from both your performances.'

Greg laughed. 'Good things, I hope.'

After that, the demands of the occasion took over as all the guests went to their seats and Greg and the others waited by the low podium. Two of the peculiar Ezgara bodyguards came into view from the right, stalking through the ruins in advance of the Sendrukans.

They were a tall humanoid race, and although he had seen shots of them on the vee, that did not prepare Greg for the impact of their presence. There were four altogether, three walking single-file behind the High Monitor who strode leisurely along with the Underminister for Culture marching briskly at his side. With a mean height of ten and a half feet, they were much taller than Humans, tall yet not spindly, their torsos broader and in proportion, and it was true – next to them, Humans did look almost childlike. Their attire was elegant, richly detailed and multilayered with semi-opaque, long-sleeved garments over stiff, almost breast-plate-like inner ones – the three attending Sendrukans wore pastel shades of yellow, green and grey while the High Monitor was decked out in striking ultramarine blue counterpointed by magenta patterns and trim. Head-dresses there were, bulbous pale-blue ones with dangling tassels for the attendants, a tall, black, oddly helical one for their superior.

As the Sendruka approached, Greg half-turned to Catriona and in a low voice said:

'I'm glad you can stay behind – the new research data is fascinating.'

'Just how fascinating?'

'Sensor scans showing passages and chambers inside Giant's Shoulder.'

She glanced sharply at him. 'Is that right? And how would you get hold of such information?'

He shrugged. 'Let's say a little space-bird told me. Fascinated yet?'

Her sharp look softened. 'Aye, okay.'

Then they were face to face with Underminister Hansen and High Monitor Utavess Kuros. As Hansen introduced each of them in turn, the Sendrukan inclined his head and then, surprisingly, politely shook hands. Kuros's hands had a light tan hue and were large with long, slender fingers adorned with a few plain red rings, and a grip whose firmness matched Greg's. The High Monitor said little beyond expressing his pleasure at being here and his anticipation of the event to come, all spoken in perfect, if accentless Anglic, his voice level, melodious, kindly. His face was broad, its features flatter than a Human's, with a high forehead and large dark eyes that seemed perpetually mournful or at least weary-wise. Despite his preconceptions, Greg found himself warming to the alien – it was an effort to remind himself of the AIs that shared these aliens' heads.

The audience settled down as the High Monitor and his attendants reclined in their specially provided chairs. Underminister Hansen gave the official welcome from the podium before introducing Greg. Greg briefly explained about the three presentations, and finished with a quotation from Haakon Greig, one of the colony's early chroniclers: 'History has much to teach us, and occasionally resorts to beating us over the head if we don't pay attention.'

A light ripple of applause accompanied him from the stage. Then, as Catriona took his place, he noticed one of the Ezgara bodyguards patrolling a stretch of the temple rampart behind the audience, a sombre reminder of his earlier encounter.

Cat was a little nervous and faltering to begin with, but she soon gained confidence as she gave a concise overview of archaeological discoveries since the colony's founding. A display screen, one of the new compact folding ones, was used to show locations and dates, then a couple of researchers brought out a few artefacts to pass round the audience. Greg smiled – the folding screen had worked first time, and no finds were dropped or broken. When she was finished the audience began applauding politely while remaining seated, but the Sendrukan Kuros got to his feet as if to accord her special approval. The other Sendrukans also rose, as did Greg, grinning widely as he clapped, glancing over his shoulder to see the rest of the audience following suit.

At that very instant he heard an odd sound like someone snapping their fingers close by. Out of the corner of his eye he noticed a figure falling backwards . . . then saw it was High Monitor Kuros, his arms flailing. Greg thought in that moment that someone must have pushed him, but when one of the Sendrukan attendants moved to help there was another cracking sound and the attendant jerked and sprawled sideways, purplish blood blossoming from his neck.

In a few seconds the orderly, polite audience was transformed into screaming, stampeding chaos.

My God! Greg thought, diving for cover. *We're being shot at*!

He scanned the shambles of overturned chairs and stragglers making for sections of wall to hide behind, desperately looking for his mother and Uncle Theo. He saw no sign of them but two of the Ezgara were there, as were the OG officers, shielding the High Monitor as the two surviving attendants struggled to carry him out of danger.

'Greg! – over here!'

Craning his head round he saw Catriona and his mother beckoning to him from the lee of a ruined wall which stretched almost unbroken to the site entrance. Reasoning that the gunman would be focused on the High Monitor, he steeled his nerve and dived across a patch of open ground to another mossy outcrop of stonework. From there he dashed to the long wall, joining his mother and Catriona.

'Are you both all right?' he said.

'We are fine, Gregory, fine,' said his mother. 'Such a disgrace that this should happen, and a shame on all of us! To think that there are still fools among us who try to solve an argument by picking up a gun. And Theodor is away to try and find whoever is . . .'

'Wait. Uncle Theo went looking for them?'

His mother sighed and nodded. 'Still thinks he is thirty-five. Says it's part of his new responsibilities.'

'Right, Mum, which way did he go?'

'He said the shots came from the ridge overlooking the site . . .'

Greg shuffled to the side, peering round and up at the mass of dense foliage and the treetops beyond.

'Are you thinking of going after him?' Catriona said suddenly.

'I am.'

'Then I'm going with you.'

Looking at her he saw that she was smiling a smile that said, *Just try stopping me.*

'Two heads are better than one,' she added.

'And certainly present a better target,' he said. 'Right, then, let's be off.'

His mother shook her head again, this time in exasperation.

'Try not to be as foolish as my brother, will you?'

16

THEO

The higher he climbed the denser the forest became, low-level branches and hanging vines intertwining with the humid undergrowth to form tangles of greenery he sometimes had to go round. Nor did it help that the ground grew increasingly uneven, weed-choked, strewn with fallen trunks, rotting branches and half-buried rocks. But despite the obstacles his sense of direction was unwavering – when that first shot hit the High Monitor, old reflexes made him follow a likely trajectory back into the thickly forested ridge, corroborated by the second shot which took down the Sendrukan attendant.

So now Theo had the sniper's location pegged in his mind, a target he was homing in on. Of course, hunting for an armed assailant while kitted out with a cudgel improvised from a piece of branch probably wasn't the wisest course of action, but it was better than no action. He grinned, knowing what Rory and the others would have to say about taking risks at his age.

Ja, gentlemen, was his imagined response. *But I've learned how to take such risks and stay alive!*

After another ten minutes of climbing over boulders and trudging across sloping, boggy ground, he reached a spot on the ridge where the tree cover thinned. Looking east he got a good view of Giant's Shoulder, the clusters of ruins and the boxy, grey-green huts and storage units. It was near here, he was sure of it.

Keeping to cover, Theo surveyed the vicinity and soon noticed a denser mass of foliage not far away. Cautiously he slipped through the undergrowth towards it, realising that it was a jutting spur of rock swathed in greenery. He slowed to a wary approach, convinced that the gunman was long gone yet keeping his cudgel ready in case. The humid air seemed suddenly warmer, the sound of birds and insects fading as his own movements became amplified in his own ears . . .

Crouching, he sidled between creeper-wound bushes, edged round a gnarled tree bole, and there it was, a sniper lair. The weedy grass was crushed flat in a long, narrow patch where the gunman had lain down and stretched himself out. And there, of all things, was the gun, a scoped Ballantyne rifle with a sculpted wooden stock, a weapon he recognised from personal experience. Of the shooter there was no sign, no belongings, no leavings, nothing but the weapon and the impression in the grass. Squatting next to it he almost reflexively reached out to the rifle's stock but stopped himself.

'Good idea, Major,' said a voice nearby. 'Wouldna want to get yer prints on it.'

Theo stood swiftly and brought up his cudgel two-handed, only to see a familiar face looking out from the foliage. It was the special forces soldier he had met at Sundstrom's villa, Sergeant Donny Barbour if Rory's informant was right. He nodded and balanced the cudgel on his shoulder.

'So,' he said. 'Business or pleasure?'

Barbour gave a sardonic smile as he stepped into view. He wore core-brown camouflage which extended to the floppy hat and hunting gloves that hung at his waist.

'Got assigned to deep patrol,' Barbour said, hunkering down for a closer look at the crushed grass. 'Was up in a tree further back, scanning the surroundings, when our boy got his first shot off. Had a good idea where it must've come frae and was looking this way when he took his second. Next thing, he came running out of here like the hounds of hell were after him.'

Theo stared down at him. 'So he just dropped the rifle and ran.'

'Aye, Major – he didn't throw it off into the bushes or anything, just put it down, got up and breenjed out. He was moving at a good speed, too, didna trip or catch himself, just flew through those trees and all they vines and bushes like a ghost.' He got to his feet. 'Not a civilian, had to be trained. Could be a mountain-man, somebody from one of the trapper towns . . . but that doesn't feel right. Why leave the rifle?'

'Couldn't he be from an elite unit?' Theo said. 'Maybe even one you don't know about.'

'Top of my list,' Barbour said with a bleak smile. 'Listen, Major, it's time we were both elsewhere – a couple of those Ezgara are heading this way and we don't want them getting any wrong ideas.'

'How do you know?' Theo said, half-suspecting the answer.

Barbour tapped his right ear. 'Got an obs link out among that audience. Now what you want to do is go back the way you came but carry on up over the ridge – your nephew and Miss Macreadie went that way. Might be wise to find them – safety in numbers.'

He grinned and pointed to the gap in the bushes through which Theo had entered. But when Theo looked back round Barbour was gone with just a few leafy sprigs nodding in his wake. He chuckled to himself and retraced his steps, found a faint animal trail marked with recent shoe prints leading up towards the crest of the ridge. A couple of minutes later he reached it, then saw that the path led along a hillside to a steeper sloping ridge further on. Picking his way along he paused on the crest of the next ridge, overlooking a shadowy, tree-cloaked gorge, and listened to the sounds of the forest. Amid the rustles of tiny denizens and the sigh of fitful breezes, he could make out voices coming from further up the gorge, from its northerly incline.

He found them on the other side of a cold, clear stream that ran between rounded rocks and the arched roots of ancient trees. Greg was helping a limping Catriona Macreadie as they emerged from a shadowy notch in the gorge wall. Twisted trees flanked its entrance and bushes sprouted high up, choking off light from above. As he drew level with Greg, he glanced into the fissure, from which a brook ran, pouring into a succession of small pools before joining the stream . . . and for a moment felt as if he was being watched from the shadows.

Greg went first, offering Catriona support as they crossed from stone to stone. Her face was pale and she gasped occasionally but eventually they were both safely on the other side, Theo offering his arm at the last.

'So what happened?' he said. 'And what were you both doing down here?'

At that, Greg glanced quickly to Catriona, who answered.

'It was my fault, Mr Karlsson – I was sure I saw footprints leading down to the stream, so I led the way, went across, and . . . and . . .'

'And Cat slipped and twisted her leg, Uncle,' Greg added, exchanging another look with her. 'I got her to rest for a few minutes before deciding to head back, and then you showed up.'

Theo smiled and nodded. *Well, that's a fine line of nonsense you're giving me, boy*, he thought. *What are you hiding? Or should I be wondering?*

He was about to ask exactly where Miss Macreadie had injured herself when there was the sound of footsteps and rustling foliage from the ridge overlooking the gorge.

'Found them,' said a voice, and several figures came into view – some OG officers and an Ezgara commando. 'Hello, Mr Cameron – are you and your friends in need of assistance?'

'We can manage, Mr Ingerson,' Greg called back. 'Did you catch the gunman? Is the Hegemony envoy badly wounded?'

'The High Monitor fortunately escaped serious injury but, tragically, his attendant is dead. The killer . . . is nowhere to be found.' He broke off and turned his attention to someone unseen on the other side of the ridge. 'Right, Mr Cameron, Major Karlsson and Doctor Macreadie – you'll have to leave the area now as the forensics people will soon be here. Let me know if there's any problem.'

With that, he retreated out of sight, although the Ezgara lingered, staring down. Theo gazed back for a moment then turned to Catriona. 'Well, girl, I don't think you'll manage that climb with a bad ankle, so in the spirit of gallantry I hereby volunteer my nephew Gregory to carry you to the top on his back.'

Greg stared at Theo, eyebrows arched in surprise, but then Catriona uttered a low, warm laugh.

'Well, now,' she said. 'It is the manly thing to do.'

At that, Greg's reserve dissolved into a grin.

'Aye, well, just as long as it's manly!'

Watching Greg ascend the slope with Catriona on his back, and hearing them both laughing, Theo smiled and wondered. Then he paused to glance back at the shadowy gap in the side of the gorge, frowning.

No, he thought. *Just my imagination, populating dark corners with spirits and kobolds, even though there's a real monster running around.*

Shrugging, he followed the others up the steep path, noting that the Ezgara was gone.

17

PATHMASTER

From the sheltering veil of shadows he watched the Humans depart, feeling something akin to amusement as the eldest of them paused to look back before likewise leaving. Then he was alone with the shadows and cold, the trickling brook and the simple creatures, as alone as he had been for nearly ten thousand years. Last of the Pathmasters, last bearer of ancient knowledge, fading remnant of cherished duty.

Was it all chance and happenstance that his essence should be drawn here on the same day that a slaying took place upon Waonwir, directly above the Sleeper's vault? And that a Human female stunningly radiant with potential should then wander close enough to get his attention? Well, the Pathmasters who taught him had always reminded him that coincidences were only the most obvious manifestations of the light touch of the Eternal. After all, the female had said, 'I've been searching for you,' and he had seen in her thoughts the fruitless outcomes of her exploring in the depths of Segrana.

Such a prize she was, the avidity of her cognitive harmony burning so brightly along the transient edge of the stable dimensions that he could almost make out the ambits of possible futures. Questions had come tumbling from her in a torrent, but he had stanched it with a command – seek out a *vudron* and undertake a vigil. For in the end it came down to Segrana, to her slow but sure perceptions, and to the reckonings she made. The immemorial awareness of the great moon-enfolding forest, vast yet thinly scattered, was close to the underlying qualities of the Eternal, which could not help but influence Segrana when the human female entered a *vudron* back there.

Then her male companion had arrived, a surprise that had caused her to lose her footing by the brook, slip and fall. The Pathmaster had allowed his visible membrane of coerced particles to melt away so that when next they looked he had apparently disappeared.

All the Humans and others were receding and he knew that there was another place he had to be, a daughter-forest where another fascinating Human was taking his ease in strange company. The Uvovo-cultivated sanctuary lay several miles away, yet for such as himself that distance was no greater than that between one thought and the next, thoughts that were long and complex, thoughts that bound this self with that succession of other selves which stretched away towards the Eternal. He formed the thought of a glade in that daughter-forest, sweet and strong offspring of Segrana, and by virtue of the entwining green weave of seed and leaf his disembodiment travelled there, slipping through to unfurl his essence in green, sheltering shade.

He found the Human, a male named Horst, sitting on a low wooden bench beneath a sunny sky, leaning sideways against the armrest, reading a book balanced on a raised knee. Next to him on the bench was a small flat device, its dark surface gleaming in the sun, while on the long grass a short distance away a young human female sat crosslegged, making chains of small flowers.

But this idyllic scene was not at all what it seemed to be. The Pathmaster knew that, like her flowers, the child was an illusion, an insubstantial image cast by Horst's cunningly wrought device. Earth Ambassador Horst was a man in the grip of grief, as much a prisoner of it as if he were weeping rather than smiling, and in his grief he had surrendered part of himself to an unthinking, visionless instrument devoid of true self.

Yet that was not the worst of it. Horst also played host to one of the Dreamless, an artificial entity of a different magnitude:

unlike the clever image of a dead daughter, these Dreamless possessed a kind of volition and a degree of self-critical awareness
very similar to their anti-life predecessors who had brought most
of the galaxy to the brink of disaster ten millennia ago.

Unlike those long-vanquished entities, however, these
Dreamless had evolved in symbiosis with a dominant species, the
Sendruka, thus spreading their influence far and wide throughout
the Hegemonic territories and beyond. The new Dreamless had
attained levels of power and existence unimaginable to those
predecessors – every artificial entity consisted of two parts, a
lesser part occupying a physical matrix in the vantage of the Real,
either a device or an implant, and a greater part that resided in
that understratum of reality known to Humans as the first tier of
hyperspace. Such scraps of information the Pathmaster had
gleaned from innumerable overheard fragments of offworlder
conversation, the occasional stray thought, and those observations of scholars and Listeners which he had received.

And the implications provoked in him a deep unease. Were the
implant Dreamless merely a manifestation of the greater, hyperspace ones, or did they possess autonomy? What was the
hierarchy of the hyperspace Dreamless and how did they communicate with their implant counterparts? That last unknown
was the most immediately worrying – did that method of communication bear any similarity to the frail bonds that linked his
essence to those former echoes of himself which were on the path
to mergence with the Eternal? His unease deepened still further
when he thought of the Sentinel asleep in its vault, and how it
communicated with deep, hidden allies.

He regarded the Human Horst once more, noticing how the
man's attention was focused on a point in the air just beyond the
other end of the bench. His lips were scarcely moving but he was
speaking, softly in his throat. From a tall, broad tree nearby the
Pathmaster tentatively reached out with rarefied senses, trying to
see into Horst's thoughts, with a touch of the mind so light as be
scarcely extant.

Yet he felt the resonant disturbance of linkage, and he saw . . .

so strange, another man, tall and well-proportioned with a relaxed, even amused demeanour, yet he was an image lacking any colour. Blacks, whites and shades of grey.

They were talking, something about the sister ships of the *Hyperion*, the ones that had gone missing, a tale that the Pathmaster was acquainted with. *I've had an enquiry from another group of ship-hunters*, Horst was saying, *calling themselves the First Flight Assocation.*

And what's their pet notion? said the Dreamless's monochrome image. *That the* Forrestal *and the* Tenebrosa *were flung far back in time and their crews became the original ancestors of the Sendruka?*

No, that's the HTF Society's theory. First Flight have somehow deduced that all three ships ended up in the Huvuun Deepzone and they've asked me to persuade the Hegemony's Grand Archivist to release any Huvuun survey data into the public domain.

But Robert, don't these people realise that the Hyperion *colonists were incredibly lucky to find an uninhabited world like this, lucky not to have encountered any interstellar marauders or resource raiders, and lucky not to have succumbed to some native micro-organism? The other two crews would need similar amounts of good fortune to survive the potential hazards.*

Which are many, said Horst. *No – I fear that the* Hyperion's *luck was a fluke and that the other vessels were overcome by tragedy or violence. Perhaps in a hundred years, or even tomorrow, a traveller will find a dead hulk of a ship drifting around an uncharted star, or the ruins of a settlement on some inhospitable world, and the mystery will be solved.*

The Pathmaster listened, amused at the finality of Horst's declamation yet puzzled to see a knowing smile pass across the grey-pale Dreamless's features. And as the Pathmaster paused to ponder, he felt an echo of wrongness resonate back from that sombre verdict, as if there was something out among the stars to contradict it.

Then the Dreamless turned a thoughtful gaze over at the seated figure of Horst's daughter. For a moment all were still in that tableau, the two apparitions hingeing on Horst's state of mind.

The Pathmaster withdrew his perceptions, returning to the simpler imperatives of plantlife, to build, to grow, to put forth leaf, flower and seed, taking in the sun while drinking from the soil. The cycles and rhythms of nations and species, however, were vastly more complex than those of plantlife and the Pathmaster had come to know for certain that several ruthless ventures and ambitions had been drawn together by the discovery of Umara. Very soon these intersecting forces would bring great pressure to bear on the colony's leaders, and also on Horst, whose position might prove to be pivotal. Also, a lot would come to depend on the resilience and character of Cheluvahar, the new Artificer Uvovo. The husking of Cheluvahar would soon take place, shortly thereafter to be followed by the dispersal of Artificer teams to their appointed destinations and tasks, many secret, some formidable, all vital. Assuming that Segrana was able to carry out the husking as planned.

Now a man approached, one of the ambassador's staff, attired in a blue, high-necked uniform and perspiring visibly as he came hurrying round the forest path and into view. He would be carrying news of the shooting, the event that would set the first cogs in motion, their turning bringing certain forces into play, allowing larger cogs the freedom to turn, while other things moved and stalked between the stars . . .

As the Pathmaster watched, Horst nodded to the official then turned to the ghost-image of his daughter, speaking gently to her as if she were really there.

Reality, the Pathmaster thought. *When it comes, will it break him or will he learn how to survive?*

PART TWO

18

KAO CHIH

Outside his armoured cabin the winds of the gas giant V'Harant raged and roared as the gravity-tug *Biaolong* maintained its spiral ascent, carrying its pendant burden of six ore containers. Relaxing in the huge, ancient pilot couch, retrofitted for the human form by Roug technicians decades ago, Chih kept a practised eye on the exterior monitor and the generator gauges while deftly swapping the music tab in the couch's headrest. Like the couch and most of the instrumentation, the exterior monitor was a conversion hack, a dusty panel cased in grey plastic and fixed to the original console with webby struts. It showed a montage of views of the *Biaolong*'s hull, looking for all the world like an inverted stepped pyramid, its flanks studded with tapered blocks, while a perpetual blast of corrosive atmosphere whirled and scoured and howled.

Watching it, Chih smiled, remembering Great-Aunt Mei's assertion that the murky skies of V'Harant were really *Di-Yu*, the underworld, the abode of demons and punishment. Then he listened to the sound of that never-ending storm, muted to a low whisper by the thick alloy hull and the chemo-suppressor field, imagining it to be the fangs of a demon host grinding uselessly away, just beyond the armoured shutters. He laughed and was about to start the music, a selection of Yunan school electroniki, when the voice of his copilot, Ta Jiang, came from the headrest instead.

'Chih – number seven is sliding out of resonance.'

'Not again,' he said, leaning forward. The generator gauges

were flat displays set on brassy, octagonal plinths that jutted from the main console. Slipping on the spectrum goggles, he studied gauge 7, switching between colour lens pairs to take in all the 3D data. The Roug's willingness to modify the instrumentation had not extended to the antigrav generator displays, stemming from the conviction that all operators had to adapt their sensory perceptions to the equipment in order to preserve the conceptual integrity of the primal schemata. Fabulously intricate assemblages of motors, gyros, gears, levers, mirrors and crystals constituted the control systems of the gravity-tugs, the mines down on V'Harant's core, the orbiting refineries, and the cities of the Roug, floating somewhere in the gas giant's turbid atmosphere. Three generations of human engineers had been unable to persuade them to introduce even the most basic digital upgrades, and with never a reason given beyond a veneration of the original designers.

'Right, Jiang,' Kao Chih said, lifting his goggles to catch a glimpse of the main console's powerflow display, then it was back to the rainbow data-forms of gauge 7. 'It's radial pair nine in the crystal array – you'll need to rebalance it by three increments . . .'

'Okay . . . is that it?'

'Just a moment – yes, Jiang, perfect.' He grinned. 'I'll buy the *ch'a* when we get back to the Mountain.'

'That is very noble of you,' said Jiang. 'And who knows – I might have time to finish it before we go out again!'

Chih laughed as he tugged off the goggles. After docking, the copilot always had a longer journey to the airlock as his monitor station was near the core of the tug, which left him with a significantly shorter break than the chief pilot.

The remaining hour and a half of the *Biaolong*'s ascent was uneventful. Once the tug was clear of the upper atmosphere, Chih opened the cabin viewport's shutters and gazed out at the sullen, roiling face of V'Harant while the headrest played old, poignant synthesiser motifs softly in the background. From this altitude the turbulent globe did suggest a place of torment like *Di-Yu*; Great-Aunt Mei once had scandalised Kao Chih's mother and father by saying that V'Harant might even be a Chamber of Hell reserved for those who betrayed friends and family, abandoning them to ruthless enemies. The elder Kao's rebuke had been calm and measured, reminding her of how their forebears had been forced to flee destruction twice, firstly aboard the *Tenebrosa* when she and her sister ships fled the Swarm, and secondly when Hegemony mercenaries attacked their settlement on Pyre. He also pointed out that the ignoble character of her comments was a dis-service towards the sept's collective sorrow.

'Our sorrow?' Great-Aunt Mei had retorted. 'How do our trials compare with the bitter, wretched misery of the thousands who were left behind, and that of their children and their chil-dren's children? Deng Guo was a fool to lead us off into the fog-between-stars – if my father's father had been elected *duizhang* of the Retributor the sept would have sought out allies, not ended up here, indentured to cruel aliens . . .'

Which was what such arguments about the past usually came down to – the flight from Pyre and how Great-Aunt Mei's grand-father would have made a better *duizhang*, or captain. Kao Chih suspected that he would have been no better, or possibly worse if Mei was any guide to her forebear's temperament. In any case, the 1,500-strong Human Sept's contract of indenture still had thirty-two years to run, after which they would be permitted to contact Earth and appeal for assistance for both themselves and the colonists on Pyre, if any remained alive by then. One hundred and ten years of servitude and silence, that was the price the Roug had asked in exchange for sanctuary from Suneye, the Hegemony-based corporate monoclan which had seized Pyre for its resources.

Outside the pilot cabin, great cyclonic systems the colour of tilled earth moved slowly across the face of V'Harant. Kao Chih could see how an observer might consider it to be a place of pun-ishment, yet in truth that was where the great floating cities of the Roug lay, shrouded by planetary storms in a system veiled by vast interstellar streams and clouds of dust and debris, the fog-between-stars which the Roug called Ydred. He smiled sardonically – anyone would think that they had something to hide.

The Roug name for their main orbital was Agmedra'a but the humans called it the Mountain. It had a wide, roughly circular base from which clusters of refineries, silos, labs, yardfacs and residential structures rose, close-packed and tapering towards the apex. A shining, glittering spire in the full light of the sun, Busrul, or a conical mass of lights, beacons, and decorative holos when in the planet's shadow, as it was now. The glowing motes of hopcraft and other maintenance drones darted among the towers while the great, slow silhouettes of freighters came and went.

But the upper reaches of the Mountain were closed to all members of Human Sept, who were restricted to the sublevels and the underdocks where they seldom encountered any crewmembers from visiting ships. Kao Chih guided the huge mass of the *Biaolong* into the embrace of a pair of mooring booms, which latched on, drawing it and its underslung cargo into the gloom of a large docking bay. Already unstrapped from the couch, Chih grabbed his ageing black jacket, told Jiang he would have the *ch'a* hot and ready for him in the canteen, then headed out and along to the personnel airlock.

The metal decking quivered slightly underfoot. Muffled thuds signalled the decoupling of the six huge ore containers that hung beneath the gravity-tug. As he approached the big airlock he heard clanks and the rough hum of motors, a moment's wait and the hatch opened with a brief pressure sigh accompanied by the smell of hot oil. It was normally a short walk along the dockside concourse to the tug-crew operations hall but as soon as he stepped out of the sinuous connecting tube a familiar voice called out his name in Mandarin.

'Pilot Kao Chih!'

Turning, he was surprised to see the tall, spindly form of a Roug approaching. Members of other indenture septs – furred Gomedra, six-limbed Bargalil and birdlike Kiskashin – hastened about their own tasks, careful to stay out of the Roug's path.

Like all its kind, it was swathed from head to foot in tight wind-
ings of what looked like thin leather that gleamed with a dull
coppery sheen. The legs were thin, the feet flat and toeless, and
the long arms had two elbows and nine-fingered hands, but it was
the silvery badges on the conoid head that confirmed its identity.

'Noble Tumakri,' Kao Chih said. 'Unusual to see you out here.'
Tumakri was assistant overseer of tug-crew assignments, and thus
seldom seen outside the operations hall.

'Not usual, Pilot Kao Chih, but necessary!' The Roug's voice
had a whispery, papery quality and came from the wrappings just
below the almond-shaped meshes that protected its eyes. 'Special
assessors have arrived from Chissu'ol, the reigning city on
V'Harant, bearing edicts from the High Index – a Conclave of
Purpose is to be held aboard your sept's chief vessel, and you are
to be present.'

The sounds of the busy dockside washed around them as Kao
Chih stood in astonishment for a moment. 'Me, Noble One? They
wish me back on the Retributor? Must I depart soon?'

'Immediately, Pilot. A hopcraft is waiting in a nearby rectifier
dock and I am to accompany you and deliver you safely to the
conclave. Another pilot will take your place aboard the *Biaolong*
but you will still be credited for a full shift.' The Roug made an
odd shrugging gesture. 'This, I confess, is unheard of, unprece-
dented, yet we must comply. Please follow me, pilot.'

So I get a paid half-day off and a trip to the Retributor? he
thought, grinning as he hurried after the Roug. *Why not?*

The hopcraft was small and cramped and had the unclean fur
smell of the Gomedran techs who usually flew it and others like it.
The rectifier dock's mooring booms flung the little maintenance
boat out of the underhull where Kao Chih's companion ignited
the reaction motors and set course. The Retributor's orbit kept it
in the vicinity of the orbital Agmedra'a and it took less than half
an hour for a bright pinpoint to grow into the grey, irregular,
pockmarked shape that he knew so well.

The Retributor had originally been one of a family of asteroids
that orbited Pyre. After landfall, the colonyship *Tenebrosa* was

cannibalised into a number of small vessels and soon after that one of the asteroids was chosen as an orbital platform for planetary survey and as a base for mining operations. Decades later, after the first probing attack by the Suneye mercantilists, the star drive from the hulk of the *Tenebrosa* was hauled up into orbit and mounted on the adapted asteroid, then simply called the Rockhab. In the end, however, the mercantilists had returned with a force of mercenaries so overwhelming that the Rockhab's captain, Deng Guo's, only choice was surrender or flight.

And here we are, he thought as the ugly, retrofitted mass of the Retributor drifted closer. *Dispossessed twice over, trapped by the Roug contract, confined to certain areas of Agmedra'a and the core mines, but at least we're still alive.*

The Retributor's exterior was littered with protruding structures, coolant pipes and vanes, vents, bot hutches, antennae clusters, hatches, loading bays and hardpoint where defensive weapons had apparently once been mounted. Kao Chih knew that encrusted carapace, knew the inner geography that lay beneath those untidy features. Then he noticed that Tumakri was staring fixedly out at the Rockhab.

'Tell me, Pilot Kao Chih – is your sept's homevessel safe?'

Chih gave a small smile. 'Well, I have to admit, Noble One, that seal repairs are permanently ongoing, the airscrubbers always need purging, and the grav-decking can be a little uneven in places, yet 1,500 of my people are happy to make their home there. They work hard at keeping it safe.'

'A candid reply, Pilot. I am reassured by your words.'

Kao Chih nodded and went back to studying the Retributor, wondering if the grapple squads had fixed the ruptured fuel lines yet.

They docked at the new loading bay, so called because it had been added soon after the Indenture, as opposed to the old loading bay, which had been part of the original facility. Stepping down from the hopcraft's hatch, they were confronted with another two Roug, both adorned with silvery hooked sigils attached to their necks. To Kao Chih's surprise, his companion hastily bowed to each in turn, which Chih was quick to emulate. There followed a brief exchange in the rapid, polysyllabic Roug tongue, which was never taught to other races, after which one of the senior Roug addressed Chih.

'Pilot Kao Chih – we are Assessors of the High Index and are commanded to escort you and Overseer Tumakri to the decision chambers of your elders, where certain materials will be examined.'

Kao Chih swallowed nervously as he went with them to the bay's main arched entryway. This all seemed much more serious than he had first thought. Had he unknowingly infringed the terms of the Indenture, or perhaps been careless when casting off from the core mines down on V'Harant? Had he left a trail of wreckage behind him, and were they about to show a recording of it to the *Duizhang*, K'ang Lo, and the other elders?

No way to know, he thought, grasping at a straw of hope. Too soon to be sure.

From the high plascrete curves of the loading bay and its busy unshipping carrels, they passed into a semicircular lobby. Rounded openings led off, up, down and sideways, and without hesitation the leading Roug assessor headed for one of the downward exits.

The Retributor was honeycombed with tunnels and chambers of every size which provided its occupants with necessities and amenities. As Kao Chih followed the Roug into the dim, biobulb-lit passageway known as Shang Street, it was the cooking smells that leaped upon his senses first, as always. No matter the shift, there was usually someone somewhere steaming vegetables, baking bread or whipping up a spiced stirfry. It was the essence of home, of normality, of an unexciting ordinariness which right then he longed for. The presence of the Roug, however, was anything but ordinary. Eyes, some amazed, some fearful, some fascinated to see Kao Chih in the company of aliens, followed their progress, heads craned out of doors and windows for a look and mouths whispered once they were past. This was an event, a source of gossip that would, he knew, be refined and refashioned endlessly over the next few days. Who could tell what they might be saying about him in a week!

For a stretch Shang Street's right-hand wall looked out through a line of louvred windows and down into Many-Voices Hall, the Rockhab's main marketplace and gathering hub. As he walked Chih caught sight of some familiar places, the Steel Dragon tea-house, Cho Lai's repair shop, and the small balcony where Old Mother Yao gave I-Ching readings. Part of him wished he was down there, but in truth he was glad that none of his friends could witness his shame.

Before long they reached the administration and command levels, quiet, carpeted corridors where amber-suited assistants hurried serenely on errands, and where the walls and ceilings emitted a pearly, ambient light. After turning a couple of corners they came face to face with two guards standing either side of a wooden door. On it were the five symbols of the Pyre colony – a tree, a bear, an open scroll, two crossed spears, and at the centre the t'ai chi, each one beautifully carved and inlaid with silver from the regalia of the original colonyship, the *Tenebrosa*. That was because it led to the *Duizhang*, K'ang Lo's, strategy room.

This is it, he thought as the guard stood aside and the Roug assessors led them in.

It was worse than he had feared. The eyes of more than three dozen formally attired people looked round at the newcomers and Kao Chih realised that everyone of consequence was present, clan elders, duty directors, command staff, and his father, Kao Hsien. In the background, rows of empty chairs waited.

I'm doomed, he thought, resigned to fate – until he saw a certain look in his father's eyes, the kind he wore when he knew that a game of wei-chi was his . . .

'Ah, Pilot Kao – at last you are here.'

K'ang Lo was a tall, barrel-chested man on whom the blue-and-black, long-sleeved *duizhang*'s coat looked natural. At once Kao Chih came to attention and gave a sharp bow of the head.

'Sir, I . . .'

'Not now, Pilot. Explanations will come later, once the mystery is revealed, neh?'

He turned to the senior Roug and gave a slight but gracious bow, then made a small gesture to the attendants. The light began to dim gradually and everyone went to find a seat as one of the Roug set up a slender tripod with a glittering device at its apex. Kao Chih and Tumakri found theirs off to the side. Meanwhile, the other Roug addressed the seated elders in perfectly inflected Mandarin.

'Most diligent and industrious members of Human Sept – what you are about to see was very recently disseminated across all first- and second-tier news feeds in the greater general region . . .'

The first Roug straightened, stepped back from the tripod, and at once a holo appeared and began to play. A series of human commentators, Caucasian, Asiatic and African, was shown, interspersed with views of what looked like villages and towns on a lush, fertile world far from Earth. The commentary and dialogue was mostly in Anglic and Russian but someone – Chih assumed it was the Roug – had added Mandarin subtitles. As the story emerged and became clearer, excited whispers rippled around the room, because those towns and villages belonged to a Human settlement founded by one of the original colonyships which had fled Earth at the height of the Swarm War, taking random hyperspace jumps into the depths of space.

The *Tenebrosa*, the *Forrestal* and the *Hyperion*. It was an old story for Kao Chih's generation, resonant with the pain and grief of defeat and exile. But for the *Hyperion*'s crew, the world which they had made their home – and named Darien – just happened to lie well within a deepzone which kept it hidden from other civilisations for a century and a half. And now Earth was reaching out to them with the promise of friendship and aid, as well as the prospect of opening up relations with nearby cultures and races. Then the commentators mentioned that Darien's neighbours were the Brolturan Compact, an offshoot of the Sendruka Hegemony, and the mood in the room changed. All knew from decades of underdock buzz and unofficial summaries, as well as the

sufferings of relatives still captive on Pyre, what Sendruka involvement really meant.

Indeed, one of the smaller septs working on the Agmedra'a
orbital called themselves the Sundered, a race whose homeworlds
had been seized by the Brolturans nearly three centuries ago. The
Brolturans had once been a fundamentalist faction within
Sendruka society until prophecy and an intensification of their
shared zealotry drove them to seek independent territory outside
the Hegemony, and the Sundered were the main victims of their
aggressive colonisation. As a pacifist race without allies, the
Sundered were uprooted and evicted from their handful of planets. Roughly half of them ended up eking out a miserable
existence in scores of refugee cantonments scattered around the
region while the rest travelled from star to star in ageing, decrepit
cryostore ships, seeking aid or petitioning for intercession. But
since the Brolturan Compact was now a close ally of the
Hegemony none was willing to risk its wrath and the predictable
consequences.

The report included interviews with some of the ordinary citizens of Darien colony, a strange people with round eyes and
brown or red hair yet full of a vitality that Kao Chih immediately
felt a connection with. Then there were shots of some indigenous
creatures and sites of great natural beauty, followed by a brief,
intriguing glimpse of excavated alien ruins that the colony's
researchers were investigating along with the help of diminutive
humanoid sentients from the planet's inhabited moon. Chih was
amazed, and smiled to see Tumakri leaning forward to stare more
closely at the half-buried stone remains while muttering dry,
incomprehensible things to himself.

The holo-sequence ended with the reception of the ambassador
from Earth and his short speech to the crowd of onlookers and
reporters. Then it was over and the lighting came up as the Roug
collapsed the projector and its stand down to a small flat unit
smaller than a woman's fist.

I'd wager that's a digital device, he thought. *Wonder how that
squares with their non-digital preferences.*

'Honourable K'ang Lo, and assiduous leaders of Human Sept,' said one of the senior Roug. 'The events shown took place less than two days ago and came into our hands during the last sleep cycle. It is an unfortunate fact that this world Darien is located in deepzone territory currently claimed by two opposing powers, the Imisil Mergence and the Brolturan Compact. The Darien system is very far from Earth and still further away from us, and the Human colony there is small and weak, thus the prospects of survival seem poor.

'However, strength is not always measured by the capacity for military violence. The plight of the oppressed and the destitute, when openly declared for all to know and see, exerts a moral power which weakens those that rely on violence to attain their goals. In the light of this, and of the assessment we compiled, the Contiguals of the High Index have decided to act. We are instructed to offer to Human Sept cancellation of the indenture contract, provided there is agreement on three conditions.'

There was a sudden outburst of delighted, almost disbelieving chatter, and Kao Chih stared at Tumakri.

'Noble One, did you know of this?'

The Roug's features were hidden by the tight, coppery swathes, but there was a certain tension in its movements that suggested surprise.

'Pilot Kao, I am as unprepared for this as you.'

Then the *Duizhang* stood, his face stern, his dark eyes glittering as he raised one hand for silence.

'Noble Assessors, please state your conditions, that we may determine their fitness.'

'As you wish. Condition the first, that Human Sept shall aid us in the necessary training once a replacement sept has been chosen. Condition the second, that the leaders of Human Sept shall agree to dispatch an emissary to the Darien colonyworld, to meet with the authorities there and to request permission for all surviving Pyre colonists to settle and join with their Human compatriots. This task must be undertaken promptly and without announce-ment or even communication with either Darien or Earthsphere –

were the Suneye monoclan or the Hegemony to learn of this too soon, the consequences would certainly hamper the evacuation preparations.'

Kao Chih could scarcely take it all in. *Evacuation?*

Duizhang K'ang Lo looked equally stunned. 'The greater part of my people still endure captivity on the world Pyre, Noble Ones. Are they included in your kind and generous plans?'

'They are, *Duizhang*. As soon as the Darien leaders issue their invitation, our vessels shall travel to Pyre and carry out the evacuation. Any attempt to interfere will be dealt with harshly.

'Condition the third, that the emissary shall be Pilot Kao Chih, son of Kao Hsien. He has been the subject of close assessment, most recently by Overseer Tumakri, and we are satisfied that he meets the criteria for such a crucial role. We shall provide him with a small but durable craft and a Roug companion, Overseer Tumakri, who will be able to impress upon the Darien authorities the true nature of the Sendruka Hegemony, and thus the need for secrecy until all the colonists have departed Pyre.'

Kao Chih sat back in his chair, astonished. Next thing he knew, people were leaning over to pat his shoulder or shake his hand, smiling and congratulating him. Mostly he felt elated, but nervousness assailed his stomach, as if he were about to step off a precipice.

Out into deep space, he thought. *All the place and races I've heard about and now I'm going to see them!*

Then a hush settled quickly over the room as K'ang Lo broke away from hasty consultations with his advisers, facing the Roug again.

'Noble Ones,' he said. 'We are humbled by the extent of your generosity. Indeed, there are scarcely words to express the depth of our gratitude, yet a few of us insist that we ascertain the reason for this sweeping, purposeful benevolence. May we ask how your people would benefit from it?'

For a moment or two there was silence. The Roug assessors were motionless, as was Tumakri next to Kao Chih, who thought that the *Duizhang* must have comitted some grave offence. But then one of them spoke.

'Honourable *Duizhang*, we are not accustomed to giving explanations, but these are unusual circumstances so we shall endeavour to put your mind at rest. We are an old race, so old that the world V'Harant is not our original home, nor are these bodies the original physical form of our species. Yet once we were as novices to an alliance of ancient races whose wisdom and intellect puts us to shame even now.

'They fell in a vast and cataclysmic war, sacrificing themselves to ensure the defeat of a terrible, pitiless enemy. The last of them charged us with the duty of overseeing this part of the galaxy, and in the aeons since we have from time to time moved to undermine or eliminate certain forces that posed a serious threat to galactic civilisation. For the last 25,000 cycles – in human terms, a little over 10,000 years – a degree of calm has held sway, but now, unfortunately, the Sendruka Hegemony is working to bring it to an end. Its proxy, the Brolturan Compact, is currently in dispute with the nations of the Erenate over who controls the bulk of the Huvuun Deepzone, where Darien is located. If a military response can be provoked from the Erenate, this would justify an overwhelming intervention by the Hegemony; the resulting conflict would draw in all the Erenate nations and could spread to Milybi or even the Indroma. It would be an interstellar war of horrifying ferocity.

'The discovery of the lost colony on Darien has fundamentally altered the balance of power. Humans are involved in the heart of it, which means that Earth and by extension the Earthsphere federation are also involved. The Aranja Tesh are already keeping a close watch on Hegemony strategy, as are the Indroma Solidarity, and this will only heighten their interest. And when it emerges that the survivors of a second lost Human colony are to settle on Darien, having been rescued from captivity under the harsh rule of a Sendruka monoclan, the Hegemony will be forced to punish Suneye or lose face. The Darien colony will gain too much sympathy and tiernet attention for the Hegemony to risk putting its plan into operation, so it will go into abeyance. During which time we hope that saner minds will prevail and reshape certain policies.'

Again K'ang Lo conferred with his advisers and the leading elders, and to Kao Chih's eyes he seemed less than happy. But before a consensus could be achieved, a diminutive old man, bald and leaning on a stick, stood up from amongst the rest, scowling. This was Great-Grandfather Wu, once deputy to an earlier *duizhang* and father to another, and one of a handful still living who remembered Pyre. He was also well known for his acerbic tongue.

'*Duizhang*, come now, why this delay, heh?' he said. 'Everyone here is eager to see the start of something good for us – please, more haste.'

'Most venerable Wu,' said one of the elders, Tan Hua. 'There are several uncertainties which need to be resolved. Be calm, all shall proceed correctly.'

His condescending tone infuriated Wu.

'Be calm! You hesitate and quibble over petty details while a precious gift waits to be accepted, and you expect us to keep calm?' He gazed about him for a moment. 'I cannot speak for anyone else here, but I yearn to feel solid ground and honest grass beneath my feet before I die! Honourable K'ang Lo, do not listen to the squeakings of this *hsiao jen*. We *must* accept the noble Roug's offer, and young Kao Chih there *must* leave for Darien without delay!'

Approving voices rose on all sides and heads nodded vigorously. An argument broke out between one of the clan elders, an ally of Tan Hua, and someone seated at the front, who was then egged on by the crowd. But before tempers became still more heated and the language less than courteous, K'ang Lo clapped his hands loudly twice and shouted, 'Enough!'

Abruptly, all fell silent, and those on their feet shamefacedly sat back down. His expression thunderous, the *duizhang* turned to the waiting Roug.

'Noble Ones, despite the reservations of a few, it is clearly the will of the elders of Human Sept that we accept your most generous proposal. In accordance with your wishes, I shall see that all conditions are met.' He looked round, straight at Kao Chih. 'Pilot Kao – come forward.'

Once more the focus of attention, he rose and went to stand before the *duizhang*.

'Pilot Kao, you are called upon to be our emissary, our representative to the leaders of the Darien colony, indeed to all our brothers and sisters in the great family of Humanity. You are to be our voice, our face. Be honourable and courageous but not foolish. Use the tactics of fox and lion when either is appropriate.' He turned back to the tall Roug. 'Noble Assessors, how soon must Pilot Kao depart?'

'Within the hour, honourable *Duizhang*. A scout-craft has been made ready and is in transit from Agmedra'a as we speak.'

'Very well. Pilot Kao, my technical officer shall prepare a datachip containing various files documenting all the adversities endured by our people, and including a personal greeting from myself. May the spirits of our ancestors protect and guide you in your mission. Now, you have little enough time left to you, lad, so spend it with your family, neh?'

Never had he experienced such a frantic sixty minutes. In between grabbing mouthfuls of food and trying to pack a small assembly of clothes and belongings, he attempted to reassure his mother that no, hyperspace was quite safe, and yes, he would be cautious and wary in busy places, and yes, he would stay near his Roug companion . . .

His father was quick to undo such placating talk, pointing out that he was a man, not a child, and he was engaged on a great task that did not require any mollycoddling. And during all this, his elder brother, Feng, made up and enacted ridiculous exploits and perils which, predictably, served to make his mother still more anxious. In contrast, his younger sister, Ti, periodically burst into tears. In addition, other relatives and family friends came to deliver their farewells, dallying to partake of Kao Hsien's peach brandy before departing.

Then suddenly there were less than fifteen minutes to grab his jacket and kitbag and dash through the tunnels and chambers, hurriedly waving and greeting other acquaintances along the way to the old loading bay. His thoughts whirled as he half-walked, half-ran, thoughts about this ship of theirs, about his destination, about all the unknown worlds and creatures waiting for him out in the vast black distance. The rest of his family was catching up as he entered the big oval space of the bay and saw K'ang Lo and all three Roug waiting off to the right, near the end of the dockside walkway. Nearby, resting in the worn, battered arms of a berth cradle, was a shining, metallic-grey ship some 30 metres long, its main drive nacelles jutting on curved vanes that mirrored the vessel's swept, beaklike prow and superstructure.

There was the final leavetaking, last words of encouragement and well-wishing as well as tearful pleas from his mother, and his father gave him a jade fu-dog pendant, an old good-luck charm reputedly brought from Earth, then firmly clasped his shoulders before turning away to blow his nose. The *duizhang* K'ang Lo handed him a small red pouch containing the datachip and a scroll bearing ribbons and seals, a declaration of Kao Chih's role as supreme envoy for the colonists of Pyre. He and Tumakri bowed to K'ang Lo and the Roug assessors, then together mounted the long, overswung gantry which led up to the hatch in the scout's upper hull. And his thoughts began to slow down, settling on the minutes, hours, days to come and the realisation that he was leaving the Roug system, possibly for good, heading outwards on a great adventure, every young man's dream.

'So, noble Tumakri, what do you think of our fine ship?' he said as they clambered down into the vessel, where small lamps illuminated a cramped space.

'It is a Henkayan two-seater, Pilot Kao, a *Shobrulig*-class fast courier with cross-fractulate shields, full-boundary thrusters and a Tier-1 hyperspace drive . . .'

Inside, Chih was confronted with the walls of a narrow passage just tall enough for his companion. The inner wall was cluttered with niches, hinged flaps, shelves, pullout storage racks, and two long sleeping compartments set into the lower half. Kao Chih flung his kitbag into the lower recess and went forward after the Roug, who was still talking.

'. . . but has a new environmental unit and sufficient basic supplies to keep us nourished for the maximum estimate of six days.
Ah, and I believe that this craft's Henkayan designation translates
as *Castellan*, and although we are not armed we possess some
detection countermeasures . . .'

His voice tailed off and his head dipped a little. By now they
were both strapped into the cockpit couches, while a rumbling
came from outside as the massive inner doors closed to seal off
the dockside. A whine of servos then a thud and hiss signalled
that the hatch behind them was closed.

'My apologies, Pilot Kao,' the Roug said, his voice subdued.
'But I must confess to a certain anxiety about the task ahead.'

Kao Chih stared at him. 'I'm not sure I understand, noble
Tumakri – you have flown one of these before, yes?'

'Oh yes, my appraisal was more than satisfactory. It is just that
I have never travelled beyond the borders of our system, and my
briefing suggests the possibility of a perilous voyage.'

'In what way perilous?'

'Due to the clandestine nature of our mission, we cannot proceed via the main tier-ports. Sendruka agents and machines will
be alert to any Humanlike species, and even the presence of a
Roug may be enough to raise suspicions, therefore the authorised
hyperspace conduits will be closed to us, which means that we
have to use illegal ports and purchase course schemata from unlicensed dealers. I have been given several detailed itineraries and a
few linguistic enablers, as well as the names of trusted intermediaries who have been told to expect us. Our onboard navprocessor
is already imbued with our first destination and the autopilot will
guide us out. Hopefully, this is sufficient preparation.'

There was a sudden roaring rush as the outer bay doors
cracked open, venting the atmosphere in a pale burst of flash-
frozen vapour. There was a slight jolt, then the sensation of
motion, acceleration pushing Kao Chih back as the scoutship
Castellan shot out from the great irregular mass of the Retributor.
Seconds away, attitudinal thrusters came to life, sending them
along a shallow trajectory away from V'Harant. Once they were

a set distance from the gas giant, the flight systems would bring the hyperdrive online and take them into the many-tiered continuum of hyperspace.

'So, Tumakri,' Kao Chih said with forced cheerfulness. 'What is to be our first port-of-call?'

The Roug took a small oval documenter from a waist pouch and read from its screen. 'Blacknest: an illegal way-station engaged in illicit commerce and the harbouring of a variety of outlaws, pirates and other transgressors. It is located in the Qarqol deepzone, just beyond the Erdindeso border, and we are to exercise . . . great caution at all times.'

'Ah yes, standard operating procedure,' Kao Chih said casually, ignoring the nervy panic that seemed to radiate from the Roug. 'Nothing to worry about – when we get to this Blacknest we probably won't even have to leave the ship. I imagine your people's contact there will have everything in hand. Just sit back and relax . . .'

And I'll try not to think about what Great-Aunt Mei said to me earlier . . .

Less than an hour ago, in his parents' house, he had just finished a bowl of rice and vegetables and was digging his old kitbag out of a chest when a finger had prodded his shoulder. The finger was attached to Great-Aunt Mei, who studied him with her hawkish black eyes.

'I heard that old fool Wu got up and singed Tan Hau in front of the Roug – is that true?'

'Indeed it is, Great-Aunt, and quite a sight it was . . .'

To his surprise, her stern, wrinkled face had then broken into a gleeful, gap-toothed smile.

'Heh, he always knows too much, old Wu, so all he can be is the wise fool!' Then her features had grown sombre. 'And how are *you* feeling, boy? Frightened?'

'I'm excited, Great-Aunt! – it's a great adventure . . .'

'Adventure, hah! The young always fail to see the whole of the road ahead, so off they rush. But then, you don't know enough to be scared, which makes you a young fool.' Then she had grasped his shoulder, pulling him closer. 'Listen to me, boy – pain will come to you, hurts and wounds the like of which you have never felt before. You must fight and kill them or they will eat you up, like hungry river serpents!'

Leaning back in the copilot couch, he watched a shielding layer of hexagonal platelets roll out across the cockpit viewpane, preparatory to the hyperdrive jump.

His first hyperdrive jump.

He leaned back, hands gripping the armrests. *Well, Great-Aunt Mei, I may not have been scared then, but be assured that I am now*!

19

KAO CHIH

On approach, the rogue port Blacknest looked vaguely intestinal, like the digestive tract of some huge, grotesque monster. Within spidering meshes of metal frameworks, silver, grey and blue flexitube corridors spread in coils and undulations, connecting polyhedral modules of various sizes that were embedded in the mazy tangles like geometric tumours. The blocks and cylinders of the original station were still visible beneath the improvised accretion of past newcomers, and it was from the largest conglomeration that a substantial docking hub protruded on a squat tower.

'Is that where we're going?' Kao Chih said, studying the hub's busy traffic on the long-range imager, comparing it to the Roug orbital, Agmedra'a.

Tumakri, his Roug companion, peered closely at the multi-coloured symbols on his small console screen, hesitantly touching a few with one dark, spindly finger. 'It seems not, Pilot Kao,' he said in his dry, papery voice. 'At first we were, but now we have been redirected to a secondary landing stage. Our syncsystem is already plotting a new guide-path.'

He looked round at Kao Chih, who smiled and nodded. 'That sounds reasonable – the main docking hub looks pretty busy,' he said, trying to sound both relaxed and businesslike. Soon after exiting hyperspace in the Blacknest vicinity, Tumakri had given him a linguistic enabler, a package of Human-configured nanobio receptors in the form of a translucent golden pill. In half an hour he was able to understand and respond in the Roug tongue, and by the time the illegal port was in visual range he was bordering on the fluent, with the result that Tumakri's erratic mental state became even more apparent.

'So tell me, noble Tumakri, who is the intermediary we are supposed to contact here?'

'One Rup Avriqui, a Voth procurer – I have since determined from our notes that in addition to providing the course data for the next stage of our journey, he will also be accompanying us. I have already sent three advice requests on the frequency tag shown in the itinerary, but thus far no response. This does not seem normal to me . . .'

Kao Chih shrugged. 'Perhaps their protocols are different in these matters, or custom . . .'

He was interrupted by a brief staccato chime from the comm panel, then a string of syllables whose intonation varied between flat, nasal and flutelike. There was a momentary jarring sensation in his mind, like sounds and symbols colliding, then suddenly he was hearing the Voth's words and understanding them. Most of them.

'. . . again to present my egremini apologies for this lapse in finsterral communications. Disturbance between rabble factions is the cause but our mezgurid business remains viable. If this addresses to the noble Tumagri and Gowshee, please to respond.'

Kao Chih and Tumakri looked at each other for a second before the latter spoke.

'Have we the honour of speaking with Rup Avriqui?'

'This is so, exalted clients-of-unrivalled-lineage.'

'Do you have the . . .'

The Voth cut him off. 'Forgiveness I beg, exalted one, but it is not wise to speak of important matters over an unsecured channel. Once you disembark, my lugosivator will bear you both safely to my hold, where we shall continue our dialogue. I bid you the short and temporary farewell.'

The channel abruptly switched to the ready-cycle's bland, atonal warbling, and Tumakri blinked.

'It seems that he is expecting to meet both of us, Pilot Kao.'

'Indeed, friend Tumakri,' he said. 'But the truth is that my appearance is distinctly un-Rouglike, and we cannot take the risk of my being recognised as Human in a place like this.'

'Yes,' said Tumakri, slumping down into his couch. 'I was hoping to persuade you to undertake the encounter by yourself, somehow . . .'

Kao Chih leaned forward, amused. 'In that case, we shall have to be creative, perhaps even inspired. What did you bring in the way of spare clothing?'

'A standard long-excursion miscellany,' the Roug said. 'But almost none of it will fit you. . .'

'Not to worry,' Kao Chih said, getting up. 'It's the details that matter, so we'll have to have a good rummage through the storage lockers . . .'

Nearly an hour later grapple-nets were hauling the fast-courier *Castellan* in beside two larger vessels that were moored to a gim-balled docking duct. A flexitube concertinaed out to fasten its mouthlike seal around the smaller craft's hatch. On opening the hatch they found a prismoid dock ID tied by a length of finefibre to an eyehook, drifting in zero-gee. After a weightless clamber through the grubby, much-patched transfer tube, then along the docking duct, squeezing by all kinds of passengers coming and going from other ships, Kao Chih and Tumakri finally emerged in some kind of lobby. The Roug wore an ankle-length, sleeved cloak of a thin, grey material that clung from neck to waist, while Kao Chih had opted to don the emergency environmental suit but without the helmet. Around his head he had wrapped bandages from the medikit, being careful not to obscure the dark, faceted goggles he had put on beforehand.

And since Tumakri's itinerary notes had warned of Blacknest's imperfect eco-cleanliness they were both wearing small breathing masks. For Kao Chih, heavy gloves and boots completed the hopefully convincing non-Human picture.

There were three turnstile gates at the lobby exit, each with a queue of arriving sophonts, most of whom were bi-, tri- or quadrupedal: did swimmers, crawlers and fliers have their own docking areas, he wondered. A buzz of conversation enveloped them, voices conversing in all manner of whoops, whistles and words, while the air was a swirl of odours. In a hubbub like this, Kao Chih's linguisitic enabler tended to lie partially dormant, only translating when he focused on a particular voice or when someone spoke clearly and from close by.

He had prepared himself for a long wait, based on his observations of similar entry procedures on Agmedra'a. But it soon became clear that new arrivals were being processed with haste by three anxious Henkayans in dimpled blue uniforms. Each was using one pair of stubby arms to pass a fan-snouted sensor over each lifeform while the other pair dealt with forms and charges.

Then it was their turn. As the gate attendant began waving his handheld sensor at Tumakri, he took one look at the prismoid dock ID and said:

'Smallboat berthnetted, minimum fee seventy keddro.'

Tumakri produced a slender black credit stem, banded in gold.

'You may deduct from this,' he said.

'Nogood, nogood,' said the Henkayan, jerkily shaking his head. 'Creditransfer network offline, you mustpay keddro now or returnship.'

'But this . . .'

'Nogood, nogood! Yellowfists here soon – pay now or leave!'

Tumakri swayed on his feet and Kao Chih steadied him with an outstretched hand.

'What's wrong?' he said. 'Don't tell me you didn't bring hard currency.'

'I do have such, but it is supposed to be for later in our journey.'

'If you don't pay the man, we won't be able to meet Avriqui and there won't *be* any more journey.'

Clearly unhappy, Tumakri dug into a waistpouch and surrendered four glittering black triangles, three inlaid with gold, one with crimson. Their dock ID was imprinted with a strange curlicue pattern and they were each presented with a blue plastic tag embossed with a string of symbols before being hurried out into Blacknest Station itself.

The corridor floor was covered in a dingy grey ridged matting, as was the ceiling, which was also a floor. A variety of sentient creatures was bustling along the gravplate pathway that ran the length of the ceiling, most of them, Kao Chih noticed, hurrying in the same direction. Then as he watched, several yellow-garbed figures leaped out from the overhead pedestrian flow, as if taking a collective nosedive towards the floor. Fearful cries went up from the gate attendants – 'Yellowfists! Yellowfists!' – and Kao Chih then saw the tethered lines on which the newcomers swung through the air to land clumsily before the transit lobby entrance. Regaining their feet/paws/hoofs, they pulled out slot-nosed sidearms and gestured threateningly at the attendants.

'Time we were elsewhere,' Kao Chih said, grabbing a near-paralysed Tumakri and dragging him along the half-deserted corridor. They had just reached the next corner when an odd, jingling voice spoke:

'Masters Gowchee and Tumagri? . . . up here, good sirs.'

Kao Chih looked up and saw a boxy, yellow cart with six fat wheels and a telescopic pole tipped with a cluster of glittering lenses which were angled down at him.

'Indeed we are,' Kao Chih said cautiously. 'You are . . .?'

'I am Master Avriqui's number 2 lugosivator – I am to take you to his hold straight away. If you step onto the sidepath and join me, we can be quickly under way.'

The lens arm pointed to a strip of grey matting that curved off the main corridor into a recess and up the wall, joining the one directly above. Without delay, Kao Chih stepped onto the branch path, feeling his stomach bounce a little as he adjusted to walking up the wall then stepping onto the ceiling strip. Behind him, Tumakri groaned, holding on to the sides of the recess as he followed. The yellow cart had seating within a curved, transparent carapace. Flexible doors popped on either side and moments later they were strapped into sideways-facing bucket seats as the vehicle sped away from the chaotic scenes further back.

'Apologies are tendered for the lack of proprieties,' said the lugosivator. 'Master Avriqui had intended to greet you in person but reports of incipient violence caused him to remain at home.'

'Are such incidents considered normal here?' said Tumakri.

'No, Master Tumagri, but unfortunately Blacknest is experiencing one of its periodic outbursts of interclan rivalry in which revenue sources, such as the embarkation gates, become strategic prizes to be defended or captured by force.'

'Fascinating,' Kao Chih said. 'What about ships in dock? Are they also considered prizes?'

'Docked vessels are inviolable, Master Gowchee,' said the cart. 'Certain categories of passenger, however, are seen as legitimate quarry at times like this.'

Kao Chih and Tumakri exchanged a worried look.

'Would we fall into that category?' he said.

'Yes – you arrived in your own craft with no personal bodyguard and no protection brevet. Data spotters will have already sent your profiles out to several gang bosses . . .'

Tumakri hunched down in his seat, staring this way and that through the cart's transparent hull.

'. . . which is why I have brevets here to give to you, signed by Master Avriqui.' A thin tray slid out from a black panel below the windscreen – on it were two documents, folded sheets of light blue textured plas imprinted with lines of text in Tralesk, a trading language. Underneath was a swirling character written with a double-nib, which Kao Chih took to be Avriqui's signature.

'How long till we reach Master Avriqui's hold?' he said.

'We shall be arriving shortly,' said the cart. 'From the next junction we follow a vascule out to the tubeworks and our destination is not far beyond that.'

Kao Chih nodded and glanced out at the busy corridor. Away from the contested arrivals lobby, the station took on the kind of appearance he had been expecting, archway and doors along the corridors revealing markets, kiosks and tiny workshops enveloped in a hum of activity, a jostling flow of creatures and sentients from every corner of the galaxy. A red-and-black-furred hexapedal

Bargalil gestured with a small forearm to a Gomedran selling light-splines and bubbles, while nearby a reptilian biped Kiskashin garbed in hooded leathers tended a stall where clusters of tarnished pipes smoked amid gauzy veils and glittering trinkets. A muscular Henkayan was raking through boxes of hardware with all four arms, examining finds with a headband scope. On the other side of the stall, an old battered mech shaped like an upright dumb-bell was doing the same thing with microfields while floating on its suspensors.

Relaxing a little, he smiled, enjoying the view which he was seeing from above as Avriqui's lugosivator trundled along the tall corridor's ceiling path. The shops and stalls went on and he wondered if most of Blacknest was like this. He saw a pair of Gomedrans haggling with a half-shelled Naszbur arms dealer; an octopoidal Makhori coldly eyeing passers-by from the opacity of its tank; a long-bodied Vusark propped up on a metal frame, its many sets of legs flexing rhythmically . . .

And a pair of beady eyes in a small, snouted face that stared straight up at him for an instant then broke away. Kao Chih had the merest glimpse of a cowl around the observer's head before it vanished into a side turning. He was about to mention this but the cart's sentience spoke.

'Sirs, my master wishes to communicate with you.'

A translucent panel appeared in the cart's forward windscreen and darkened into a display showing their adviser and prospective travel companion, Rup Avriqui, sitting in a high-backed wood-and-leather armchair. Behind him were the glows and shadows of a low-lit room. Rup Avriqui was a Voth, a squat bipedal race which bore a superficial similarity to a presentient Earth species called orangutans. The Voth certainly had long arms but also had broader torsos and shorter legs, larger ears and flatter faces. They also had a liking for bulky, concealing garments – Avriqui was wrapped in layers of clothing, some finely woven and intricately patterned, others coarse and plain, while on his head he wore a strange cap comprising beads and tiny mirrors over padded cloth.

'Ah, most viable our business, noble visitors, and most efficient my preparations. Soon we shall be discoursing upon the urgent matter of your task and my part in its workings.'

'Please accept our thanks for the brevets,' Tumakri said. 'Reassurance is a gift which lights our way.'

'I am gratified to be able to confound the misfortunes of the current unrest,' the Voth said. 'I must confess, however, that I had to nominate Master Gowchee's species profile as being Roug in order to dispatch the brevets with my lugosivator. Now I see by the evidence of my own eyes, as well as the profiles obtained just moments ago, that Master Gowchee is not of the exalted and ancient Roug.' The hooded eyes regarded Kaò Chih. 'Humans are not popular, you see, thus there is danger for you at every turn. Fortunately, you will both soon be within my hold and I shall have the brevets modified . . . what *is* that noise?'

A faint knocking sound had suddenly become a loud banging. Muttering angrily, the Voth levered himself out of his seat and moved out of sight, shuffling footsteps receding. For a moment all was quiet onscreen, then there was a shout followed by the sound of running feet. Rup Avriqui abruptly rushed into view, his headgear askew, his eyes bulging as he lunged at the controls near the vidcam.

'Exigency nine, exigency nine!' he shrieked, stubby fingers scrabbling at the panel as a pair of hands, one metal, one flesh, grabbed his shoulder and dragged him screaming away. Then the screen went opaque for a second before melting into transparency. Kao Chih and Tumakri stared at each other in horror, then grabbed the edges of their seats as the cart jerked to a sudden stop halfway down the corridor wall.

'Passengers must evacuate at once,' said the vehicle as its sides sprang open. 'Deepest apologies for unforgivable treatment, masters, but the Avriqui hold has been compromised, therefore this unit can no longer guarantee your safety.'

'But . . . but what must we do?' said Tumakri, voice quivering with shock.

'Return to your ship is the safest course – the safest course – safesafesafesafe . . . please return to your seats there is no danger we will soon arrive at residential unit stem nine radial twelve . . .'

Fighting a surge of panic, Kao Chih jumped up from his seat and dragged Tumakri away from the suborned lugosivator.

'It was right,' he said. 'We have to get back to the ship!'

'. . . yes,' said the Roug. 'Yes, we must!'

Then he shrugged off the Human's support and leaped into a headlong sprint back the way they had come. Amazed, Kao Chih took after him, but with his longer legs Tumakri soon opened up a good lead. The Roug wove between stalls and knots of sentients, ignoring Kao Chih's shouts to slow down. So intent on his destination was he that he never noticed the gang of fur-snouted Gomedra rushing out at him from a side passage until it was too late.

Kao Chih saw the ambush, shouted Tumakri's name . . . and in the next instant felt something tangle his legs, causing him to dive forward and land with jarring force.

'Bind him!' said a guttural voice.

Half-dazed, he fought against rough hands that tied his wrists and fixed a gag to his mouth.

'The Blacktooth vermin are escaping with the other one,' came another nasal, rasping voice.

'Then render him worthless,' said the first.

Fearful, Kao Chih tried to yell around the gag and struggled against his captors. Instead, he was hauled upright in time to see an armour-clad Bargalil raise a hexabow and fire off three bolts. There was a brief, high shriek and Kao Chih knew with horrible certainty that Tumakri was dead.

'Sack this one and bring him to our new nest!'

A cloth hood stinking of machine oil enfolded his head and, grasped lengthways, he was carried off, friendless, soundless and wrapped in darkness.

20

ROBERT

He hated to be late for meetings, hated being out of breath and feeling sweaty and grimy, but sometimes the only thing to do was accept it and move on.

'My most sincere apologies to you all,' he said as he entered the president's private conference room, a low-roofed chamber with green-textured walls. 'Communications with my government have proved very slow overnight.'

'That is quite understandable, Ambassador Horst,' said Sundstrom. 'But now we can proceed – I assume you recognise everyone present?'

There were seven people at the large oval table including Robert, Sundstrom; Deputy-President Jardine; the intelligence chief, Vitaly Pyatkov; Theodor Karlsson, an adviser to the president; General Morag Soutar, the C-in-C of the Darien Volunteer Corps; and the sixth, a heavily built, middle-aged man in a dark sober suit, whose name escaped him until Harry appeared nearby and said, 'Edvar Storlusson, master-provost of Trond and Sundstrom's unofficial deputy-president for the Northern Towns.'

Robert smiled and nodded, partly for Harry but mostly for the gathering. 'Indeed I do, Mr President.'

'Good, then before we discuss this terrible event, I want us all to take stock of the latest reports. We'll start with you, Vitaly – tell us about the High Monitor and his staff, then what your investigations have uncovered.'

Sundstrom sat back in his wheelchair, looking weary but also,

Robert thought, sustained by the anger and outrage he had expressed during his vee broadcast to the colony last night. The man had articulated a burning repugnance for the attempted assassination in language of such lyrical force and delivery that Robert was able to imagine what Sundstrom must have been like in his younger, healthier years.

'High Monitor Kuros,' said the intelligence chief, 'is well and fully recovered from the shock and distress of the attack. He and his staff will be holding a private mourning ceremony later today for their murdered colleague, Assister Morild. As to the attack itself, we have determined that the gunman opened fire from dense forest cover overlooking the Giant's Shoulder excavations. The murder weapon was a forty-year-old 8.5 calibre Ballantyne rifle, modified for hunting with a 15x50 telescopic sight and a sculpted, rebalanced wooden stock . . .'

Photos of the weapon were being passed around, and General Soutar was quick to comment.

'Practically an antique,' she said in a booming voice. 'Aye, and pricey, too. But deadly in the hands of a marksman – wouldn't you agree, Major Karlsson?'

There was a brief but uncomfortable silence, then Karlsson gave an unflustered smile. 'The gunman was probably a good shot, certainly, General. He also has excellent woodcraft and stealth skills, but then so do most of the faraway hunters and trappers. What I'm puzzled about is why he abandoned the rifle – he must know that it will inevitably furnish us with information.'

'We are trying to trace the rifle's origins and previous owners now,' Pyatkov said to him. 'Although the killer left no prints or any other evidence, we know from the flattened grass that he was of average height with a fairly lean physique. One of the High Monitor's bodyguards took away swab samples from the rifle to see if any DNA evidence can be recovered.

'As for suspects, we have brought a number of known sedition-ists and extremists in for questioning, but although some claim to be members of the FDF no one can name their leaders or give a coherent summary of their aims beyond a handful of slogans.'

Sundstrom nodded. 'There may be a degree of disquiet amongst the general populace about some aspects of the new situation and its consequences,' he said. 'But there is no grassroots support for violence and killing. Every call to my office, and to every other legator, has condemned the shooting, often in vigorous and colourful language! This has extended to my decision to cancel the Founders' Victory Day celebrations, but you can't please everybody.'

There were a few laughs and knowing grins around the table. Robert smiled.

'It is most reassuring to know that the Darien Colony is united in its opposition to this act of terror,' he said. 'Whether they turn out to be this Free Darien Faction or someone else.' He paused. 'Has anyone claimed responsibility yet, Mr President?'

'No one at all,' said Sundstrom. 'It's as if they were expecting their vile act to start an uprising but nothing happened.'

'They're not finished,' Karlsson said grimly. 'The next one will be worse.'

'We have to make sure that there isn't a next one,' said Sundstrom. 'The Hegemony is adamant about that.'

'So you've spoken with High Monitor Kuros about this matter, Mr President?' Robert said.

'No, Mr Ambassador, but informal channels between ourselves and the High Monitor's advisers have remained open.'

'I see.'

Robert sat back, stroking his chin thoughtfully. His AI companion Harry leaned on the back of his chair, bent close to Robert's ear and said, 'You'll have to give them some idea of what they're in for if these attacks don't stop.'

He nodded slightly and sat straighter, facing the waiting Dariens.

'My friends, the Hegemony takes attacks on its officials very, very seriously indeed – if this shooting had occurred on Hegemony territory they would have instituted the severest measures. Curfews, confiscation of firearms, a ban on public assembly, restrictions and censorship of all public media . . .'

'That's outrageous,' said Storlusson, the provost of Trond.

'I've not finished, sir. Satellite surveillance would be employed in conjunction with positioning tags fixed to all vehicles and, if necessary, to all civilians. Communications would be filtered and spying devices of every kind and size would become omnipresent.'

'But this is not Hegemony territory,' Pyatkov said.

'True, but the Brolturans have made a claim to this region of the Huvuun Deepzone and I have just learned that they have dispatched their ambassador to Darien aboard a line warship – originally it was to be a diplomatic corvette but news of yesterday's attack has altered their posture. So you see, it really is in your interest to show High Monitor Kuros that you mean to keep him and his staff safe while doing all you can to capture this murderer.'

The others listened with worried faces, exchanging glances when he finished, all eyes eventually turning to Sundstrom. The president was silent for several moments, his frowning gaze fixed on the tabletop before him where he slid and turned a pencil through his fingers over and over.

Have I gone too far? Robert thought. *Perhaps I painted too bleak a picture . . .*

'This is all . . . illuminating, Ambassador,' Sundstrom said at last. 'What is your position on this? What advice might you have for me?'

'My government fully supports Hegemony policy on acts of terrorism,' he said. 'Most of the measures I've described have in the past been enacted by Earthsphere authorities in response to attacks carried out in our domains. My advice to you, which my government has approved, is to pre-empt the High Monitor's request for heightened security arrangements – offer a detachment of your best troops as permanent guards for the Hegemony embassy and as an escort should he or any of his staff need to move outside its confines. Consider the measures I mentioned – I'll have a list sent over later – and go as far as you can to put them into practice.'

'You'll never get the Northern Towns to agree to the likes of censorship and weapons confiscation,' said Storlusson. 'They'll fight it all the way.'

Robert shrugged. 'Then at least propose curfews and restrictions on public assembly. Also, you might like to think about temporary legislation to help enforce anti-sedition options – that would persuade the Sendrukans that you're serious.'

Voices were raised but Sundstrom cut them off with a sharp sweep of the hand.

'Ambassador Horst,' he said. 'I would like to formally request the prompt deployment of Earthsphere marines to aid the security needs of my government.'

'I'm sorry, Mr President,' he said. 'I have been instructed that no Earthsphere troops are to be dispatched to the colony at the present time. You see, the Brolturans would interpret such a move as staking a claim and the Hegemony would tend to support that view.'

'So what material assistance can you offer us?' said Pyatkov.

'Some intelligence, some training for police units, but weapons or support equipment – that would be seen as technology transfer, which is strictly forbidden under multilateral treaty. Look, Mr President, I know this seems very unhelpful but you have to be patient and try to help the Sendrukans to feel that you're on their side. To that end, I strongly advise against appealing to the representatives of other nations or blocs for aid – that the Hegemony and the Brolturans would regard as an unfriendly act.'

He stood, glancing at the large oval clock on the wall. 'Now I must take my leave – I am shortly to meet with High Monitor Kuros's senior assisters and after that the *Heracles*'s first officer.'

The rest got to their feet, apart from the wheelchair-bound president.

'Thank you for explaining your government's position so candidly, Ambassador,' Sundstrom said. 'We shall give serious thought to your observations and recommendations. I should also like to consult further with you later this afternoon if that is convenient.'

'I'll tell my office to expect your call, Mr President.'

A courteously slight bow to either side of the table, then he was outside the conference room, following his personal attendant round to the main elevator with Harry striding along beside him.

'*Well you can't say you didn't leave them wanting more,*' the AI said, smiling drolly.

Robert waited until he was alone in the descending lift before replying.

'It's a grave situation, Harry, with the potential for turning nasty if the Brolturans get the wrong idea . . .'

He sighed. The Brolturan Compact, like Earthsphere, was a close ally of the Hegemony; however, their origins as an offshoot of Sendrukan society and their willingness to act as the Hegemony's military proxy gave them a kind of favoured-ally status which amplified both their arrogance and their endemic paranoia. Robert had on several occasions encountered Brolturan priests and military (which often amounted to the same thing) and knew that they would have to be treated with kid gloves.

'*It wouldn't have hurt to let them know that you asked for permission to deploy the marines down here.*'

Robert shook his head. 'It would have softened the blow. I want to shock them into the reality of their situation and our role here – they can't afford to harbour any illusions.'

'*Yes, Robert,*' said Harry without a hint of irony. '*We can't have illusions getting in the way of stark reality, absolutely not!*'

21

THEO

Depressed and angry at Horst's response, Theo was crossing the Darien Assembly's wide foyer, making for the entrance. The three sets of ogival arched double doors lay at the foot of a huge mural of the First Families done in a variety of woods, their colours carefully arranged. He was a few paces from leaving when one of the azure-uniformed government couriers caught up with him.

'Begging your pardon, Major Karlsson, but the president asks if you would care to join him in the diplomatic suite.'

'Did he say what it's about?'

'No sir, only that you would be glad you came.'

Theo's frown turned into a smile. *More presidential hugger-mugger, eh? Well, could be instructive, maybe even entertaining.*

'I'm game, lad,' he said. 'Lead the way.'

The diplomatic suite was a comparatively recent extension of the assembly complex. Three levels constructed on pillars at the rear with plush room and conference chambers whose big curved windows looked out over the Kalevala Gardens. The young courier led him to the third floor and past several OG guards to a room adjacent to the big, half-domed auditorium at the end of the corridor. As the courier smiled and turned away, one of the guards opened the door and ushered Theo inside.

It was a long, narrow room with small tables along one side. The windows were opaque and the wall-mounted uplights gave off a soft yellow radiance. More OG guards stood behind Sundstrom, who sat at a table, flanked by Pyatkov and Soutar, both of whom looked sombre. When Theo entered, Sundstrom smiled at him then nodded to a guard officer, who hurried off to the other end of the room and left by a second doorway, where another guard was on duty.

'Come and join us, Theo,' the president said. 'This is quite a sight.'

On the table before him was a portable display. From a low vantage point it showed a wide section of the diplomatic suite's roof, which was marked out with a landing grid. Moments later he heard the sound of an approaching craft, its engines a blend of deep bass drone and high-pitched whine, then a strange, webbed cluster of angular modules came into view, the blast of its drives sending dust and leaves flying as it banked, straightened up and drifted to the centre of the grid. The craft, Theo noted, was a uniform dark, matt, coal-like grey, and he wondered if that was evidence of stealth technology. Then landing legs unfolded and it descended, its entire structure flexing as it settled onto the roof.

'Our guests are disembarking from the other side,' Sundstrom said. 'So they'll be with us shortly.'

'And who are these guests, Mr President?' Theo said.

'If we're lucky, valuable allies. Otherwise, we may at least be able to rely on considerable sympathy.' He turned his wheelchair a little. 'My friends, I have a small admission to make. For more than two years my administration, i.e. myself and a few trusted colleagues, has been in touch with officials from the Imisil Mergence, one of the nine star nations that make up the loose alliance of the Erenate. I have had many exchanges with one of their senior diplomats, Javay shtu-Gauhux, a Makhori of long and distinguished lineage. Soon after we got the first messages from the *Heracles* he predicted that something like this situation would arise and that the Earthsphere response would be weak and subservient to Hegemony interests.' He smiled bleakly and spread his hands. 'This meeting is to formalise relations between Darien and the Imisil Mergence, but we will also be introduced to a representative from the Cyclarchy of Milybi, an immense confederation whose territory borders the far edge of the deepzone.

This emissary is from a race known as the Chatha who are, I'm told, insect-like in appearance . . .'

Theo knew that the Makhori were an octopoidal species, but he wasn't expecting the strange, small object that glided through the doors at the far end, flanked by diminutive Gomedran escorts. It was an antigravity platform with a transparent carapace beneath which the Makhori ambassador sat, its long pseudopods nestled under an inner rim.

'My good friend Holger! It is most refreshing to meet you face to face at last!'

The Makhori's voice was a synthesis of Human speech but the cadences and emphases seemed slightly awry: what made it remarkable was the musical accompaniement, soft, fluty notes that gave an undertone to every syllable. As the words were spoken, Theo could see one of the Makhori's pseudopods working a little panel with a cluster of stubby palps. Theo held back from smiling – it was like having your own personal orchestra.

'Ambassador Gauhux, I am most pleased to welcome you to Darien,' said Sundstrom. 'I regret that this could not take place under more relaxed conditions.'

'Indeed. It appears that the warmth of your welcome is not shared by the Earthsphere forces which are in control of your orbital environs. I do not mean that they mistreated us, merely that they extended the minimum of courtesy and consideration.'

'I can only apologise, Ambassador.'

'There is no need – such is only to be expected within the ambit of Hegemony influence.' The Makhori's floating pod turned slightly so that its large oval eyes could take in Theo and the others. 'You have companions with you, I see.'

'Yes, Ambassador – may I introduce Mr Pyatkov, director of our intelligence service; General Soutar, commander of the Darien Volunteer Corps; and Major Karlsson, my personal adviser.'

Personal adviser?

Theo had to focus hard on keeping any surprise from showing at this promotion. And from the stiff glance Pyatkov gave over his shoulder, he wasn't the only one caught unawares.

'Fellow sentients,' the Makhori said, 'I am very pleased to meet you and thereby expand the boundaries of my knowledge. Sadly, this must be a brief encounter – my travelling companion is a cautious and highly circumspect being and wishes to return to our ship as soon as possible – ah, he approaches.'

As Ambassador Gauhux drifted to one side, a pair of odd, bird-like creatures, tall and feathery in rich shades of blue and ochre, strode in through the doors at the far end. They had no wings or arms and in the place of a beak they possessed a long, prehensile snout ending in four bony fingers. Each one held a glassy, poly-hedral device whose facets glowed and glittered. The strange sophonts calmly pointed these things at everyone in the room before facing each other, bowing, and pressing a stud on each device. For a moment all were still, then a newcomer entered.

Theo's first thought was that this was an emissary from a machine race, going by the four slender metal legs, but in the next instant he realised that, like the Makhori's antigrav plat-form, this was a mobile carriage. The Chatha was larger and bulkier than the Makhori, and although it bore a vague similarity to an Earth-type spider, there were some clear differences. Rather than hairs on a hard exoskeleton, the Chatha had a leathery, greenish-purple hide with a pebbly texture, and instead of a low-slung body there was an oval hump which rose to a wedge-shaped head with an occipital ridge running from the smooth, rounded back of the skull forward to a tapered, beak-like proboscis. There was a pair of eyes on either side of the head, giving it about 270 degrees of vision, Theo guessed, while a curved opening under-neath, at the neck, was probably its mouth. The Chatha's real legs, he realised, must be quite short and had to be interfaced with the powered, mechanical ones which extended from the open pod in which it sat. The Milybi emissary looked grotesque to Theo and he felt uneasy in spite of himself.

The trunk-armed attendants presented their devices, which the Chatha took with its short limbs, examining each in turn. Then it stowed them away inside its pod, approached the table where the others were waiting, and began to speak.

The words were a stream of liquid vowels pronounced with a wide range of pitch, then the speech changed into a sequence of hard but expressive sounds, interspersed with an occasional deep hum. Then suddenly it was speaking Anglic.

'I am Estimator Jeg-sul-Mur. I greet you in the fair language of the Great Cyclarchy of Milybi, in the formal tongue of the Chatha, and in your own language. I am deeply gratified to see that none amongst you is contaminated with the machine virus which afflicts the unwise Sendruka. Similarly, your race seems to lack any significant mind-force faculty, which for weaker races can be a burden rather than a benefit.' The twin eye-pairs considered them all one by one, ending with the octopoidal Imisil ambassador. 'Colleague Gauhux, if you would designate.'

'With pleasure, Colleague Sul-Mur. This is the foremost leader of the Darien Humans, President Sundstrom, and his diligent attendants.'

Once again a smile laid siege to Theo's lips. While 'diligent attendant' felt more natural to him, he knew that the General thought otherwise, at least going by the dark look on her face.

'President Sundstrom,' the Milybi emissary continued, 'I am able to tell you that interlocution between your collective and ours is acceptable but not possible under these circumstances. And unfortunately, prognosis indicates that the Hegemony or their Brolturan proxies will soon seize control of your world and use it as a staging post for further strategic expansion throughout the deepzone.'

Theo was taken aback by the emissary's frankness – even Sundstrom was visibly shaken.

'I knew that we faced a perilous situation, Estimator,' the president said. 'But you seem to think that our cause is lost even before the struggle has begun.'

'I understand your distress,' said the Chatha, tilting its long head forward so that all four eyes could regard Sundstrom. 'But galactic history is littered with instances of the fate of small communities when they become an obstruction to powerful hierarchies. Perhaps my Imisil colleague has related a few more recent and relevant examples.'

'Estimator Jeg-sul-Mur,' Sundstrom said. 'Your confederation is large and powerful – if we were to appeal directly to you for assistance, would you give it?'

'The Great Cyclarchy of Milybi is indeed large and powerful, President Sundstrom, but it is also pragmatic and far away – my echelon senior would be swift to point out that we have no inter-ests to defend in this part of the deepzone.' The emissary paused. 'However, I can tell you that your predicament is developing with unseemly haste. We have studied the various ploys which the Hegemonics or their proxies have deployed against a number of victims, and it would appear that one or more are in play here. Your world is clearly of great value to them and they have in the past proved themselves adept at presenting themselves as the injured party. I extend my fulsome sympathies but I regret that I am unable to offer you any direct support.'

Theo's growing frustration was diverted by the Chatha's final words, which seemed to imply that the Hegemony envoy Kuros was behind his own attempted assassination. Unless Kuros was a sacrificial pawn in a game played by someone else on his own staff . . . his thoughts spun, trying to assimilate the implications of such a conspiracy. But then his critical faculty rebelled – how could they locate a skilled marksman (and infiltrator) amongst the Darien colonists so quickly without raising suspicion?

'I am grateful for your considered remarks, Estimator,' Sundstrom said. 'A time may yet come when I can invite you to Darien for a longer, more relaxed period.'

'Against the weight of history I hope that this will happen,' said the Chatha. 'I would urge you and your trusted echelon to exer-cise great caution in all of your dealings with the Hegemony and any of its servants. Alternatively, if you need an escape from encroaching jeopardy, I am certain that diplomatic sanctuary may be sought with the Imisil delegation . . .'

'Yes, Holger,' said Ambassador Gauhux. 'This avenue is open to you and your immediate circle.'

'My thanks for this generous offer but my place is here on Darien.' Then he laughed. 'Gentlemen, there is an old human saying, "It's not over until it's over," which I intend to keep in mind at all times.'

'I applaud your determination in the face of great odds,' the Milybi emissary said, then began to speak in the alien tongues again, ending with: 'I bid you farewell in the name of the Great Cyclarchy of Milybi – may the Infinite and the Benign watch over you when you walk in dark places.'

Then with the two feathery attendants, the Chatha steered its carriage back along the room, retracing those deliberate insectile steps. The Makhori Gauhux watched him go for a moment then looked to Sundstrom.

'My friend,' it said melodically. 'I must accompany my colleague back to our ship and help him prepare for his departure – our auxiliary vessel will transport him back to Erenate space and the nearest Milybi mission. In the meantime, I shall remain and make plans for a modest residency . . .'

'Does our situation really look that bad, Gauhux?' Sundstrom said.

'I'm afraid so, Holger.' The Makhori's large oval eyes seemed to be full of sorrow. 'My own analyst concurs with my Chatha companion – the Sendrukans are operating a deep scheme against you. Either one or more of your fellow Dariens have thrown in their lot with them, or the Sendrukans have brought a couple of humans with them for the purpose. Whichever is true, you'll have to stop them before they bring disaster down on you all. Now I must return, so until we meet again, good fortune . . . and hunt well.'

'Safe journey, Gauhux,' said Sundstrom.

As the Imisil glided out of the room Sundstrom turned his wheelchair to face the others.

'Any thoughts?' he said.

'They seem very certain that the shooting is a Hegemony ploy,' said Pyatkov. 'And unsurprised.'

'I think we should plan for the worst, Mr President,' General

Soutar said bluntly. 'For example, if you were killed, then Jardine would become president, correct?'

Sundstrom's lips twitched with a ghost of a smile. 'I'm afraid so, General.'

Soutar nodded. 'And if both of you were killed, what then?'

'Then the cabinet would vote on a successor, in closed session.'

'And if the entire cabinet was wiped out?'

'General!' said an angry Pyatkov.

'Hush, Vitaly,' Sundstrom said. 'I understand the General's reasoning. Well, in the unlikely event of such a catastrophe it would fall to the Speaker of the Assembly to either assume the office himself or attempt to negotiate a government of national unity.'

'Unless the military takes control, of course,' Theo said.

It was Soutar's turn to be outraged. 'That's a damnable accusation coming from the likes of you!'

'Really? And just how would you define the likes of me?'

'Verra easily! – as a disloyal turncoat who . . .'

'Right, that's enough from the both of you!' roared Sundstrom with a stentorian fury that made even Theo step back. 'This carping is of no use . . .'

At that moment the climbing drone of the Imisil shuttle's engines came through from above, interrupting tempers and sharp words. As the sound faded Sundstrom began to point out that divisions would only help their adversaries, but broke off when Theo's comm chimed from his inside pocket.

The president frowned. 'I'd hope you would have had it muted.'

'It was,' Theo said, taking it out, staring at the oval bluescreen. 'Only emergency calls can get through – and I don't recognise this number.' Swiftly, he thumbed the answer. 'Hello, who is this?'

'*I'm disappointed, Major,*' said a man's voice. The accent was vaguely Russian and his manner quite relaxed. '*I thought that you at least would have understood, you, Major Karlsson, Black Theo, Viktor Ingram's right-hand man . . .*'

'Understand what?' he said, miming to the others for something to write on.

'*That this is our land, our world, the place where our fore-fathers found sanctuary and fought and slew a pitiless enemy.*' The man laughed softly. '*Ah yes, sounds like a song, doesn't it, Major? Like a saga. And now our time of testing has come and we also have an adversary to fight.*'

'You mean the Hegemony?' Theo said as he wrote on a piece of notepaper – IT'S THE ASSASSIN. 'That's a sizeable party to choose as your rival, boy. I mean, all the First Families were up against was a crippled machine-mind . . .'

'*It's not just the Hegemony, Major, it's all alien offworlders, all those twisted abominations. Like the ones you just said goodbye to.*'

'How do you know about . . .'

'*I have sources, Major, and a good view from an office building across the square.*'

'So what's your creed – us against the galaxy, is that it?' Theo said.

'*They need to learn that this is our world, our place in creation,*' said the voice, now more earnest. '*And the Free Darien Faction is going to teach them that they're not at liberty to wander where they like, that they're not wanted.*'

'You'll be stopped, boy. We'll see to that!'

'*You're welcome to try, Major, but I think you'll find that you've got your hands quite full . . .*'

At that moment Theo heard the sound of an explosion, a loud, echoing boom not far away but muffled by buildings. For one horrible moment he thought that the Imisil shuttle had been sabotaged, but Pyatkov was already on his own comm, talking rapidly. Looking down Theo saw that the mysterious caller had cut the link.

'It's the Founder Square zeplin terminal,' Pyatkov said, still listening to his comm. 'Both mooring towers blown off, fallen into the square . . .'

Then the president's comm began to ring, along with the general's. Moments later, Pyatkov was getting a fuller picture.

'There were three devices, two on the towers, one in a waste basket by the entrance . . . no reports so far of fatalities but many seriously injured . . . emergency response teams already there and the Assembly marshal has begun lockdown procedures.'

Sundstrom was motionless as he listened but his eyes burned with anger. 'The scum is going for soft targets, trying to show that it's not just the Hegemony he wants to hit . . .'

Then Theo's comm pinged and looking down he saw the symbol for a new voice note, as well as its origin number.

'I think this is from him,' said Theo, holding out his comm so they could all hear it when he pressed the play button:

'As I said, they need to learn that they're not free to wander where they like. Don't worry, I'll get them, every last one of the offworld filth – that was just the second instalment of my course of instruction. I hope you all learn the lesson.'

22

CHEL

Rain was falling through the dusk, falling on the dense, lantern-speckled mass of Tapiola, as Chel made his solitary way up a steep path towards the tree line. There was little wind and the hiss of the rain came from all around him in the darkened valley, filling the distance with a vast, hollow murmur against which the drips and patters from nearby bushes were soft and muffled. The ground was spongy underfoot and the air was cold, moist, redolent of foliage.

Forty years before, when the daughter-forests of Segrana were being planted in the soil of sad Umara, the senior Listeners of the time had asked the Human community to give names to them all. After much deliberation, the Humans decided to name them after great writers, all except the most northerly, which they called Tapiola. This was the name of a mystical forest from an ancient Human saga called the *Kalevala*, composed at a time in their past, long before books and devices, when singers and devout keepers committed great histories and song cycles entirely to memory.

As we still do, Chel thought. *Even though we have a written tongue and small archives exist in Segrana, we continue that tradition.*

Subdued lamps grew brighter as he drew near, a string of hazy glows leading further into Tapiola Forest, and the tall, hooded form of a Listener stepped into view and waited. When Chel got to the edge of the forest the Listener stretched out one bony hand, palm outwards.

'Name yourself and say why you are here.'

'I am Scholar Cheluvahar of the Benevolent Uvovo,' he said. 'I have come to be husked in the sight of sacred Segrana.'

'You will give up that which you were?'

'I will.'

'Are you ready to cast off the shell of the now and don the veil of becoming?'

'I am ready.'

'Then enter, Scholar Cheluvahar, and know that this is the last time you will be called as such.'

Chel shifted the weight of his travelsack to his other shoulder then stepped out of the rain and into the welcoming shadows of Tapiola.

Few Uvovo actually resided in the daughter-forests: scholars, gardeners and herders watching over the plants and animals. But here there were dozens, gathered up high, in or near temporary shelters made from vinework and leaf layers, the lamplight from within making them resemble giant cocoons. The Listener, who did not introduce himself, wordlessly led Chel to a clearing from where a sturdy-looking rope ladder curved up to one of the lower branches of a huge ironwood tree. A couple of female Uvovo who were conversing nearby as they approached fell silent, smiled and bowed to the newcomers.

'May Segrana make you welcome,' said one.

'May Segrana show you the Eternal,' said the other.

'Sisters, I thank you.' Chel bowed, then seized the ladder and began to climb.

He had attended huskings before, back on Nivyesta, and knew the significance of the climb, symbolic of the rise from the commonplace to the astonishing, from the familiar to the sublime, from ignorance to perilous knowledge. He had always imagined that his own husking would happen back on the forest moon, guided and cheered by his own family and friends, not here in this cold, austere place, watched by no one that he knew well.

From the ironwood branch another rope ladder led up to a higher branch, and from there across to another tree. Then straight up and across to a truly massive tree, looming like a many-armed giant through the gloom. This one had dozens of branches sprouting quite close together, making it easy to follow the sequence of little lamps that spiralled up the gnarled, mossy trunk.

At last he and the Listener came to a sizable platform of woven branches where a group of Uvovo wearing thin brown shifts and pale yellow caps waited. They were known as the Unburdeners and to them he gave his travelsack, his outer and inner garments, his knee and feet protectors, and the *zoza* stone he wore about his neck. Then, following the Listener's directions, he climbed naked up to the platform known as Contemplation, where, as was customary, he paused to gather his thoughts and prepare himself. Not far above was the final stage, Threshold with its *vodrun* chamber, and a solitary Unburdener who was waiting to offer him the Cup of Light.

Chel shivered. It was colder at this height, dark and misty beneath the canopy, with occasional droplets coming down through the foliage. He though of Gregori, who had given him one of the new music devices as a parting gift, and wondered if the murderer had been caught. Then he thought about Catriona and her obsessive search for the Pathmasters, knowing that she would only find them if they wanted to be found. And he thought about Listener Weynl and Listener Faldri and the nameless Listener below (whom he thought might be a Starroof Listener called Eshlo) and tried to imagine his own body changed, bones lengthening, flesh stretching. Would there be pain, and for how long . . .?

Wishing suddenly that Greg and Catriona were there, he breathed in deep and turned to face the last ladder.

I am to be unmade and remade, he thought. *No more delay.*

With renewed determination he climbed to the Threshold platform, where a pair of lamps hung from curved poles. A masked Unburdener stepped forward and offered a small oval bowl, which he accepted, then drank from its narrow end. It tasted fresh, like skyleaf water only carrying a variety of subtle flavours that eddied slowly across his tongue. The door of the *vodrun* lay open and without hesitation he crouched to duck inside then sat on the plain bench carved from the interior. Fleetingly he wondered where the Listeners had found a seedpod of the immense *vunris* tree, supposedly extinct on Umara. By the lamplight he could see that the *vodrun*'s inner surface was covered with fine carving, patterns, faces, creatures of Segrana, and some strange shapes that looked like erratic, random outlines . . .

The Unburdener stood in the doorway, his wooden mask regarding him.

'Segrana awaits you,' came a female voice. 'Her purpose will show you all the pathways of the Eternal – be ready.'

Chel smiled, bowed his head. The Unburdener stepped back and swung the door shut, plunging him into darkness.

With eyes closed he leaned back against the rough podwall. He knew that the Cup of Light was meant to unfasten the moorings of his mind, but so far he felt quite calm and unchanged. The flavours from the strange drink still lingered in his mouth but were steadily fading, tastes of nuts and berries dissolving away to nothing – and just then he caught a whiff of smoke. He sniffed, quickly then deeply, sure that something was burning just outside the *vodrun*. Then he saw a glow next to the floor, bent down and saw a tongue of flame extending up the curved wall, splitting and spreading, a fine network of fire.

He called out and banged on the door, but it was shut fast from the outside and no answer came. Chel began to panic and fumbled on the floor for the stoppered flask of water that was usually left there. Nothing. The blazing web expanded, covering the whole of the pod's wall till he was crouched down in the centre, enclosed in a shell of quivering, rippling flames. The carven creatures crawled while patterns contorted and faces turned to him and spoke in harsh voices, demanding, commanding and condemning. The voices all ran together, echoing and changing as the flames fragmented and shrank, sinking into the wall of the *vodrun* until it glowed a rich reddish yellow.

The shapes and patterns carved there looked far more detailed now. Fascinated, he moved closer to study, just as more colours streamed across the wall, shades of dark green spreading up to and along one of those odd, erratic outlines while a deep blue flooded and filled the other side of it. Then an obscuring mass of opaque greyness drifted slowly across the upper part of the wall he was examining. All distress forgotten, he stared, suddenly realising that it was a coastline seen from orbit. He giggled and looked closer, following the shore round and down a long, curving stretch to a short peninsula shaped like a hook.

Just like the one where the Humans have their stilt buildings, he thought. *Pilipoint Station . . .*

The details drew his gaze; engrossed, he looked still closer and the coastline leaped a little nearer. More details emerged, the texture of Segrana's vast expanse, the rough, dark surface of the Silversong Sea, then nearer still with coves and inlets becoming visible . . . vertigo stirred in his head, his chest, his stomach, and he tried to pull away from the dizzying vista.

Then the wall of the *vodrun* melted away, and with nothing to brace against he fell, limbs flailing as he shrieked, plummeting through layers of cloud in a headlong dive towards the ground. Soon he could make out treetops and wheeling birds, lines of waves and tiny figures walking along the shingle. And Segrana rushed up to embrace him.

Through layers of foliage he fell, a battering descent of broken branches, collisions and glancing blows. He felt every one, yet there was no pain, no sense of bones broken or blood spilt. He tumbled and rebounded down into the cool, humid darkness of Segrana's interior, down towards the forest floor, towards a sheltered pocket of old, impenetrable shadows where an ancient swamp lay. It quivered as he plunged into it, a black, gritty wetness grasping his struggling limbs, dragging him down further down . . .

Return to the soil, return to the seed of things . . .

He was drowning yet not drowning, while immense thoughts coursed through his mind.

. . . to your soil, to your seed . . .

The swamp faded, its enfolding dark trembling into misty night strewn with stars and swirling haze, and the rich light of a planet turning slowly overhead. Umara, the beautiful blue orb that he had watched countless times from the high towns of Segrana. But his gaze was drawn to another distant quarter of the sky where an array of glittering points moved steadily nearer, stretching across almost half the firmament, and behind it was another vast formation and behind that another and another. Then his mind . . .

His mind was within one of those points, a vessel crammed with metallic shapes, incomprehensible devices, all webbed with furious energies while lodged at the vessel's heart was a creature, an intelligent being . . .

An enemy to be pitied, a knight of the Legion of Avatars, the truncated remnant of something that had once walked upright. Their race became entangled in its own technical hubris, eventually surrendering to a union with the machine, inveigled by promises of immortality. They hate the flesh and its flaws, a hate that bred fear and a hatred of other species less invaded by technology . . .

Suddenly Chel was back, staring up into the deepness of the night as arrow-formations of glittering points swept towards the spreading web of Legion vessels. An eyeblink and he saw the graceful lines of the newcomers, long contours adorned with curved wings and vanes yet seemingly too few against the swarming attackers.

In their millions the Legion invaded from another universe, and battles like this bloomed in hundreds of star systems. Facing desperate odds, the High Ancients rallied together and wrought a terrible weapon in the cause of the Great Purpose . . .

As battle was joined he was shown fleeting glimpses of clashes near other farflung worlds, saw scientists and workers of many races working without cease to finish the weapons that would end the Legion's destructive rampage, tunnels bored down into the deep layers of reality – warpwells.

Vast amounts of power were needed to bring the warpwells to life, so hundreds of millions of High Ancients gave up the energy

of their minds and bodies to create those vortices of destruction.
Witness their dignity as they sacrificed themselves to the greater
good. A hundred thousand years ago, a sacrifice long forgotten by
almost all, yet our memory is everlasting and we will deny the
Unmaker a final victory . . .

Chel saw the warpwells reach out to drag everything into their
dazzling maws, dust and meteorites, the debris of battle, lifeless
bodies, warships of either side. Some Legion craft on the edge of
the conflicts tried to escape but the High Ancients gave more
minds to fuel the warpwells and their reach extended out to the
space between the stars. He saw Legion vessels by the thousand
drawn inexorably down, many reduced to wreckage, spilling
vapour and ragged fragments, while others still grappled with
the larger High Ancient warships, all funnelled inwards, crashing
together, hull against hull. Then Chel was . . .

Chel was in the middle of it, hurtling downward amidst the
grinding shriek of metal, the buzz of horrifying weapons and the
roar of the warpwell vortex, whose ice-blue-spear-black light
blurred everything. Suddenly, a world loomed – his second
descent – rushing upwards, a dazzling bright eye that gaped, a
lacuna of energies into which he plunged.

From all sides came glimpses of strange worlds and stranger
firmaments, deranged landscapes, inconstant tracts, distortion,
decay and desolation, fleeting and fading, a shadowy succession
of realities through which he fell. Openings began to appear,
pulling great swathes of mangled machines and vessels, and Chel
seemed to see this from outside, see all the warships, Legion and
High Ancient alike, disintegrate and scatter across the dark, deep
layers of hyperspace. He realised that the same thing was happening at all the other warpwells, the utter destruction of the
Legion of Avatars, millions, perhaps billions of them, a cataclysm
to stagger the mind.

Could anything survive such a descent? The rushing blur
slowed as he fell with the battered, broken remnants into a foggy
abyss webbed with flickers of silver radiance, slowing still further,
drifting down past black cliffs . . .

Many died that still many more and their successors might live on . . . yet Unmaker takes many forms . . .

The cold shadows faded, and he blinked slowly as he looked up. Once more he stood on that high place, gazing at the planet overhead and almost crying out when he saw that it was burning from horizon to horizon. A few stretches of pockets were still green but smoke veiled the surface of Umara, great wings and tails of darkness sweeping across forests, plains and mountains.

Ten thousand years ago Unmaker came again as the Dreamless . . .

Something crossed the bright edge of the planet, a strange cluster of spikes growing as a large silhouette came into view, a solid curve of blackness, some kind of disc with antennae and probes radiating, Chel guessed. Then a rod of polychromatic light stabbed out and something exploded in planetary orbit, shedding a burst of illumination upon the silhouette. Chel saw that it was a massive globe covered with countless columns and spires of varying sizes, wavering like the spines of a colossal sea creature. And there were others drifting in from the lightless gulf of interplanetary space, black bristling orbs unleashing glittering barbs that fell on the world below.

From a mountaintop on Umara he saw them strike and tear apart the land, great slabs of ground and forest rising up, twisting and disintegrating in the grip of a terrifying destruction. But the Uvovo held their positions throughout the burning, tormented forests. Chel could see them in underground chambers, in hilltop strongholds, in fortified caves, all working with strange mechanisms through which the green force of the planet-girdling forests was channelled.

As I once was, with unity and with a voice . . .

He saw the Waonwir temple in its original state, pillared, open floors rising from the hollowed-out prominence, Uvovo everywhere engaged in serious tasks. Its uppermost levels tapered to a slender tower that sprouted numerous leaflike vanes which shimmered with energy. Periodically, a massive flash obscured great stretches of forest and a glowing membrane of light would leap up into the sky, straight and fast, flying up out of the atmosphere and wrapping itself around one of the Dreamless vessels. Spines sheared and snapped, the globular hulls cracked, the energy membrane surged inside and found . . . nothing.

So weak, the last remaining, yet an old ally came . . .

Chel knew the story in his heart – at the darkest moment of the battle, when it seemed that the Dreamless had won, the Ghost Gods arrived – and now he was seeing it. Their ships were immense and fashioned to resemble ferocious beasts, four- and six-limbed, winged and serpentine, many-tentacled and carapaced, all bigger than mountains and numbering but thirty all told. When battle was joined they were like giants assailed by insects, but the Dreamless were relentless. Wave after wave, horde upon horde of their machines was hurled against the Ghost Gods' massive vessels, and while most were destroyed a few got through the weapon barrages and shields. Of those even fewer survived the defences and Sentinels, managing to break through the hull, and of them just a handful evaded the interior guards.

But that was all that was needed to seed ducts and pipes with swarms of deadly metal vermin, to infect the vitals with contagion. Eventually, even these colossal craft began to succumb one by one to the pitiless tide of Dreamless machines, to fail and break apart amid blossoming clouds of fire.

And Segrana, knowing that defeat could now be avoided only by paying a terrible price, gave up the greater part of itself. The forces of the world-forest were diverted into opening a way to the domains of hyperspace where the Dreamless kept their vast citadels. There went the greater essence of Segrana to infiltrate those strongholds, to spread itself transformed and unseen across every sense and knot of fleshless mind, every source of power, and to perish in a cataclysmic destruction from which not a single machine escaped. The interlinked meshes of communication and domination which had given them such strength were also the cause of their downfall.

Such a victory, such loss, yet Unmaker never wholly dies.

The vision of ships and fortresses burning in star mists faded.

These new Dreamless know of our great well, the last, and they hunger for it.

Sky-filling planetary vistas rolled away into shadow.

Weak and untested, still we must prepare for battle, for invasions, for desperate sacrifice.

Cold silence enclosed him, limbs held fast, body curled up, thoughts at rest, eyes tightly shut.

Your time approaches. Elders wish you remade but I want less from you, much more later.

Was he inside a shell or was he the shell that was going to crack open and reveal something new? Some kind of pressure eased and he could relax fingers from gripping, arms chest-wrapped, shifting his limbs a little, then shakily standing, feeling with eyes still closed for the *vodrun* chamber inner wall, running a hand over the rough carvings.

'Are you well, seeker?' came the Unburdener's voice from outside.

Chel smiled as he heard the sound of the door being unfastened and cracked open his eyes to the lamplight pouring in.

And screamed.

As soon as he heard the screaming, Listener Eshlo broke off from his meditations and climbed quickly up to the Contemplation platform then to the Threshold. It was not unusual for the freshly husked to be overwhelmed and distraught, although such a vocal outburst was quite rare. But when he clambered onto the small shelf he was helped to his feet by a panicky Unburdener who pointed to the *vodrun*. Its door stood open and the naked, unchanged form of Cheluvahar lay slumped half inside, head bowed in the shadows, shoulders trembling as he wept uncontrollably.

'My son,' he said. 'Compose yourself, stem your sorrow.'

The sobbing abated a little.

'Pain . . . Master, in everything I see . . .'

The Unburdener gripped Eshlo's arm. 'His eyes, Master!'

Eshlo met her fearful gaze for a moment then put aside his own unease and reached down to drag Cheluvahar out of the *vodrun* chamber. The scholar cried out, shielding his face from the lamp-light. But not before Eshlo saw the four new eyes spaced across his forehead, blinking and watering.

'Sister Unburdener,' Eshlo said, barely able to keep his voice from shaking. 'Tear a strip from your robe – our brother needs a blindfold.'

23

KAO CHIH

He was dreaming, a disjointed reverie of arguments held in odd, shadowy halls, and inexplicable searches through dusty, half-lit shelves, all the while evading threatening, dog-headed men in a pursuit that led through the storerooms and backstages of a strange and immense theatre. Then he came to a towering, cavernous corridor that sloped down towards a colossal door of fire which was the sole source of light as well as a smothering warmth. A series of wagons and carriages passed by, filled with beings from every species, a noisy, chattering cavalcade that seemed unaware of their journey into fiery doom. He ran alongside them, away from the blazing portal, shouting and trying to warn them, but they took no notice.

The carriages grew larger as the procession moved onwards and downwards, became interstellar vessels, tierliners and freighters, garbage scows and warships, then great cityships and immense orbitals of wheel or cone or helix or cluster configuration. And, impossibly, entire planets and their moons joined the parade, sailing ponderously past, their cloud-strewn surfaces tinged reddish-gold by the furnace that awaited them.

Then suddenly he was on one of the great, open-topped carriages, accelerating down towards the stupendous flaming maw. There was no way to escape – he was hemmed in by oblivious sentients as the heat grew intense and the incinerating light flooded his senses, blinding, burning . . .

And he awoke, stretched out on a wooden floor, bound hand and foot, with a bright light shining in his face.

'It's awake,' said a sibilant voice. The words were in a guttural 4Peljan variant, but the linguistic enabler Tumakri had given him made them understandable.

'Good,' said another, deep and hoarse. 'Get it on its feet and move that band up to its knees. It can walk – I'm not carrying it.'

With the light trained on his eyes, one of his captors hauled him upright then slid the restraint from ankle- to knee-level. Kao Chih felt groggy and full of aches from erratic sleep and lack of food – he didn't know how long he had been held prisoner but guessed it to be nearly a day. They had locked him in an upper-floor room in poor Avriqui's residence, during which time he had been given nothing but a plastic bowl of brackish water.

Now, as he was led along a low passageway by a rope tethered to his neck, he was able to see his guards more clearly. Both were Henkayan, a brawny, four-armed race of humanoids taller than Humans by head and shoulders. However, one of these two was if anything slightly shorter than Kao Chih, scrawny and walking with a limp. This was the one with the torch, still held carelessly, and who suddenly became aware of Kao Chih's regard. Without turning the Henkayan paused and buffeted the side of his head with an upper hand.

'Why you looking, Human scum?'

'Leave it alone,' said the other. 'Munaak wants it undamaged.'

'But it stare at me. Curses with eyes, maybe.'

'Everyone stares at you, Grol, trying to understand why you're so ugly.'

Grol shook the torch in anger. 'You shut, Tekik, you shut! You scum-eater . . .'

'Shut up your vlasking,' said Tekik, voice louder and threatening, 'or I'll ram that light down your gullet and Munaak will shove a spikel up your waster – if you don't get a move on!'

Kao Chih stared at the floor, his gaze never lifting as he was steered up a narrow stairway consisting of many shallow steps. Earlier, while lying awake in the darkness, he had almost been overwhelmed by the grimness of his situation, lost far from home, his only companion, Tumakri, almost certainly dead, while he himself was in the hand of ruthless brigands. Even if he could somehow escape, all the border documents and the ship ID tag had been in the Roug's pocket, along with the hard cash and the credit spines. But without his or Tumakri's live presence, they were useless to whoever had them, which wasn't much of a consolation. Yet somehow the worst of the bleak dread had ebbed as the hours had dragged by, aided by a small voice of hope insisting that they had to be keeping him alive for a reason.

Up on the next floor he was led straight through a dark open door into a small, wedge-shaped room lit by a long console of screens and displays. Several large, indistinct figures were gathered on either side of a high-backed chair on a swivel pedestal. Kao Chih was alternately dragged and pushed over to the chair then made to kneel, close enough to hear an odd-sounding dialogue. There were two voices deep in conversation, except that one of them seemed to have a whispery echo. Then the chair turned.

A pair of reddened, piercing eyes regarded him from the hollow-cheeked face of a Henkayan who Kao Chih took to be Munaak. Lenscups protected those eyes, magnifying their appearance, while puckered cicatrices criss-crossed the hairless scalp. The Henkayan wore long black robes marked with symbols in pure white, and Kao Chih almost failed to realise that he was missing both right-side arms. But the upper shoulder had something else attached to it – a head.

'This is the Human creature we reluctantly brought under our protection,' Munaak said in a smooth, rich voice, and as he did so the head muttered and whispered, quickly repeating the sentence but mingling its phrases while the shrivelled eyes stayed tightly shut. 'Does it meet your requirements?'

Over Munaak's shoulder, something moved on one of the screens, a shadowy cowled form against a dim background, shelves, racks, yellow light gleaming on glass and chrome objects.

'My . . . my requirements call for many, but you have only one.' The hooded figure's voice sounded vaguely metallic and blurred. 'Was this one alone?'

'It was travelling with a Roug but we killed it rather than let some biter vermin gain a commodity . . .'

'A Roug?' The shadowy figure leaned back. 'An old race with strange abilities – might they not pursue, seek redress?'

Munaak made a derisive sound. 'An old race, but weak and without allies – they will not venture this far. Now, you know the price so will you pay?'

The cowl inclined. 'I will enable the fund transfer now and arrange collection of the specimen in three odas.'

The screen blanked and was replaced by swirling blue patterns. Munaak regarded Kao Chih for a moment with his large, gleaming, unwinking eyes then switched his gaze to the two guards.

'Take our specimen down to the vehicle bay,' he said, with the head whispering disjointedly. 'Lock it in the storeroom, and no delays for any reason!'

Kao Chih kept his head bowed and his mouth shut as the Henkayan guards roughly and swiftly dragged him out of the room. He had learned early on the value of silence and now all he could do was hold to both his sanity and a few shreds of hope.

But now my fate rests on my value as merchandise of some kind, he thought bitterly. *We were foolish to come here so rashly – where there are no laws the weak become property.*

Neither of his escorts said anything as they hurried him down a steep stairway in which the gravity plating was decidedly uneven. Soon they arrived at a heavy, moulded pressure door that swung sideways to admit them to a gloomy parking bay with curved walls. A pathway of spongy, grubby gravplates led along one of the walls, between the reinforced struts, to what looked like a rectangular box with a window. The brawny Tekik opened a door in its side, paused to snap another restraint around Kao Chih's ankles, then thrust him inside. He gave the cluttered interior a brief look and stepped back, but before the door closed the scrawny Grol poked his head round.

'Human scum going to new owner,' he sneered. 'Soon wish he was back with good Henkayan friends – we not scientists!'

He let out a burst of cackling that stopped abruptly when a

large hand grabbed him by the throat and yanked him back out. The door slammed, a locking click, squabbling voices receding, the pressure door closed with a soft clank and the hiss of the seal. Silence.

Kao Chih squirmed onto his back in the darkness and managed to get into a seated position, leaning against the wall. Feeling drained and shivering a little, he tried to take stock of his surroundings. A faint blue radiance came from a small console set into the grimy window's lower right corner and as his eyes grew accustomed a few details became apparent. Dozens of small objects, parts maybe, were scattered over most of the floor, and the air stank of degraded machine oil. Cupboards gaped, revealing rolls of some mysterious material and heaps of tools, wires, junk. A large metallic cylinder, a lubricant tank perhaps, was fixed to the wall, above a few rows of indistinct tools on hooks . . .

'Are they gone?' said a voice.

Kao Chih caught his breath in surprise, senses suddenly alert.

'Who's there?' he muttered. 'Where are you?'

'First look out of the window and see if either of those cretins is standing guard.'

Guessing that the hidden speaker might be a survivor from Avriqui's household, Kao Chih struggled to his feet and shuffled over to the window.

'No one there,' he said, peering out. 'Must have gone back in . . .'

'Good – one less obstacle to overcome.'

Pale, bleached light bloomed in the small room and Kao Chih turned to see the wall cylinder flicker like a display with a bad feed. Then, in an instant, it went from a two-metre drum-like fixture with flat ends to a somewhat dumb-bell-shaped object about a metre tall. The meagre light from microfield projectors showed up the scratched and battered casing as it drifted over to the window.

'Nice trick,' Kao Chih said slowly. It was a sentient mech of unusual config, yet there was something familiar . . .

'Camouflage projection,' the mech said. 'It has its uses, now and then.'

Recognition dawned. 'I've seen you before, at that market in the big corridor where . . .' He faltered, vividly recalling Tumakri's last moments.

'The Roug who was killed yesterday was your friend?'

'Friend and travelling companion,' Kao Chih said.

'And you are a Human.' The machine paused. 'Your race is most uncommon in these sectors, yet greatly disliked.'

'So it seems,' he said. 'Were you an associate of Rup Avriqui?'

'You speak in the past tense so I assume that the vile Munaak has taken his life, and now he's looking for a buyer for you . . .'

'He's found one, a scientist of some kind.'

'Ah, a vivisector in other words.' The mech's microfields showed a glittery diffraction pattern for a brief moment. 'Now I shall be most honest with you – although I knew Avriqui slightly I could not be considered his associate. However, when your Roug friend was ambushed and killed on Nibril Concourse I was nearby and chased off those Gomedran scavengers. Even with a bolt in his head he was still conscious enough to urge me to take certain items from his garment while repeating a name over and over, saying I had to find this person, Gow-Chee. This is you, correct?'

'Indeed, yes,' Kao Chih said, hardly daring to hope.

'You may call me Drazuma-Ha*, although my full name involves audio frequencies your species is unequipped to hear.'

The last syllable of the mech's name sounded like a strange metallic chime, but he made no mention of it and gave a short, formal bow.

'I am very pleased to meet you, Drazuma-Ha*. Now that you have found me, are you prepared to help me escape?'

'I would be more than happy to help you flee this moron-infested junkheap altogether if you take me along with you.'

A number of questions came to the forefront of Kao Chih's thoughts – why did the mech want to leave and where was it heading, among others – but none seemed urgent.

'That would be most acceptable – could you begin by removing these bonds?'

Microfields extended tendril-like from the mech's upper and lower bulbs, there were faint clipping sounds and Kao Chih's ankles, knees and wrists were free.

'My sincerest thanks,' he said, trying to ignore the uncomfortable needling of returning circulation. 'What plan do you have for leaving this place? Will we have to fight our way out?'

'That is one possible route,' said the mech Drazuma-Ha*. 'However, I did think that leaving by the bay doors in one of Avriqui's lugosivators would be less hazardous to life, limb and circuitry.'

Kao Chih's eyes widened. 'Like the odd cart that Tumakri and I rode in? Are they fit for hard-vacuum travel?'

'Barely,' the mech said. 'Well, we only need to get from here to a general maintenance lock, near the Secondary Docking Lacuna, which it should manage adequately.'

'There is a small problem,' Kao Chih said. 'Rup Avriqui was to provide a hyperspace course dataset for the next stage of our journey, which he was supposed to join us on. It must still be in his system somewhere . . . would you be able to access it from here, perhaps?'

The mech was silent for a moment, its aura displaying strings of geometric symbols that pulsed with a soft, pearly glow then vanished.

'These controls,' the mech said, pointing a microfield extensor at the small window console, 'are not linked to the hold's higher data functions. I will *have* to go up into the hold itself and *hope* to find a terminal nearby without encountering any of Munaak's thugs.' The machine glided over to the door, which clicked and swung open. 'Wait here, and please don't make any loud noises.' It left the storeroom, crossed to the pressure door, which opened and closed behind it.

Kao Chih gazed around him, looking for something he could improvise as a weapon, and came up with a long-shafted autoauger and a good, solid panel sledge. That took about five minutes. Fifteen nail-biting minutes later the pressure door opened again and Drazuma-Ha* re-entered the garage hold.

'Do you have the course data?' Kao Chih said, emerging from the storeroom.

'I do but time is against us – I had to stun one of the guards, which means he'll be missed before long. Quick, climb up to those stalls while I open their shutters. And you may as well leave the low-tech arsenal behind.'

Kao Chih shrugged, tossed the autoauger but decided to hold on to the sledge. Then he stepped gingerly off the gravplate walkway, grabbed one of a series of tethered handholds and pulled himself along in zero-gee over to a now-open alcove in which a lugosivator of a cheerful blue colour was anchored. As he drew near, its windowed cowling popped open and Drazuma-Ha*'s voice came from the storeroom.

'You'd better get in now, Gow-Chee – it seems we will have to depart in a hurry.'

Once he was inside, the little vehicle shuddered and leaped out of its recess, sealing itself as it swung towards the ribbed bay doors. Kao Chih, thrust sideways by abrupt acceleration, held on to the seat while panicky questions crowded his thoughts – where was the mech, how did you steer this thing, and what if he hit something?

There was a thud from above, and looking up he saw the metre-long shape of Drazuma-Ha* lying on top of the cart, its microfields extended in a web that gripped the cart's upper casing.

'No need for anxiety, Gow-Chee. A brief journey along this side of the station and we shall be back inside and on our way to your ship.'

The bay doors concertinaed open and the flash-frozen atmosphere burst all about them in a glittering cloud as they flew out. For one breathtaking moment it was as if they were hurtling through a miniature galaxy, past swirls, clusters and ripples of tiny gleaming pinpoints. Then the cart slewed round as braking thrusters flared and off they sped.

The exterior of Blacknest Station was an accurate reflection of its inner disarray, a maze of spars and cables, conduit bundles, blobs of vacglue moulded into handholds, bulging (and frequently damaged) nets of trash, old pinhole leaks fantastically bearded with spiny icicles. Improvised bucketseat funiculars provided safe crossings while a horde of drones, probes and bots of every size darted about on mysterious errands. Drazuma-Ha* seemed to be steering the cart in the same direction as a couple of diamond-shaped bots bearing a red smiling moon symbol, and minutes later they were sharing the filthy, battered drum of a maintenance lock. There was a chorus of grinding, scraping noises as it turned, flashes of bright light, the loud hiss of repressurisation, and the lock swung open to reveal a cluttered, narrow workshop and a surprised Bargalil botmaster, its stocky, hexapedal form draped with tool belts and pouches of spare parts.

'Thank you for the use of your lock, good sir,' Drazuma-Ha* told it as Kao Chih clambered out of the cart. 'Please accept this excellent, deluxe-model mini-loader as a token of our gratitude.'

Then they dashed out of the workshop, leaving behind the pleased yet confused Bargalil, his gaze moving from abandoned cart to empty doorway and back.

'We must be as quick as we can without arousing suspicion,' said the mech as a lateral slot opened in its upper section and a bundle of objects protruded – the boarding passes, dock ID, Tumakri's credit stems and hard cash. 'At the gate, be polite and calm, and if the new attendants ask for additional payment pay it without argument. Tell them that I am travelling with you – if they ask for more details, say that I am your contracted technical support adviser. If they aren't aware of how vital commercial confidentiality is to a place like Blacknest I shall be more than happy to enlighten them.'

In the event, their passage through boarding control went smoothly, and Kao Chih had to pay only a fairly small amount to meet the 'one-off staff surcharge'. He felt almost giddy with relief as they reached the other side of the gates and hurried down towards the variously sized portals. Following a glowing telltale on the dock ID, they had just reached one of the medium oval exits when the mech paused abruptly, and glancing back Kao Chih saw the gate officials angrily gesturing at two bulky drones who were pushing their way past the desk.

The next thing he knew, Drazuma-Ha* had bodily lifted him with pressor fields that held him against the mech's casing, arms and legs held straight and immobile.

'My sincerest apologies, Gow-Chee, but speed is of the essence!'

Kao Chih let out a wordless sound of surprise as the mech launched itself up the docking duct, swooping and dodging around other passengers.

'Is there something you'd like to tell me, Drazuma-Ha?' he said loudly as they slowed to edge past a family of reptilian Naszbur.

'I shall explain it all,' the mech said. 'Once we are aboard and safely under way. Do not be alarmed, however – my predicament is no cause for concern over my integrity.'

Nice of you to let me know, Kao Chih thought as they reached a circular door which detected his dock ID and opened like a flower, leaves sliding aside.

Then they were in the flexible transfer tube, dimly lit by a few glostrips and the docking lacuna's own floods, filtered through the tube's opaque membrane. Released from the mech's pressors, Kao Chih kicked and hand-steered himself along to the *Castellan*'s airlock, a sight he'd thought he would never see again. He brought the dock key up to the verifier panel and held it there while poking his little finger into the biosampler slot.

Something moved outside, occluding the light from the nearest dock flood, then suddenly it loomed closer and collided with the tube.

'Does it usually take this long?' said Drazuma-Ha*, now poised quite close by.

Kao Chih glared at the machine. 'Is that another of your predicaments? – look, it's trying to cut its way in!'

A metre or two back from the airlock, the tube's heavy-grade material was being pinched. Kao Chih stared at the deforming plastic with panic and a growing sense of unreality enhanced by the hammering sounds coming from the access port at the other end of the tube. Then to his vast relief the verifier panel beeped and the airlock hatch slid open. Courtesy was not uppermost in his mind as he dragged himself in round the edge of the coaming, closely followed by the mech. Once they were inside he punched the hatch button and a moment later they were sealed off.

'Show me to the pilot controls,' the mech said. 'We must leave immediately.'

'This way,' Kao Chih said. 'But why the haste now that we're safe?'

As they reached the main console he heard distinct hard knocks and thuds coming through the hull.

'Who are those droids?' he muttered. 'And what do they want?'

'Collectors,' said Drazuma-Ha*. 'Chasing an old debt. A moment, please.'

Microfield extensors sprang out from the mech's aura to the console, connecting with several interface ports. Readouts and symbol telltales flickered in waves across the cockpit and one of the auxiliary screens unfolded from its niche to reveal an exterior shot of the *Castellan*'s hull, underneath, near the midsection. A strange, angular machine crouched there on several articulated limbs, reflected light from further back casting it in silhouette. A second screen showed the other two droids now in the access tube and making cumbersome progress towards the airlock. Then a faint whining noise came from underfoot, beneath the deck.

'It's drilling through the hull,' Kao Chih said, striving to stay calm.

For a moment the mech made no reply, then:

'All is ready, Gow-Chee – shall we depart?'

'Without delay!'

The *Castellan* gave a lurch and suddenly he realised he should have been strapped in. Hurriedly he did so while keeping most of his attention on the exterior displays. The access tube had unfastened from the airlock and was retracting into its housing with the two droids still holding on. The third still clung to the ship's underside and the drilling sound continued unabated. On the screen, the jumbled shapes and structures of Blacknest receded as their reaction thrusters burned a departure trajectory.

'We will soon be far enough away for a safe jump into hyperspace,' the mech said. 'But there is a problem.'

'What kind of problem?' Kao Chih said hoarsely.

'The hyperjump course data I obtained from Avriqui's system is supposed to take us to Bryag Station near the Indroma border, but the value set is several hours out of date. Clearly he meant to recompile it just before departing with you and your deceased companion . . .'

Kao Chih's heart sank. 'We could emerge inside a sun or a planetary atmosphere . . .'

'No, not with the safety features built into this vessel,' Drazuma-Ha* said. 'We would be safe from such perils, including the one currently attached to our hull – it would detach itself the moment the hyperdrive initiated its first phase. But our destination will be indeterminable.'

'And if that breaches the outer hull, we're finished.' Kao Chih gripped the arms of his couch. 'Do it!'

'You're certain?'

'Just do it now!'

The shield layer rolled across the viewpane and he murmured a brief prayer to his ancestors as the hyperdrive gathered all its forces and hurled the *Castellan* into the void.

24

GREG

He was almost a dozen metres down the southern face of Giant's Shoulder, shivering in a cold night breeze, when his comm chimed. He called out to Teso and Kolum, his Uvovo accomplices, to stop lowering, then answered the call.

'Greg Cameron here.'

'Hello Greg, it's Catriona. Just thought I'd call you before the shuttle leaves.'

'Ah, thanks Cat, that's, um, very thoughtful of you.'

'So, what are you up to this evening? Sounds like you're outside . . .'

'Oh, just studying some pillar carvings, y'know, trying to figure out if they're ritual or ceremonial . . .' He felt himself break out in a cold sweat, more from the gnawing sensation of vertigo, suspended there in the high darkness with a handilamp hanging from his neck, lighting up the rock face right in front of him.

'Just a moment,' said Catriona. 'Are you . . . dammit, you are! – you're climbing down the side of Giant's Shoulder *in the middle of the night*. Are you completely insane?'

Greg sighed. In the aftermath of the shooting yesterday he had showed Catriona the scans revealing the passages and chambers beneath the temple, and together they had started planning how to reach the opening that led inside. But Cat had been ordered back to Nivyesta, leaving Greg to pore over the scans and and an assortment of pictures of Giant's Shoulder dug out of the files.

Then came news of the bombings, which seized his attention for the rest of the day.

'Look, I'm fine, I'm safe, the equipment is the best and I've got friends helping me,' he said, exchanging waves with the two Uvovo smiling down at him. 'I'm more worried about you, to be frank.'

'I'm okay. Did you get hold of your mother and your brothers?'

'I did, and they're all well – no one was anywhere near Founder Square or the Ros Dubh sports centre, but there's been no word from Uncle Theo since yesterday . . .'

'Greg, I just wish you'd give up this midnight expedition and wait for daylight.'

He smiled, thinking – *Ah, she really does care. Things are looking up.*

'Och, don't worry, Cat,' he said. 'I'm strapped into a body harness with about a thousand D-rings and plenty of that Uvovo heavy-bearing line . . .' He gave the line a playful tug. 'Safe as houses . . .'

Which was when the composite strap junction at his back snapped. He yelled as he swung to the right and down, head dipping. Through his cold terror he was aware of his lamp slipping off and falling away into the blackness, but most of his attention was on trying not to slip out of the loops that still gripped his legs and left arm. The two Uvovo called down in fearful voices but he tried to reassure them – then cursed when he realised that he had dropped his comm. By now he had worked himself into a more upright position, holding on to the safety line with a gloved hand.

Gods, Cat was right! I must be mad to be doing this . . .

He glanced down and started to tell the Uvovo to haul him up, then paused, staring at a faintly glowing spot on the rock face a few feet below. He stared, held his breath and listened . . . and, just on the edge of audibility, heard a tiny voice calling his name. Catriona! He laughed shakily – his comm must be lying on a ledge or in the tangle of a cliffside bush – and shouted to her to wait a minute or two. Quickly, he rigged the loose strapping onto the safety line with toothhooks to take some of the load off the

damaged strap junction, then told the Uvovo to lower him. Slowly
he descended towards the glow, which he now reckoned might
well be sitting in a niche in the rock. Then he came level with it
and saw his comm, resting in a tangle of dry, dead roots that
spilled out of a sizable gap in the cliff face.

Reaching in he grabbed it and saw that Cat had disconnected.
Quickly he sent a note saying that he was okay, then activated the
comm's little torch and shone it inside the opening. He stared in
surprise for a moment, then chuckled – beyond the opening was
a small passageway sloping down towards the front of Giant's
Shoulder. The opening was just wide enough to crawl into, which
he did, pausing halfway in to undo the harness then shout to the
Uvovo to pull it up. When he told them he was exploring a cave
they became agitated, imploring him to return.

'I'll be perfectly safe,' he yelled back. 'Just get the replacement
harness from stores and listen out for me.'

'Old places are dangerous, friend Greg,' came Teso's strained
reply. 'Please be very careful.'

'I will be, don't worry!'

Then he turned his attention to the passage. It was quite
narrow and low, just a little over average Uvovo height. The walls
were smoothly worked with even curves, as was the opening
through which he had entered. Shining his torch further down he
could make out another similar aperture, but choked with coils of
redthorn as well as the decaying detritus of dead plants. This had
to lead to the opening he had seen on the *Heracles* scans, and
which he had intended to find tonight.

Perhaps this will be safer than hanging about in the air, he
thought as he tugged out his forest blade and attacked the tangle
of vegetation.

The passage went on for another ten metres or so, blocked at
regular intervals by bushes or creepers that had taken root in the
soil-caked floor near the openings. He was sweating freely by
the time the passage turned back the other way: the water-worn
vestiges of steps were just visible under the layers of dirt and decay.
Insects glimmered and settled in the slim beam of his comm-torch,

which chimed just as he started hacking at another wall of desiccated twig. It was Cat. He took a deep breath and answered.

'Hi, Cat!'

'Right, what the hell happened?'

'Eh, nothing serious, just juggling with my comm . . .'

'Dammit, Greg, I . . . was worried . . .'

He heard the catch in her voice and instantly regretted the off-hand remark.

'I'm sorry, Cat, I'm okay, just had a wee fright when a clip broke. But I rigged a repair and I'm now inside the rock face of Giant's Shoulder and making my way down a passageway.'

'Is it safe?' she said. 'What does it look like?'

He gave a brief description and assured her that he was not in any danger.

'Aye, well watch out for doubletails – they nest in dark, dank places.'

'And they're usually found further to the north than this,' he said. 'But I will keep my eyes open, I promise. When's your shuttle flight?'

'Less than an hour.'

'I'll call you when I reach the opening,' he said. 'Or wherever this is leading to.'

After murmured goodbyes, he thumbed the torch back on and resumed chopping away dead foliage. Another thirty-odd minutes later he had hacked, kicked and torn his way through several barriers of roots, creepers and bushes, most of it dead growth. His exertions had raised wafts of dust which clung to his clothes and hair, working its way into the creases of his hands and face – he felt indescribably grimy and often coughed in the hazy gloom. But beyond the last clump of vegetation he came to a level landing and a large square door in the rock. Opposite the door was a semicircular window that was blocked by a curtain of heavy-leafed creeper, some of which had spilled inside.

Beyond the dark threshold of the door was a pitch-black corridor. With his torch lighting the way, Greg followed it inwards for about twenty paces before encountering a double row of pillars that completely blocked the way. The pillars were square and the rows were set close together in a staggered formation that obscured what lay further on. Frowning, he called Catriona.

'Took ye long enough,' she said.

'I've been doing a bit of pruning,' he said. 'Have you ever seen square pillars in a Uvovo building?' As he spoke he took out a small field cam and took a few pictures.

'No, never.'

'Well, I'm looking at some now.' He described them for her, then examined their tops and bottoms. 'The dirt and dust buildup is solid around the bases but up at the ceiling there's a definite gap, as if the pillars slid down – maybe this is some kind of primitive stone portcullis . . . wait a second, what's that?'

After probing the gap around one pillar he had pushed it to see if there was any give, and immediately a sequence of four glowing symbols had appeared on its face, one by one down its length, and faded away. A moment later the sequence repeated itself and he swiftly took more pictures while describing what was happening.

'What do the symbols look like?' Cat said.

'Nothing like any of the glyphs that the Uvovo use, now or in the past.' He bent down for closer study. 'They're composed of straight and curved lines, some crossing others, some not.'

'Could be ideograms,' she said. 'But what kind of technology can embed glowing characters in stone and still be functioning thousands of years later?'

'Aye, those ancient Uvovo sure had a few tricks up their sleeves . . .'

Suddenly there was more light in the passage as several triangular symbols lit up on the adjacent pillar.

'Why have you gone quiet? Greg, what's happening now?'

'Seven triangles have appeared on the next pillar . . . wait, the one at the bottom has gone out so there's six . . .'

'Hmm, odd. Has it come back?'

'No, and another just went out, the top one, when the four symbols went through the sequence.'

'Hang on, the Uvovo use the triangle to symbolise an imperative demand for an answer so those other four ideograms . . . must be some kind of question you have to anwer before all the triangles are gone . . . I think . . .'

'So how do I answer the question?'

'No idea – how many triangles are left?'

'Two.'

'Get out of there, Greg, now!'

He dived away from the pillars and dashed for the entrance. As he did, a rumble came from the surrounding rock then cracking sounds and a cluster of heavy impacts. Dust billowed out and settled on his shoes and trouser legs.

'Greg, are you okay?'

'I am,' he said. 'And now I'm going back inside for a look.'

'If I could reach through this comm . . .'

'There're more pillars, Cat, about fifteen paces in this time.'

The new obstruction was identical to the first but pristine, no windblown dust or dry leaf fragments nor insect remains.

'Don't touch it, Greg – in fact, don't even go near it. Promise me you'll go back up and wait till morning. Then you can speak with Foyle at the Institute and get hold of one of the Listeners to see if they recognise those symbols.'

'Aye . . . okay, Cat,' he said, retreating to the entrance. 'Maybe you're right. I'll head back up top, get some rest.'

'Good, you sleep well and I'll . . . send you a message when I'm home.'

'Okay, safe flight.'

For a few moments after the line disconnected, Greg stood there, smiling thoughtfully, wondering where this thing with Catriona was going – if it actually was going somewhere. Then he shrugged.

Hard to be sure now that she's away back to Nivyesta, he thought. *As for this puzzle . . . perhaps I'll wait for Chel, see what he thinks of those symbols, and when I've got something solid, then I'll tell Foyle at the Institute . . .*

He shone the comm torch back along the corridor one last time, peering at the pillars in the dimness. Then he saw something he hadn't noticed before, that the walls were covered in the familiar Uvovo raindrop pattern, incised lightly into the stone. Except that here the drops were depicted sideways as if they were streaming into Giant's Shoulder.

And there was something else, an extra detail he had never seen before; every drop had a round dot in it, making it resemble an eye, and the more he stared the more they really did look like eyes, hundreds, thousands filling either wall, rushing into the heart of Giant's Shoulder.

Chel, old friend, he thought as he produced his camera once more, *I hope you can help me figure out what this means before I have to hand it over to the Institute*!

25

THEO

Sixteen hours after the bombing in Founders Square, with dawn still an hour or more away, Theo and several others were hurrying through the streets of High Lochiel. Rory was in constant contact with the teams staking out the house while Ivanov, Hansen and Forshaw provided armed escort, their semi-automatics hidden by long coats. Theo was likewise prepared with a 48-calibre hunting revolver holstered at his waist.

'How much further, Rory?'

'No' far, Major – the house is three streets away and we'll be goin' in the back door of the building across the road. Our main obs post is on the top flair.'

'How many exits? Who's covering them?'

'It's a three-storey rooming house, two exits – Fyfe's team is covering the front, Brunni's at the back wi' his boys and a sharpshooter.'

'What about comings and goings?'

'Two women entered about an hour ago – Benny says they were both totally hammered, must've been at a party – and a man not long after them. Our boy stayed in his apartment and is still there.'

'Good – tell Fyfe and Brunni that we'll move in the next twenty minutes.'

It was the rifle which had led them here. Its serial number dated back to the time of the Winter Coup, and came from a government shipment of arms that Viktor Ingram's men had seized just before Theo Karlsson's small army marched into

Hammergard and occupied the Assembly buildings. After Theo's surrender and Ingram's suicide, the shipment had been broken up and hidden away in various locations, apart from one portion that was ditched in the sea by its couriers while in transit north, pursued by a coastal patrol. The two men involved, Grieve and Orloff, were later reported dead in a house fire in Trond. The surviving arms ended up years later as part of Theo's assets. But Rory had a record of all the assets' serial numbers and found that the scope rifle came from the missing weapons cache, supposedly lying in 200 feet of water due east of New Kelso. It seemed unlikely that they had ever been dumped in the sea at all, but the rifle's number provided no useful lead.

They had more luck with the scope. It was custom-made but had no makers mark, leading Theo to visit a smoky trappers' bar in Hammergard's wharfside district. There, a leathery-faced veteran hunter called McTavish studied the wallet of images Theo had brought along and identified the craftsman as Maxim Lirmenov, an optician of High Lochiel. Theo and Rory then travelled the 35 miles up the North Highway to High Lochiel, reaching its outskirts in the early evening. The light was still on in Lirmenov's shop and the moment they entered Rory recognised the optician as being none other than Kazimir Orloff, one of Ingram's supposedly deceased gun runners.

With Rory's autopistol pressed against the back of his neck, Orloff had quickly caved in, admitted that he'd sold the scoped rifle to a man called Denisov. There was an address for him in the sales record but Orloff said it was probably false; while returning from a client in the north of the town last night he had chanced to see Denisov using a key to enter a run-down rooming house. With that address, Theo had Janssen get a couple of local reliables along there to watch the place while Rory drafted in some lads from Landfall and Gagarin.

The observation post was in a disused office on the fourth floor of a rickety building that sat between a lumber yard and a low warehouse. The stairs were lit by a couple of minimal glostrips while the room's inky darkness was broken only by a red lamp sitting on the floor. As they entered, a diminutive woollen-capped man glanced round from the tripod telescope positioned at the window.

'Hello, Rory, Major Karlsson – would you like to see?' he said, rising from a three-legged stool.

'Thanks, Benny,' Theo said, taking his place. 'Any change?'

'No, sir, he's still there, sitting and reading, drinking a cup of tea, as if he's waiting for something.'

'Or somebody,' said Rory with a lascivious chuckle. 'Like a lady friend!'

Theo gave a half-smile as he looked into the telescope. 'I doubt that he's the kind to take such risks.'

Through the lens he saw a third-floor window with patterned curtains almost fully open and a leanly built man reclining in an armchair reading a copy of *Crag & Coast Monthly*. Denisov was wearing a short-sleeved red shirt and dark trousers and wisps of vapour rose from the cup on a nearby table.

'And that's all he's been doing?' Theo said, frowning.

'Mostly, for the last hour or so.'

Theo thought a moment then nodded. 'Okay, I don't think we should wait any longer. Rory, tell Fyfe and Brunni to get ready to—'

Just then Rory and Benny's handsets crackled into life.

'Activity at the rear,' said a voice. 'Guy in blue workwear just came out – he's carrying a toolbox and taking a bike out of the shed . . .'

Theo squinted down the telescope. 'He's still there.' *But something doesn't feel right.* He beckoned for Benny's handset and thumbed the reply.

'Brunni, this is Karlsson – describe the man for me.'

'Short, stocky build, receding hair – looks harmless but I can have one of my lads grab him if you like.'

Theo stared at the man who called himself Denisov as he calmly sipped his drink and turned a page.

'Let him go,' he said. 'We don't want to alert Denisov before we have to.'

'Right . . . that's him pedalling away now.'

'Okay – Brunni and Fyfe, move your men up to front and rear doors. When you're both in position, move in: do your best to take Denisov alive.'

'Understood.'

Theo stood up to get a better view of the street while using his binoculars to keep an eye on the target. Three men were heading for the rooming house's front door, again long coats concealing weaponry from any chance observation. Theo watched, feeling a knot of tension in his stomach as he listened to the murmured voices on the handsets. One of the three forced the lock then the door was open and they were inside.

'Remember – we want him alive,' he said, raising the binoculars again. Denisov still sat in his chair, reading, drinking. Theo's uneasy feeling sharpened as the open channels relayed the team's stealthy progress up the main stairs. Denisov never changed and Theo was about to order a pause when a woman started screaming inside the house. Denisov didn't so much as flinch. Seized by a rush of dread, Theo was drawing breath to order a retreat when the upper floor erupted in flames and a roaring crash.

Theo threw up his arm instinctively as the explosion ripped off part of the rooming house roof and blew out the walls of Denisov's apartment. The windows of the observation room rattled in the shockwave and a few of the small panes shattered. When Theo straightened and looked outside, the rooming house's top floor was engulfed in fire.

'My God, a trap!' said a horrified Benny. 'It was a trap . . .'

Theo ignored him, instead snarled into the handset. 'All teams report! – Brunni and Fyfe report!'

'Major, this . . . is Uvarov – Brunni and Fyfe are both dead. We've got another three injured and only myself and Dewar unhurt, but there's people trapped upstairs – should we go in after them?'

Theo moistened his lips and tightened his grip on the handset. He could hear the agonised cries from the window.

'Do what you can, but get any weapons out of sight – Rory's

on his way, Benny too . . .' He glanced up to see Benny following Rory out of the room at a run. 'Emergency services should be along soon so the story is you were enquiring about rooms to let when it went up, okay?'

'Got that, sir.'

'And tell me – who was it that screamed?'

'A woman opened the door across from Denisov's flat and must have seen our guns – after that everything went to hell.'

Alarms were ringing, some in the burning building, others in adjacent houses. Then came the pulsing wail of fire trucks.

'Is Rory with you yet?'

'He's here now, sir – he's got all the guns and radios.'

'Right – give him yours when I sign off and don't forget to stick to the script.'

'Yes, sir.'

'Rory – local police will be here any minute so you and Benny get over here and wait at the back door. I'll pack the gear and meet you there.'

'Got ye, Major. We're on our way.'

Theo put down the handset, slipped the binoculars into his pocket and began to dismantle the telescope.

The man in the blue workgear was Denisov, he thought grimly. *It had to be. When he got to a safe distance he must have watched my men go in then waited a few moments before triggering the boobytrap, just to maximise casualties.*

So what had Benny been watching for the last couple of hours? Some kind of hologram projected by an offworld device, maybe? If so, it was probably rigged for self-destruct when the main detonation went off, leaving no traces, no evidence.

With everything stowed in a heavy backpack, Theo slung it over his shoulder, picked up the red lamp and headed for the stairs. Rory and Benny were waiting just inside the back door and as they slipped off into the night, he wondered how he was going to explain all this to Sundstrom. And, more importantly, to the families of his dead men.

26

GREG

Even wrapped in his wool-lined jacket, he shivered as he leaned on the ancient, cracked rampart and stared down at the misty coastal plain. It was a grey morning, the air cold and moist from the night rains.

'So how bad is it?' he asked his brother.

Captain Ian Cameron, wearing full field camouflage, rested one booted foot on a low notch in the wall.

'There's a lot of suspicion,' he said. 'Folk in the towns just won't trust travellers or strangers, anyone who's noticeably out of the ordinary.'

'That accounts for most of the faraway hunters and trappers I've ever met,' said Greg.

Ian smiled. The eldest of the three brothers, he was taller and rangier than Greg and had always been the most physically active of them all.

'Aye, some of them have been on the receiving end of it. I mean, the bombings are bad enough, but there was a street protest in Gagarin last night in support of this Free Darien Faction, which really got some locals angry.'

Greg shook his head. 'Who were they?'

'Just some college hotheads waving placards, a few dozen of them, but they made plenty of noise going down Tylermans Walk, upsetting the locals, who started arming themselves, but at least the police were quick to escort them out of the area.' He rubbed his neck. 'Then that house went up in High Lochiel last night. Not good.'

Both were silent for a moment.

'It's hard to believe that community spirit is that fragile,' Greg said.

'Things could be worse,' said Ian. 'I was talking to some old Norj trappers yesterday, real hill-viking types, and they were telling me a few tales from the time of the Winter Coup. Reminded me of some of the stories Uncle Theo used to tell – didn't take them seriously back then, but now . . .'

'So where is he?' Greg said. 'I've not heard from him since the shooting up here, neither has Mum, and she's worried sick.'

Ian nodded. 'Officially, he is a special adviser to the president's office, but there's no doubt that he's been getting up to some skulduggery with the Diehards, something to do with the bombings.' He swept his gaze around the temple site. 'The Office of Justice has stepped up security at several locations as well as here, and not just because of your guests.'

Greg glanced over his shoulder at the grassy area well to the rear of the main site. Several awnings had been set up for the dozens of Uvovo who were gathering there to await the arrival of the Listener who was to lead this new offshoot, the Artificer Uvovo. Greg knew that it was supposed to be Chel, but he also knew that the husking ritual radically altered the Uvovo physique and sometimes the personality too. Would he be anything like the Chel he had come to know, and would he even recognise Greg?

Just then a corporal approached with a clipboard of supplementaries which Ian read over and signed.

'There's a dirij headed our way from the north,' he told Greg as the soldier hurried off. 'Should be their Listener. I'll just have our comms operator let company HQ know.'

As Ian strode off, Greg steeled himself and straightened. At least there were no reporters present by order of the Institute, for which he was grateful. Lee Shan's coverage of the shooting of the Sendrukan Assister had depicted the security arrangements as amateurish and ineffective, despite the involvement of Kuros's bodyguards. It had also included a shot of Greg's encounter with

the Ezgara commandos, complete with his every barbed witti-
cism. The Ezgara and other offworlders might not understand
the sarcasm but the Darien audience and those back on Earth
could not have failed to pick it up. Not long afterwards, of
course, the bullets had started flying.

Not exactly a crowd-pleaser, he thought, heading over to his
hut to change.

Fifteen minutes later, a cigar-shaped dirigible drifted in towards
the zep station, the drone of its engines tailing off as mooring
cables were made fast. It swayed gently by the platform, its bulbous gasbag looking pale grey in the morning haze. Greg could
make out a small huddle of hooded figures as they disembarked,
some making their way up the wide path by foot while a few
others went ahead in one of the motorised buggies. By the time
the buggy arrived at the entrance to the site, Greg and his brother
were standing alongside Listener Genusul, expectancy of one kind
or another in all their features.

Three hooded figures emerged from the vehicle, the last of
them Chel, who looked unchanged and unaltered, much to Greg's
relief. But the reaction of the Listener at his side was noticeably
different, concern to the point of distress visible in his gaunt,
long-jawed face. Chel met him halfway, said something in a low,
urgent voice, then turned to Greg.

Greg's positive feelings cooled and his smile faltered. Physically,
Chel seemed the same but his features were drawn and his eyes
had a bleak, sharp quality as if he was under tremendous strain.
Just above the eyes a strip of dark cloth was stretched tight across
the forehead, and Greg wondered if it was a dressing for a wound.

'Greetings, friend Gregori,' the Uvovo said with a faint smile.
'I've learned about these bomb attacks – I do hope that your
family is safe.'

'They are, Chel – my mother has been giving me almost hourly
updates. My brother Ned has been helping at one of the hospitals
where a lot of the injured were taken.' He hesitated. 'How about
you? You look pretty much the same, apart from needing a couple
of days' sleep, maybe.'

A look of amusement softened the Uvovo's weary, strung-out expression. 'Yes, the husking did not proceed quite as I or anyone else expected. Yet it has left its mark . . .' Chel paused as one of his cowled companions signed to him; he nodded and continued. 'Gregori, regretfully we must resume our talking later – I have a very important forgathering to attend.'

'I understand – I look forward to hearing about your travels.'

'I promise I will explain what I can,' Chel said cryptically. 'Till then.'

For the next three hours or more Greg went over a bundle of field reports filed by teams of Uvovo scholars who had been surveying the valleys northwest of the Kentigerns. Periodically he had to go over to the large eco-samples hut to examine this or that specimen – he would have asked the reports' authors but they were attending the conclave of this Artificer Uvovo. As he shuttled back and forth he could see that the numbers were growing steadily as newcomers arrived via the densely forested ridges rising to the west. There seemed to be a lot of discussion, groups walking to and fro, lone speakers addressing small crowds, knots of Uvovo milling about. Fortunately the weather was mostly dry, with just one light passing shower which freshened the air and made everything gleam in the cloud-fractured sunlight that followed.

At last a young, wide-eyed Uvovo brought a message from Chel asking Greg to meet him in the excavated area known as the Stairwell in half an hour. He spent the time eating a snack of baroham and gramato sandwiches while catching up on the news headlines on the radio, then, with minutes still to spare, he decided to head over anyway.

The Stairwell was a perfect example of the problems inherent in excavating Giant's Shoulder. It did have some stairs, two flights descending beneath the flagstoned expanse, but after that further steps had been improvised out of broken masonry uncovered by earlier explorers during their excavations. However, due to the unstable, cavity-riddled nature of the interior, those pioneers found that the baulk sides of their digs quickly became prone to serious collapse the deeper they went. After several cave-ins and one fatality a couple of decades ago, the bottom ten metres of the twenty-metre hole were filled in and planked over. Further investigation was restricted to stratification studies and a few cautiously shallow side trenches.

Chel was already there when he arrived, seated on a bench in one of the older side trenches, just out of the fitful sunlight. He raised a hand in greeting as Greg descended the few steps and joined him on the bench.

'Chel, I could say that you're looking great,' he said. 'But that wouldn't, strictly speaking, be true.'

'The truth, friend Gregori, is that I feel worse than I look,' the Uvovo said with a tired smile.

'Was your gathering a success?'

'In the end, yes. There was much doubt to overcome, and more distrust and pessimism than I anticipated.' He gazed up at the ragged clouds. 'They were expecting a fully-fledged Listener but instead they got . . . something else.'

Turning to face Greg, he launched into an account of his visit to the daughter-forest Tapiola. Greg listened intently, fascinated at first by the husking ritual and ensuing hallucinatory trance. But when he spoke of having visions of the past and hearing the voice of Segrana in his head, Greg began to wonder if the drug had affected his mind – Chel seemed convinced that these experiences were not fanciful creations of his mind but came from outside, from Segrana.

Chel paused and regarded him a moment. 'Earlier, many of my brothers and sisters thought that part of me was still in thrall to the husking sap – do you think that I have lost my reason?'

'You seem quite rational, Chel – I'd be reluctant to judge until you've finished your tale. What happened to you in there? Why didn't you turn into a Listener?'

Chel gave him a considering smile. 'Because I became something else.'

He pushed back his cowl, reached up to untie the dark grey bandage and lifted it away.

Greg stared, open-mouthed, at the row of four closed eyes on Chel's forehead. As he watched the outer pair fluttered open while Chel kept his own, original pair tightly shut, along with the centre pair. The new eyes swivelled to look at Greg, who smiled uncertainly.

'What do you see?'

The eyes looked around the shallow trench, its sloping sides of compacted soil and masonry debris, then up to the sky for a moment of searching before gazing down at the Stairwell and its gloomy depths.

'I see Umara's hidden face,' Chel murmured. 'I can see glimpses of lost and forgotten histories. That block for example—' He pointed to an irregular piece of stone with a smooth outward surface, '—was once part of an archway, and that one just along from it was part of a supporting wall. Or I can look at your face, Gregori, and see your mother and father, very clearly . . . and also a thin-faced man with an ear missing, and a woman with long black hair and a white streak through . . .'

Greg could suddenly feel his heart pounding. 'My grandfather Fingal was a hunter who lost an ear to a cragwolf, and the woman with the white in her hair can only be my great-grandmother Moira – Chel, how . . .'

The Uvovo regarded him with those eyes, their darkness a mingled hue of brown and green. 'Segrana's gift, with which to carry out Segrana's work.'

Greg could not help noticing the undertone of resentment in Chel's voice, but now that the initial shock was past his mind was focused on the Uvovo's new abilities and what they implied.

'And the other eyes,' he said. 'What do they do?'

'I am not entirely certain,' Chel said, replacing the strip of cloth then opening his ordinary eyes. 'I have not yet learned how to interpret what they show me – sometimes it is as if I can see a kind of language underpinning things around me, then if I look at symbols or written words or even pictures it feels as though part of my mind is trying to wrench a different kind of meaning from them.'

'Are all these eyes meant to work together, perhaps?'

Chel gave a bleak smile. 'I have attempted that – once. The effect is . . . hard to describe, as if my head is filled with a thousand arguments except that it is not voices that war with each other but meanings! When I came out – *crawled* out of the *vodrun* I really thought that my mind was going insane, like a storm flooding and tearing apart a town, a city, while all I could do was watch the destruction from a nearby hill. If Listener Eshlo had not acted to cover these eyes . . .' He left the sentence unfinished.

Could it really be true? Greg wondered. *Is Segrana actually an aware entity, some kind of distributed sentience capable of radically altering individual Uvovo*? He had never heard of any Uvovo being born with extra eyes, yet here they were before him, which suggested that they had to be part of Uvovo DNA. Which also begged the question, were these characteristics the result of survival adaptation or of genetic engineering?

'Chel, have you looked at any Uvovo carvings or symbols with the outer pair?'

'A few times,' Chel said.

'Did any appear unusual?' he said, adding, 'but in a rational way?'

'In Tapiola there are several ground dwellings and the one where I recuperated is decorated with a number of meditation pieces, wooden figurines and tablets. One bore the symbol *hmul*, meaning "release of burdens", but when I opened these eyes it became a word – *elishum*, meaning "work of calmness".'

Greg nodded, his smile growing as facts fitted together.

'Chel, my friend, I think you might be able to help me solve a little problem.' Then he told the Uvovo about his encounter with the *Heracles*'s xeno-specialist, Lavelle, and took him over to his hut to show him the scan printouts of Giant's Shoulder. As Chel stared at the images by the light of a desk lamp, Greg went on to tell of his midnight expedition, the strange passage and the pillar traps blocking the way. The pictures he took down there had turned out slightly distorted or blurred but he showed them to Chel anyway. Chel studied the pictures closely then shook his head.

'I cannot make out these symbols, Gregori.'

Greg grinned. 'Would you like to go and look at the real thing? Now?'

Chel needed little persuading. Half an hour later, with the help once more of the Uvovo scholars Teso and Kolum, they were lowered down the south face of Giant's Shoulder, first Greg then Chel, entering this time through the creeper-curtained opening. Equipped with a torch each, they ventured into the cold, dark passage. Chel stared about him at the eye-motif carvings on the walls but made no comment, just nodded thoughtfully. Greg slowed as they approached the pillars.

'Be ready for when the symbols appear,' he said. 'When that countdown starts it goes by very quickly.'

'Very well, Gregori, as you wish,' Chel said, removing the headband and opening those strange eyes. Then he walked the final few paces, bringing him right next to the row of square pillars. He looked them over carefully while Greg watched, tense and edgy, and they both waited. Five minutes went by without incident then five more. Chel looked questioningly at Greg, who shrugged.

'Friend Gregori, did you not say that you touched the pillar while examining it?'

'Well, when I touched . . . I suppose you could say it was a bit of a shove . . .'

Chel nodded and gave the nearest pillar a firm push. There was no give to it but almost immediately four familiar, glowing symbols appeared on the middle pillar. Chel saw them, gasped and staggered back a step and shook his head, as if dizzy.

'Are you okay?' Greg said.

Chel glanced at him with his ordinary eyes while keeping the new ones focused on the pillar. 'No cause for alarm, friend Gregori. Every time I need to adjust a little . . . ah now . . .'

Leaning closer, the Uvovo examined the four intricate symbols, just as a column of glowing triangles appeared on the adjacent pillar.

'And that right there is your countdown, Chel,' he said but the Uvovo waved him into silence, his stance almost that of someone who was listening intently. After a moment or two of standing stock-still he suddenly straightened, his small, neat features creased by a smile, then he sang a sequence of syllables in a clear, loud voice. There was a grinding sound, deep vibrations from above, and trickles of fine dust fell as the double row of pillars ascended into the ceiling. Beyond it, Greg could see by torchlight the previous ones and another three sets after that also rising.

'That,' he said, 'was well done.'

Chel was gazing up at the pillar ends, resting flush against the plain, unadorned stone ceiling. 'At first I thought the *celfs* – the symbols – were showing me words but when I looked deeper at each one I heard musical notes which I sang in the order of the words and . . .' He gestured at the now-open corridor.

'If only Cat was here to see this,' Greg said, laughing. 'Right, let's see what's along there.'

'Tread carefully, Gregori,' said Chel. 'There may be other tests.'

Twenty paces on, the passageway turned a corner and steps went down to a chamber where four columns stood in a group before three stone doors in a curved wall. The room was icy-cold – it was like walking into a storage freezer. Greg shivered, his breath pluming like silver fog in the torchlight as he went up to the door on the left. Before he could get near it, though, Chel said:

'Gregori, wait, don't touch it! There is danger in this room, another test to overcome. These columns . . .' The Uvovo reached out to one, grazed it with his fingertips and snatched them back. 'Very cold, sharp as talons, and something else . . .'

Greg stood back from the stone door, and moved his torch beam up the heavy frame and across the lintel and the wall above, illuminating panels of relief carvings of forest imagery alive with creatures of every kind, including Uvovo. Then he noticed something in the wider cone of torchlight, a circular, seemingly blank panel amid the carven foliage, and when he turned the torch rightwards he saw others.

'Chel – look.'

The Uvovo turned to see, adding his own torch beam to Greg's as he examined the discs, standing motionless with only his strange eyes staring. After several moments he let out a long sigh, bowed his head and muttered something in the Uvovo tongue. When he looked up again his original eyes were open as well and full of a dark, relentless concentration. The light from his torch trembled on the wall and Greg didn't know whether to speak or keep silent. Then Chel drew in a shuddering breath as he turned away, all eyes closed, shining torch dangling from his waist.

'It says, "Choose Your Path To Death".'

'How cheery,' Greg said.

'But in the Iterants of the Eternal it says that all paths lead to death and all deaths lead to the Eternal . . . so why three doors?' The new eyes were closed but his own glinted in the torchlight. 'And why four pillars?' He approached the nearest, aiming his torch at it as he placed his empty hand against it.

'Careful, Chel,' said Greg. 'Frostbite.'

'I can resist it for a short while, Gregori. There is something strange about these pillars . . . could you shine your torch here a moment – thank you.' Under the combined light, Greg could see that the column had a slightly slick, dull sheen. Chel shook his head. 'This is not stone. Like the ones out in the corridor it signi- fies something but I cannot *see* it . . . with these or these.' He indicated his normal eyes then the new outer pair.

'What about the other ones?' Greg said.

Still looking at the pillar, the Uvovo said, 'Are you asking me to risk my sanity, Gregori?'

'I could never do that, Chel,' he said. 'If the risk for you is too great, then we'll go back up top and see if there's another way to solve this – your call.'

Chel smiled. 'There is risk, certainly, but as I now have a responsibility to the Artificer Uvovo I must investigate this mys- tery with all of my abilities. Otherwise I would not be worthy of Segrana's gifts and purpose.'

He closed all his eyes and stood there for a moment, head slightly bowed. Then he straightened suddenly and on his brow the centre pair of eyes snapped open, glanced very briefly at Greg, then stared at the pillar before him. Greg looked on, trying not to think about the cold, pitiless volition he glimpsed in those eyes for an instant.

Chel's gaze seemed to bore into that column. Occasionally he flinched, a slight twitch of the head, and his lips began to move soundlessly. Then without warning he stepped away and went over to the next pillar, his features fixed in a wide-eyed grimace. After some moments he proceeded to the next and finally to the last. When he retreated from it his eyes were all tightly closed and his face was a mask of pain. As he fell to his knees, Greg lunged forward to slow his fall, helping him to rest on his side; the hand he had used to touch the pillars was cradled by the other, and when Greg reached out to the wrist he felt shockingly stone-cold flesh.

Guilt washed over him. *God, what have I done?*

'The test demands . . . demands the correct path to death,' Chel said hoarsely. 'Each pillar is a meditation focus that fills the meditator with a particular creed of thought, an overriding set of beliefs and instincts.' Levered up into a seated position, he pointed with his good hand at the pillars one by one. 'Fear, escaping from enemies; dominance, destroying or preying on the weak; arrogance, reaching out for godhood; serenity, changeless and creating no change.' The Uvovo gave an unsteady smile. 'If I had been a fully husked Listener, or had approached with all these new senses open, and chosen the wrong pillar, I would have been overwhelmed by it and, soon after, dead from whatever trap the doors conceal.'

'We'll be calling you "lucky Chel" next,' Greg said.

'I would wear the title gladly,' the Uvovo said, getting to his feet. 'Once we are through safely. Now I must open myself to the pillar of serenity . . .'

'And that's the correct one, is it?'

'So the Iterants of the Eternal say.'

'How much will it affect you?' said Greg. 'Will you be safe?'

'It is only a temporary veil over the mind and fades soon after.'

'You hope.'

'Exactly so.'

Greg stood over to one side as Chel approached one of the rearmost pillars, facing it with all three pairs of eyes now open, hands clasped across his chest. In the frozen stillness Greg resisted the urge to stamp his chill-bitten toes, instead rocking back and forth on the balls of his feet, keeping the circulation going. Then, before he knew it, Chel was heading towards the middle door of the three, arm half-extended, hand raised palm-outwards. He moved with a swift, gliding gait and reached the door before Greg was even halfway there. At his touch the carven stone block swung inwards and the Uvovo continued on through without breaking step.

Just as Greg reached the doorway there was a swelling pulse of pale green light and fearing the worst he stopped at the threshold, peering in. But at the other end of a short passage he saw Chel standing a few paces onward, swinging his torch beam around and above him, gazing into the pitch-darkness.

'The way is open, Gregori,' said the Uvovo in a dreamlike voice. 'Join me.'

Nevertheless he felt a prickling sweat as he hurried through to the other side.

'Such power waits here, Gregori, a vast slumbering might.' Chel's voice was measured yet slightly drowsy. 'The legacy of the Great Ancients.'

For a moment or two Greg didn't respond as he looked about him, trying to comprehend what he was seeing.

They seemed to be in the huge circular chamber shown in the deepscan images, standing near the sheer wall which rose perhaps 30 metres to a level ceiling. There was a second waist-high wall, 4 metres in and made of rough blocks, which ran round the chamber. By torchlight he saw no decoration on the walls or ceiling, but when he looked over the low wall he was amazed to see patterns incised into the dark, polished stone, strange interlocking, semi-geometrical designs, symbols and characters quite unlike the glyphs and ideograms of the Uvovo language, completely covering the circular floor as far as he could see by his torch's beam. From the scan printouts he had guessed the chamber to be roughly 250 metres across, which made this vast, ceremonial decoration a staggering find, not to say a mysterious one.

Following the low wall, he considered climbing over for a closer look, but then further along, just visible by his torch, was a gap. As he drew nearer he saw that there was a wide platform set into the main wall at about head-height with steps leading up to it. He glanced back at Chel, thinking to draw his attention to it, but the Uvovo was seated cross-legged on the stone floor, eyes closed, his torch lying beside him, throwing a fan-shaped shaft of light across the stone.

He'll see it all when he comes out of that trance, he thought and climbed the steps two at a time. The steps split halfway up into two stairways flanking a curved shelf which jutted from the platform like a pulpit. The platform itself was about 2 metres deep and empty but on the jutting shelf was a square plinth with an odd pyramidal depression in its flat top. Standing there he could almost feel the ancient darkness congeal about him. The air was cold and still, yet it didn't seem in the least bit stale.

Was this an altar? he wondered. Or a vantage point, since the great circular floor was the undoubted focus of this immense chamber?

Greg descended the stairs. The gap in the low wall lay directly before him and without pause he walked out onto the fabulously incribed floor.

A sudden, fleeting sensation passed over him and he could feel hairs prickle on his scalp and the backs of his hands. It didn't feel any colder out there yet there was an instinctive uneasiness quivering in him. Frowning, he crouched down with his torch to get a good look at the patterns. The lines were smooth and precise and had been incised in the stone with a fine, sharp implement, yet the edges of every groove were rounded and worn while the untouched stone surfaces looked pitted and eroded. He reached down and touched the stone, which turned out to be slightly warm. Then with a fingertip he traced one of the pattern lines, a long curve with several small loops, feeling the rounded edges and the rougher stone on either side . . .

Next thing he knew a bright gleam appeared in the groove beneath his finger and began to race along it in both directions. He snatched his hand away but it kept spreading like a silver thread dividing and coiling and entwining and surrounding. Seized by dread he stood, intending to head for the gap in the low wall . . . and was stopped by an invisible barrier. Fearful, he turned, took a step and came up against another one. It was solid and entirely transparent: shining his torch at it caused a faint ripple effect that quickly faded. Trying not to panic, he turned, pointing his torch, and saw an open area but before he could take a step he heard Chel speak urgently nearby: 'Gregori, as you value your life stay exactly where you are – don't move!'

27

CHEL

The meditation pillar for serenity had made everything so clear to him. With all eyes open and his every sense ready, Chel had looked into the pillar and the pillar had sung to him a gorgeous, interlocking river of concepts and revelations that flooded his thoughts with intrinsic truth. *Be changeless and leave the world unchanged*, the highest aspiration, the supernal truth.

And of course, if all paths lead to death it does not matter which door you take, thus when he chose the middle door it let him through without hindrance. A few steps on and he had to stop, his senses overwhelmed – the huge chamber was alive to his eyes! The glow of torches, the walls decorated with brightly coloured hangings, the pulse and pattern of energies, messages sent and received, visitors coming and going, greetings and farewells, conversations, commands and prayers. With the eyes of serenity Chel could see the changes wrought by the past: changeless he could perceive the warpwell in all its slumbering glory, its use as a journeying portal expertly operated by those ancient Uvovo.

He tried to communicate something of this to Gregori, who had then wandered past him, eyes blind to all the glory yet clearly still struck by the chamber's dimensions and the subdued undercurrents of the warpwell's mighty purpose. In Chel's eyes, the well's surface was a murkily opaque layer, a thick translucent plate covering nebulous depths. Not dead but not awake, the warpwell slept.

Chel had sat down on the stone floor to rest his limbs and allow his thoughts to drift into a true changeless state. But something was amiss, something was holding his mind back, keeping it from the soothing, joyous certainty of indivisible serenity. And whereas before, just minutes ago, every precept of the serenity path had stood pure and whole in his mind, now they seemed vague, uncertain. Troubled, he strove to reclaim that cherished state of being, to shore up its bulwarks and reaffirm its foundations . . .

Then through all these muddled thoughts he heard, clear and sharp, the impact of Gregori's first footfall upon the surface of the warpwell.

He scrambled to his feet, the serenity meditation falling away like misty tatters. The reverberations of those footsteps were like hammerblows and were being channelled downwards by the patterns in the stone. And glittering webs were shimmering in the gloom beneath the warpwell's opaque covering plate. Something, some part of the well was responding and if it was in self-defence . . .

He dashed along the walkway. Gregori was several paces out on the surface, his torch aimed at the stone as he crouched down and touched the patterning. At once, glowing tendrils spiralled downwards beneath the human while restricting veils sprang up around him: meanwhile, wider, surrounding patterns were starting to glow. The warpwell was trying to protect itself from its enemies . . . and its last enemies were the Dreamless, artificial, inorganic entities, and Gregori's boots contained artificial elements.

Gregori had just realised that something was very wrong when he collided with the pattern walls. Quickly, Chel leaped onto the wall and called to him;

'Gregori, as you value your life stay exactly where you are – don't move!'

The Human froze and looked his way. 'Chel, what's happening?'

'You are standing on an artefact built by the Great Ancients at the world's dawn. Its defences have awoken and will kill you if you don't get back over this wall – now, remove your boots, your socks too. Roll up your jacket sleeves, as high as they will go, and your trouser legs.'

Wordlessly, Gregori did so and finished with his boots hanging around his neck. He grinned.

'This feels like getting ready for some obscure country dancing ritual.'

Chel stared at him – sometimes Human humour was incomprehensible, but especially so now.

'Turn to your left,' he said. 'Reach out and feel your way along the pattern walls.'

'Why am I doing this?' Gregori said as he began.

'I am guessing that replacing the dead materials of your boots with the living flesh of your feet may cause these defences to either slow down or go into abeyance.'

'But you don't know.'

'I can see . . . I have seen fragments of the past . . .'

Fleeting images now to his six open eyes, scattered and fading in the rising heartbeat of an ancient, buried power. *And this is what they are here for, Kuros and the Hegemony – this is what we must defend, if it does not kill us first.*

'How am I doing, Chel?'

Gregori had turned a corner and was following a long, curving wall through the patterns, but the ominous machineries were still escalating beneath him. Were the warpwell's Sentinels following some ingrained, inflexible purification ritual?

'Keep going,' Chel said, walking along to stand at the gap in the wall, staring at the patterns all around Gregori, pushing at them with his mind, trying to wrench answers from them. What was this buildup of power meant to achieve and how dangerous would it be?

Gregori was a couple of paces from the gap when another pattern wall winked into existence before him.

'Follow it to the right,' Chel said. 'The other way leads back into the pattern.' And a few moments later Greg was an arm's-length from Chel, who then stopped him from leaping the remaining distance. 'First, drop your boots behind you.'

Gregori unslung his boots from his neck, tossed them back the way he had come then grasped Chel's outstretched arm, which hauled him off the warpwell pattern.

'Now what?'

Chel heard the sudden change in the building energies and felt a strange vibrancy in his muscles, his nerves, his eyes.

'Run!'

They took off in a mad dash back to the entrance. Gregori had the longer legs and got there first, ducking along the short passage and swinging round into the cold chamber, leaning against the wall. Hard on his heels, Chel saw he had stopped and dragged him towards the stairs.

'Don't . . . stop . . .'

They made it to the top of the steps when the warpwell defences finally surged, a soundless eruption. Chel's eyes were closed but still he felt the edges of that purifying reflex – for a second at its peak he found he could stare though his eyelids and right through the rock of Giant's Shoulder, as if it was foggy glass, to see the dazzling webs of energy that were pouring out of just that small section of the warpwell pattern to scour the entire chamber. Then the ferocious radiance subsided, leaving him in the dark.

Opening just his ordinary eyes he saw Gregori crouched at the top of the stairs, eyes wide and blinking.

'Chel? Are you still there?'

'I am, friend Gregori – what can you see?'

'Hmm, a familiar-sounding blur.'

Chel laughed. 'Your sight will return to normal soon. I'm going back down to inspect the chamber – do you wish to accompany me?'

'I think I'll sit this one out . . . Aye, and don't do anything risky, mind. Take it from one who knows.'

'I shall not be long,' Chel said, descending the steps.

The warpwell chamber looked exactly as it had before,

although he was using only his ordinary eyes. The air was as icy as before but now it had a faint mineral odour, like stone ground down to fine dust. The incised patterns on the surface of the well seemed dull and lifeless, and of Gregori's boots there was no sign.

Not dead but not awake, he thought, recalling the visions he had seen during the husking, the vast funnel of energies reaching out to seize the ships of the Legion and the Great Ancients alike, dragging them down into the warpwell then further down through the levels of hyperspace, through crushing, shredding strata to dark and narrow places. *Yet still potent. Will it be any use against our enemies? Will we have time to puzzle out its workings?*

For a moment he was tempted to open his husking eyes and gaze upon the fleeting ghosts of the past, but instead he replaced the cloth headband, tying it at the side. No, he had to meet with Weynl and the other Listeners to seek guidance and determine if any useful knowledge survived from those far-off times.

And he would have to give an explanation of some kind to Gregori, who had appeared at the door to the meditation chamber, his torch a bright knot in the inky darkness. Chel grinned and waved, then hurried to join his friend, wondering how much he should tell him.

28

KAO CHIH

'Ah hmm, so if I may summarise,' said the droid recycler, a Voth called Yolog, as he prodded the small pile of money with a long, stained finger. 'You wish to hire me to recover your corrupted course data, so that both you and your fine mech companion may travel onwards to the outlaw anchorage of Bryag Station . . . and this is all you have?'

Kao Chih smiled and spread his hands.

'Honourable artisan Yolog, at every stop in the journey that awaits us we shall make a point of mentioning you and the unequalled excellence of your work. Now if you had to buy that kind of advertising, how much would it cost? – yet here we are, offering it as part-payment for a comparatively minor data recovery job. Isn't that a good deal?'

The Voth regarded him with one large, dark and doleful eye and a stubby hexagonal lens unit that jutted from the other socket. The biograft was part of a close-fitting headpiece which wrapped around the back of the skull and down around the hairy neck to join with an odd body harness. It looked brown and shiny and had beaded black tendrils running to the exoskeletal sheaths that enclosed the Voth's arms. Yolog sat in a small mobile chair whose metal framework spread out above his head, a fan of interfaced tool housings, extensors and component trays. The Voth seemed to be quadriplegic and Kao Chih would have pondered further on this had his mind not been focused on the predicament at hand.

'You are by far the most amusing Human I have ever met,' Yolog said, his expressive lips twitching into a half-smile. 'But this data recovery is not so minor – since my own processors are fully occupied recodifying droids for certain paying customers, I would have to rent time on the Tagreli hubway which would require authenticated fund transfer. I fear that I must decline your kind offer to become my publicity agent.'

Despite his growing sense of desperation, Kao Chih maintained his unflappable, business-like exterior, complete with bright smile, even when the mech Drazuma-Ha* began displaying in its nimbus a message in Mandarin characters – Told you it wouldn't work – Told you it wouldn't work – Told you it wouldn't work – Told you it wouldn't . . .

'Thank you for your kind consideration, honourable Yolog,' he said. 'Perhaps you could suggest an alternative method of payment?'

'I am not ungenerous, Human Kaachi,' said the Voth. 'I would be prepared to accept payment in kind, such as any redundant or superfluous components from within your singular mech.'

Kao-Chih stared at Drazuma-Ha*, expecting a scathing response suitable to their surroundings, Yolog's spare-parts store. It was a dingy hold full of shelves crowded with defunct bots and droids, casings, effector arms, power cores, and motility sub-assemblies, bins full of supply connectors, servos, processor nodes, handler units, and several wall racks on which a few large industrial bots hung. Gloomy, grimy and smelling heavily of oils, it was undoubtedly a droid graveyard.

'I have no superfluous components,' Drazuma-Ha* said at last. 'The very notion is impolite.'

'I would be prepared to pay very well,' the Voth said, his flesh-and-blood eye staring hungrily at the mech for a moment before snapping back to Kao Chih. 'I will be frank with you – the likes of such a machine have not been seen in this vicinity for centuries.' He addressed Drazuma-Ha*. 'Are you not a Strigida sentient drone of the Ninth Iteration, fabricated during the final period of the Salgaic Synerge?'

'Broadly speaking, you are correct,' said the mech. 'And broadly speaking, you are also lacking in courtesy.'

Yolog gave an odd, harness-constricted shrug. 'Courtesy also has its price.' He looked back at Kao Chih. 'A great shame – Strigida parts are highly sought after.'

'Why?'

'The Salgaic Synerge was one of several promising civilisations that were obliterated by the Uncog Fecundemic, a replicating machine horde which erupted from the Qarqol deepzone over ten thousand years ago.'

Kao Chih was fascinated. 'I've never heard of this – what were they like?'

'Oh, typical dumb-smart machines – they all looked the same, dark globes bristling with weapon spines, but they came in all sizes, some large enough to be considered planetoids. They rampaged coreward for hundreds of lightyears, destroying every opposing force, effacing every inhabited world in their path until they reached the Huvuun Deepzone, where they unaccountably stopped. Every Uncog, whether in planetary orbit or traversing hyperspace or engaged in battle, simply halted as if switched off then began to disassemble, entire fleets of the things turning into vast clouds of debris. Unfortunately, they had by that time wiped out the Salgaic Synerge, the Interim Qudek, and a dozen other starfaring nations . . .'

'An interesting history lesson,' said Drazuma-Ha*. 'But scarcely helpful, since my components are not negotiable.'

The Voth sighed.

'Your options are limited, Human Kaachi. The only other medium of exchange that interests me would be unusual cultural artefacts. Might you possess such items?'

Kao Chih's thoughts raced, in his mind rummaging through the personal effects in his holdall back on board the *Castellan*. Unwashed clothing, hygiene flims, indoor shoes, a woollen hat, a deck of cards (missing the Prince of Veils), some pens, a notepad, pictures of his family, a couple of book tabs (mostly adventure stories written by Pyre exiles), and . . .

He stopped and smiled.

'Most honourable artisan Yolog – do you like music?'

An hour and a half later, the three of them were seated in the cramped cockpit of Yolog's cargo shuttle as it flew towards the huge cluster of domes and esplanade docks that was Tagreli Openport. Positioned at the pilot console, the Voth's head was bobbing in time to the music emanating from the audiobuds he had in his long-lobed ears. Removing one of them he turned to speak.

'Hmm, yes, very good, Kaachi, very good indeed, a most intriguing range of styles and execution. Your species appears to have dedicated a great deal of thought and effort to this pastime, resulting in some fascinating, hmm, product.'

'Do you have any favourites yet?' Kao Chih said.

'I'm not so keen on that electroniki you recommended – very mannered and precise yet somehow bloodless – but this rokinrol is, ah, crude, harsh and fully alive, especially the Deep Purple, the Black Sabbath and the Led Zeppelin.'

Kao Chih smiled and nodded. His wallet of music tabs had been a last-minute addition back on the Retributor, and had proved a wise one. After hearing a selection of compositions from various eras, Yolog's demeanour had changed markedly and he made an offer which covered the cost of his services and increased their store of hard currency.

'I had thought that your preferences would be the other way round,' Kao Chih said.

'Matters of taste are scarcely fathomable, friend Kaachi. Your electroniki is just the kind of thing my brother Yash would find irresistible, but not the rokinrol. What is certain is that many of my contacts will be eager to obtain entire suites of music once they have heard a few samples.'

The Voth replaced his audiobud and went back to monitoring the displays, head nodding, fingers tapping. Outside, the immensity of Tagreli Openport was looming ever closer as Yolog guided the craft towards one of the main esplanade docks. Kao Chih leaned towards Drazuma-Ha* and in a low voice said:

'Have you learned any more about this place? Are we safe?'

Soon after the corrupt course data brought them here, the *Castellan*'s comm system had managed to link into the local data-plex, but only at a low level. They knew they had arrived near Tagreli Openport but access to almost anything other than ad-chains, job agencies and product catalogues was restricted to secure idents. So while the mech tried to glean background information they posted a request for a data-recovery tech on one of the agency hireflows and Yolog responded not long after. The Voth's storage hold was part of an ancient, demilitarised Indroma troop transport, a gigantic hulk sitting in a parallel orbit to Tagreli's, along with several other decrepit vessels converted for warehousing, food production, manufacturing and even prisoner detention.

'I have determined a few more details,' the mech said. 'Tagreli Openport lies at the border of three nations, Sul, Weh-Alzi and Iroaroa, impoverished client states of the Sendrukan Hegemony. The port is tightly controlled by the Abstainers, a clan of very old Henkayans wholly dependent on a combination of mechanised life extension and anti-agathic drugs. Tagreli operates ostensibly as a neutral port open to anyone, but the Abstainers know that the Hegemony is boss. And are we safe? – well, if someone was looking for us it would not be hard to find us. The sooner we conclude this commerce and leave the happier I will be.'

Kao Chih nodded and looked round to see the bows of an immense grey-and-green ship filling most of the viewport. The vessel's entire forward section was long and straight with a rhomboid cross-section, its flat prow occupied by three large weapon ports, probably composite beam cannons, he guessed. The flanks were studded with more weapon clusters, domes and turret mounts; the mid-section flared to the aft, which was wide and Y-shaped, its corners tapering to three huge, rotating weapons carrels while the main drive tubes jutted from the stern. There was also battle damage, scorching, broken and melted shield antennae, and hull breaches around which repair drones and tekneers were gathered.

'That's the *Heshgemar-Kref*,' Yolog said. 'A *Chastiser*-class Hegemony battleship. It's just back from the Yamanon Domain, where it got into a skirmish or two with the remnants of the Dol-Das regime.'

'What's that smaller ship?' Kao Chih said, pointing.

As the Voth's shuttle progressed the battleship's other flank came into view, as did a second ship moored nearby at the esplanade end of the great open hangar. This one was roughly a tenth the size of the *Heshgemar-Kref* and was all sleek, dangerous lines, as if modelled after a sea or airborne predator, its long narrow hull lacking obvious weaponry and sensors while slender wings curved forward from the rear; the wings' leading edges were open for repairs, exposing the extendable weapon arrays. It was a lightly armoured vessel built for speed and aggressive manoeuvrability, and its livery was dark blue with silver high-lights and a series of symbols along its dorsal line.

'An Ezgara ship,' said Yolog. '*Ambusher*-class, almost certainly assigned as escort to the battleship. The names of Ezgara vessels are seldom posted on the dockflows but this one has eleven kill sigils on its hull, which means that it could be the *Chaxothal*, which was supposedly responsible for the destruction of the Dol-Das navy's flagship during the Yamanon liberation.'

Kao Chih had known little about the liberation of the Yamanon Domain, beyond the fact that the invading coalition included Earthsphere and the Sendrukan Hegemony, and that the occupation had been dragging on for nearly four years. Since embarking on his mission to Darien, however, he had noticed many details, overheard scraps of conversation in public places or reports on news channels, which gave the impression that the occupation was very unpopular and provoking a grassroots insur-gency rather than fostering peace and reconciliation.

Then the shuttle's flightpath took it past the next open hangar and Kao Chih's eyes widened. The vessel moored there was gigan-tic, perhaps three or four times the size of the Hegemony battleship. In shape it was like a four-cornered, gleaming gold and red arrowhead set on its side, its edges curving in to join with a

massively domed aft section, its surfaces bizarrely adorned with
creatures and figures, symbols and lines of characters as well as
great banners and flags. The bas-relief forms were worked into
the warship's exterior features: mouths gaped around launch bays
while beam weapons jutted from eye sockets. The entire hull was
a fabulously baroque façade, as if enemies were to be awed into
submission by its relentless ornamentation.

'Ah, yes, hmm, the *Kho-Maurz*,' the Voth said. 'A Brolturan
ship, which they call a Strategic Offensive Conveyor but its really
an ancient super-carrier built by the Ufan Oligarchs during their
war with the Sarsheni-dominated Indroma nearly five hundred
years ago.'

'Impressive,' Kao Chih said.

Yolog gave a little smile. 'Just so, and yet the flagship of the
Yamanon navy was produced by the same yard around that
time – it was a super-heavy carrier and was twice the size of that
one.'

Kao Chih blinked and looked at the Voth. 'And that Ezgara
ship . . . it's practically a boat in comparison.'

'Yes, yes, but the Dol-Das regime was basically a gang of
incompetents – a quarter of that flagship's weaponry was out of
commission, fifteen of its seventy decks were sealed off due to dis-
repair, and just four out of its twelve launch bays had a full
complement of close-support fighters. Rumour has it that the
Chaxothal gained entrance to one of the disused bays and proceeded to blast a tunnel through the ship's interior to the stern
where it wrecked the drives and set a number of charges. Once the
Ezgaran ship left the way it had come, the flagship was torn apart
by several devastating explosions.'

Teams of engineers worked all over the *Kho-Maurz*'s glittering
hull, which slid out of sight as the Voth's shuttle climbed towards
a line of smaller hangars sitting on top of the big ones. But Yolog
steered past them and through the slow traffic of ships and pilot-
tugs towards a tower around which other similar docks were
spaced. Staring at this tower, Kao Chih took in the wider view
and suddenly realised that Tagreli Openport had a spoked-wheel

configuration with each of the six spokes ending in a secondary axis tower, and it was one of those that was their destination.

Soon they were docking in what appeared to be an access shaft for automated garbage scows. Yolog's craft clamped itself to a recess in the shaft and a segmented transit tube swung out, neatly settling over the shuttle's airlock. Minutes later Kao Chih and an oddly quiet Drazuma-Ha* were following the Voth into what he called his 'business premises'. Ceiling arrays of coloured lights came up to reveal a showroom with rows of pristine-looking bots and droids. Wide double-doors led into a well-equipped workshop where machines hummed and odd-shaped displays showed strangely blurred strings of data flowing in patterns, coils and grids. Yolog blanked them with a gesture then moved smoothly over to a terminal with a large, convex oval screen.

'If you please, Kaachi, your course data.'

Kao Chih handed over a small memory crystal which was swiftly slotted into a curved console with silvery beadlike keys. Moments later datastreams began to flow down the screen, with an inset showing analysis results flowing left to right. Drazuma-Ha* was floating a few feet away and Kao Chih was letting his gaze wander around the workshop, the benches, the assembly rigs, and the ceiling-mounted scanners, when the mech spoke.

'Yolog, this equipment appears to be malfunctioning.'

The machine was hanging before a large sloping cabinet on which various lights and symbols were flickering.

'It is only a battery-charging stall,' the Voth said without diverting his attention. 'Pay it no heed – the cut-out will shortly . . .'

A loud bang came from the cabinet and pieces of its shell and sparks burst outward, showering Drazuma-Ha*. The Voth cursed, turned from the silver keyboard and sped along to the cabinet, reaching out with one of his exo-supported arms to shut off the power.

'My good clients, I am deeply sorry for this unfortunate accident,' Yolog said, moving in Drazuma-Ha*'s direction. 'Are you damaged, most valued machine? Do you require repair or systems check, hmm?'

Kao Chih rushed over, full of anxiety, but the mech was retreating from the Voth, then gliding towards the exit.

'I am undamaged,' it said. 'But I intend to wait in the shuttle. Please continue with your work.'

Kao Chih watched the mech leave then turned sharply to Yolog, who was trundling back over to the console.

'What happened?' he said.

'I do apologise. Most unfortunate – a discharge from a faulty charging stall,' the Voth said as his long dextrous fingers played the bead keys. 'Much of my equipment is obsolete and in serious need of upgrades yet my orderbook is so full that I cannot afford to have machines standing idle. Certain older devices, however, retain their usefulness, like this manual interface which, despite its anachronistic nature, permits a more relaxed approach to neural tasking.' Suddenly Yolog ceased keying and lifted his hands from the silvery keys. Then a short melody of soft, descending notes sounded and he plucked out the memory crystal and returned it.

'Your course data, fully restored and updated.'

'Thank you, honourable Yolog. You have been most helpful.'

The Voth grinned, showing off a spectacular set of ochre-hued teeth.

'Yes, hmm, well, our transaction has certainly lightened my mood and provided a new store of musical mysteries to explore. And now you must return to my shuttle, which will take you back to my parts hold from whence you can continue your journey.'

'Are you accompanying us?'

'Work detains me, Human Kaachi – the repair of that junkheap of a charger, amongst others.'

'Then goodbye, Yolog, and good fortune.'

The Voth smiled, nodded and went over to examine the cabinet.

Back in the shuttle's small cockpit, Kao Chih found the mech floating lengthwise against the low ceiling.

'Our business is concluded, I trust,' it said.

Kao Chih held up the memory crystal, which was quickly probed with a brief needle of icy blue light.

'It seems to be in order. What delays our host?'

'Yolog says that he has to work on that faulty charger and . . .'

'Passengers aboard,' interrupted an autovoice from somewhere in the cockpit. 'Are passengers ready to depart? – answer yes or no.'

'Yes!' Drazuma-Ha* said loudly. 'Before I am forced to deal with more trickery.'

'What do you mean?' said Kao Chih.

'That piece of theatre with the charging cabinet was meant as a cover for the burst-scan which was simultaneously directed at me from a ceiling-mounted device. But I had already reconfigured my sheathing shields before arriving here – his scandata will show something besides what he expects.'

'Which will be what?'

'Detailed schemata for a household valetbot, not unlike those on display back there.'

Laughing, Kao Chih wedged himself into the pilot couch and pulled the straps tight just as the shuttle declamped from its mooring. There was a lurch, a faint thrum of motors, and the Voth's craft flew sedately out of the garbage scow access. Drazuma-Ha* declared that he was suspending activity functions in order to runs a systems check. Kao Chih nodded and leaned back, feasting his eyes on the vast intricacy of Tagreli Openport, its glittering clusters and spokes and hangars, the vessels of all sizes and shapes that came and went, and the innumerable hopcraft, taxis and pleasure-boats, all set against the muddy grey-green world around which it orbited. And wished his family and friends were there to see it too.

Back in his workshop, with the showroom lighting muted, Yolog sat at his console, looking at the female Human whose face filled half the screen.

'Got your message – what do you have for me?'

The Voth smiled hesitantly. 'Well, friend Corazon, I have a lead on a Human and a mech who needed their course data recovered . . .'

'Are you saying that they were in your grasp and you let them walk out? Were they part of a larger group?'

'Ah, no, they . . .'

'That wasn't part of our deal, friend Yolog.' The woman smiled, cold and dangerous. 'You are supposed to securely detain solitary Humans . . .'

'It was the man's mech,' the Voth said hurriedly. 'It's an old, very powerful and cunning sentient machine, which foiled my attempt to scan it. If I had tried to imprison the Human it might have attacked me, even killed me!'

The woman, whose full name was Corazon Talavera, shook her red- and black-furred head. 'If they've left, they are no use to me.'

'I have a copy of their course data,' Yolog said. 'They're going to Bryag Station and I had one of my remotes put a tracker on their ship while they were over here.'

'Better, if not ideal,' said Talavera. 'What are their names?'

'The man is called Kaar-Chee and the mech is Drazuma-Ha*.' With a shaky hand he fingered the silvery bead-keys. 'I'm sending you all the data I could obtain on them, image files and statistics as well as the parameters of the tracking signal.'

'Bryag Station, eh? Not easy to get there before them.' Corazon Talavera glanced down, no doubt seeing the data packet arrive, then gave Yolog a hard, appraising look. 'But when I return we are going to have a little talk, just to remind you how our agreement is supposed to work.'

Then the screen was blank, leaving Yolog trembling and sweating. For a second he sat there, utterly relieved that she was gone, then anger welled up and he raised his exo-clad arms, clenching his fists.

Gods of infinite space, how he hated Humans, and the Talavera woman especially. Were all their females so cruel and pitiless? Many years past, he had made a small, very small mistake which had led to the tragic death of one of the aged and venerable Henkayan Abstainers, all purely through a chain of chance and accident. He thought that only he knew the truth until that cursed

Human had turned up and showed him the damning evidence which she had locked safely away, so long as he did what he was told.

Yolog thought about packing his essentials and valuables and fleeing Tagreli, off into the depths of known space, but that was a well-worn fantasy, just like the one where he fled instead to the Aranja Tesh, to some world near the Yamanon border, and helped build combat droids for the struggle against the Hegemony and their despicable Human lackeys.

He uttered a bleak laugh, knowing that only imminent, life-threatening catastrophe could make him leave. On the other hand, it was not impossible that the imposing mech Drazuma-Ha* might deal fatally with Talavera should a confrontation take place.

With that happy thought, he put his earpieces back in and began checking shipment manifests while the sweeping rhythms of a song called 'Kashmir' filled his head.

29

CATRIONA

From her viewport she could see glimpses of Nivyesta's single massive landmass through breaks in the cloud cover as the shuttle made its banking, spiral descent. The green of Segrana was rich, dark and mysterious from this height, yet the clouds looked soft, inviting. Whenever she saw them during a shuttle journey she imagined them to be a strange, floating terrain of pure whiteness with its own flora and fauna . . . until the shuttle scythed through them. Then there were only moisture droplets crawling across the outside of the viewport while steely-grey fog rushed past.

As they swept on through cloud, her thoughts drifted back to her encounter with that apparition which looked so like a Pathmaster, or how she imagined one would look. *Seek out a* vodrun *and undertake a vigil – all will become clear to you*, it had said in a sighing, sibilant voice, but why would it say such a thing? And had it been real or had she just imagined it? If the latter, it called into question her mental stability and fitness for her position and responsibilities . . . and if it *was* real? She knew from research with male and female Uvovo that those who underwent the *vodrun* vigil said that they experienced the feelings of Segrana and heard her thoughts, so perhaps she should attempt it, although how she would obtain permission from a Listener was as yet unfathomable. She would ponder this – later, when she got back to the enclave.

Soon, the cabin staff announced the final approach and everyone strapped in to their couches. Catriona's fellow passengers numbered eleven, mostly ecologists and biologists with a pair of Uvovo scholars well into their maturity going by the grey tufts behind their ears. In addition there was one mystery man, seated a row in front and on the other side of the aisle – during the nine-hour flight he had eaten nothing and drunk only a few cups of water, spoken to no one, read nothing, listened to nothing on his couch phones and watched nothing on the overhead display. All of which convinced Cat that he was one of the Enhanced. She didn't recognise him, but then the project directors had rigorously segregated all the coactiles of students with the aim of enforcing a tight group loyalty. The faces of her own coactile were vividly and accurately recollectable, yet others who were there at the same time were scarcely more than vague blurs.

The dear brothers and sisters of my coactile, she thought sourly. *A smothering straitjacket of peer pressure, all individuality subsumed to the group, an identity controlled by those directors, who were interested only in creating living processors capable of high-level computation. Walking calculators . . .*

Sighing, she relaxed back into the comfort of the couch and wondered how to find out his name, maybe even discover what an Enhanced was doing on Nivyesta. From that early, cloistered part of her life she knew that many Enhanced ended up working for the government in their Special Designs Division. But what would the SDD be doing here on Nivyesta?

The approach and landing took another twenty minutes. Vibration came in successive waves, as did the loud moan of the engines applying staged braking. The impact of landing on water made the craft shudder and the pitch of the engines altered. Soon they had taxied up to Pilipoint Station's floating dock, a large, curve-roofed structure capable of accommodating two shuttles. As the passengers gathered their belongings and donned outdoor garments, Cat found herself wondering, not for the first time, what Greg was up to back at Giant's Shoulder, knowing full well that for him the temptation to go back into that puzzle-trap corridor would be irresistible. As it would be for her.

Please stay out of trouble, she thought. *Or at least go looking for it with someone you can rely on.*

She grasped her holdall and was quick to get behind the mystery man as the cabin lock cycled open. Slowly trooping to the exit, she overheard the steward call him Mr Yurevich and saw him take two substantial pieces of luggage from the stowing booth before stepping through the airlock. One was an ordinary barkleather suitcase but the other was a tall, grey case on small wheels; its sides had stickers saying HANDLE WITH CARE – PHOTOGRAPHIC DEVICES but she recognised it as a standard transport case for lab equipment as used in the Enhanced project.

A moment or two later she emerged from the shuttle's smelly recycled air, setting foot on the combiplas decking of the dockside and taking a deep breath of Nivyesta's atmosphere. Yurevich was hurrying away but that was okay – his name and description and the 99 per cent certainty of an Enhanced status was more then enough to trace him through the whisperway. Now, however, she faced the onerous duty of reporting to Professor Forbes, who had no doubt seen coverage of the shooting at Giant's Shoulder and probably read the preliminary reports.

What she had to do was put herself in a resilient, unflappable frame of mind. It was not a question of whether or not Forbes would be objectionable and mean-spirited, merely a matter of how it would show itself.

But all this was forgotten as she entered the low-ceilinged, slightly shabby transit lounge. The lounge had two vees, usually tuned to sports and light entertainment, but right now both were showing news and were surrounded by dozens of anxious-looking people. On the screen was one of the better presenters, grey-haired Jan Kronagen, addressing viewers from the studio, so she paused to see what it was all about.

'. . . but members of the Sendrukan Hegemony delegation have still declined to make any comment, and since there is as yet no Brolturan Compact representative on Darien we must gather viewpoints from where we can. Let us return to the *Heracles*, where our spot reporter, Serj Tanilov, has obtained more views of the Brolturan vessel, as well as some hard data. Serj?'

'Yes, Jan, thank you. More information on the Brolturan ship, which is called *Purifier*, by the way – its official designation is a Tactical Dominance Enabler . . . Ah, we have it now? . . . Right, we can show more vid as supplied by a Gomedran freelancer who was on board one of the *Heracles*'s atmosphere boats when this leviathan took up stationary orbit above Darien.'

The screen abruptly switched to a view of the stars from orbit, the nearest of them blurred by the dustclouds of the deepzone. But the foreground was filled with an immense, gleaming, fabulously ornate ship, its forward sections bearing a passing resemblance to a sweeping, stepped pyramid while the stern tapered slightly towards the blocky main drive manifold. The view swayed a little and suddenly zoomed in on the prow, where a huge statue of a Brolturan in archaic battle armour emerged from the hull. In one hand it cradled a mirrored polyhedral while the other held out a long, straight sword, pointing forward.

The Gomedran freelancer then panned slowly up the length of the warship, showing decks, launch bays, weapons arrays, missile batteries, all amid the most incredible embellishment Cat had ever seen outside some of the Rus chapels. During all this, the reporter was reeling off statistics – the *Purifier* was nearly 700 metres long, had a crew complement of 12,000, a support and interceptor complement of 2,800, a troop transport capability of 10,000 alert or 20,000 cryo, and the commander probably held the rank of father-admiral . . . Tanilov added that these were not official figures, having been gleaned from various tiernet sources, and a few enthusiasts from amongst the *Heracles*'s crew. Back in the studio, Kronagen reminded the viewing audience that an ambassador had been expected from the Brolturan Compact, thought not in such an imposing ship.

Shaking her head, Cat shouldered her holdall and headed for the shuttle-dock's small lobby.

They might have sent an ambassador, she thought, *but that ship constitutes undiplomatic language. Maybe we're supposed to*

be intimidated by its scary ornaments or something; if so I think
they're in for a surprise . . .

The way to the exit led past a small bar, and as she drew near
she noticed Yurevich, seated in one of the easy chairs, talking to
someone. Walking further on she saw that it was a woman with
short dark hair whose face slowly came into view past the foliage
of a plantpot. She was just a few paces away when recognition hit
her so forcefully she almost stopped in her tracks. At that moment
the woman looked round, saw her, straightened, put out a hand
to silence Yurevich then rose and came over.

'Catriona! – it's been many a year. How are you?'

'I'm well, Julia, I'm fine. How are you? You're looking . . .
well.'

Julia Bryce, Julia of the warm camaraderie smile and the icy,
disapproving stare, ruler of their nine-strong coactile, her tiny
empire, ruthlessly manipulative and tactically generous. She was
taller than Catriona, pale skin accentuating her elfin good looks,
dressed in a long, dark coat over fashionable dark green formals.

'Certainly, Catriona, I keep active, as always. I'm here to work
on a research project, very dry and unexciting but worthy. I have
Albrecht and Gustave working with me – they'll be delighted to
know that you're on Nivyesta.'

Cat made herself smile. So the ice-queen still had her two
favoured minions in tow – Albrecht and Gustave had played the
role of willing instruments who were also clever enough to conduct their own little psycho-dramas from time to time. It was
unimaginable that they would be 'delighted', considering what she
had called them on her last day as an Enhanced.

'You must pass on my fond regards.'

'Of course. So tell me, have you work here?'

'Oh yes, eco-social studies of the native Uvovo, including cultural and biological aspects. It's cross-disciplinary and very
demanding but I enjoy it.'

'That is fascinating.' The look of bland regard in Julia's face
didn't change. 'You know, it's such a shame that your enhance-
ments failed at the last – poor Catriona, it must have been such a

struggle. But you have work and that's so important. Well, I must say goodbye – perhaps we'll run into each other again.'

A smile tinged with satisfaction, a nod, and Julia Bryce was strolling back to Yurevich. Cat kept the fake composure plastered on until she had turned the corner out of the lobby and into Pilipoint Station's narrow concourse.

Bitch! She's working 'on a research project' but I 'have work' – makes it sound as if I pour the tea and deliver the mail. Chrome-plated bitch!

Then she slowed down, in her thoughts as well as the furious pace she was marching along at, while comprehension dawned. Eighteen years on from that tight, fevered hothouse of a coactile group, and Julia could *still* prod her temper and stir up feelings of low self-esteem. She had nothing to be ashamed of and every reason to feel good about her achievements, yet self-justification was not what she needed, rather it was a tougher skin.

Then she stopped entirely, realising that she had walked right past the entrance to the small foyer where an elevator gave access to the floor where Forbes had his office. And on the spur of the moment she decided no, she wasn't going to go up there and endure Forbes's verbal thuggery. If he truly, urgently, needed a report she would be more than happy to send him a text version via the satgrid.

Feeling liberated, at least for the time being, Catriona strode along the low-ceilinged concourse, past the small shops and empty café, heading for the main security doors beyond which lay Segrana. Or rather a small community of Uvovo traders dealing in fresh fish and fruit, and a couple of *trictra* sheds. She knew that the security autosystem would sense her ID tag and log her out when she left, and that Forbes would find this out not long after. But she was eager to get back to the trees, back to Segrana to see if there was anything on the file from Galyna, but most of all to ponder the Pathmaster apparition's words.

Seek out a vodrun! – the words had come in a kind of blackened whisper. *Undertake a vigil . . . all will become clear to you . . .*

A vigil. What might she learn from it? Something to give her investigations an urgency in the eyes of the Institute, perhaps, and to bring a certain measure of fame her way? Perhaps even enough to ensure that Julia and her minions heard about it.

Well, it might not be the healthiest reason for seeking fame and fortune, she thought as she emerged from the station and made for one of the *trictra* sheds. *But it's the way that makes me feel good!*

30

THEO

He was recalling the disaster at High Lochiel as he, Rory and Janssen crouched next to the ground-floor fire escape in a side alley. Sundstrom had been appalled at the casualties and furious at the security lapse, fearing that the media might piece it all together. But since the woman who saw Theo's men had also died in the explosion, there were no witnesses to their involvement beyond that of bystanders. Pyatkov had urged the president to exclude Theo from taking any further part in anti-terror operations, but then Rory had appeared with a lead on a man who was behind a couple of riots and some false flag incidents, inciting antagonistic groups to clash on the streets. Rory's informant said the man, known as Olgren, was taking orders from another staying in his loft apartment in southwest Hammergard.

So, after a hectic cross-town dash, during which Rory made certain that both men were still there, Theo and his men were assigned to secure the fire escape while Pyatkov's other teams took control of all the stairways and the lifts. The building had eight floors and was a mixture of owner-occupier and rented property . . . and Theo's anxiety was winding tighter and tighter. What if this was another elaborate setup? – what if Rory's inform-ant had been fooled by another high-tech illusion? Advance reports from the High Lochiel explosion said that a small device, possibly a hologram projector, had been recovered from the charred ruins of the top floor. Could they be sure that they weren't walking into another deadly trap?

He stood up.

'Okay, no more waiting,' he said. 'Let's go.'

Rory grinned as he got up, but gave Theo a narrow-eyed glance.

'Thought we wuz waitin' for Pyatkov's order, Major.'

'I want to be sure it's not another pit of spikes we're getting into, Rory.'

'Well, ma boy Vlad says he seen 'em both in the last hour . . . but aye, yer right, don't want tae get our teeth handed tae us again like they did last night.'

'Okay, Janssen – lead the way, and tread lightly.'

It was a nerve-racking climb, trying to use the wooden flights as cover from above while careful to avoid any creaking steps. At last they reached the top landing and crouched outside the emergency exit.

'Rory,' Theo whispered, pointing at the door.

Rory grinned and produced a small device with a plastic dial and a metal tongue which he fitted to the bottom of the door. A minute later they were inside, crouching below the height of the windows in the doors at either end of an empty, white-painted corridor. Theo crept to the one leading to Olgren's apartment, took out a pocket S-scope and peered into it.

What he saw was both alarming and confusing. The apartment was airy and spacious with half-height partitions sectioning off small sleeping areas in both of the far corners. An open-plan kitchen/lounge occupied the centre of the apartment and tall windows with their slatted shutters flung wide let in what remained of the day's sunlight. But in the nearer half of the room sat what looked like automatic gun sentries, low, tripod-mounted and positioned to provide deadly crossfire on anyone entering by the main door.

What confused him was the two men, one sitting near the far side, the other standing near him and engaged in a comm call while staring out of the window. Both had shaven heads, and the seated one was looking down at some kind of grey device which was attached to his upper arm.

Just then he felt his own comm vibrate in his jacket pocket. Passing the scope to Janssen, he took out the comm and answered in a low murmur.

'Karlsson.'

'Pyatkov here – we're about to head up. Start your ascent.'

'Word of advice, Pyatkov – don't charge the door to the apartment. There are two autogun sentries guarding it.'

There was a moment of silence. 'You're up there already, aren't you? Damn you, Karlsson, you disobeyed my orders . . .'

'And you should be thanking me, but we can argue about that later, yes? When you are in position, we'll move first and try to shut down the autogun on the left, okay, sir?'

'Acknowledged – proceed.'

Rory grinned as Theo put away the comm. 'So, is Mr Pyatkov still on our side?'

'Oh yes, but I don't think we'll be getting a Christmas card this year.'

'Something's wrong,' said Janssen. 'They're agitated.'

Theo grabbed the scope and looked. Both men were now standing over a terminal, one of them tapping on the keyboard. They stared at the screen for a moment then went into a burst of activity, gathering together small satchels and several weapons. The odd grey device went into a green backpack.

'They know someone's coming,' Theo said. 'Sensors on the stairs and in the elevators, maybe . . . and one of them is headed this way!' He turned to the other two. 'When he comes through, I'll shoulder through this side going the other way so while he's looking round at me the pair of you bring him down.' He thumbed his comm's quickkey and when Pyatkov answered he said, 'We've only seconds – they're on to you so we're going in!'

Theo just had time to stuff the comm into his jacket and ready his rifle, a Makarov semiautomatic, when the shaven-headed man pushed open the door.

Immediately, Theo charged through the other door. The man cried and whirled, bringing a handgun to bear, but Rory and Janssen kicked away his legs and wrestled him to the floor. The

other man looked round and Theo saw him smile just before the
nearest autogun opened up. As rounds hammered holes in the
walls and floor, Theo dived for cover behind a long display case
full of seashells of every kind. He lobbed a concussion grenade
round the side of it towards the autogun then ducked his head,
covering his ears. The explosion burst apart the display, blew out
most of the windows, made the floor lurch underfoot and left his
head ringing.

Covered in wood splinters and shell fragments he sneaked a
glimpse round the partition corner and saw the second man wearing a backpack and crouching on the ledge of one of the tall
windows, now empty of glass. Seeing Theo he laughed and
snapped off a shot to make him dodge back. When he chanced
another look it was in time to see the man tip sideways and fall
out of sight.

'No!' he bellowed and rushed to the window. There was gunfire
behind him but he ignored it as he stuck his head out the
window – and immediately heard a motorised whine coming from
his right. There was a fist-sized object mounted on the outside wall
more than an arm's reach away, and a taut, vibrating cable was
running out of it. He pushed himself a little way out onto the
ledge and looked down to see, in the gathering dusk, a figure landing lightly on his feet on the flat roof of an adjacent building.
Sparks spat from the winch device and the severed end of the
cable fell away. Theo brought up his rifle and squeezed off a
couple of shots but the man was off at a zigzagging run, dodging
between the cover of venting ducts and outlets. Reaching the other
side of the roof he simply rolled over the edge and was gone.

Theo cursed, then noticed that he had cut his arm on the jagged
remains of the window and cursed again, wearily this time. Back
in the room the two autogun sentries had been reduced to smoking wrecks and Pyatkov was standing before the other man, who
was now tied to a chair with Rory and Janssen immediately
behind him.

'The second man got away,' Karlsson told Pyatkov. 'He lowered himself with a light cable winch fixed outside the window.

He got to the south wall of the next-door building then I lost sight of him.'

Pyatkov nodded wordlessly and issued abrupt commands on a corps-issue handset. Theo glanced at Rory, who was nursing a grazed chin.

'Is this Olgren?' he said.

'Aye, and a right handy lout he is, too. Interesting tats, though.'

Theo regarded the man, who sat there unresponsive and apparently unperturbed. He was wearing shorts and a sleeveless shirt, revealing the tattoo patterns which encircled his ankles, upper arms and neck. Pyatkov put away the handset and faced Olgren.

'You're in very serious trouble, Mr Olgren, but you can help yourself by telling me who that other man is and where we can find him.'

Olgren smiled patiently. 'Utlaginn goes where he's needed, sir, resisting the enemies of Darien. All of you should be helping the FDF, not hindering us.'

Theo grimaced – 'Utlaginn' was old Norj for 'outlaw'.

Pyatkov regarded the man with stone-cold eyes for a moment. 'What are those tattoos for?' he said, pointing.

'They symbolise the FDF's unity and purity of purpose.' Olgren shook his head. 'Sir, beyond explaining the Faction's principles, I have nothing to say.'

Pyatkov leaned closer. 'You know, I'm glad that you feel secure and armoured by your beliefs – it means that when you do break you'll give me all of it, without hesitation or resistance. It's just that these tattoos . . . well, in years to come they will only serve to remind you of what you betrayed. Very sad.' He straightened. 'Take him away.'

Olgren gave no trouble as he was led away and at almost the same moment that he disappeared down the main stairs, another figure came up and entered the apartment. Clad in a brown leather town jacket, it was Donny Barbour.

'Mr Pyatkov,' he said, 'I'm on an urgent assignment and require some additional personnel – I wonder if I can borrow Major Karlsson and his men, if that's not inconvenient.'

Pyatkov regarded Barbour coolly for a moment and Theo could almost hear his thoughts – *You're on an assignment and I've not been informed?*

'Very well, Mr Barbour, but be sure that they follow orders, yes?'

'Excellent, my thanks . . . Major, if you and your men could follow me . . .' Then in a lower voice, once Pyatkov had moved away, 'Sorry for the short notice but we've got a possible lead on the guy that just dived outa yon window and we have to move now!'

Theo glanced at Rory and Janssen, who both nodded.

'Lead the way,' he said.

Rather than wait for the lift, which was already on its way down with Olgren, they took the stairs at a swift pace. Barbour's spinnercar was parked across the road, its motors humming on idle. Theo was about to climb into the front passenger seat when Barbour said, 'I'll need you to drive, Major, while I operate the tracker.'

Once behind the wheel, he checked the controls and instruments then turned to see Barbour hunched over a circular display panel whose raised rim was speckled with mysterious glowing symbols, and had a line of oval, black studs along the bottom edge. Rory poked his head through from the back seat, spotted the strange display and opened his mouth, but Barbour spoke first.

'It's a signal mapper,' he said. 'It can isolate a single comm call within a radius of 100 metres, match its frequency and piggyback it through the switching node network to its destination, which then shows up as a street address. Takes time, though – your boy made a call just before all the fun started but he was only on for twenty to thirty seconds. Needs at least a minute . . .'

'Can ye listen in, like?' Rory said.

'Nah. This wee baby is Imisil tech rush-adapted for use with our somewhat backward comms . . .'

Just then the circular screen lit up, showing an odd schematic of radial spikes and funicular shapes that moved around in 3D.

'Is that what I think it is?' Theo said.

Barbour nodded. 'Target's making another call . . . keep talking, you scumsucking dog . . .'

Moment ticked away as Barbour tracked a glowing line through a strange shifting maze of cones, helices and blocks of numbers, occasionally switching to a Hammergard map for a quick look. About a minute and a half later the signal went dead, but Barbour had the address.

'Abercromby Hall on Athole Road – it's a Corps training barracks.'

'Is that off Westerling Street?' Theo said as he engaged the spinner.

Frowning, Barbour nodded. 'Why are they interested in a training barracks?'

'Could be a staging area?' Theo said, heading north. 'Maybe just a meeting place?'

'Could be,' said Barbour, sounding unconvinced.

The even darkness of night had fallen by the time they reached Abercromby Hall, a modest brick building set between a furniture warehouse and a garment manufacturer. Theo and the others waited by the car while Barbour went to speak with the duty officer. Moments later he was back, his face grim as he thumbed the keys on his comm.

'Everyone back in,' he said. 'We've got trouble.'

'What kind of trouble?' Theo said, ducking back inside.

'The worst – there's no trainees or cadets stationed here just now, but last night they were providing temporary accommodation for an escort squad on detachment from the Second Division. This is the squad assigned by the president to guard High Monitor Kuros; Kuros and Ambassador Horst are at Port Gagarin, where the Brolturan ambassador is about to arrive . . . he's the target, has to be.'

'My God,' said Theo. 'You think someone in that unit is collaborating with the FDF?'

'Or our gunman has substituted himself for one of them . . .' he snarled, and tossed his comm onto the shelf above the dashboard.

'And I'm not getting through to anybody in Port Gagarin on this thing! Right, let's get moving and drive there . . .'

'They've got nearly half an hour's head-start,' Theo said as he swung the spinnercar round in a U-turn and headed for the coast road.

'Maybe we'll get lucky,' Barbour said. 'The Brolturan shuttle might develop a fault and be called back, the weather might have the same effect, or the hitman might already have been caught . . . or he might miss . . .'

'Aye, right,' said Rory from the back seat. 'And the *baro* might not shit in the woods, and the bishop of Trond might turn out tae be an atheist! – is that whit yer saying?'

Theo glanced at Barbour and saw him grinning. 'You'll have to excuse him – his glass is a bit half-empty tonight.'

'Better a half-empty glass of truth,' Barbour said, 'than a keg full of deluded hopes, is that it, Rory?'

'Better a cynic than a sucker, sir.'

'Remind me not to be marooned on a desert island with you – the optimism would kill me.'

31

ROBERT

The passenger lounge serving Port Gagarin's Landing Bay 2 was closed to the public and the rows of seating had been moved well back to make room for the Hegemony and Earthsphere entourages – one with nineteen members, the other with just two.

Harry, dressed in a long grey coat over a dark formal suit circa 1930s America, was smiling as he observed the High Monitor Kuros and his escort of four Ezgara commandos, twelve DVC soldiers and three attendants.

'Robert, sometimes I don't think the Diplomatic Service takes your safety seriously enough – hell, you don't take it seriously enough. Yesterday, Sundstrom offered you your very own personal escort, just like Kuros, but you turned it down. Why?'

'I've told you already,' Robert said in a low murmur. 'My secretary and his assistant are both armed – any more would be an unnecessary burden and would get in the way.'

'Yes, well, I didn't believe you yesterday and I don't believe you now, so what's the real reason?'

Robert glared at his AI companion, which elicited only a sunny smile in response. He sighed.

'If you must know, an openly armed escort would make me feel as if I really was in danger. If this was a non-Human world, like when we were on Giskhn 4 a few years ago, I could see the point. But here . . . well, it would feel like an admission of defeat. These are our people – we can't fail them so we must make sure that the special accord between Earthsphere and the Hegemony actually means something.'

'I'm sure it means something to the exalted Kuros,' Harry said. 'Loyal dependability, for example.'

For a few moments they regarded the Hegemony envoy. The tall Sendrukan was attired in a more martial manner than on previous occasions, his sleeves and leggings resembling ancient metal armour, his headgear looking more like a helmet than a hat. Also, oblivious to his guards or Robert, he was clearly in conversation with his own AI companion, going by the lip movements and infrequent hand gestures. Robert realised that in the absence of reporters and their cams – banned from this event – Kuros felt more able to relax. Even the terminal security cams had been switched off by the express wish of Diakon-Commodore Reskothyr, the Brolturan ambassador to Darien.

The other main condition of Reskothyr's visit was that President Sundstrom not be present, since the Brolturans insisted on dealing initially only with responsible authorities, i.e. Earthsphere. Inevitably Sundstrom was annoyed but he had quickly grasped the diplomatic realities and displayed considerable leadership qualities by the speed with which he reconciled himself to the situation.

'I've met him, you know,' Harry said. 'Kuros's companion.'

Robert stared at him. 'You've met him? You can communicate with Hegemony AIs?'

Harry gave him a droll look. 'It's not such a hard concept to grasp, Robert – avenues for dialogue exist, according to stringent protocols laid down by both governments, and quite recently I chanced to encounter the High Monitor's companion.'

'I'm fascinated – what was he, or it, like?'

'He's an ogre. His persona is a detailed remap of one General Gratach, who was a Principal Abrogator during the Three Revolutions War, an especially gory episode in Hegemony history.'

'I've seen some recordings from that period. Gory doesn't begin to cover it.'

'Well, old Gratach was up to his elbows in it, helped put the first Serrator Hegemon on the throne – both times. If he's Kuros's companion it might be worth going over some of his campaigns, just to get a feel for his strategic style.'

Robert nodded. 'I wish I'd known about this a couple of days ago, Harry.'

'Well, when I say quite recently it was really pretty recently. Like last night.'

Robert was about to reply when his comm beeped softly – it was Gagarin Terminal's security chief, Porteous.

'Mr Ambassador, I am to inform you that the *Purifier*'s shuttlecraft has landed and that the Brolturan delegation will be with you very shortly.'

'Thank you, Mr Porteous. Please extend my sincere gratitude to all your staff for their efficient professionalism today.'

'You're very kind, sir – I shall do so at the earliest opportunity.'

'Incidentally, any news on the comm network?'

'Sorry, sir, we're still restricted to a local service. I understand that engineers are working on the local hub now.'

Harry grinned as Robert put away his comm.

'Relax, it's probably just a blown fuse or melted circuit, given the backward state of the cell network here. I've seen the plans – it's a wonder it works as well as it does.'

Robert shrugged. 'It's my job to worry. How else do I earn the fabulous salary they don't pay me? But never mind – what about Kuros? With a brutal old Hegemony general for a companion, you'd think he would be rather less than even-tempered . . .'

He broke off, seeing figures descending a spiral staircase which lay beyond a tall glass wall at the other end of the passenger lounge. He turned and signalled to his secretary, Omar, who hurried over from the seats with the welcoming gift, a hand-carved chess set. Glancing over, he saw Kuros also receiving a package from one of his assisters.

'Could be awkward if it's another chess set,' said Harry.

'Kuros strikes me as more of a poker player,' Robert said. 'Keeping his cards close to his chest, that sort of thing.'

'What about our new guest?'

'His game of choice? Something with the ornate quality of chess and the brute directness of boxing, maybe.'

The Brolturan procession had reached the foot of the spiral stairs and turned towards the wide open double doors that led into the lounge. Reskothyr's livery ran to blood-reds and silver-grey, as manifested in the attire of the four bodyguards and six officials, while he himself wore perfect black, a collarless, knee-length coat of austere cut: his head was bare and shaven, his hands covered by gleaming black gauntlets. Before them strode two standard-bearers dressed in plain crimson uniforms and grey metal helmets. As Robert made Omar stand a pace behind with the wrapped gift, ready to hand it forward, he realised that there was some kind of music coming from the approaching entourage, a deep vocal drone.

Then the procession came to a halt, except for the standard-bearers. They continued several paces further on then diverged, one carrying his standard over to the Hegemony envoy, the other to the Earthsphere ambassador. As the choral droning grew louder Robert realised that it was coming from a small black cube at the top of the standards. Then with the huge Sendrukan looming over him, Robert bowed to the standard, a long banner of thick, dark blue cloth fringed with jewelled honours and car-rying the duty and family crests of Diakon-Commodore Reskothyr.

That was when the shooting began.

PART THREE

32

KAO CHIH

Drazuma-Ha* had explained about Bryag Station's singular security precautions, the outer perimeter markers, the sensor web enclosing several cubic lightyears of emptiness, and the semi-random route that the station followed through it all. But Kao Chih could not help but feel a gnawing exasperation when they encountered the third marker buoy. According to Tumakri's itinerary notes they had been due to contact a Piraseri at the station almost three days ago.

Seeing the marker-buoy signal on the console display, he shook his head and slumped back in the couch.

'Another one?' he said. 'This is beyond paranoia.'

'If I could shrug,' said Drazuma-Ha*, 'I would. But it's their security and their rules – to my certain knowledge, Bryag has only suffered two attacks since deploying this system a century ago, once by an Earthsphere operative, the other by a Kiskashin blood smuggler with a grudge against the ruling Vusark Enclavol – both times damage was minimal and no one died . . . well, no one of consequence . . .'

Just then the intership channel clicked and a synthvoice spoke in 4Peljan, a Vusarkic trade language that Kao Chih recognised from his dockside work on Agmedra'a. His linguistic enabler translated it perfectly.

'Attention vessel 433 dash 2506 – you are being scanned to ascertain your fitness and trustworthiness with regard to a Bryag Station boarding permit . . . scanning . . . all passengers must remain still for 12 seconds . . . scanning . . . speech pattern scan will commence in 15 seconds . . .'

Which was a word-for-word repetition of the last two encounters, both of which had resulted in being offered course data for a 'stage continuance' or an 'area exit' microjump. Of course, both were essential, since the vast sensor web – and thus Bryag's wanderings – were confined to the fringes of the Omet Deepzone where dense, swirling clouds of dust and things they hid distorted any attempt at hyperspatial computation. Travellers had to rely on Bryag's course data or not bother travelling there at all.

As they waited, Kao Chih gazed out of the viewport at the foggy darkness of deepzone space. Here and there the concentrated light of stellar clusters and the nearest stars managed to pierce the dust veils that glowed muddy orange and purple, distorted whorls of amber, stretched ripples of violet. The Omet Deepzone, as Drazuma-Ha* reminded him, was the source of the great Achorga Swarms which 150 years ago had torn through hundreds of star systems in the vicinity, ravaging and wrecking entire planets, amongst which was the homeworld of Humanity, Earth. That particular Achorga outbreak was not their first and others had occurred since, many of them sweeping into Indroma territory, causing havoc and destruction on a vast scale.

Somewhere out there, he thought, in the dark heart of all that dust and debris, was the world of the Swarm, the Achorga. Without them there would have been no Swarm War, and no desperate, blind launch of the three colonyships. The *Tenebrosa* would never have plunged blindly through hyperspace and arrived at the beautiful world which the first settlers had named Virtue In The Valley, nor would they have suffered those attacks and the sight of their world being mined and scoured around them, the long indenture for those who escaped . . .

'Scan complete. Permit approved.'

Kao Chih sat up straight, gaping then grinning as the marker buoy went on.

'Please state course required – station access or area exit?'

'Station access,' Drazuma-Ha* said swiftly, a neon yellow

microfield extensor flicking out to operate the com panel. 'Polydigital channel open.'

'Fastchaining data . . . fastchain complete. You may now depart.'

'And not before time,' said the mech, who was already merging the new course data into the navigationals. Kao Chih just had time to strap in before the hyperdrive forcewaves cohered and twist-hurl-dropped them back into the first tier of hyperspace.

Another half-hour microjump during which he again went over the notes in Tumakri's documenter, making sense of the Bryag Station contact – a Piraseri vacsuit vendor named Milmil S'Dohk – and how to recognise his suspensor-mobile establishment. After that he spent a further twenty minutes playing halfboard chess against the ship's gaming subsystem until hearing the strap-in alert. Moments later the *Castellan* emerged-fell-spun from hyperspace just a few klicks away from their destination. Drazuma-Ha* powered up the manoeuvring thrusters and soon they were vectoring in on a guidance beacon.

Set against the dust swirl colour-glow of the Omet, Bryag Station was a sight. Coasting along on its never-ending peregrination, it looked to Kao Chih oddly like a colossal bivalve seashell, like a cockle gaping wide open, the central hinge pointing the way ahead. Each half was full of structures, towers, domes, globe clusters, spars, cables, as well as scores if not hundreds of bots, hopcraft and jetsuited creatures darting this way and that. The outer surface of the station's hull halves were dark grey carapaces of heavy plating, shielded ducts, maintenance housings and armoured drive vents, pitted and scored by the Omet's plentiful dust and micrometeorites.

Pairs of docking booms of various sizes fringed the lip of either half, berthing capacities increasing towards the station's stern. The *Castellan*'s pilot system followed the guidance beacon in towards a boom dock on the leading edge with a learned grace. Grapplenets unfurled from the booms, snared then drew the small ship through the glitterglow of an atmosphere shieldfield and into an auto-adjusting cradle. From the viewport Kao Chih could see three levels of walkways running the length of the dock and wide gantries extending tongue-like between the berths.

Excited, Kao Chih made sure he was first at the airlock as it went into equivalence mode and opened fully. Across the gantry was their neighbour, a Makhori organics miner, its hull resembling a glued-together cluster of large, leathery-brown and misshapen ovoids entwined in numerous cables and ribbed pipes. Engrossed in it, he had just stepped through the lock with his left leg when someone collided with him. Reversing out of reflex he caught his heel on the edge of the hatch and fell back inside, thumping into a protruding lower drawer handle. He uttered a strangled cry, assaulted by pain from both foot and shoulderblade.

'Please, please, please, can you help me? . . . please help or they'll . . . they'll take me and . . . and . . .'

Grimacing with the pain, Kao Chih sat up and saw a slender young woman, a human female, cowering inside the doorway. She wore a zip-pocketed canvas jacket over a grubby blue teklabourer onepiece, a little shoulder bag of some transparent material, and a pair of heavy, paint-splashed miledriver boots. Her disarranged hair was a rich brunette and her face, smudged with something oily and stained with tears, was arrestingly beautiful.

'You *are* Human, aren't you?' she said, almost pleading.

The linguistic enabler Tumakri had given him a few days ago was clearly working perfectly – he hadn't even noticed that she was speaking Anglic.

'Yes,' he said carefully. 'I am. Who is it that wishes you harm?'

'They're . . . they're . . . horrible monsters! – they took my friend Telzy and cut her up . . .' She began weeping again and darted along to the cockpit. 'Don't let them take me, please!'

Kao Chih got to his feet and went after her, hearing Drazuma-Ha* say:

'Young woman, you may not stay here. We have come to Bryag on serious business and cannot leave you in our craft alone . . .'

'Why not?' Kao Chih said. 'I'm sure we could lock out the controls and avoid any accidental tampering and leave our guest

with some food and water while we go and find this Milmil
S'Dohk.'

'Of course, Gow-Chee, this is your vessel and your mission – I
merely anticipated that you might wish to keep the ship as secure
as possible. My apologies for . . .'

'Please don't leave me alone,' wailed the girl from beneath the
console where she had wedged herself.

'What's your name?' Kao Chih said, starting to feel harried.

'Co . . . Cora,' she said between sobs. 'They were following me! –
they might come here! Please help me, please please please . . .'

'Okay, okay . . .'

'Are they coming? Are they here? Please, you've got to close the
hatch . . .'

'Wait, just wait,' Kao Chih said, heading for the airlock. 'I'll
take a look . . .'

Quickly he ducked out of the hatch, scanned the walkways in
either direction for any commotion and saw nothing out of the
ordinary. There was a heavy thud from inside followed by a fearful cry, and when he re-entered the cockpit he saw Drazuma-Ha*
lying on the floor, his field nimbus rippling with silver and red distortion patterns. Cora was tearfully watching it from the other
side of the cockpit.

'There's . . . something wrong with your droid,' she said.

'Don't worry,' he said, crouching down beside the dumb-
bell-shaped mech. 'He should recover his systems soon . . .'

Just then he felt her fingers press something against the side of
his neck. He whirled round, even as a cold numbness flooded
through his limbs, and he slumped over to sprawl on the floor.
Out of the corner of his eye he saw Cora, now composed and
grinning, lean over to say, 'And now there's something wrong
with you,' just before he passed out.

When he came round he found he was strapped into the
copilot couch with hands and ankles bound, an ache in his head
and an awful taste in his mouth. The background chorus of shipboard hums and the hexagonal patterns of the viewport shield
told him that they were under way, back in hyperspace. Next to

him, in the pilot's couch, was his captor, watching him with unruffled amusement, her hair now silver-blonde and braided tightly against her scalp. Her clothes, the jacket, onepiece and her boots were all the same and she was still as beautiful as before but Kao Chih knew from something in her eyes that he was in terrible danger.

'Awake, KC? Good. Mouth taste like month-old spew?'

Kao Chih grimaced. 'Somewhat, yes.'

'I'll give you a drink soon – I may even untie your hands. But see these?' She took out a paper strip of white circular patches. 'I took you down with one of these – give me any trouble and I'll slap another one on you. Clear?'

'Who are you? How did we get away from Bryag Station? Where . . .'

'Whoa, too many questions for cargo – okay, I was recording everything you said from the moment I got here, fed it into a digimask then used it to tell Docking Control that news of a death in the family meant I would have to depart immediately.' She made a mock sad face. 'They went for it and here we are, KC, on our way to meet my business associates.'

'What kind of business?'

'Well-paid business,' she said. 'Oh, and I'm Corazon Talavera, and you are my cargo.'

When Kao Chih heard that he suddenly recalled that moment back in Avriqui's hold when he was on his knees before Manuuk and the hooded buyer on the screen behind him. *Is that what this is about?* he wondered. *Is this Manuuk's doing?*

'What did you do to my mech?'

'Used a stasis limpet,' she said. 'Strigida drones have a reputation for being tricksy so I had the limpet configured and it worked perfectly. Two valuable pieces of cargo, all neatly packaged, ready for delivery.'

'Delivery to whom?' he said, desiring yet fearing the answer.

'Hmm, I shouldn't really tell you . . . but what's the harm. To certain revolutionaries of my acquaintance who are always in the market for new recruits.' She laughed. 'Which I suppose makes me their recruiting sergeant!'

Kao Chih swallowed. 'But I'm not trained for fighting – I've never even fired a weapon.'

She smiled and gave him a little pat on the cheek. 'KC, for what they've got in mind for you, that hardly matters.'

Kao Chih looked away, stomach knotted with fear, mouth dry, throat feeling irritated.

'Can I have that drink now? I assure you that I will be no trouble.'

She nodded and a moment later he was sipping from a hot cup of the ship's Roug-style infusion.

'Your name is Chinese,' said Corazon. 'What were you doing out here – scouting for some big Earthsphere *gongsi*?'

Kao Chih thought quickly. 'I'm freelance now – I was on my way to collect articles for a client . . .'

There was a thudding jolt that Kao Chih felt through the solid frame of the couch as well as underfoot. Cora suddenly directed all her attention to the instruments.

'What was that?' he said. 'It sounded like something hitting the ship, but debris drops back into normal space, doesn't it?'

'Shut up,' Cora said, emptying out the contents of her transparent shoulder bag and fitting together some odd-looking objects.

Tense silence followed for some moments before there was a second thud, making Kao Chih jump. Then a hum that he took a few seconds to realise was the sound of the airlock's outer hatch opening. His heart began to race.

'Are we . . . being boarded?' he said, feeling panicky. 'How can we be boarded in hyperspace? That is not possible . . .'

'Shut up,' she said again, pointing a peculiar, skeletal handweapon at him. 'Keep silent or it's narcopatch time! Yes, it's supposed to be impossible but I've heard rumours . . . never thought I'd get to see one though . . .'

By now she was along the side passage, poised near the airlock's inner hatch, weapon at the ready. Seconds ticked away and Kao Chih found that sweat was prickling his neck and trickling down his back . . .

The airlock popped and slammed aside and a grey, bulky figure flew out, arms spread. Cora got off one shot which knocked the attacker sideways, just before a foot came swinging out of the airlock and kicked the odd gun out of her grasp. As it bounced and clattered back into the cockpit, Cora lunged after it.

Kao Chih was trying to make sense of what he was seeing – the first boarder lying still and sprawled at the end of the passage as a second one, garbed in dark blue body-armour and a face-concealing helmet, dived on Cora. Then they were half inside the cockpit, fighting on the floor, Cora with the gun in one hand, her attacker grabbing at it with one pair of hands while a second pair fought to choke her throat . . .

He stared, realising with horror that they had been boarded by an Ezgara commando. He had never encountered one but everyone on the Retributor had heard the rumours about these fearsome, quad-armed mercenaries. It was said that a company of them carried out security tasks aboard the Suneye trading station that orbited Pyre.

So who is this four-armed monster after? – me or her?

Then Kao Chih saw that the Ezgara was gaining the advantage. With his partly untied hands he loosened some of the couch straps, allowing him to move round and start lashing out at the helmeted commando with his bound feet. Yet he was still too far away, only managing to clip its arm. It wasn't even distracted.

But he kept thrashing away in hope that seemed to collapse when the Ezgara managed to wrench the weapon out of Cora's hand. In response she arched her back, heaving her attacker off with unexpected ferocity, pushing his upper body sideways in Kao Chih's direction . . . just as his tied-up feet swung round and connected full-force with the Ezgara's chin. The helmeted head twisted savagely, there was an audible crack and the four-armed commando sprawled motionless on the floor, helmet knocked off by the tremendous impact.

Kao Chih was only wearing deck shoes and his toes were throbbing with pain, yet he let out a whoop that was equal parts relief and exultation. Then his gaze fell upon the Ezgara's head and he saw an exposed ear, nose, side of a mouth, eye and hair that looked very Human.

'Is he dead?' Cora said, scrambling over to the still body. 'Is he . . . yes, he is, you idiot!'

'He looks Human . . .'

'Noticed that,' she said, manically dragging the corpse along towards the still-open airlock hatch. 'And you had to kill him.'

Kao Chih stared in confusion. 'But I thought you wanted him dead.'

'I wanted him unconscious,' she gasped, hauling the commando over the raised edge of the hatch. 'But now that he's dead, a binary liquid explosive is mixing up and down his intestines and will blow this ship apart if I don't get him out in time . . .'

She slammed the airlock shut and hit the cycle-through button. The servos hummed, there was a brief sucking sound of the airlock contents evacuating to hyperspace vacuum. For a second Kao Chih imagined that the body had snagged on the hatch exit and was about to explode and tear open the *Castellan*'s hull. Then he heard Cora sigh and knew that the danger was past, and when he glanced down he saw that her gun was lying a few inches from his left foot.

Without hesitation he picked it up and straightened to see her watching him coolly from the passage. They looked at each other for a moment.

'I don't want to hurt you but I will,' he said.

She shrugged, put her hands in her canvas jacket pockets and leaned against the bulkhead.

'You're in charge,' she said.

'He was Human, the Ezgara,' Kao Chih said. 'Did you know that they were Human?'

'There's always been lots of rumours surrounding those goons,' Cora said. 'But the Hegemony's been known to use genetic material of other races to breed useful servants of one kind or another. The fact that they seem to have done that with Humans, their biggest ally, just stinks of very nasty politics, which I don't want to know anything about.'

'How did they find us in hyperspace? And why?'

Cora smiled. 'Has to be you, not me. You've got the ship, which is easier to track. They probably used a hyperspace leech-probe adapted to carry an operator rather than a shipkiller payload. They went to a lot of trouble just to get at you – I wonder why.'

Kao Chih frowned, worried that his family and the rest of the Human Sept back at the Roug homeworld were at risk. Then he tried to reassure himself by imagining that the Roug would not allow them to be endangered.

'Okay,' he said. 'First, I want you to undo my ankles, then get my mech companion out of the rest bunk and deactivate that stasis device.'

'Hmm, I don't think so,' she said as she moved casually towards him.

Kao Chih pressed the fire stud several times but nothing happened. Cora firmly took the slender weapon from him with one hand while the other came up and thumbed a white patch against his wrist.

'Party's over – time to go bye-byes.'

He tried to speak but it came out as slurred nonsense as Cora and the entire cockpit turned grey and tilted away from him.

33

GREG

'It is terrible, Gregory, absolutely terrible. I have never known such a feeling of . . . of dread,' his mother said on the comm. 'And that horrible murder at Port Gagarin last night – God knows I remember how bad it was before the Winter Coup but it was nothing like this, not at all. At least that was just us fighting among ourselves, but this? – did you see that battleship on the news? . . . The size of it . . .'

'Aye, Mum, I did,' he said. 'So much for all the Hegemony talk of peace and cooperation.'

He was standing in the large stone window in the north face of Giant's Shoulder. Behind him the passage ran straight through the rock to the icy room of pillars, beyond which was the warp-well, as Chel had called it. Chel and Listener Weynl were there now, according to a message he'd got earlier that morning while reassigning the sector surveys. Most of his Uvovo field researchers were involved with this Artificer business, but luckily the Rus and Norj teams had agreed to take up the slack. Vaguely irritated by Chel's message, Greg had been on his way to the winch-lowering spot at the wall – now covered by a gazebo – when he got a call from his brother Ian asking him to call their mother and say something to ease her worries. Once he was down in the passageway he had done so, only to find himself agreeing with her bleak outlook. He had seen a news summary that morning and all of it, from the slaughter at Port Gagarin to the Brolturan troops fortifying the Hegemony embassy, was grim.

'Surely the Sendrukans and the Brolturans and the Earthsphere people won't let this get worse,' Greg said. 'Sanity has to prevail.'

To his surprise, she laughed. '*Only if sanity is backed by heavy weapons, my dear. Do you remember your father's elder brother, Piers?*'

'Uncle Piers? Vaguely – bit of a black sheep, wasn't he?'

'*Yes, you could say that – he was on Ingram's side during the Winter Coup, helping organise support in the trapper towns and further out, but his heavy-handed methods backfired on him and he supposedly met a grisly end away in the north. Anyway, he had a favourite saying – "Screw negotiations, break out the ammo" – which I suspect these Brolturans would identify heavily with.*' She was silent a moment. '*I worry about the three of you so much, because I fear that it will all get much worse before it gets better. Ian is a soldier and Ned is a doctor, so danger will come searching for one of them . . .*'

'Mum, you shouldna worry so much, and especially not about me – all I do is rattle about with my stone carvings and dusty potsherds.' *Aye, and a mysterious, underground chamber built by a vanished race, probably Forerunner.* 'But we'll also be looking out for each other, and Uncle Theo.'

'*Ah, I spoke to him this morning – he said that he was on the trail of those who killed the Brolturan ambassador but he was too late to stop it. He's so angry, at himself too. Oh look, I've talked long enough. I should let you get on with your work . . . oh, I meant to ask if your friend Ms Macreadie is still working at your site.*'

'No, she's away back up to Nivyesta, Mum. She really only was here for that official visit a couple of days ago.'

'*Right, of course. Well, goodbye, dear.*'

After their farewells, Greg put his comm away and headed along the passage, burdened by guilt, knowing he should be in touch with his mother more often, actually making the call rather than leaving it to her or, in this case, Ian.

Perhaps I'm just not a very good son, he thought gloomily as he walked down into the room of pillars.

Chel and Listener Weynl were out on the chamber's patterned floor, at roughly the spot where Greg had lost his boots the day before. Barefooted, they were crouching down in the cold golden light of a lamp sitting on the boundary wall, a short strap anchoring it to a shoulder pack. Warily, Greg approached the gap and sat on the wall, legs kept safely away from the floor patterns.

Chel glanced up and smiled. 'Friend Gregori, good to see you.' He was wearing the headband over his new eyes and seemed more relaxed and rested than last time.

Then Weynl straightened and gave him a measured look.

'May I address you as "Scholar", Mr Cameron?' the Listener said. 'It feels far more appropriate considering all that you have done for the Uvovo, all the clues you have found, culminating in this amazing discovery.'

'I would be honoured to accept the title, Listener,' he said. 'Is there a ceremony involved?'

'Yes – it consists of a day and a half of meditation in a *vodrun*, followed by individual visits to your family and friends to sing the Song of New Leaves. However, there is no *vodrun* within easy travel and the pressure of events allows little enough time for even the most vital of tasks.'

Greg hesitated, not expecting the seriousness in Weynl's words and his demeanour. Even Chel's smile was sombre.

'By events, do you mean this diplomatic row with the Brolturans? Once we catch those murdering maniacs, we'll get back to negotiations and it'll all blow over. And anyway, what bearing does that have on our work here?'

'Do you remember what I told you yesterday about this place, Gregori?' Chel said.

'You said that it was built a hundred millennia ago by a race, no, an alliance of races called the Great Ancients. And I said, well now, that sounds similar to these Forerunners I've been hearing about in the news and on the vee, who were supposedly wiped out in a cataclysmic war about a hundred thousand years ago.' Greg smiled. 'And I said, so what did this big chamber actually do, what was it for, and you said that you'd get Listener Weynl to explain it to me . . . and here we all are. I assume that it has something to do with my dazzling experience yesterday.'

Weynl nodded. 'A defence – the well has a vigilant Sentinel, watching tirelessly, guarding against anything that might be considered a threat.'

'Like my boots?'

'The Sentinel is very wary of unnatural or processed materials,' Weynl said. 'You'll notice that our feet are bare. If you take off your footwear you can join us – it's quite safe.'

Greg held up his hands. 'Once was plenty, thank you. So, what are you doing, and how does it relate to what this place is for?'

Chel looked up from the pattern grooves, which were gleaming where he had touched them, although Greg noticed that the radiance faded when he lifted his fingers away.

'We're trying to rouse the Sentinel,' Chel said. 'Then hopefully speak with it.'

'Speak with it and warn it,' added Weynl. 'The Great Ancients built this place and others like it on a hundred other planets, wells of power to counter the terrible might of the Enemy; numberless in their vast hordes, they sought to smother and strangle all who opposed them, but the wells could reach out into the starry blackness, drag them down and swallow them, sending them down into the darkness below the darkness, the emptiness within the emptiness.'

Greg stared at the older Listener, not knowing what to say, feeling oddly embarrassed, but he knew that he could not dissemble.

'Listener Weynl, I've heard the Saga of the Ancient Roots and I've read the transcript – I'm sorry but it's a legend, a myth. All societies and cultures have stories like this in the bedrock of their prehistory . . .'

But Weynl was smiling at him, not quite in pity, more like tolerant amusement.

'Friend Gregori,' said Chel. 'This is not a matter of faith for the Uvovo – we know it to be true, as true as the War of the Long Night.'

'Chel, you've seen our work . . .'

'Gregori, you saw what happened here yesterday – you were blinded for several minutes by the forces that came up out of the pattern.'

'I'll concede that this is a technological artefact from some vanished civilisation,' he said. 'But there's not a shred of evidence to connect this place to the Uvovo myths.'

'Scholar Cameron,' said Weynl. 'I tell you in all honesty that this chamber is the reason why the Hegemony is so interested in Umara. They know of this place and they want it – its powers would make them invincible.'

It was an amazing statement and lent a growing sense of unreality to an already bizarre situation. But Weynl said it with such steady conviction that Greg took a mental step backwards – could it be true, he wondered. It explained several coincidences, yet for all that it was a tantalising conjecture his ingrained scepticism demanded empirical evidence.

'How may we convince you, friend Gregori?' said Chel.

'Proof,' he said. 'Show me undeniable proof that it's all connected – Segrana, this chamber, the Forerunner Catastrophe, the Uvovo – and I'll . . . well, I'll know better.'

'If we can persuade the Sentinel to speak,' Weynl said, 'would that suffice?'

'That would certainly get my attention, aye.'

Smiling, the Listener looked at Chel, who nodded. As Greg watched, the Uvovo crouched down, examining the incised stone, muttering to each other as they ran fingertips along the lines of the patterns. Silver threads shone in their wake and he noticed that each Uvovo was delineating a cluster of lines, symbols and curves distinct and separate while just a few feet apart. After working on them for a few minutes, first Weynl then Chel rose and took three paces out towards the middle of the floor, crouched down and again scribed out glowing patterns on the stone. Their squatting forms appeared dim and shadowy a few yards from the lamp, but the patterns gleamed like mercury.

Chel stood and came back over to the nearer pair, crouched

and began tracing a line from one pattern cluster to the other, while Weynl did the same at his end. When the links were made, the pattern pairs brightened suddenly then faded – the Uvovo grinned at each other and nodded. Then Weynl bent down and began to scribe a bright thread from his patterns back to Chel's. Just before the end he paused, smiled up at Chel and Greg, then closed the gap.

All four pattern clusters brightened significantly and the wall at the opposite side was now just visible. Like the last time Greg felt a change in the air, which became neither warmer nor cooler, with no change in humidity or odour or even pressure. It was as if abruptly something was present in the chamber, something impassive. . .

TUUL-RAAN-SHAYH

Greg jumped as a massive voice spoke. It came from all around, and while it was not overly loud there was a deep, resonant timbre to it which made the hairs on his arms tingle.

Chel and Weynl looked stunned and uncertain. The Listener started calling out greetings in the Uvovo tongue while Chel whispered suggestions. Greg however felt sure that those three words were not from the Uvovo language.

SHUUL-TANN-RAYH

'Do you know what that means?' Greg said.

The two Uvovo glanced at each other before Weynl spoke.

'I cannot be sure, Scholar Cameron. At first I thought it was an ancient dialect of our tongue, or even a high idiom used by senior Listeners, yet there is no recognisable sense to these . . . sounds . . .'

'But did you notice with the second announcement that the initial consonants shifted?' Greg said, a nasty suspicion forming in his thoughts. 'If it shifts again . . .'

RUUL-SHAAN-TAYH

'Right,' he said. 'I think we should get out of here, actually . . .'

'But why, friend Gregori?' said Chel.

'Remember the tests you and I went through?' he said as he got to his feet. 'Remember what happened to my boots?'

Chel smiled. 'I really don't think that we're in danger, Gregori.'

'How do you know?'

'I have been using my new senses to study the well and what lies beneath it, and I can tell you that the flow of powers is very different from before.'

'Hmm, either you're very trusting,' Greg said, moving in the direction of the entrance, 'or very optimistic.'

SHUUL-RAAN TAYH

'I think that sometimes I am a distrustful optimist,' Chel said, while Listener Weynl continued calling out greetings in a variety of Uvovo dialects.

'Well I'm an orthodox sceptic,' Greg said. 'So I'll be waiting back at the corridor while you see what happens . . .'

Chel grinned and waved and Greg left the chamber. He was near the head of the stairway when the comm in his jacket beeped, alerting him to a message. He took it out, thumbed the keys, saw it was from Catriona and began to read while walking along the entry corridor.

'Hi Greg,' it began. 'I tried calling you but the node hub said you were out of range so I'm sending a comnote instead. Just to let you know that I'm going to try something different in my hunt for the Pathmasters – a Listener I know suggested I spend a few hours in a *vodrun* chamber, contemplating the mysteries of Segrana in the hope that *she* might see fit to let me in on a few Pathmaster secrets. Anyway, by the time you read this I'll probably be in the *vodrun*, especially given the signal lag between here and Darien. I guess you're back down there in that chamber – wish I was there too. Bye.'

The comnote had been sent nearly half an hour ago but had only reached him when he left the chamber and came to the corridor. Suddenly anxious, he began keying for a return call but before he could put it through, that deep, reverberant voice spoke again from below . . .

HORON

Reflexively, Greg turned to the stone wall, clamping his hands over his eyes. For telescoping moments all was dark and silent, no remorseless, hammering light pouring into his optic nerves, turning the world into white fog. Cautiously, he peered from behind his fingers, then lowered his hands – all seemed fine, but just to be sure he hurried back to the stairs, pausing halfway down.

'Chel, are you both okay?' he shouted.

'All is well, Gregori,' came the faint reply. 'No need for concern.'

'Great!' he yelled back, then retraced his steps, waiting till he reached the window, where the body harnesses hung, before making the call to Catriona.

34

CHEL

Listener Weynl had been in the middle of an elaborate greeting delivered in a whispering hinterland accent when that great voice spoke again.

HORON

. . . and simultaneously the four glowing pattern clusters went dark, leaving them in the faintly golden light of the solitary lamp. It cast their shadows in long black paths across the intricately carved surface of the well, making all the incised lines, curves and symbols appear harshly cut, and the stone look like grainy, corroded metal.

They both stood there for a moment then, to Chel's surprise, Weynl began to laugh quietly, his shoulders shaking with mirth. Chel found himself starting to smile for no apparent reason, and was about to ask what had set off this display of merriment when Greg's voice came from far off, probably the main passage.

'Chel, are you both okay?'

'All is well, Greg,' he shouted back. 'No need for concern.'

'Great . . .'

On hearing Greg's distant yelling, however, Weynl went into another bout of hilarity which provoked in Chel a slight but growing irritation.

'Listener, are you well?'

'. . . I'm . . . sorry, good Scholar . . . all this marvellous construction dedicated to preserving the Great Ancients' work and when we awake their Sentinel we cannot understand a word.'

He smiled. 'But a Human shouting from outside we can comprehend quite well . . . my apologies, it seemed overwhelmingly funny . . .'

'Understandable, Listener,' he said, feeling disapproval at Weynl's amusement, then wondering why he would feel that way. *Am I turning into some kind of strict, humourless traditionalist? Perhaps I'm the one in need of a dose of merrymaking!*

Suddenly, Weynl fell silent and turned to face Chel, his eyes wide, mouth open.

'Foolish I've been, yes, and blind!' He stretched out a hand to the well surface. 'The Great Ancients built this place, so might it not be expected that their Sentinel would speak their language?'

'Exactly so,' said a sighing, whispery voice from nearby. 'Disappointing that you took this long to discern it.'

In the air above the golden-glowing lamp hung the tenuous outlines of a vague, hooded figure, its spectral contours formed from minute particles of dust hanging and glittering in the heat rising from slots in the lamp cover.

'Venerable Pathmaster,' Weynl said, bowing. 'Then it is true – the Sentinel speaks only the Great Ancients' tongue.'

'I seem to recall that it was fluent in a great many forms of communication, not all of them spoken. However, I do remember that it could be slightly irascible in temperament. Perhaps I can persuade it to be more forthcoming.' The Pathmaster paused. 'Cheluvahar, I see the changes Segrana has made in you – I expect you were surprised.'

Chel almost smiled, imagining how Gregori would answer such a comment.

'Yes, Pathmaster, surprise was indeed one of the emotions I experienced when I came out of the *vodrun*.'

'Your importance cannot be overstated, newest of Listeners,' the Pathmaster said. 'Segrana has not husked forth one such as yourself since the War of the Long Night when hundreds of Seers were needed to guide the Scholars. There were battles in the high skies, but there were also battles here on the ground against the lesser servants of the Dreamless, metal things that crept, ran, flew and swam and which infested the forests and the plains, the hills and the valleys. They strove to disrupt the defiant unity of the Uvovo but ultimately failed.

'Segrana knows that we need the Seers again but she is weak – the War of the Long Night took something from her that can never be replaced, thus she can only do what she may with the little strength that remains.'

'Venerable one,' Chel said. 'I thought my abilities were similar to those of a Listener, yet you named me a Seer . . .'

'There are aspects to your senses that will make themselves known to you in time. Realise this, too – the path from Scholar to Listener to Pathmaster is in the gift of Segrana, but a Seer cannot become a Pathmaster.'

Chel was intrigued. 'So what *does* a Seer become? What *will* I be?'

'After the upheavals and struggles that lie ahead?' the Pathmaster said. 'Alive, with any luck.' The Pathmaster's form blurred a little. 'Now, please leave me to converse with the well's Sentinel – go with the Human back to the encampment above. I will come to you in a while and relate what has happened.'

The Pathmaster fell silent. Chel stared at the attenuated form, hazed, almost fragmentary outlines quivering in the golden heat-haze of the lamp. Then he glanced at Listener Weynl, who gave a slight shrug and bowed to the Pathmaster. Chel did the same and both Uvovo stepped off the patterned surface of the well and headed round towards the chamber exit.

'Phruson,' Weynl said thoughtfully as they crossed the room of the four pillars.

'Excuse me, Listener?'

'Phrusonemejas was one of the three great Pathmasters who survived the War of the Long Night – in the centuries that followed all three eventually gave up their failing flesh and began their journey to the Eternal. Although the remains of two were discovered where they had lain down for the last time in the embrace of Segrana, Phruson's were never found.'

'Do you believe that *he* is this Phruson?'

Weynl smiled. 'It would be hard to determine, but it is an explanation of sorts, which is better than no explanation at all.'

But if it is wrong, Chel thought, *is a wrong explanation better than none at all?*

35

PATHMASTER

All was silent now in the cold gloom at the rock's heart. The Pathmaster let the outlines of his old physicality, maintained for the younger Uvovos' benefit, drift and blur like the vestiges of a snuffed candle's smoke trail. Before him yawned the great aperture of the ancient warpwell, its inscribed control patterns stretched faint and wispy across those penumbral depths. The Pathmaster's senses could cut through appearances to essences and he knew that the Sentinel of the well was always there, always alert, always listening.

'Greetings,' he said in the long-forgotten language of the Great Ancients. 'I do know that you could have responded in the Uvovo tongue yet you did not. I wonder why.'

I WAS NOT ACCORDED MY DUE RESPECT NOR ADDRESSED CORRECTLY . . . IT HAS BEEN MANY CYCLES OF THIS SUN SINCE ANY OF THE AUXILIARIES HAVE VISITED THIS DORMANT PLACE, APART FROM YOU AND THE WEARER OF THE EXTREMITY COVERINGS.

The Pathmaster smiled to himself, knowing that this was a reference to the Human Scholar Greg's boots. In any case, the Sentinel knew that the War of the Long Night had killed most of the Uvovo on the planet and trapped the rest on Segrana's forest moon, until the arrival of the Humans – it was just being petulant.

'The times of peace are ending,' he said. 'War is almost upon us. You know of the Humans and the interest being shown towards this world?'

I HEAR MUCH AND BELIEVE LITTLE. THAT WHICH IS
KNOWN IS INVARIABLY SHOWN TO BE INCORRECT OR
INCOMPLETE.

'A commendable scepticism, if kept within limits,' the
Pathmaster said. 'This place is now known to our enemies, an
immense empire of the stars called the Hegemony – they are
secretly dominated by their servants, machine-minds whose
power extends to the underdomains of the Real.'

THE DREAMLESS! I HAD THOUGHT THEM DESTROYED
ALONG WITH ALL THEIR INSTRUMENTALITIES.

'This appears to be a distinct genus with no apparent links
with those earlier counterparts,' he said. 'Their need for aggressive
domination is nearly identical, however.'

THE UVOVO MUST BE MADE READY FOR BATTLE –
UMARA'S DEFENCES MUST BE STRENGTHENED.

'Such preparations have begun, but resources are thinly spread
and untried, and Segrana is seriously weakened. I would like to
speak with the Construct, if he still exists, to ask for advice and
aid.'

I CONVERSED WITH THE CONSTRUCT A SHORT TIME
AGO – HE SAID THAT YOU WOULD SOON VISIT ME WITH
THE INTENTION OF CONTACTING HIM.

The Pathmaster felt a quiver of surprise. 'Did he say more?'

HE TOLD ME TO SAY THAT AID WOULD BE RECIPRO-
CAL. HE SAID TO ASK YOU TO PROVIDE HIM WITH AN
ENVOY, PREFERABLY ONE OF THE HUMANS BUT A
UVOVO SCHOLAR WOULD SUFFICE – THIS ENVOY WILL
HELP TO OBTAIN THE AID YOU REQUIRE. THERE WAS
NO FURTHER MESSAGE.

Possibilities flickered through the Pathmaster's mind. Until his
husking, Cheluvahar would have been ideal for such a task, but
now he had a new purpose and the abilities to go with it. It would
have to be another of the Scholars, or . . . or a Human, such as the
scholarly Gregori? It seemed unlikely that he, or indeed any of the
Humans involved in the work of the intellect, would consider an
undertaking like this. Then there was the matter of secrecy.

Keeping the Humans ignorant of the warpwell and its entrance would prevent such knowledge falling into the hands of the Sendrukans and the Hegemony machines, although that might delay them only for a while.

'Did the Construct reveal the nature of the aid that he might provide?' •

HE DID NOT, BUT IT IS CLEAR THAT HE IS EXTENDING HIS CAPACITIES AND AWAKENING SELECTED CADRES OF THE AGGRESSION IN RESPONSE TO SOME THREAT IN THE LOWER DOMAINS OF HYPERSPACE. IF YOU WISH TO SPEAK WITH HIM IN PERSON I CAN TAKE YOU TO HIM.

The Pathmaster almost laughed out loud. 'My incorporeal state makes it impossible for me to undertake such a journey. However, please convey to the Construct my gratitude at his offer – I shall give it the most intense and immediate consideration, and return with a reply tomorrow. In the meantime, if you would excuse my younger companions their earlier lack of courtesy and engage them in dialogue, I am certain you would find them a most appreciative and respectful audience.'

I SHALL DO THIS. DO YOU WISH ANY LIMITS PLACED ON WHAT I MAY SAY TO THEM?

'None, although perhaps you should be vague about some of the warpwell control patterns.'

NOW THAT I AM APPRISED OF YOUR UVOVO COMPANIONS, I SHALL ENSURE THEIR SAFETY.

'Thank you – I am gratified.'

There was no response. The Pathmaster listened carefully in the deepening silence, widened senses soon confirming that the Sentinel's immediate presence had receded.

The Pathmaster thought on what he had learned. The Construct, a near-mythical ally of the Great Ancients, had apparently known or guessed that he would try to make contact: did that imply that the Construct was somehow monitoring events here on Umara? Then he recalled the reporters who kept up a flow of information to their offworld organisations and the arenas of the tiernet beyond, and realised that the Construct had access to more than he could know.

The request for an envoy was strange, however, and curiously lacking in detail, which he would return to tomorrow. Also, the mention of cadres of the Aggression being awoken to deal with an unspecified threat was sufficient to provoke unease. Many centuries ago, when he was young enough to still have a physical form, he had travelled via the warpwell to the Construct's stronghold in the unsettling underdomains of hyperspace, the Garden of the Machines. During his stay he had been taken to a gloomy vastness where the Aggression waited, sleeping, an immense phalanx of war machines: he remembered the inactive hush that hung over the motionless serried rows, columns and files stretching back into shadow, thousands upon thousands, yet knowing that even these great numbers would have been swallowed by the Legion of Avatars.

None of the Aggression had been awoken during the War of the Long Night, but some were now. It was a conundrum which implied much and begged many questions.

Which I intend to have answered tomorrow, he thought as he drifted from the chamber.

36

CATRIONA

The darkness of the *vodrun* was broken by the tiny flame of a luring candle, the kind some Uvovo used to catch certain insects for the wing casings they shed. Catriona lay back against the cushion she had brought for her back, both hands cupping a beaker of turnsprig tea, breathing in its vapour and occasionally sipping as she waited for it to cool. There was no way to get hold of the special sapdrink that the Uvovo used in their rituals, so she had made up a flask of turnsprig for its relaxing, de-stressing properties, which turned out to be invaluable.

And so here she was, following the mystic utterances of the spectral Pathmaster whom she might or might not have seen. In fact, the stress of the situation derived not from the Pathmaster's promptings but from the possibility of being discovered. True, this *vodrun* was part of a high-canopy town which was empty due to the steady migration down to Darien, but travellers and traders, humans and Listeners still tramped along the nearby branchways. It was not impossible that someone might chance to pass by and see that foliage had been cleared away from the *vodrun* . . .

Catriona smiled, shook her head, and took a mouthful of her tea, which had lost some of its heat. Eyes closed, she could feel the warmth spread through her, calming, relaxing. She sipped again, cleared her throat and, with a yawn, settled further back into her cushion's comfort. Suddenly it was easy to keep her eyes closed, to breathe deeper, to feel that simultaneous heaviness of limbs and lightness of thoughts that floated free to pursue the whims of unfathomable intent.

The first definite thread of her dream was the thing she was holding in her hands: a datapad, a tech-functions model with a battered alloy casing and worn keys. She turned it over, examining it, recognising it as the one she had used during her early Enhanced years. Deliberately she looked up and found she was standing in the small, cramped room she had occupied at Zhilinsky House. There was the bed, the desk, the bookshelf, the always-closed window shutters, yet everything was pale, colourless and grainy. She was also aware that she was dreaming, conscious that she was still in the *vodrun* while also standing there in the doorway, staring along an empty corridor. Out the corner of her eye she caught sight of herself in a square, wooden-framed mirror – dark hair tied in a bun, grey nondescript uniform, a face that looked on edge and showed her to be about twelve or thirteen.

Catriona walked, datatpad in hand, shoeheels rapping loudly on wooden floors. Zhilinsky House seemed deserted and she smiled as an idea occurred to her. *It's my dream, so let's go and take a look at the director's office, see what my file really says!* She took the main stairwell to the second floor and was halfway along the south gallery overlooking the senior dining room when a door opened in the north gallery on the opposite wall and Julia Bryce stepped into view. Amid the monochrome surroundings, the soft greys and inky blacks, Julia was a knot of rich colour, the pale pink of her skin, the dark mahogany of her hair, the sky-blue dress uniform, the shiny brown shoes. The moment she saw Catriona, her eyes widened and she rushed to the railing.

'Catriona! – I need to speak to you . . .'

But Catriona didn't wait to listen and dashed for the door at the gallery's end. Then it was up the fire stairs to the next floor and quickly along to the opening that led into the annexe. As she fled she noticed other students beginning to emerge, peering out from behind cupboards or sitting in corners or ducking back into doorways as she passed.

'Join us, Catriona! Join me!'

She gasped. She was up on the balcony in the minor gym and Julia was down in the centre of the court, gazing up.

'I need you, Catriona!'

She ran.

Out the annexe side door, down the garden, past the brolly-berry trees and back into the main building. A windowed corridor led past the junior canteen where a few others sat singly here and there, their colouring as grey-shaded as the environment and the food on their plates. Then a boy hurried down a stairway in the centre of the canteen, and came over to the window where Catriona stood on the other side. Like Julia he was in full colour – red hair, blue shirt and shorts, and a grin that she knew, although he had never been at Zhilinsky, simply because he was a normal. She placed him at perhaps fifteen, but it was definitely Greg.

'This is my dream,' she said. 'Why are you and Julia here? I'm aware that I'm dreaming so I should be able to guide it where I like . . .'

'That would be true,' said the young Greg. 'If this was a dream. Cat, you've got to speak with her.'

'What, with the Julia in my head? Aye, as if I'm going waste my time.'

Greg smiled. 'She's not in your head, Catriona – you're in hers.'

Suddenly fearful, she stepped back and continued along the corridor which she remembered led to the east lobby, but once through the door she found herself in one of the lecturers' offices, a small wood-panelled room with a cluttered desk, a wall of filing cabinets, a small window up high . . .

The door clicked shut behind her and she whirled to see Julia standing before it.

'We're all in terrible danger,' Julia said. 'Two of their servants arrived last night but I have lost them, somewhere within my abundance . . .'

'This is all very un-Julia-like of you,' Catriona said sharply. 'But then you did put me through the help-remorseful-Julia-redeem-herself playlet a few times, I seem to recall. Not this time, though.'

'I cannot see them, and who can tell what they are planning?' She stretched out her hands. 'Please, Catriona, I have been blind for so long – join with me and be my eyes. You are special, so different from the People of the Leaves, and so rare, even among your own kind . . .'

A chill went through her, the cold realisation that this truly was no dream, nor was this in any sense Julia.

She's not in your head, you're in hers.

An unreasoning terror welled up in her, wiping away the room and the pleading Julia – and suddenly she was wide-eyed and awake, fumbling the *vodrun*'s door open, tumbling out to sprawl on damp mats, gasping for breath.

Was that Segrana? she thought. *What did it mean by 'join'?* Then she remembered something else – 'Two of their servants arrived last night . . .'

She shivered in the fading light. Nivyesta's orbit would soon be carrying this part of Segrana into night-time but for now some sunlight filtered down from above, striking gleams and glitters from the raindrops that had fallen while Catriona had been in the *vodrun*. And she thought about how it was dark and shadowy down on the forest floor, and found herself imagining soft-footed intruders skulking through the undergrowth, weapons in hand and malice in their eyes.

Still seated on the high, narrow platform, she hugged her knees and tried to think.

37

THEO

To get to Sundstrom's villa, Theo had to go with three security guards through the adjacent property's grounds to avoid the dozen or more reporters camped outside the villa's main gate. It was overcast and unseasonably mild this early in the morning, with the promise of more rain to follow last night's succession of showers.

It had been raining steadily by the time Theo and Donny Barbour and the others had reached the Port Gagarin terminal, only to find it sealed off, jumpy local police and DVC soldiers covering every exit, while all flights had been grounded. They soon found out why, which contributed to Donny's ill humour, itself sharpened by news that the DVC squad assigned to Kuros had been disarmed on the say-so of the Earthsphere ambassador and were being interrogated by Brolturan officials and officers. Nothing Barbour could say was enough to get him through the cordon – the comm system hubs might have been out but the order had apparently come through on one of the old landlines, express instructions from the deputy-president to allow the Brolturans to conduct an investigation unhindered.

Theo had been astonished to hear this and only a little more surprised at Barbour's cold and impassive response.

'The port is theirs,' he had said in low, clipped tones. 'No point in staying here – we should get back to Hammergard.'

He had then turned and strode off back to the spinnercar, followed by Theo, Rory and Janssen. Pausing by the car, Donny tried his comm once more, got nothing, weighed it in his hand for a second before hurling it with sudden violence against a nearby brick wall, where it shattered into pieces. Saying not a word, he calmly opened the driverside door and got in. Janssen merely arched his eyebrows for a moment, but Rory had grinned and nodded. 'Ah wiz worried there,' he had said as they climbed in and Donny drove off.

Once back in his apartment, Theo had made for the lounge, thinking to check a news channel on the vee, but then exhaustion started dragging at him with a hundred hands and he had found himself swaying on the spot.

I may be a fit fifty-year-old, he thought. *But I'm still fifty*.

Almost without thinking, he had staggered into his bedroom, where he fell asleep fully clothed.

Until he was roused by an insistent hammering on his door about three hours later. It turned out to be a government courier with a handwritten note from Sundstrom pleading with him to come to the villa for a 'crucial advisory meeting'. Bleary-eyed, he had stared at the note and the courier, then sighed.

'Right . . . okay . . .' He jabbed a thumb over his shoulder at the kitchen. 'Coffee's in the brown jar, beakers are on the board – I'll be having a shower.'

'It's all right, sir. I don't want anything to drink.'

'It's for me, laddie – my need is greater than yours!'

Now he was following one of the security guards through a cleverly masked gap in the hedge then along the side of the villa to a porticoed side entrance. Theo wondered what would be on the agenda as he was shown into a dim passage then up a flight of stairs. It wouldn't be hard to guess, going by the radio reports he'd heard during the drive here. It seemed that the Brolturans had determined that the Darien soldier who assassinated their ambassador had died in a grenade explosion only moments after the murder. Some of the DVC soldiers present had been released into the Office of Guidance's custody while a few others were still being questioned at the terminal. In addition, the Brolturans were fortifying the Hegemony embassy on the basis that the next ambassador would be based there. The perimeter wall had been heightened overnight in several places and various mysterious devices were being installed at intervals around it. Local residents also reported the comings and goings of small transport craft; it was not known if the Brolturans had obtained permission to over-fly Hammergard. Staff at Port Gagarin air traffic centre were said to be tight-lipped about the matter.

I'll bet, he thought as he was escorted up to the second floor. *No one wants to look a fool, especially when it might make your boss look one too.*

Moments later he was ushered into Sundstrom's office, exchanging nods of greeting with Pyatkov and Donny Barbour, who were already seated at a small, ornamental table occupied with heavy-bottomed glasses and a bottle of Urquhart. A wood-cabinet vee was murmuring in the corner, showing *Macroscope*, the 24-hour news channel.

'So, has the Hegemony taken over yet?' Theo said, pouring himself a drink. 'Has Horst finally caved in?'

Pyatkov's smile was thin. 'Not really. The Brolturans are push-ing the "we are the victims" line and Starstream are giving them plenty of coverage, along with Kuros and Horst, who are play-ing the compassionate sympathisers' role for all it's worth. The *Purifier*'s commander, this Father-Admiral Dyrosha, even gave an interview – on Starstream, of course – expressing his outrage that peaceful Brolturans were slaughtered by, quote "savage settlers", unquote.'

Theo stared at the intelligence chief. 'He really said that? – "savages" plural?'

'The father-admiral was quite concise in his meaning,' Pyatkov said.

'Savages,' Theo echoed. '*Ja*, and we know who brought them here! Why don't we go get some of those reporters in here and tell them who really has been behind all of this?'

Donny laughed, but Pyatkov was unimpressed.

'Because we have no proof that the Hegemony has sent Human-like agents among us . . .'

'Apart from Mr Olgren and his singular tattoos,' cut in Donny.

'Who's now lying in the morgue,' Pyatkov said.

'Aye, in pieces.'

Theo glanced from one to the other. 'What's this about Olgren? How did he die?'

'Dismembered,' Donny said with a savage relish as he refilled his own glass. 'Seems they tattoos weren't just for decoration . . .'

'My officers had brought him to the OG detention centre and were taking him to Processing when he collapsed on the floor, yelling and gasping,' Pyatkov said. 'Those tattoos were starting to constrict his neck, arms and ankles.' He grimaced. 'Suddenly there was blood everywhere and his escort were looking at a dismembered corpse.'

'My God,' murmured Theo.

'Tells ye one thing, though,' said Donny, looking straight at Theo. 'These people mean business.'

'That may be so,' said Pyatkov. 'But certain events seem to have no rationale, like the rifle left behind after the Giant's Shoulder shooting. They must have known that someone would have traced the scope to High Lochiel and eventually to that rooming house.' He shrugged. 'Was that what it was all about, setting up an elaborate trap? I cannot be sure but my instinct says no.'

Donny hunched forward. 'There's no doubt that all those attacks were supposed to exhaust the OG's resources and divert its attention. Add to that the really convenient comm hub blackout earlier, along with the security cameras in the Bay 2 lounge having their plug pulled just before the Brolturans arrived.'

'Horst requested that,' Pyatkov said sourly. 'Prompted by Kuros, no doubt.'

Theo snorted. 'So there's no record of what happened.'

'Apart from the one apparently made by one of Reskothyr's retinue,' Donny said. 'Which they've promised to release to the news media later today – oh, and to us, in the spirit of cooperation.'

'So where's Sundstrom?' Theo said.

'Trying to cope with a political crisis,' said Pyatkov. 'Storlusson, the master-provost of Trond, has told him that if he cannot restore order and persuade the Brolturans to withdraw their troops, the Northern towns may reform their League as a temporary security measure. Also, he is facing a vote of no confidence when the Assembly meets in emergency session in a few hours. The Consolidation Alliance are pressing him hard while certain elements of his Civil Coalition are badly shaken.'

'Could he lose?' said Theo.

'It's on a knife-edge – there's a handful of Legators who are certain to switch to the Consies if he can't stabilise the situation. If that happens and he then lost the vote, he would most likely step down in favour of Jardine. Holding an election under these circumstances is unthinkable . . .'

'Jardine,' Donny said with undisguised distaste. 'That windbag . . .'

Just then, the other door opened and Sundstrom entered in his wheelchair. He looked as if he had aged in the hours since Theo last laid eyes on him, yet a kind of dogged tenacity still burned in those embattled features.

'Gentlemen,' he said, steering his chair over to their table. 'Thank you for coming at such short notice, and my apologies for shortening your sleep.'

'Sleep?' Donny said to Theo. 'What's that again?'

Theo grinned while Pyatkov kept a stone face.

'I've read Vitaly's report on Olgren, which I assume the both of you are privy to,' the president went on. 'What none of you know is that you're here to witness the conference call I am about to take with Ambassador Horst and the High Monitor Kuros. Depending on the outcome, we may have to adjust our short-term tactics.' He leaned forward to pour himself a generous measure of Urquhart and knocked it back in a single gulp. He exhaled pleasurably through gritted teeth and set down the glass. 'My doctor will be most displeased. And now, gentlemen, as my father used to say – it's showtime!'

He propelled his chair over to his desk, fingered its control pad and picked up his comm while turning to face the pair of view screens that had come to life above the low bookshelves at his back.

'My friends, could you move that way, out of the screens' two-way sensors?' Then into the comm he said, 'Is that it? Good, then you may put them through.'

A moment later the screens blinked, one after another, and presented the faces of Robert Horst and the Sendrukan Utavess Kuros. Sombre greetings were exchanged, although Theo thought that Horst seemed the least grave of all three.

'Ambassador, High Monitor – I am sure we are all aware of the despicable act that took place at Port Gagarin last night, and may I reiterate my sorrow and condolences for the victims and their families.' He paused a moment. 'As you might realise, the events of the last few days have had repercussions for my government, especially me. I can tell you that the death of Ambassador Reskothyr has brought things to a head . . .' And he laid out the details as Theo and Donny had been told a short time before.

'A tricky situation, Mr President,' said Horst. 'If I may be blunt, if you were to stand down, would Mr Jardine be able to form a stable government? Is that what this call is about?'

'No, sir – Deputy-President Jardine would be unable to maintain the Civil Coalition, thereby losing his majority in the Assembly and facing his own vote of no confidence, which he would inevitably lose. While this is happening, Trond and her neighbouring towns would, I've been assured, re-establish the Northern League, triggering protests, arrests, expulsions and general civil unrest. Any attempt to run a general election amidst such upheaval would be almost impossible, and the full consequences would of course be broadcast for all to see.'

Both the offworld diplomats were now soberly attentive.

'What this call is about is my persuading you, High Monitor, to withdraw the Brolturan troops, and you, Ambassador, to provide Darien Colony with, say, a company of Earthsphere marines to assist my government in maintaining security and stability, as well as deepening ties with the homeworld. What do you say?'

Theo exchanged astonished looks with Donny and Pyatkov.

A hard gleam had entered the Sendrukan's gaze. 'This is scarcely diplomatic language, Mr President. Father-Admiral Dyrosha would be far less understanding than I.'

Sundstrom smiled and nodded, all evidence of his earlier fatigue seemingly vanished. 'High Monitor, I agree that my recommendation lacks the diplomatic niceties, but I am sure that the honourable father-admiral will understand it if you tell him clearly. If you as yet remain unconvinced by my determination, then let me acquaint you with some recent developments. Last night my security service detained a man known to be a member of the Free Darien Faction, a man whose body was decorated with bands of tattoos. Soon after he was taken into custody, these tattoos turned into some kind of implants which then constricted, dismembering him in minutes, so that he quickly died of blood loss and shock. Analysts tell me that these skin implants can only have come from offworld, which forces me to conclude that Darien's internal affairs are being interfered with.'

'Are you accusing the Hegemony of responsibility for this incident, for which you have presented no proof?' said Kuros.

Sundstrom shrugged. 'To be honest, High Monitor, I don't know what to think. However, in a few minutes I shall be holding a press conference, and if I have to announce my resignation I shall tell the reporters why in detail, including a coroner's report on the FDF agent's body and additional testimony from my analysts.'

'Sir, this behaviour is outrageous!' said Horst.

'Indeed it is, Ambassador, but when you have a weak hand you have to make every card count.'

Theo grinned, enjoying this display of old-fashioned political rough-house.

'You have a talent for negotiating, Mr President,' said Kuros. 'Let me first put your mind at rest regarding Hegemony involvement in any insurgent activities here on this world – we Sendrukans do not engage in illegal activities that would threaten stability. That said, I do feel that, on reflection, your proposals have considerable merit. I am certain that Father-Admiral

Dyrosha can be persuaded to draw down the Brolturan peace-keepers. I am likewise sure that Ambassador Horst can easily see how continued stability can only be beneficial to all concerned.'

For a moment Horst's face stared blankly from the screen. Then he blinked and life came back into his features.

'Well, eh . . . if my Sendrukan colleague is willing to per-suade . . . persuade the Brolturan commander to scale back the troop presence, that puts matters in a different light. In the inter-ests of cooperation and stability my remit would allow me to offer the kind of military assistance previously mentioned.'

'Your words are most gratifying, gentlemen,' Sundstrom said. 'You have no objection to my announcing the main points of our accord to the waiting reporters?'

Assurances were given by Kuros and Horst, along with strained smiles, then farewells and the confrontation was over. Theo joined the others in an impromptu round of applause to which Sundstrom gave a sardonic smile and bow of the head.

'That Horst,' Theo said. 'The man's a hand-puppet . . .'

'Aye, he just caved at the end, there,' Donny said. 'I thought he had more spine than that.'

'Well, we've no way of knowing what advice he was getting from his AI implant,' said Pyatkov. 'Or how much control it has over him.'

'Then there's no point in speculating,' Sundstrom said. 'In any case, this is a temporary reprieve until Kuros decides on his next move. Pyatkov, Barbour – could you wait downstairs in the conference room? I just need to have a private word with the Major.'

The two men nodded, rose and left. Theo returned his empty glass to the ornamental table and went to sit on the edge of Sundstrom's desk, silent, waiting.

'The assets, Theo,' the president said at last. 'You've got to move them again.'

'Again?' His heart sank. 'Why? And where to this time?'

'Away from the towns and settlements. The Uvovo know of many a hiding place in the East Hills – I'll put you in touch with one of the Listeners. And why? – well . . . time is against us, Theo, even though my steamroller-ambush ploy bought us a little more.'

'What happens when time runs out?'

'Occupation, maybe internment for the hard cases, with some kind of justification proclaimed loudly along with declarations of their generous and enlightened intentions towards us. I've seen several reports documenting the Hegemony's "generosity", worlds where every city is reduced to rubble, or where the eco-sphere has been deliberately poisoned, or where tailored micro-organisms were released to expunge a staple crop or a vital food animal. Which is what would have been in store for us had we not been a colonial offshoot from their principal ally.' His eyes were full of a ferocious resolve. 'There has to be resistance, Theo, a guerrilla struggle against the Hegemony that will deny them the right to be here.'

'Surely public opinion back on Earth wouldn't stand for Hegemony occupation?'

Sundstrom smiled. 'Public opinion depends on public percep-tion, and across Earthsphere, especially amongst Human sectors, that perception is shaped by a news media consensus led by . . .' He raised a hand towards Theo, expecting him to finish the sen-tence.

'Starstream,' Theo said sourly. 'What have they been saying about us?'

'That we're a bunch of ignorant, hairy-arsed throwbacks. Oh, there have been any number of pretty documentaries about Darien's flora and fauna, but otherwise the general slant is that we're a parochial, clannish rabble.'

Theo remembered hearing about his nephew Greg's run-in with one offworld reporter. 'Is Lee Shan with Starstream?'

The president chuckled. 'He's a piece of work, that one – I saw one of his reports on Darien politics that went out on a culture and politics channel which isn't fed through to Darien, surprise, surprise. It was cleverly done, subtle and nuanced, managing to be both accurate and completely misleading.'

'You mentioned seeing reports on the Hegemony and now this

one by Lee Shan.' Theo paused. 'Have these come from the Imisil, Mr President? If so, can they be trusted?'

'More than that, Theo, we had one of the OG's newest surveillance terminals, modelled on one from the *Hyperion*, patched into a data nexus on board the Imisil ship in orbit. We were able to access the tiernet itself, that vast interstellar network; my God, Theo, there are oceans upon oceans of information out there, the knowledge and culture of thousands of worlds, and that is how I came to find out the foul history of the Sendrukan Hegemony. And can they be trusted? – I have no doubt that they have an agenda, but equally I am sure that our interests and theirs coincide.'

'Good, so we can expect a shipment of advanced weapons very soon, yes?'

Sundstrom gave a half-smile. 'Soon, perhaps. That Brolturan ship has seeded Darien's orbital shell with probes and detects that track everything in the planet's vicinity out to beyond Nivyesta's orbit. If something happens to disrupt and divert attention, the Imisil ambassador will seize the opportunity.' He thumbed keys on his desk and the wall screens behind him went dead. 'Now, time you went about your business and I tended to mine.'

'Donny Barbour and Mr Pyatkov?' Theo said. 'Why the separate meeting for them?'

'Actually all three of you are to be briefed separately and privately by me,' Sundstrom said. 'Thus the capture of one cannot jeopardise the others.'

'A practical approach, Mr President, if a bit pessimistic,' Theo said. 'What if they capture you?'

Sundstrom laughed. 'Trust me, no one is going to capture me alive.'

The two men shook hands.

'Now go,' Sundstrom said. 'Good luck and good hunting.'

'You too, sir.'

And as he left the study, Theo was struck by a foreboding that this would the last time he would see the man alive.

38

ROBERT

After the conference call with Sundstrom and Kuros, he sat there at his desk, feeling an odd exhaustion of the mind. His thoughts were like worms slowly pushing themselves through a dark, muddy cave, taking an inordinate amount of time to reach the other side.

'Robert, how do you feel?'

How *did* he feel? He blinked, breathed in deep and turned to see Harry in a patterned grey lounge suit, seated at the end of the desk with concern in his features.

'You look tired, Robert,' he said. 'It's my fault, I pushed you too hard on the deployment matter . . .'

'Harry, Harry . . . you were only doing your job while I was just, well . . . wrong-footed by Kuros. Just wasn't expecting it. And Sundstrom – I was so furious at that gambit of his, and yet I can admire the way he played it, played *us*.'

'Politics is politics, whether it's on a backwater planet or at the Great Assembly on Earth.'

Robert nodded and sighed, gazing out of the first-floor window. The road was quiet, deserted, lit by a teardrop-shaped lightpod hanging from a question-mark lamp-post, and as he watched it began to rain, bright flecks falling within the radiant halo, dark spots speckling the ground.

'So what will you do about the marines?' asked Harry.

'Order Captain Velazquez to deploy them down here,' Robert said, turning to beckon Rosa over. 'After a quick game of chess.'

From a desk drawer he took a folding board and a box of pieces. 'Black or white, my dear?'

'I'll play . . . black,' Rosa said, and as she sat on an opaque high stool, sixteen translucent black pieces appeared on her side of the board while he patiently set out the white side. This was a joy, he thought, playing a relaxing game of chess with his daughter after a hard day's work. But look at the lateness of the hour! – he would have to see her safely tucked up in bed once this game was over and not a moment later.

Robert played first, then move followed move, white pieces and dark, opaque grey pieces staking out territory, threatening assaults, shoring up defences.

'Robert, Lieutenant Heng is still in the building,' Harry said. 'I'm sure he would know the state of readiness of the *Heracles*'s marine complement. Might be prudent to know this.'

'Hmm, you think so?' He pondered a clash of pawns on the board before him. 'Very well, have him come up.'

It seemed only a moment or two before there was a knock at the door. He called out and a young man in an Earthsphere olive-and-brown uniform entered, approached and gave a stiffly formal bow.

'Mr Ambassador,' he said.

'Ah, Lieutenant – my daughter, Rosa.'

A moment's hesitation, then the officer bowed again. 'Miss Horst.'

'A pleasure to meet you, Lieutenant,' Rosa said.

Horst nodded. 'It is very good of you to answer my summons at this hour. I shall shortly be issuing a request to Captain Velazquez for a company of marines to be redeployed down here, but in advance I should like to know what their state of readiness is.'

'I understand, sir. The *Heracles* carries two full marine companies, complete with lowalt fliers, ATVs and med-mobiles. Either or both companies can be scrambled and ready for deployment in under an hour, and a full company can be translocated to the planet's surface in about six hours, if all three shuttles are available.'

'Excellent, Lieutenant, and how would you describe morale at the moment?'

'Very good, sir. Everyone's keen to do whatever they can for the Darien colony.'

'Of course, which is only natural and which we are already achieving!' Rosa moved a bishop across the board and placed it on a square occupied by one of Robert's knights, then poked her tongue out at him. He smiled and removed the knight. 'So, Lieutenant, when do you return to your ship?'

'The cutter is supposed to leave Port Gagarin at 9 a.m., sir, but we have been advised to be there by 7.30 at the latest so I thought it advisable to start out as soon as possible.'

'Then I shall detain you no longer, Lieutenant. Be on your way, and pass on my warmest regards to your captain.'

'I shall, sir.' He bowed to Robert and again to Rosa, who smiled sunnily.

As the young officer left, Robert returned to the game and after a moment's scrutiny saw that he was a few moves away from a complete defeat.

'Another game, Daddy?' said Rosa.

'Young lady, if your mother were here she would be outraged to see you still up at this hour. . .well, perhaps one more. . .'

'Robert, you were going to issue that order to Captain Velazquez,' said Harry, who was standing at the other window. He was smiling in that narrow-eyed, head-tilted manner that signalled disapproval.

'Oh, but I'm busy with Rosa, Harry – would you patch into my messenger and send a note for me? You know the basic details.'

Harry was still and silent for a second, then he said:

'That's it done, Robert. Do you want to retire to bed now? Since you decided not to cancel tomorrow's engagements, I would recommend catching up on some sleep.'

Robert frowned as he rearranged the pieces. Why was Harry being such a nuisance? Couldn't he understand that a father had obligations to his daughter?

'Really, Harry, I've just agreed to play another game. I'm sure that I'll be able to meet the day's . . . the day's . . .' He paused, feeling a little dizzy and seized by an irresistible need to yawn. The room dimmed and seemed to grow pale as if a grey veil fell upon everything.

Were those his hands that were carefully putting away the chess board and pieces? Was that his voice that said 'Goodnight' to Rosa and his fingers that switched off the intersim? His legs that carried him upstairs to change into his sleepwear, his bed into which he slipped? Grey hands, grey veil, grey voice, just like that moment during the conference call when his mind seemed to stumble but something in him carried on. Grey voice, grey hands, grey veil, his mind like a grey cave across which he crawled, sinking at last into grey sleep.

39

CATRIONA

Morning sunshine speared down through Segrana's upper canopy as Catriona guided her *trictra* along the branchways, heading back to that deserted village, back to the *vodrun*. The cold air was laced with damp odours of leaf and flower stirred and swirled by the heat of the sun. Rising wafts of warm air carried insects higher to unfurled, nectar-beaded blooms, new luscious leaves, overnight fungi and tiny water pools held in the crooks of tree limbs. Seeing this, Catriona knew that every insect had its predator, whether it was a bigger insect or a bird or some small, furry pseudo-mammal. Or even a plant, luring with sweet smells and bright colours, trapping the quarry with snapping leafy jaws or sticky, smothering leaves or steep-sided drowning sacs. There was even a tree which enticed insects into a crack in its bark which closed convulsively when an intruder tickled certain fibres within.

And as Catriona travelled, always her thoughts circled back to last night's strange dream in the *vodrun*, to the warning about invaders gliding through Segrana's shadows. Predators stalking prey . . .

After that unsettling and curtailed vigil, she had returned to the Human enclave and a restless night of shallow, inconstant sleep. Rising early, she had tried to focus on her backlog of research work, sorting and cataloguing samples, but her mind wandered back to that dream, her childhood at Zhilinsky House, Julia . . .

Yes . . . Julia. Then she had taken out her comm, pondering the fact that there were people she could contact and favours she could call in. In the event, however, the reliable details she gathered provided only a sketchy picture. For about a year the government's Special Designs Division had been maintaining a research post at Pelagios Base, the old oceanography platform ten miles up the east coast. Then several weeks ago a dozen or more additional personnel had arrived but were taken off Pilipoint in a large launch which headed for Pelagios Base. There was never any mention of Pelagios and its staff in any public announcement or memo or directive from Pilipoint's administrators, but the community's rumour-mongers took it for granted that the new people had been Enhanced. Another handful had arrived in the week following, of whom Yurevich was the most recent, all of them with that aura of lofty intellect. And then last night, while she was getting ready for her vigil, some eighteen to twenty of them had left on a special shuttle flight back to Darien, including Julia Bryce – a friend on the embarkation staff had noticed the name on a passenger manifest before it was removed.

Beyond that, there was little of substance. Nothing on Enhanced identities, and not a clue as to the nature of the research taking place at Pelagios. And certainly no explanation for the evacuation, although it wasn't impossible that the Brolturan ambassador's murder had played a part.

It was a setback, this near-perfect information blackout, but not that much of a surprise. The Enhanced and their minders were secrecy obsessives and habitually paid great attention to details, ensuring the integrity of that blackout. Catriona realised that it would take more digging to find out anything useful, more time than she had today.

Instead, she had made a few more calls to fellow researchers in other enclaves dotted around the continent-spanning forest of Segrana. She was looking for any reports of odd happenings or sightings and found herself being offered innumerable reports on the curious and often inexplicably purposeful behaviour of the forest's flora and fauna. But when she made it clear that she was after more mysterious, unattributable incidents documented in the last couple of days, she was left with a handful of accounts:

a set of bipedal prints leading up the sandy beach of Emmerson Bay on the north coast; four perfectly circular holes drilled into the 200-foot-wide bole of one of the five pillar trees that made up the outer northeast buttress cluster; the cut-up carcasses of five crab-analog *ogmi* found beside one of the eastern underlakes, every incision smooth and precise; the sighting, on the night before last, of a large, dark bird swooping low over the dense heartlands of the Great Central Uplands before lazily flapping away eastwards.

Catriona brought the spiderlike *trictra* to a halt on a natural shelf of interwoven branches and tied it up within easy reach of edible foliage. Then it was a brief downward climb to the small platform where the *vodrun* waited. She thought about those singular reports and what they might mean if yesterday's dream-vision was right, the possibility that offworld intruders were lurking somewhere, watching, planning . . .

In her left hand she held a plastic tub on a cloth strap – inside were some biscuits, nuts, a small flask of turnsprig tea and a luring candle fixed in a seashell holder. Then with her right hand she took out her comm and called Greg, imagining the signal flying up to one of Nivyesta's comsats and then tight-beamed to another orbiting Darien, then down to the local hub node. After several moments a breathless Greg answered.

'Yes? . . . hello? . . .'

'Greg, it's Cat,' she said.

'Well, hi . . . did you get my message? Did you . . . did you go through with it?'

'I did, and I didn't.'

At the other end Greg chuckled quietly. 'I detect a wee note of indecision there.'

'Not so much indecision as blind terror,' and she gave him a terse summary of that unnerving vision, including her encounters with the younger Greg and Julia, which also entailed a brief explanation of Julia's role in her past.

'Uh huh, so you were dreaming about me, eh? I'm honoured.'

She smiled and shook her head. 'No, Greg, there wasn't any

dreaming involved. I'm certain, now, that I was talking to Segrana and that she was using images from my memory . . .'

'I must admit that sounds pretty wild,' Greg said. 'But I had my own share of surprises last night . . .'

She listened as he told of the huge chamber and the pattern-inscribed floor that Chel and Listener Weynl called a well, and how the Uvovo had awakened some kind of automatic defence (which had apparently obliterated his boots during the first expedition).

'Your boots?' she said, laughing.

'Aye, took exception to certain aspects of their manufacture, it seems.'

'I think I'd rather be down there than up here,' she said.

'Ach, we are where we are.'

'Homespun philosophy, Mr Cameron?'

'Straight from my mother's knee to your ears, Miss Macreadie. So – are you going to try again?'

How did he guess? she wondered.

'I think . . . I think that I have to,' she said. 'It's the precautionary principle – *if* Segrana has been talking to me and *if* there are hostile intruders around, then it's wise to be prepared. In the vision she said I could help – now I'm going to find out how.' She laughed drily. 'And if it turns out to be a wild goose chase, I'll be on the next shuttle back to Darien to join the resistance!'

'It's not quite got to that stage,' Greg said. 'In fact, Sundstrom has somehow got the Brolturans to drastically reduce their troop presence at the Hegemony embassy, and persuaded the Earth people to send some marines down from the *Heracles*.'

'Some good news at last – maybe I'll not have to leave Nivyesta after all.'

'I don't know – we could need a Uvovo expert on call when we get round to studying those underground chambers!'

Their shared laughter was easy and warm, but brief.

'Sorry, Greg, but I'll have to go and get this over with while I'm still convinced.'

'Aye – I have to go, too. Promise me you'll call the moment it's done.'

'I will, I promise. Goodbye, Greg.'

'Bye, Cat.'

Call ended, she tucked the comm away, breathed in deep. . .then swung round, tugged open the *vodrun*'s circular door and ducked inside. Moments later, the candle was lit, the tea was poured and the door wedged shut with a wad of leaves.

Right, she thought as she sipped the hot, herby infusion. *I'm here so let's get to work.*

40

CHEL

The zeplin pilot was a Finn named Varstrand who kept up a stream of gossip and rumour as they flew out from Hammergard, heading southwest across Loch Morwen towards the Savrenki Mountains, a southerly offshoot of the Kentigerns. Varstrand's craft, the *Har*, was essentially a true dirigible with a gondola slung beneath a gas-filled envelope shaped like a fat cigar. The gondola's twin-prop motors could run on either alcofuel or battery power and solar cells glued to the outer skin provided an emergency backup.

Chel was seated behind Varstrand, in a wire-and-wicker couch that seemed as rickety as the construction of the creaky gondola. He was wrapped up well against the chill and the icy draughts that slipped through cracks in the hide-and-canvas hull. The noise of the engines added to the discomfort but this was his first visit to some of the Burrows to which he had dispatched the teams of Artificer Uvovo over a day ago. He would sit it out – there were worse things to be endured.

A two-hour journey under grey skies took the rest of the morning and, following the map scribed by Uvovo scouts, brought the *Har* to a bushy ridge in the foothills of the Savrenkis. Chel clambered down a rope ladder to be greeted by Tremenogir, the Scholar in charge. Then together they grabbed the mooring lines let down by Varstrand and tied the zeplin between a couple of sturdy trees.

'How long you be, Listener, sir?' Varstrand yelled down.

'Not very long, Pilot Varstrand,' Chel called back. 'Maybe half an hour.'

'Good! – I have book . . .'

Chel grinned and waved then looked round at Tremenogir.

'Let us begin, Scholar Trem.'

'It is a great relief to have you here, Listener,' the Scholar said as he led the way down the other side of the ridge then up into a steep-sided gully. 'Our findings are astonishing.'

Chel thought about correcting the Scholar's use of the Listener title, but since he was not entirely sure of the difference himself he decided to leave it until he was.

Rocks, bushes and age-twisted trees cluttered the gully, carved from the hillside over time by a stream which splashed and gurgled down a notched rock face at the gully's end, where four immense boulders were piled to one side. A stair of flat rocks led up onto the second-highest boulder and a dark gap where the third boulder leaned against the gully's undergrowth-swathed slope. Chel followed Scholar Trem into the gap, which became a low, narrow, curving passage, clearly hewn out of the tilted boulder.

The passage widened, wood-shored sides showing many signs of recent repair. *Ulby* roots and tethered *ineka* beetles shed enough blue-green light to see by as they continued further into the hillside.

'So, Scholar Trem, your findings,' Chel said as they walked. 'What makes them so astonishing?'

'The expected followed by the unexpected, Listener,' said Trem as they entered a small, shadowy room where three young Uvovo sat at a table, scribbling by the light of a candle. Hastily, they stood and bowed.

'My assistants, Jont, Flir and Kamm – it was Jont who literally stumbled upon our discovery. But first, the roothouse.'

The Scholar showed Chel through a doorway leading off to the right and down stone steps into cold depths. The carapace glows of a few *ineka* beetles speckled the inky darkness. Soon they came to a low, arched entrance where Trem paused, took a shell candle from a waist pouch, lit it with a Human match then continued. The air was dry and musty, like the faint emanation of an ancient decay. The passage was about a dozen paces long and showed many holes and gouges where plant growth had eaten into the stone, most of which had been cleared away except for one thick, rough root which had burst through then snaked along to the other end. And this was the very least of it, as Chel saw when they emerged into the roothouse and Trem raised his lamp.

Twisting, coiling and knotted, rootworks filled the high, circular chamber before them. Through the tangle Chel saw vague suggestions of carved images on the walls, all buried beneath encrusting filth, except for a massive, fallen shard of rock which stood at an angle across the chamber, webbed with roots. He could also tell that several other passages led outwards from the round room – ten or twelve all told.

'I had Flir and Kamm clear away some of the roots from the bottom,' Trem said. 'There's enough room to crawl over to one of the laving galleries.' He crouched down and pointed. 'That one.'

As they crept under the mass of entwined roots, occasionally snagging clothing on twiggy protrusions, Chel went over in his thoughts what Listener Weynl told him about the Burrows. They had been built well before the War of the Long Night as a means of bringing greater focus to the powers of Segrana-that-was, the Segrana whose embrace had once enclosed both planet and moon. Each Burrow, Weynl said, was the meeting point of hundreds of roots, thousands in the larger ones. With the use of nutrients and other balms provided by some of Segrana's most specialised plants, the growth and extent of the forests and jungles could be managed; likewise, Segrana's harsher powers could be channelled and intensified and, if necessary, put forth in anger. This was the Artificer Uvovo's urgent task, to find out if anything useful remained, at least in those Burrows in the immediate vicinity.

A few paces into the laving gallery they were able to stand up and survey what it had come to. From the grey, dust-choked remnants of ducts and wall channels, Chel could see how the roots entered from above and curved down through one or more stone basins, where they were fed specific fluids. Now a snarl of uncontrolled roots filled most of the gallery, grey roots, grey dust, grey webs.

'This has been abandoned for a very long time,' Chel said. 'And it provokes in me a certain sadness rather than astonishment.'

Trem nodded. 'As it did in me until Jont found something more interesting in another gallery.'

A few moments later, in the root-framed entrance to that gallery, they were standing over a rectangular hole in the floor.

'While clearing away dead roots and dried-out debris, Jont tripped and fell to his knees right here.' Trem squatted down beside the opening. 'Some rotted framework gave way beneath and he would have plunged into darkness had he not caught the edge and climbed back out.'

A narrow set of steps was visible by the meagre light of Trem's shell lamp as he led the way down. Chel immediately smelled something different from the roothouse – a hint of damp, a woody odour, then the pungency of mould. Something was growing down here.

The steps ended in a small alcove just off a corridor, but the way was blocked by a large pipe. *No, not a pipe*, he realised as Trem went over to it with his lamp, but a huge root. Like the Scholar he ducked under and saw a high-walled passageway not unlike the galleries above, except that here the roots were big and alive, some bulbous, some bifurcated, some sprouting pale rootlets that spread across the walls, over faint, labyrinthine traces of previous rootlet webs. And there in the quiet, underground dimness he heard the sound of droplets falling from high onto roots or plinking into small puddles. He was tempted to tug aside the blindfold and open some of his new eyes to all this, but his perceptions were still unpredictable so perhaps another time would be better.

'Yes, Scholar Trem,' he said. 'Astonishing is the right word.'

'Thousands of years,' Trem said. 'Thousands of winters and summers and still it functions – if we'd brought more lamps you would see the *fenfinil* roots where they come down through the ceiling then push through the cutting collars that feed the sap down to the spouts – true, there is mould and moss everywhere, but never so much that they staunch the flow.'

'Well, Scholar Trem, if the roothouse is above us, then what is this place?'

Trem smiled and gave a little shake of the head. 'I can only make a tentative guess, Listener, that it may be some kind of master regulating system which we've stumbled upon by chance. But if the other Burrows also have something similar, we may have to think again on its purpose.'

If only I had known of this before leaving Hammergard, Chel thought. But Weynl and the other Listeners had banned the use of radios to ensure that positions were not given away by signals easily detected by those in orbit above. Thus all communication was by courier, either on foot or by dirigible. Which was what Chel would have to do now, take Varstrand's zeplin back to Waonwir rather than continue on to the next Burrow. The other Listeners would have to be informed and then enough messengers would have to be dispatched to discover if there were similar galleries elsewhere.

He explained this to Trem, who nodded.

'A sensible approach, Listener,' he said. 'Would you like any or all of my assistants to return with you and give what help they can?'

'No, Scholar Trem – I need you all working hard here. If your Burrow turns out to be the only one with a gallery like this, we will need to know all there is to know as quickly as possible.'

'I shall get them back to work at once,' Trem said.

'Good. Now I shall return to my zeplin and be off back to Waonwir. We must use the Humans' flying craft for swift travel while we are still able to do so.'

'Are the Dreamless close to assuming control?' Trem said as he led the way back up to the roothouse.

'Not yet,' Chel said. 'An emissary from the Brolturans was assassinated soon after landing at Port Gagarin, which the

Brolturans then used as an excuse to start sending troops down from their huge warship, supposedly as protection for the Hegemony envoy. Yet the Humans' president somehow persuaded them to withdraw while obtaining Human soldiers from the Earth ship.'

'This Human Sundstrom has great cunning,' Trem said, helping Chel up out of the floor opening. 'I have heard some Listeners speak highly of him.'

'Cunning may not be enough,' Chel said. 'I have been told that the Dreamless are as numerous amongst the Brolturans as they are across the Hegemony. I fear that it is only a matter of "when" not "if" they reach out to take what they want.'

'I fear you may be right,' Trem said. 'Ah, now we have made several sketches of the roothouse and the galleries since our arrival. Would you care to take them with you?'

'That would be most useful, Scholar, my thanks.' By now they had reached the narrow passage leading to the exit. 'Shall I send you more paper with the next courier?'

'That and more blankets,' Trem said, as they emerged blinking into the daylight. 'There are centuries of cold in those underground stones and it feels as if I am getting to know it all too well!'

41

THEO

Grimy, sweaty, streaked with dirt and grease, weary and aching, Theo, Rory and the Firmanov brothers staggered into the Bell and Cat, an old-fashioned dockside pub. Outside, sunlight gleamed on cobbles wetted by a brief shower; inside, it was as murky and smoky as it would be by the evening, though perhaps not quite as crowded. As Alexei Firmanov went to buy the first round, the others found an empty barrel-table and some stools, and moments later Theo was slaking his thirst with a hefty swallow of Golden Lever ale.

As it went down he sighed.

'I swear it's never tasted that good before.'

'Aye, Major, right enough.' Rory had already downed half his pint. 'Reckon we deserve this, and more.'

Nikolai nodded vigorously then lit up a pipe, grinning hugely around the stem as he reminded them how Maclean had his lunch eaten by a forest *baro* then later lost his cap to an inquisitive *ginibo* monkey. Theo laughed along, feeling that mixture of camaraderie and pride reserved for officers who shared a deep level of trust with those under their command. Yet the Diehards were not a formal military unit, which made their trust – and therefore his responsibility – far more daunting.

Ja, we've done well today, he thought. We managed to move all the weapon caches again and stow them in some very out-of-the-way places, just like Sundstrom wanted. But what happens now that the Brolturan troops have left? – will we have Earthsphere marines patrolling the streets with the DVC?

He had heard news coverage and comment on the radio while travelling around all morning and most of the afternoon. The consensus of opinion among both the studio quackers and the public phoning in seemed to be optimistic, yet he thought he detected a fearful edge to it, even a reluctance to contemplate any kind of worst-case scenario. Then again, the radio studios could well have been screening out any phone-ins that voiced such opinions.

Well, whatever the outcome, at least this moment was a restful one spent in the company of good friends. The rest of the Diehards were returning borrowed trucks and vans or heading back to homes and families in Port Gagarin or High Lochiel or easterly towns like Laika and Rannoch. And as he gazed around the pub, a grey-whiskered man in a ragged-brimmed hat seated at the counter caught his eye and they exchanged a friendly nod. Poacher Zargov, that was, a reprobate scoundrel who was just one among several other old-time drinking buddies that Theo recognised. Nick the Spring, a sly and patient trapper who once drank Viktor Ingram under the table; Swedish Harry, a tracker from Trond; Stamper Nadine with her bandolier of fine metal-working tools; and here, heading towards their table with a balding Earther in tow, was Father Josef Terekhov, a respected trawler captain.

'Theo, *gospodin*,' Terekhov said, his glare enhanced by a magnificently bushy beard and moustache.

'Josef,' he said. 'You're looking well. Would you care to join us?'

'A kind offer, my friend, but I am just here to give this fellow into your custody, and so prevent him from annoying the other patrons with questions about you!'

Terekhov's glare softened and a slight change in his beard indicated that he might be smiling beneath it.

'My thanks, Josef,' said Theo. '*Spaseeba balshoye*! I shall take charge of our guest and deal with his questions.'

Terekhov nodded, raised a hand and went back to his table. Theo turned to the newcomer, a young man with receding hair and a nervous manner.

'Pull up a seat and join us, Mr . . .'

'Oh, ah . . . Macrae, Barney Macrae.'

As Theo made brief introductions round the table, along with handshakes, Rory frowned at the offworlder.

'Macrae's a good Scots surname, but ye speak like a . . . whit are they, again? . . . American, that's it.'

Macrae nodded. 'Yes, sir, that is correct. One of my distant ancestors emigrated from Scotland, back in the 1800s, I believe. My own branch of the family is from Boston in the ESA . . .'

Rory was about to come back with another question but Theo cut in.

'So, Barney, Father Terekhov said you were asking after me, so what can I do for you?'

'Okay, first you should know that I'm a freelance reporter working under a Starstream licence. . .'

Rory snorted. 'That lot.'

Macrae shrugged. 'I know what you're thinking, but a Starstream licence was the only way to clinch an assignment I was offered by a prestigious edumedia netcorp . . .'

'Barney,' said Theo. 'May I ask if you have an AI implant?'

Macrae gave a wary smile. 'No, Mr Karlsson – I do have a gofer-AI back in Boston but his codecore was done up by a local indie . . .' Meeting blank stares, he went on. 'Anyways, the answer is definitely no – my thoughts are my own.'

'Well, then, Barney, what's your point?'

Macrae paused, chewed his bottom lip then leaned forward and murmured, 'I've got a recording of the Brolturan ambassador's assassination.'

There was a stunned silence around the table while the normal hubbub of the Bell and Cat went on about them.

'Do you have it with you?' Theo said, suddenly tense.

Macrae nodded, patting the chest of his jacket.

'And how did you acquire it?'

'I had got to know one of the soldiers guarding the Hegemony envoy – before her unit was assigned to him, I should say – and persuaded her to carry an eyebead on her uniform.'

'Whit's that, then?' said Rory.

'A tiny videocatcher, smaller than the head of a pin,' Macrae said. 'I had her put it on her jacket shoulder. But after the attack the Brolturans detained your soldiers for questioning and she was among the last to be released. I only got it back this morning, and when I saw what was on it I knew I couldn't just sit on it.' He began to reach into his jacket. 'I can play it for you if you like . . .'

Theo shook his head and put a restraining hand on Macrae's elbow, then glanced at Nikolai.

'Ask at the bar for a key for one of the pool rooms upstairs.'

Five minutes later they were gathered round a pool table, watching Barney fiddling with a small, notebook-sized device in featureless beige plastic which was leaning against one of the cushions. Then the device's flat surface flickered suddenly into soundless video, a view of the back of a DVC soldier marching along a wide corridor adorned with glowing adverts, somewhere in Port Gagarin, Theo guessed. The procession came to the lounge and as the Darien soldiers formed a rank behind the towering Hegemony Sendrukans, the viewpoint showed the Earthsphere ambassador and his assistants, the high walls and viewing gallery, and the glass-fronted stairwell from which travellers usually emerged. Then, as the picture swung back towards the High Monitor Kuros and his delegation, Macrae froze the recording with a black, penlike remote.

'See here?' He pointed to a cluster of dark blue figures, each standing with upper arms folded and lower arms hanging straight. 'Those are Kuros's personal bodyguards, four Ezgara commandos. That's what Lenya saw when she entered the lounge, four of them.'

The recording resumed and events played out just as the news reports described. The Brolturans emerged from a pair of wide-open double doors that led out of the lounge. Two standard-bearers led the way, followed by four bodyguards and six officials, flanking Reskothyr himself, attired in a black knee-length coat of austere cut: his head was bare and shaven, his hands covered by gleaming black gauntlets. The procession came to a halt, except for the standard-bearers, who continued forward, one carrying his standard over to the Hegemony envoy, the other to the Earthsphere ambassador. Just as they bowed to the standards set before them, unseen attackers opened fire.

A volley struck members of Reskothyr's retinue to the left. Cries went up and Reskothyr's own guards hustled him off to the right. The Earthsphere ambassador and his aide retreated towards the seats as the Ezgara and the DVC soldiers began firing back at a dark glass-fronted gallery overlooking the lounge. But one DVC soldier had broken from the rest and was heading round to the right, against the wall, aiming his weapon not at the gallery but at Reskothyr. The assassin opened up, bursts of automatic fire cutting down Reskothyr and the Earthsphere ambassador's aide, as well as one of the standard-bearers, who charged with his banner pole held like a spear. He went down in a welter of blood, one hand blown off. Then the gunman shot dead a few others before dashing towards a door in the corner, but one of the Ezgara hurled a grenade after him. There was an explosion and the already jerky viewpoint swung wildly, showing glimpses of other DVC soldiers diving for cover. Then the picture spun back round in a blur, showing clouds of dust and smoke hanging over a scene of devastation, a wrecked wall, pieces of debris lying over a wide area, and the still bodies of casualties. Members of Reskothyr's retinue stumbled through a grey haze, some shouting into communicators, some weeping, all in silence. Then Macrae froze it again.

'Okay, my friends – how many Ezgara commandos do you see?'

The moment he asked the question, Theo understood. And sure enough, when the distinctive blue-armoured figures were counted there were five.

'The fifth Ezgara didn't enter by the concourse doors,' Macrae said. 'There were no Ezgara in Reskothyr's entourage and that side door led into a storeroom with no other exit.'

'You're saying that the assassin dived through that doorway, survived the grenade, then changed into an Ezgara uniform?' Theo said.

'Sure, why not?' Macrae said. 'They could have rigged up a temporary blast shield for the shooter to get behind, along with one of those combat armour rigs that they wear. And yeah, I know they say that they recovered a DVC soldier's body from the wrecked room – so what? Kuros's people had effectively sealed off that lounge more than an hour before Reskothyr's shuttle touched down.'

'But why?' said Nikolai. 'It makes not any sense to me. They pulled their troops out overnight so what was it all for?'

Macrae gave a gleeful little laugh. 'The Hegemony is fond of big, simple dramas – they love to put on a show, and that's what this was. I think I heard that they're going to release their own recording of the attack, is that right?'

'Seems so,' said Theo. 'The question is, why bring this to me?'

'Because your president has to see it!' Macrae said. 'I watched that press conference last night and I could tell right away that he'd played Horst and Kuros perfectly. Some guy, that Sundstrom.'

Theo smiled. 'Indeed he is, Barney, but he's not the one who has to see this first.'

'Then who . . . you can't mean . . .'

'Yah, Horst! – get him on our side and we might stand a chance of seeing that big battleship of theirs sailing away.'

'I don't know,' said Macrae. 'Horst . . . he's pretty staid, pro-Hegemony, pro-alliance to the core.'

'That's why we have to tell him that we have copies of this in Sundstrom's hands and circulating round the colony.' Theo grinned. 'So if he wants to avoid a public outcry and diplomatic scandal all rolled into one and then seized on by every reporter within reach, he'll have to get Kuros and his pet Brolturans to send their peace-boat home.'

'Sounds like a flare,' Macrae said. 'But it might fly. So how do we get this to Horst as soon as possible?'

'It so happens that I know exactly where he is, right now,' Theo said. 'At the Falls of Gangradur on the southern shore of Loch Morwen . . . well, at the Mistwatcher Guesthouse that overlooks the Falls. I know that he's been touring a local fishery and the Veiled Caves and that he's to spend the night there, which presents our opportunity. In my role as presidential adviser I can get in to see him and show him Barney's recording, safe in the knowledge that Kuros is twenty-odd miles away.'

'How do we get there, chief?' said Rory. 'Take the coast road?'

'We'll charter a zeplin,' Theo said. 'Fly straight across the loch and be there in an hour. What say you, Barney?'

'It's a great story, Mr Karlsson,' Macrae said, slipping the display unit back inside his jacket. 'I'll follow it all the way.'

Theo looked at the others and they all nodded.

'Just as long as my brother stops for a quick shower,' Alexei said, jabbing his thumb at Nikolai, who sniffed at him then wafted his hand before his face.

'I'm not the only one . . .'

'Depending on how long we have to wait when we get to Northeast Fields, we can clean up a bit,' Theo said.

Everyone stood and drank a toast to luck and the hunt before leaving. It was a ten-minute walk to Northeast Fields, after which half an hour was spent looking over the available charters in the hires room. Given a bid marker by the hires allocator, they went looking for berth 18 and found a curious, block-shaped zeplin beneath which sat its captain, a stocky Dansk named Gunnar. Business was transacted and ten minutes later they were climbing into the sky over Hammergard, heading south. As the roofs and streets of the city dwindled and slid away, Theo suddenly remembered that he had meant to contact his sister and arrange to go round and see her. 'Damn . . .' he muttered, resolving to call her when he got back, Greg too. It felt as if the whole crisis was cutting him off from his family, especially the ones he really cared about. Yet he knew that part of him was enjoying it, or at least enjoying the intensity of tactical judgement, the threat and the risk.

Just as long as it doesn't put the ones I love in danger, he thought. *That's what matters.*

A little over an hour later, the zeplin was descending to a

stubby mooring platform, engines running down as its fore and aft cables were hauled in by motorised winches. Theo paid Gunnar his fee and a retainer and they all disembarked, waving to the winchmen as they did so. The mooring platform was situated in a field bordered by bushes and a stand of whistler trees to the west, their odd-shaped leaves causing an eerie piping chorus in the faint breeze. These were the grounds of Mistwatcher, and as they followed a gravel path through the trees, the guesthouse came into view, a conglomeration of circular buildings raised stiltlike up on pillars. This area was about 50 feet above sea level and not far from the shore of Loch Morwen. But it was dwarfed by the gigantic spur of stone that jutted from a towering slope that led up to a high valley so immense it was almost a plateau set against the grey outlines of massive peaks. The spur tapered and sloped downward to a blunt prow from which water fell in a white column 800 feet through clouds of mist to a boiling cauldron which spilled down a brief series of rapids to Loch Morwen.

The constant roar of Gangradur Falls grew louder as they approached the guesthouse. Mistwatcher's entrance and admin building was identical to the circular residence modules, only larger and situated at ground level. At the front desk, Theo presented his government ID and asked for directions to Ambassador Horst's suite. When permission was granted, he took Barney and Rory with him, telling the Firmanovs to wait in the lobby. A spiral staircase took them up to a large, covered platform from which walkways radiated to the modules. A green-uniformed attendant seated in a booth pointed out which one led to Horst's residence and minutes later they were standing before its front doors. Theo presented his ID to the visitor sensor and the doors slid apart to admit them to a small, tiled, oval hallway. A slender young man in a dark brown, high-necked suit came forward to greet them.

'Major Karlsson,' he said in a surprisingly deep voice. 'My name is Carolian – I am Ambassador Horst's secretary. The desk said that you wish to speak with the ambassador on an urgent matter.'

'That is so,' Theo said. 'It concerns the events at Port Gagarin yesterday.'

'I see.' The man Carolian took out a small grey pad which he studied for a moment. 'Our sensors say none of you is armed but one of you is carrying a digitact of some kind.'

Theo put his hand on Barney's shoulder.

'My associate, Mr Macrae, has a device containing new information about the attack which the president is keen for the ambassador to see.'

'Very well, I will see if he is ready to receive you.'

Carolian left by a side door then reappeared moment later to beckon them in. Theo led the way and was ushered through to a well-lit kitchen/breakfast bar where the ambassador sat at the table, playing chess with a ghost.

'It's a hologram,' Macrae murmured. 'Supposed to be his dead daughter.'

The translucent figure was of an attractive young woman, early twenties perhaps, with long brown hair, wearing a many-coloured flowery shift over patterned blue trousers. Theo knew the background from news reports and Pyatkov's briefings, which said that Horst's daughter had died a couple of years ago, yet the sight made the hairs on his neck prickle.

'Good day, gentlemen,' Horst said, rising to face Theo. He was wearing a calf-length house-gown of some olive green material, fastened loosely with a yellow sash. 'Major Karlsson, yes? The president's adviser . . .'

The two men shook hands. Horst's grip was firm, dry and steady, yet Theo got the impression that there was some concealed frailty to the man.

'My thanks for agreeing to see us, Ambassador. These are my colleagues, Mr Macrae and Mr McGrain.'

More handshakes. Rory had blinked on hearing his surname and his wide-eyed stare flicked between the ambassador and the opaque hologram. *Come on, Rory,* Theo thought. *Don't let me down, lad.*

'And this is my daughter, Rosa.'

The hologram girl smiled at the three men, who gave brief, nervous bows. Theo glanced at Macrae, but he seemed unruffled so he tried to appear unconcerned himself.

'So, Major,' Horst went on. 'You have more information regarding yesterday's horrific events, information so urgent that it could not wait till my return to Hammergard.'

'Exactly so, sir – we have a recording of what happened.'

A look of unease passed across Horst's face. 'A recording? Is it from the Brolturans?'

Theo shook his head. 'Another source, Ambassador. May we show it to you?'

For a moment the ambassador was silent, his eyes glancing sideways for a moment before he gave a sigh and nodded.

'Very well, Major, do you require any equipment?'

Theo turned to Barney, who already had his displayer in hand. 'Um, would it be okay to use the ambassador's vee screen?'

'Certainly,' said Horst.

Macrae produced a coil of tendril-thin cable, hooked up the displayer to the vee screen, fingered the screen controls, and moments later was ready. But Horst made him wait while he spoke with the hologram.

'I'm sorry, Rosa, dear, but I have some work to attend to. Can we continue our game later?'

'Of course, Daddy – I'll remember where all the pieces are.'

As fondnesses were murmured, Theo exchanged baffled looks with Barney and Rory. Then the hologram winked out and Horst slipped a flat, octagonal unit into the pocket of his house-gown, put away the chess set and turned back to the others.

'Proceed.'

Barney pointed the black rod remote and the recording played out silently as before. Barney paused it as before, pointing out the number of Ezgara commandos before and after the assassination. When it was over, Horst sat there looking stunned, even a little shrunken in the baggy folds of his gown. But then he stared off to one side, frowning, lips moving, shaking his head slightly as if having a private conversation . . .

His AI implant, Theo realised. *That's what he's listening to . . .*

'Ambassador . . .' he began.

'Ah, yes, Major, yes . . .' Horst put finger and thumb to the bridge of his nose, eyes squeezing shut as if in discomfort. 'How confident are you of this information's provenance?'

'My colleague, Mr Macrae, is the one who obtained it,' and at Theo's prompting Barney told the ambassador how and why the recording had come to be made. By the end, Horst's expression was weary but grim.

'This is very serious,' he said. 'I would be the first to admit that the Hegemony has in the past employed questionable methods in pursuit of its interests, but to do *this*, and to their closest ally?'

'It looks like a justification for a military intervention,' Theo said. 'But if anything they've stayed their hand.'

'Darien Colony would be in upheaval now if Sundstrom had not manoeuvred us into looking bad to the media.' Horst stared down at his hands. 'If I'd known about this before I would have deployed the marines sooner and in greater numbers.'

'Can this be done now, Ambassador?' said Theo.

'Yes – I have a subspace comset in my luggage . . .' He paused and looked to one side. 'It's all right, Harry, I know what I'm doing.' As he got to his feet his attention came back to Theo. 'It's through in the stowaway – I'll just . . .'

The door flew open and the secretary Carolian rushed in, clearly upset.

'The news channel, Ambassador! It's about you . . .'

Quickly, Horst reached for the vee screen's keypad control and thumbed it on. Up came the Darienwave news channel with one of the regular presenters, Oxana Rugov, and with Horst's face in an upper corner box.

'. . . just to recap on our breaking story, the Brolturan delegation has issued a statement accusing Earthsphere Ambassador Robert Horst of planning and ordering the terrorist attack at Port Gagarin yesterday, resulting in the murder of Diakon-Commodore Reskothyr and four others on his staff. The statement goes on to claim possession of damning evidence, eyewitness accounts and a testament given by a DVC soldier who Ambassador Horst allegedly tried to recruit.

'Shortly after the release of this statement, a communication was received by all media outlets from Father-Admiral Dyrosha, commander of the Brolturan vessel *Purifier*. It says, quite simply, that a Decree of Arrest has been issued, naming the ambassador and demanding that he present himself to airborne units which have been sent forth to detain him . . .'

Horst staggered back from the screen and dropped into a chair at the table, looking pale.

'It's preposterous . . . outrageous! . . . I had nothing to do with . . .'

'Ambassador, you've got to get to safety,' Theo said. 'Can you call the *Heracles* and get them to send a shuttle to pick you up?'

'Yes, I can,' Horst said, getting to his feet. 'I'll get my comset . . .'

'I'm sorry, Ambassador,' said Carolian. 'But you and your visitors will have to remain here until the arrest detachments arrive.'

The slender secretary, poised and composed, was holding a handgun with a strange oval barrel sporting curved flanges along its sides.

'Carolian,' said Horst. 'What the hell are you doing?'

'Following orders, sir, which means that you will have to follow mine.'

Everyone froze. Theo cursed the demented bad luck of Horst having a Hegemony agent on his staff, even though it was only to be expected . . . and then he realised that Rory wasn't in the room. Now he glimpsed movement along the short passage that connected the kitchen with an adjacent room, probably a formal dining room. Carolian hadn't noticed Rory's absence yet, so a diversion was called for.

'You're walking a razor's edge, you know,' Theo said. 'The captain of the *Heracles* won't permit this and Sundstrom will put all military units on high alert.'

'Don't be ridiculous, Major,' Carolian said. 'The *Purifier* outguns the *Heracles* by roughly ten-to-one – if Captain Velazquez tries to interfere he will be fired upon and you'll be dredging pieces of his ship out of the ocean for months to come. As for any forces under Sundstrom's command . . . well, they don't present any kind of serious threat, I can assure you . . .'

And that was when Rory's left hand slammed Carolian's head into the wall while his right shoved the secretary's gun hand up at the ceiling as it went off. A bright barb of energy punched through the plaster and woodwork, causing a spray of dust and splinters, while Rory tore the weapon from Carolian's fingers and then punched him to the ground. Leaning over the moaning, bloody-nosed secretary, he said, 'How's that fur a serious threat, matey?'

'Well done, Rory!' said Theo. 'How . . .'

'Ah was over at that window in the corner when he came in, and I could see a gun in his back pocket and I thinks, well now, whit's this all about, so when he pulled it out I hopped up and through that wee delivery hatch smart as ye like. Came round the other side and nabbed him.'

'Excellent. You and Barney get him tied up. Ambassador, let's dig out this comset of yours.'

But when it was unearthed from a large, wheeled trunk the device turned out to be dead. The power cells registered full but nothing was being activated.

'But I used it this morning to speak with Velazquez,' Horst said.

'Your secretary must have disabled it soon after,' Theo said. 'Advance preparation – he couldn't have known that we were coming or what we had to show you.'

'So he knew that Kuros was planning my arrest,' Horst said slowly, then glanced sideways. 'They are? Thank you, Harry . . . Major, it's not safe here. Those Brolturan fliers will soon be here.'

'Then we need transport,' Theo said, trying not to think about the AI as he took out his comm and called Alexei, who was still down at the entrance with his brother.

'Yes, Major?'

'Alexei – Brolturan troops are on their way here to arrest the ambassador so I need you and Nikolai to head back to the zeplin and tell Gunnar to cast off, fly over and pick us up from one of the residencies – we'll be the ones on the roof, waving.'

'We're on our way, Major.'

Theo closed his comm and turned to Horst. 'Time to go, Ambassador.'

From the viewing balcony outside, a stairway curved up to a railed-in sunbathing deck on the roof. The view of the thundering Gangradur Falls in the rosy late afternoon light was breathtaking but all eyes were fixed in the other direction, towards the guest-house's mooring grove and the sparkling grey expanse of Loch Morwen beyond.

Theo had been racking his brain to think of somewhere safe to hide both Horst and themselves. Then as the bulbous, boxy shape of Gunnar's zeplin rose over the treetops he realised that there was one place which was perfect and took out his comm, hoping that he would be able to get through.

42

GREG

Greg was on his way back from having sent provisions down to the well chamber with Chel (who had recently arrived by zeplin) when his comm chimed. Seeing who it was, he grinned and quickly answered.

'Uncle Theo, good to hear from you. How are you today?'

'I'm well enough, lad. Listen, would it be all right to impose myself and a few friends upon you just for tonight? We'll be up and away early tomorrow.'

'Aye, that shouldn't be a problem, Uncle. When can we expect you?'

'We're coming in by zeplin so we'll be with you in about half an hour. Oh, and there's no need to tell the station warden – our pilot is going to let us down on that grassy stretch behind the ruins. Can't thank you enough for your help – you're a good lad. Right, be seeing you.'

As the line went dead Greg lowered the comm and stared, half-annoyed, half-amused at having been unable to get a word in.

He's almost a force of nature is Uncle Theo. What must he have been like when he was younger!

At the site huts he quickly checked the state of the rec room then looked in on the stores to see what bedding was available. He also stopped at his own hut to assess how much work he had to cover later on, then put on a heavier jacket and went back outside.

Dusk was his favourite time of the day he decided as he strolled through the darkening ruins. Dawn could be very special if it was bright and dry – a rainy dawn felt as if the world's burden was being reluctantly dragged into the daytime. Whereas dusk looked great whatever the weather, be it cloudless skies or overcast, clement or a downpour. A few times he had been out and about at sundown with mist or fog creeping down from the dense forest slopes, and every time it was a splendidly Gothic experience.

Now, in the fading, grainy light, the surfaces of ancient broken walls and columns were beginning to grow dark and foreboding, the stonework looking increasingly eroded and time-worn, until the night finally claimed them, turning them into black shapes, silently looming. Then, as the sun's last glimmer sank away, leaving only a dwindling radiance on the horizon, Greg heard the hum of approaching engines. A minute later he saw the faint edges of a light beam wavering along the cliffs that led east from Giant's Shoulder. After that it wasn't long before the bulky mass of a zeplin nosed up over the natural ramparts of the promontory, a solitary spotlight probing the gloom.

As it descended, engines idling, Greg ran over, exchanging a wave with the pilot in his glowing cockpit. When it got to about ten feet off the ground it paused, hovering, while a rope ladder was flung out of a side hatch and several figures climbed down. By his own torch Greg recognised Uncle Theo and Rory but not the other three, one of whom was dressed in what seemed to be an elaborate dressing gown. Greg went over to greet them, but before he could even say hello, Theo had a hand on his shoulder and was steering him back towards the huts.

'Good to see you, boy. I hope you didn't let anyone know we were coming.'

Behind them, the zeplin was gaining height and turning south to head over the ridge.

'Didn't tell a soul, Uncle. So, what's all this about?'

By the meagre torchlight he saw Theo's craggy features crease into what his mother once called his 'devil-may-care' smile, which was usually a sign of trouble ahead.

'Ach, well, it's quite a tale,' his uncle said. 'One that should be told with a glass of the fair dram in hand.'

'I believe that I can unearth a bottle of Glenmarra . . .'

'Good man! Always prepared for guests, that's what I like.'

But when they reached Greg's hut, Poul, one of the interns, was waiting for him.

'Poul, what's the problem?'

'Not sure, Mr Cameron, but a weird message came through to our hut terminal from the university, warning us that those Brolturans are sending troops here to search for the missing ambassador.'

'What?' Greg said. 'To search for who?'

Poul shrugged. 'Seems that the Brolturans are accusing the Earth ambassador of being involved in all the bombings and that assassination. It's been all over the vee-news since this afternoon.'

'Aye, well I've not had the vee on all day, Poul – too much to do. Look, thanks for letting me know – could you pass that on to the other teams, tell them to get ready?'

As the intern headed off, Greg looked at his uncle, black suspicion in his thoughts.

'If this has anything to do with you,' he said, 'you should tell me now.'

Theo sighed, then beckoned forward the man in the long robe, who had been hanging back.

'Greg, let me introduce you to the Earthsphere ambassador to Darien, Robert Horst. Mr Horst, this is my nephew, Gregory Cameron.'

Up close he recognised the grey-haired man from the news reports, while feeling a slight sense of unreality as he shook his hand.

'So, er, Mr Horst, what do the Brolturans want with you?'

The ambassador looked tired and haggard yet he managed a smile. 'Mr Cameron, I assure you that I had nothing to do with the murders at the airport yesterday, or any other terrorist acts. I was *there*, I saw it, I could have been killed myself! . . .' Horst's anger ebbed as quickly as it had surged. 'The Brolturans usually do what the Hegemony tells them, so I have to assume that it is all Kuros's doing. Mr Cameron, until I can make contact with the captain of the *Heracles* I must appeal to you and Major Karlsson and his friends for help. I have no wish to end up in a Brolturan interrogation chamber!'

'Greg, those Brolturans will be here soon,' Theo said. 'We need to find somewhere safe to hide, like in the forest back there. Are there any caves up behind that ridge?'

'I don't know, I think so,' said Greg. 'Some of the Uvovo scholars would know, but it would take time to reach the nearest, and wouldn't these troops have some kind of nightvision tracking technology?'

Theo nodded. 'They're bound to.'

Greg ran a hand through his hair. 'Right. Fine. Then there's only one place you can go – follow me.'

Once everyone was down in the entrance corridor, he told the Uvovo scholars Teso and Kolum (whom had he had woken earlier) to dismantle the winch and the canopy and stow them in the storage hut. They were then to reassemble them about an hour after the intruders had left. As he watched the empty body harnesses rise up and out of sight, he muttered a prayer that his instructions had been clear enough, then turned to take stock of the situation. At least everyone had a blanket, and there was a satchel filled with whatever food had been in his cupboard, along with a couple of hand torches. Which should keep them from getting too cold and hungry for a while.

'Never heard o' this place,' Rory said, glancing around. 'You scientists been keepin' it secret, aye?'

'Didn't know about it myself until a coupla days ago, Rory,' he said, and launched into a brief summary while omitting the bit about it having been built as a weapon, as well as any mention of an ancient, intelligent guardian, not wanting to have to deal with alarm, much less disbelief. His audience was nevertheless silently astonished as they followed him along the corridor and down into the icy room of pillars.

'This is incredible,' Ambassador Horst said, peering by torchlight at the carved walls. 'Could this be the work of the Forerunners?'

'Going by Uvovo histories and the few datings I've done so far, the time period seems to be about 100,000 years ago,' Greg said. 'Which apparently puts it near the end of the Forerunner era, going by what I've learned from offworld sources. But if you come through here you'll see the main attraction . . .'

Warming to his tourist-guide role, he led them into the well chamber, torchbeams lighting the way through the heavy, cold darkness. Two figures were visible off around the boundary wall, Chel and Weynl huddled over something in the lamplight. Then one of them must have heard the clatter of footsteps, straightened and looked round. Greg waved and the Uvovo stood and started towards them. As he drew near Greg saw it was Chel.

'It is a remarkable edifice,' Horst said, approaching the boundary wall. 'And you say this circular area has a ritual function?'

Greg nodded. 'There's also some kind of highly advanced Forerunner technology embedded in . . .'

A shattering, stentorian drone blasted through the chamber as spears and swirling webs of brilliant radiance erupted from the surface of the well next to where Ambassador Horst was standing. Everyone reacted the same way, rearing away from the noise and the dazzle, except for the ambassador, who was trapped in a cage of light, quivering meshes interleaving. The roaring drone lessened in force, becoming a resonant, booming voice speaking incomprehensibly in a demanding tone.

'What in hell is that, Greg?' yelled Theo. 'Is the ambassador in danger? Are we?'

'The chamber . . . the well has a guardian . . .'

But before he could continue, Chel came running up followed by Listener Weynl. Chel's forehead was bare and the outer pair of eyes were open.

'Who is he, Greg?' said Chel, pointing at Horst. 'Who is this man?'

'He's the Earthsphere ambassador.'

At the same time, Listener Weynl was shouting at the coruscating maelstrom of light, responding to the immense voice that thundered forth from it.

Chel stared at Horst, who was on his knees, looking terrified and hugging folds of his gown to his chest.

'Does this man carry one of the thing you call AIs?' he said.

'Yes, he does,' said Greg.

Chel shook his head, teeth bared. 'A Dreamless . . . we will try to save him from the Sentinel, Greg, but you must trust me and not interfere.'

Greg breathed in deep, trying to steady himself, then nodded and watched as Chel and Weynl bared their arms and crouched down near Horst. There was a moment of stillness, then they swiftly thrust their arms through the bright shifting mesh – Greg saw the short, dense fur on their arms begin to char and smoke – and touched the ambassador's head.

And the ambassador cried out, the muscles on his neck taut as cables, his eyes wide with pleading.

43

CHEL

When Greg and the other Humans appeared at the door, Chel and Listener Weynl were sitting cross-legged on the walkway floor with a blanket between them and the cold stone. By the lamp's golden glow they were examining hand-drawn copies of several patterns recently uncovered in a very old stone tile archive on the forest moon. They were comparing the tile patterns with sketches they had made of portions of the well surface, looking for similarities. The tiles also contained commentaries, but they appeared to be written in some kind of abstruse cipher which no one had thus far solved.

So it was over these that the two Uvovo were poring when Chel heard the hard, dry sound of footsteps and looked up. He had been using the outer pair of his new eyes to regard the well patterns, but now he saw a strange, spiked nimbus around one of Greg's companions. At the same time, a faint amorphous radiance was gathering at the edge of the well nearest the newcomers.

'Something is wrong, Listener,' Chel said, getting to his feet. 'The well is behaving strangely.'

Without waiting for Weynl's reply he started round towards the group of Humans. He had gone a few paces when a bright column of energies erupted from the well's edge, near where the man with the disturbing aura was standing. A cacophonous, blaring drone accompanied the outburst of light, almost painful to Uvovo ears, yet he broke into a run. He could see that the man had been caught in a bright cage of well energy, and he could hear the blasting drone subsiding into speech, words in the Uvovo tongue.

INTRUDER! ENEMY DETECTED! THE HIGH PATH-MASTER MUST INSTRUCT ME ON THE MODE OF ERASURE.

'No, Sentinel, wait,' Weynl cried out. 'This is a friend.'

CAPTIVE IS IMPLANTED WITH A FABRICATED ENTITY – THIS ENTITY MAINTAINS A COHERENT CHANNEL INTO THE UNDERDOMAINS OF THE REAL. THIS CHANNEL MUST BE SHUT OFF OR ERASURE WILL BE ENACTED – YOU ARE NOT A PATHMASTER.

Chel hurried up to Gregori, who was talking with his uncle.

'Who is he, Greg?' he said, pointing at the man in the cage. 'Who is this man?'

Gregori looked stricken by what was happening. 'He's the Earthsphere ambassador . . .'

Chel gazed at the ambassador, a terrified, grey-haired man who had slumped to his knees, holding the folds of his robe close to his chest for some reason.

'Does this man carry one of the things you call AIs?'

Chel gritted his teeth. 'A Dreamless . . . we will try to save him from the Sentinel, Gregori, but you must trust me and not interfere.'

Gregori hesitated, then nodded. Chel removed the sleeves of his body garment, as did Weynl next to him, then they knelt down on the stone floor on the other side of the energy cage from the Human ambassador. He steeled himself, his outer eyes open, staring at the intervening, shifting bright meshes, saw how they moved and saw how to move between them. Then as one, he and Weynl raised their hands and struck through to take hold of the Dreamless's host. The spikes in that nimbus signified the Dreamless's presence and gave away the nodes of its connection. Some instinct made his hands move, small, furred hands stroking the man's head, tracing out the contours beneath, applying a touch or a finely gauged pressure . . . no, not an instinct, he realised, but skills of another agency, the Sentinel of the well.

Both Uvovo withdrew their hands, and Chel noticed the band

of crisped and smoking fur on his upper arms. There didn't seem to be any pain at the moment.

'Chel, are you okay?' said Gregori as he helped him and Weynl to their feet.

He felt dizzy and there was a hollowness in his stomach. He fumbled with unsteady fingers at his waist for the strip of heavy cloth, the blind for his husking eyes. Once they were covered, he inhaled deeply, held it for a moment then exhaled a long, shuddering breath.

'Yes,' he said as the tension ebbed a little. 'I feel better.'

Then he realised that the Human ambassador was still held prisoner. The Sentinel had fallen silent, for all that Listener Weynl kept calling out to it. And now the ambassador had recovered his composure sufficiently to stand and converse with Gregori in signs.

'Chel,' Gregori said after a moment or two. 'Ambassador Horst says that his AI is absent and making no contact – why won't the Sentinel release him?'

'I confess I do not know, Gregori,' he said, turning to Weynl. 'Did it say anything before . . .'

Suddenly the deep, overpowering voice spoke:

THE DREAMLESS HAS BEEN CONFINED AND ITS TIES TO THE UNDERDOMAINS ABROGATED. HOWEVER, IT REMAINS A THREAT.

Chel and Gregori exchanged a look of alarm.

'Wait, Sentinel,' said Chel. 'There has to be a way to make it completely safe. If you release him to us, it may be possible to remove . . . the device . . .'

NONE HERE ARE PATHMASTERS. NONE MAY COMMAND ME, THUS I MUST RESOLVE THIS IN THE LIGHT OF OTHER REQUIREMENTS. THE CONSTRUCT HAS ASKED FOR A HUMAN PROXY SO THIS ONE MAY SUFFICE.

'No!' said Gregori. 'We need this man here – he can help get the Hegemony off this world . . .'

'Certainty is not . . . immutable . . .'

The words came in a dry, sibilant whisper, not loud yet omnipresent, and Chel felt a surge of relief when he saw the outlines of the Pathmaster's hooded form emerging amid the energy meshes that enclosed the Earthsphere ambassador.

'Venerable one,' he said, bowing along with Listener Weynl. Gregori was still standing nearby while Theo and the others retreated off towards the entrance.

'Sentinel,' said the Pathmaster. 'The Human bears a Dreamless which has been restrained. Why do you still hold him?'

THE ENTITY IS CAPABLE OF CONTROLLING ITS HOST, PATHMASTER. IT REMAINS A THREAT. I JUDGED THAT THE CONSTRUCT'S REQUEST FOR A HUMAN WOULD BE SATISFIED BY THIS ONE.

'Yet this Human is a senior representative of the greater Human culture,' Chel said. 'Left here, he would be able to weaken the Hegemony's position and even force their withdrawal.'

'Ah, young Seer Cheluvahar, the Hegemony Dreamless know this place exists – they will not loosen their grip, even if the Earth Humans were to turn against their Hegemony allies. No, the ambassador's presence will have little or no effect on the strife and conflict about to befall this world. The Hegemony will shortly control Umara and soon they will be walking in this very chamber.'

Chel fell silent, shocked, but Gregori was clearly upset.

'What does that mean for the ambassador?' he said to Chel in Noranglic. 'He's not sending him off to this Construct, whatever that is . . .'

'Human, the Construct was the Great Ancients' most faithful ally,' the Pathmaster said in perfect whispered Noranglic. 'And it remains a steadfast guardian of their purpose – it has promised us help in our struggle against the occupiers, and its promises are never broken. Also, it will know how exactly to deal with the Dreamless locked up in the host's head, for that is why he has come here, Human, otherwise he would be elsewhere.'

'No,' said Gregori. 'This man is our best chance of holding off the Hegemony . . .'

'Damn it!' said Theo Karlsson. 'I didn't get him away from those Brolturans just to lose him like this!'

'No, Human Karlsson,' whispered the Pathmaster. 'That is precisely why you rescued him.'

'Venerable one,' said Chel. 'Respectfully I ask, is your certainty immutable?'

'No, Seer Chel, but my judgement must be – Sentinel, send the Human onwards to the Construct!'

IT SHALL BE DONE.

For a long, agonising moment Chel stared at the horrified Ambassador Horst as he pointed and begged in silence. Then a dense vortex of well energies engulfed him, a bright maelstrom swirling for a few seconds before it began to diminish back across the boundary wall. The Pathmaster still hovered amid the fading, dissolving flow of radiance, and in those dying instants it pointed at Chel, Gregori and the rest in a single, sweeping gesture.

'Leave here – now!'

Then the last threads and grains of energy were gone, leaving them in the gloom of torchlight, hopes crushed, plans scattered, and the future . . .

The Humans wandered despondently away through the door, Gregori lingering, gazing at the darkened well. Chel went with Listener Weynl back to their small camp to gather together their sketches and papers. Yet Chel realised that, despite this dismal, dispiriting outcome, the future remained unwritten, as opaque and formless to the Dreamless as it was to themselves. Consoled by this, he followed Weynl, hastening after Gregori and the others.

44

KAO CHIH

In his dream he was being chased by a long, winding festival dragon whose head was the four-armed torso of an Ezgara commando, its four hands tipped with serrated claws, its featureless helmet splitting open to show rows of needle-like teeth, gleaming, snapping . . .

He was jolted in his couch, waking once more to a sickly mouth and a nasty headache.

'Back among the living, KC? – good. We're docking with my associates' mothership so it won't be long before you meet the leaders of the revolution!'

Corazon Talavera, his beautiful and deadly captor, sat in the pilot couch, monitoring displays, making a few adjustments, and glancing at him occasionally. The cockpit's viewport was clear, revealing a strange vista, a dull yellow sun the size of a coin, its amber radiance casting a daylight crescent over a grey-brown planet which filled about a quarter of the frame. At first sight, it seemed that clouds of asteroids hung in spreading orbits about the nameless world . . . until a dark, jagged object tumbled past not far off, catching the sunlight on torn metal edges, a faring, a section of hull. Glittering and dwindling, it fell away into the planet's gravitic embrace.

'Wreckage,' said Cora, who had been watching him. 'Debris, the smashed remains of ships, combat and civilian, big and small, armed and helpless. Welcome to the Shafis System.'

Kao Chih frowned. 'You say that as if you expect me to know what it means, but I do not.'

She arched her eyebrows. 'KC, where have you been? I'm not a newsleech but even I've picked up a few details about Shafis here and there. Okay, here's the short version – which is all I can be bothered with. Shafis is a system on the edge of the Yamanon Domain, where it shades off into the Huvuun Deepzone, and so far Coalition forces have fought three battles here. First time it was with retreating remnants of the Dol-Das fleets, then it was against an armed reconnaisance group from some Aranja Tesh civ, probably Metraj, trying to rescue survivors from that dustbowl of a planet. Third time, which was just a couple of weeks ago, it was a bunch of idiot Sageist zealots putting together a fleet to attack Coalition positions, using the high-orbit shell here as a staging post while trying to recruit from the scrabblers down on the surface. Each time, the Hegemony – and its loyal Earthsphere sidekick – stormed in with their ships and destroyed any vessel which offered resistance. And "offering resistance" was interpreted pretty loosely, I hear, resulting in these picturesque clouds of wreckage you see today. Along with a few more additions to the survivors down on the planet.'

'So why are your employers stationed here?' Kao Chih said. 'Are they scavengers as well as revolutionaries?'

'Benefactors, KC, rescuers. Since that third battle, the one with the holy armada, was fairly recent, it is possible that there may be survivors trapped on some of the hulks drifting out there, which naturally interests my employers. Who are also interested in similar individuals down the gravity well, but orbital searches come first.'

'Recruits,' said Kao Chih.

'Exactly. You're catching on.' A clunking sound came through the hull and a rasping voice spoke over the ship-to-ship in a language that seemed to defy the linguistic enabler. Cora replied in kind and fingered several controls, putting most of the pilot controls on standby. 'Time to meet your new masters.'

Kao Chih's bonds were rearranged and lengthened, then, at gunpoint, he helped her wrap Drazuma-Ha* in a sheet and together they carried the mech out through the airlock and into a much larger one made of some dark, flexible material which had formed an airtight constriction around the *Castellan*'s airlock flanges. Hatch doors closed behind and opened ahead and Cora gestured with her skinny gun to continue. His ankles and wrists were now bound with two-foot-long secure straps which made movement a chore, but he managed to back out of the raised hatch edge, carrying his end of Drazuma-Ha*. Then he turned and saw that they were in a large, well-lit hold with equipment racks, luggage nets, upper-wall walkways, through-floor risers and overhead cargo lifts. There was also a welcoming committee, a tall reptiloid Kiskashin and a Gomedran garbed in grey overalls and carrying an odd figure-of-eight device.

At Cora's direction he helped carry the quiescent mech over to the two sentients and stood it on its end.

'Congratulations, Talavera,' said the Kiskashin in deep-throated 4Peljan. 'A high-grade human and a functioning Strigida-9 drone, just as you described. Truly, you are my most prized procurer.'

So this is a revolutionary? Kao Chih thought.

The Kiskashin was nearly seven feet high, and beneath a sleeve-less, three-quarter-length bluefibre coat wore what looked liked pieces of combat armour on his arms and shoulders, grey poly-hedral surfaces worn at the facet edges, scored and pitted. Kiskashin were upright bipeds with muscular, birdlike legs and wide-toed feet. It was only after Kao Chih looked more closely that he realised that the Kiskashin's arms were artificial, having spotted the shoulder ball-joints and the fact that those arms had a longer reach than normal.

'As always, it is an honour and a privilege to serve your cause, Castigator Vuzayel,' Cora said, giving a slight bow.

'And to serve your own, hah?' the Kiskashin Vuzayel said. 'The great cause of money!' With the finger and thumb of one articu-lated, armoured, six-fingered hand he took a black velvety pouch from within his immaculate bluefibre coat. 'Selling souls for profit, Talavera – few sins are as black as that in the eyes of the Great Sower. I sometimes think about inviting you to join the struggle, to lay down your sinful burdens and follow the path taken by those you have already brought into my care. But then I realise what a loss to the cause, the Writ of Sacred Revenge, that would be so I decide to forgo my duty, to further our greater ends.'

'I am glad that I will continue to be of service to you, Castigator,' Cora said unflinchingly. 'And to be paid.'

The velvety black pouch hung there for a moment, then was whisked out of sight, stowed back inside the coat.

'Later. First, I wish you to give our newest arrival the extended tour of our mighty vessel, the *Sacrament*, show him its most inspiring sights while the Strigida drone is being redacted.' Vuzayel glanced at the waiting Gomedran. 'Take it down to the examiners.'

The Gomedran bowed then stepped over to where Kao Chih still held Drazuma-Ha* upright, the sheet having been removed by Cora. The Gomedran motioned Kao Chih back, then slapped the figure-of-eight device onto the mech's carapace, thumbed its control pad and a moment later was carrying the mech out of the hold on his shoulder as if it weighed next to nothing.

Kao Chih found himself being studied by Castigator Vuzayel, pale yellow Kiskashin eyes regarding him, occasionally tilting that narrow-snouted head to focus one of them on him.

'I do not know what barbarous gods you Humans worship,' he said. 'But when you make your offering in the name of Sacred Revenge, know that you will be redeemed. You and the other devotees are the lucky ones – we, the leaders of the Chaurixa, must put off the joyous sacrifice until the Great Sower's writ has been fulfilled, a sorrowful burden which we stoically shoulder. But before you begin your journey, Human, tell your name.'

'I am called Kao Chih, sir,' he said. 'I am a freelance chandler, so if you have any unfilled contracts I would most happy to offer my services.'

Vuzayel laughed, a horrible grating sound.

'If nothing else, you Humans are entertaining! Go in peace, Karrchi, the Great Sower awaits you.'

As the Kiskashin headed for one of the exits with a heavy tread, Cora pointed with her gun at a flight of stairs that led up to a grillwork walkway. Glumly, he followed her directions, his thoughts inevitably focusing on his mission to Darien and the erratic route that had brought him to this end, the reprogramming of his companion, Drazuma-Ha*, and his own conversion to these fanatics' cause. No doubt he would face some form of brainwashing, perhaps a combination of drugs and sense-deprivation, or maybe even some kind of immersive procedure. Whichever it was he was determined to resist for as long as he could.

Cora prodded his shoulder with her gun then indicated a pair of heavy pressure doors just along the walkway. 'Straight through and down the ramp.'

Ankles restricted by the secure straps, he shuffled forward and the doors slid aside to let them past.

'I liked the way you tried to take my place,' Cora said. '"Freelance chandler", eh? Good title. I think I'll adopt it now that you won't have any use for it.'

'I wouldn't plan too far in advance, Ms Talavera,' he said, trying to sound as if he were in good spirits. 'Your master hasn't paid you yet. But then you didn't mention our little Ezgara problem – I wonder why.'

Cora's laughter was light and edged with malice. 'Keep flapping that mouth and I'll have one of the aspirants nerve-block it.'

Kao Chih shrugged and continued down the ramp, which turned leftward twice. The Chaurixa mothership's interior décor was in simple yellows and greens with notices and signs in dark red, often hurriedly stencilled to the walls. From a couple of location guides he discovered that the ship had a linear module configuration, four large hull sections built on a central axis, the drives and engineering at the stern, the bridge and quarters in the prow segment, while the two midsections were dotted with a number of arcane-looking symbols utterly mysterious to him. He had figured out that they had docked at the third hull module from the prow and were heading forward to the second. Cora steered him round a couple of corners and into the ship's spinal corridor, up steps and through the connecting passage, and down more steps. She then had him turn left and follow the gravplating track up the portside curve of the hull past a series of opaque doors. Each door had a grey panel bearing one of the symbols he had seen on the wall guides.

'I know what's going through your head, KC,' Cora said behind him. 'You think you'll have to endure beatings and torture and drugs and crazy mind-scrambling virtsensoria . . . well, no, these people don't work that way. These people are professionals with pressing deadlines and precision needs, so they're not going to waste time trying to beat their point of view into you.'

She stopped him in front of one of the doors and the grey panel melted into transparency. Inside was a white surgical theatre where two masked and gowned Henkayans were working on a bulky form bound to a large cradle. The patient, or victim, was a Bargalil, its six-limbed body lying still and silent.

'The Chaurixa medtechs have three ways of remoulding minds to fit the task. There's viral programming, where they use tailored bugs to edit and rewrite an ordag's brain, creating new compulsions, fears and desires, whole chunks of behaviour dedicated to carrying out the mission . . .'

'What was that name you called him? Ordak . . .'

'Ordag – short for "ordained agent",' she said. 'Well, anyway, that seems like the worst way to me. You are yourself, you feel like yourself, but there's all these memories and instincts making you do things you don't understand. Creepy.'

She motioned him on to the next door. The panel went transparent, revealing a tall Sendrukan male, his eyes blindfolded as he lay strapped to a cushioned table while a hooded device on a segmented cable moved all around his head as if examining it from all directions. There was no one else in the room.

'Another way is to just simply wipe away the mind, flatten all the characteristics, leaving aside the autonomic and certain learned reflexes. Then they embed a new persona sufficiently complex to carry out whatever task it's needed to do.

'But some tasks can be too involved and socially demanding for an embedded persona, so the Castigator's clever underlings came up with kernelling – basically, parts of the cortex are scooped out and a paraorganic nanostructure is grown in its place, which serves as the residence for a partial, or sometimes a full, AI.'

'Efficient,' said Kao Chih, horrified but maintaining his composure. 'In Chinese mythology there are many hells, some as elaborate as these rooms.'

She looked at him. 'For example?'

'There is the Hell of Disembowelment where hypocrites and tomb robbers have their bowels cut out. Or there is the Hell of Sawing where kidnappers and those who force good people to do bad things are sawn into pieces.'

'You're making that up.'

He shrugged. 'Chinese history goes back a long, long way, so some things might indeed be made up. And some may not.'

She smiled and wagged a reproving finger. 'You can't spook me, KC. Besides, you haven't seen the rest of our little circle of hell yet.'

The walkway led past another couple of milky opaque doors, curving over to the starboard side, where Cora had him stop before a set of double doors. Through the clear panels Kao Chih saw a white room with a few thin-legged chairs and another pair of doors. He also saw an octopoidal Makhori laid full-length on a wheeled trolley, its pale tentacles stretched out and still while its torso showed regular, slow breathing. Its large, open eyes stared blankly upwards.

'It's just been wiped,' Cora said, giving him another prod. 'This is the augmentation area – go on in.'

He pushed through with both hands and stopped to gaze down at the immobile Makhori.

'Sometimes missions require a strength or speed beyond the abilities of ordinary organic creatures,' she said. 'So ordags are brought here for alterations, modifications, refurbs, whatever the mission calls for, occasionally the full, customised cyber-augmentation – heart, veins, muscle, blood and bone, from the roots of your hair to the nails on your toes. No sense left untouched.'

One of the inner doors opened and to Kao Chih's surprise a Human emerged, a thin, old man in a brown robe, grey-haired and stooped. He saw Kao Chih and, peering, came over.

'So they got another,' he said in a creaky voice as he held out a wrinkly hand. 'I'm Josh – what's your name, son?'

'I am Kao Chih, sir – I am honoured to meet you. How do you come to be here?'

'Likewise.' Josh indicated Cora, who was still holding her gun levelled at Kao Chih's chest. 'Came here courtesy of your friend's one-way service.'

'Did she put you to sleep as well, Josh?'

'Three times – I was a cranky passenger.'

Cora rolled her eyes, just as the inner doors opened. A green-clad Henkayan entered, seized the trolley with all four stubby hands and wheeled the insensible Makhori away beyond the doors. A second, more imposing Henkayan appeared, garbed in pale green, ankle-length robes and wearing a yellow band around his throat. His wide, tapering head was crowned with dense purple hair coiffed into stiff, upward coils and his large, coarse features were grinning as he approached Josh.

'Very good, superior one, but keep up practice of New Montana accent, become perfect. Go now to outfitters, they are expecting you.'

'My thanks, Compositor Henach. May the Great Sower's will be served.' So saying, the man called Josh straightened his posture and, ignoring Cora and Kao Chih, strode out of the main doors. The grinning Compositor Henach turned his attention to the new-comers.

'Castigator Vuzayel has spoken to me,' he told Cora. 'This one is to be sent to one of the Tertiary Grace worlds in Metraj, to assassinate a Vikantan industrialist.'

Cora made an impressed sound. 'So a partial augmenting, I'd guess.'

'Yes, and then wipe and persona overlay, not unlike my most recent patient.'

'What of the drone?'

'Will be reprogrammed and fitted with anti-personnel systems and self-destruct.'

Cora nodded and turned to Kao Chih. 'Well, this is it, KC – it's been a rollercoaster ride but we got there in the end. So see you in another life – or another hell!'

She smiled and winked, just as the Henkayan touched something cold and metallic to his neck. Immediately, everything below his head went numb and like a puppet with severed strings he fell but was neatly caught. Bizarrely, he was still conscious and fully alert but without any control over his neck muscles so that his head lolled this way and that as Compositor Henach carried him from the room.

'Your new body will be remarkable, Human – we do only remarkable things here and you will see it all.'

The Compositor placed him in some kind of cradling couch which had a row of folded surgical extensors along one edge, like the hooks and pincers of a grotesque creature, glittering and retracted. He only caught glimpses of it as the Henkayan fastened him in. Kao Chih wanted to cry out, even curse his captor, but the deadening effect encompassed his vocal chords.

'So – augmentation of legs, arms, hands, chest, and perhaps spine also.' Kao Chih could see the Henkayan lean over then heard a series of tiny clicks, and a hologram of a human body appeared overhead, an image stripped of skin and showing muscles, arteries, organs, the stark, pale orbs of his own eyes staring up, his toothy jaws gaping but unable to speak, an exhibition in red. A sense of helpless despair filled his mind.

'Hmm, no dataweave, no cranial conduit, and no implants . . . except for molecular attachment in linguistic centre . . . hmm, still largely unblemished Human brain – most refreshing . . .'

Suddenly the couch gave a slight jolt and out of sight there was a metallic clinking, and the clatter of something falling to the floor. The Compositor cursed under his breath, put his grin back in place and looked at Kao Chih.

'First, we cut open your legs, insert builder seeds and guide membrane,' he said. 'Quick, easy, you feel nothing, then . . .'

This time the entire room lurched and Henach was thrown sideways to fetch up against the wall. He let out a shriek of rage and dashed across the room towards something out of Kao Chih's sight. Outside the surgery alarms were warbling in the corridors and a moment later he heard the Henkayan say, 'This is Compositor Henach – what is happening?'

'So sorry, Compositor, but the Strigida drone has broken free of its stasisweb and caused damage to the inner hull . . .'

'I am working! – no excuses, recapture it!'

'Yes, Compositor, at once. When we find it.'

'What? How can you lose it?'

'It found a way into the maintenance interstices, sir, and the security scuttlers aren't reporting anything . . .'

The opencom voice was blotted out by a deafening crash in the room, the sight of flying fragments of what looked like deck tiles, and a terrified howl from the Compositor, swiftly cut off. For a second or two there were only the ticks and knocks of bits of debris falling to the floor and an odd, muffled, mumbling sound. Then the familiar dumb-bell shape of Drazuma-Ha* drifted into view.

'Greetings, Gowchee – I see that you are about to undergo some physical modifications, which would certainly enhance your ability to defend yourself in the future. Would you like me to return later?'

Robbed of his voice, Kao Chih could only frown, glare and mouth various demands and imprecations in an attempt to get his meaning across.

'Ah, I deduce that this would be unwelcome – very well.'

All of a sudden he was plunged back into the sensations of his entire body again, as if he had convulsively awoken from a nightmare, or into one. Shivering, itching, coughing, he scrambled out of the surgical cradle and saw that Drazuma-Ha* was restraining the Compositor with a forcefield extension wrapped around the Henkayan's mouth and neck. Rage mottled his features and despite the forcefield gag he was still trying to shout and threaten, which accounted for the muted throaty muttering.

'So, how did you . . .' Kao Chih began, but was forced to break off by a coughing fit.

'Obtain my freedom? Well, our hosts, who think very highly of themselves, reasoned that providing our female hijacker with the specifications of the Strigida design would ensure success. They failed to realise that over the course of several thousand years I might have introduced some modifications of my own, like improvements to my power grid as well as multiple redundancy in the vital systems. Thus I was able to reroute my core functions, disable the stasisweb and free myself.'

Swallowing painfully, Kao Chih looked down at the long gaping hole in the floor. 'Well, it certainly worked. What shall we do now?'

'Getting off this space-going torture chamber would be most preferable,' Drazuma-Ha* said. 'I managed to tap into the security web and sealed the intermodule access doors, but that will only last until they splice up a workaround.'

Kao Chih stared at the unrelentingly wrathful Compositor Henach. 'Does this vessel have escape pods?'

'Yes, a small number for each module, but if we departed in one it would be an easy matter to send a recovery vehicle to bring it back in.'

'We don't go,' Kao Chih said. 'He does.'

'A diversion, very good, making sure that the pod's comm device is nonfunctional. Then, I assume, we will head towards the docking ring and your ship.'

'Exactly – if you can make it appear that you have me restrained with forcefields, we can play guard-and-prisoner.'

'I have a better suggestion,' Drazuma-Ha* said as a shimmering aura formed about it, lengthened, altered its outline, swirled with colours . . . and suddenly Kao Chih was looking at two Compositor Henachs, the real one glaring with undisguised hate at his impostor.

Kao Chih grinned. 'The appearance is precise – can you sound like him?'

'Of course, puny Earthling!' said the mech in the Compositor's voice. 'My vocal simulacrum is unrivalled!'

'Then let us carry out our plan . . .'

'You may like to keep this with you,' said Drazuma-Ha*, tossing a silvery object which Kao Chih caught. It was a flattened oval with two springy arms tipped with dimpled pads. 'That is what our companion used on you – a nerve-blocker. It may be useful if we encounter difficulty.'

It was not far from the augmentation rooms to the low, narrow escape pod bay, and there were no guards to be seen. It seemed that when Drazuma-Ha* had sealed off the modules, locking all the surgery doors in the process, most of the guards were in the adjacent module searching for a missing drone.

Once the pod's comm system was disabled, the real Compositor Henach was thrust inside, his bellows of rage muffled by the closed hatch. There was a manual release in a wall niche which Kao Chih took great pleasure in pulling. A heavy thump, a furious hiss, and the pod leaped away, small chassis nozzles jetting. Another alarm started sounding so they ducked back out to the walkway and quickly made for the access door leading to the next module. Disguised as the Compositor, the mech paused nearby to crack open a wall panel, uncover the datalinks and modify the intermodule access status. As the door opened and the guards rushed in, shouting, Kao Chih assumed a listless stance, a drooping head and a vacant expression.

'Compositor Henach!' said the guard sergeant, an angry Gomedran with saliva gleaming on its fangs. 'You have left your . . .'

'Do not delay me, cretin! – this ordag must be wiped, orders of Castigator Vuzayel!'

'But sir, is this the Human recently arrived? Its machine has caused much disruption . . .'

'Are you calling me a fool? *Are you*? This different Human – fugitives use escape pods, cretin!'

'I see, I understand . . .'

'*Why are you waiting for them to escape?*'

Wilting in the face of such towering rage, the Gomedran sergeant saluted and hurried off while Kao Chih and Drazuma-Ha* proceeded through to the next module. No one stopped them as they continued up the ramp to the gantry which led along the docking ring. There was a Gomedran guard who challenged them but Kao Chih's speechless, shuffling act got him into the right place to pounce with the nerve-blocker.

This is a useful device, he thought as he pocketed it and stepped over the sleeping guard. *Wish I'd had one before Cora invited herself on board.*

Drazuma-Ha* used a field probe to bypass the docking ring security and open the hatch. Moments later they were back in the familiar, cramped, odorous surroundings of the *Castellan*'s cockpit.

'Gowchee, I rigged a two-minute delay on the docking clamp release,' said the mech, now returned to his usual, curved, featureless self. 'I would advise strapping into your couch as I am readying the main thrusters for a fast burn . . .'

One of the transparent console screens gave a blink of static before showing the Chaurixa leader, the Kiskashin Vuzayel.

'My friends, why such a hasty departure? – there is so much we have yet to discuss, and I would rather exchange words than weaponsfire . . .'

The *Castellan* lurched free of the docking ring. In the next moment acceleration slammed Kao Chih back into his couch and left him struggling to breathe against the sudden pressure. He had wanted to make an obscene gesture at Vuzayel's image but Drazuma-Ha* cut the link.

'Vile creature,' Kao Chih said. 'And a vile place, Drazuma-Ha*. How soon can we leave . . . oh, but have we any usable course data?'

'I'm checking that now . . . interesting, they had already commenced merging several course data sets into the navigationals, purely as place-holder templates.'

'So those course data are out of date?' Kao Chih said, spirits sinking.

'By about thirty-six to forty-eight hours.'

Kao Chih groaned. 'We went through this trying to escape

from Blacknest! Are we going to have to make another blind hyperjump out among the stars?'

'It may come to that, Gowchee, assuming we can evade the small craft that are now gaining on us.'

The screen in front of Kao Chih flashed to a rearward view, showing two bright objects following – the perspective jumped closer to one of them, revealing a tapered wedge shape with a large impeller drive and two gimbal-mounted work arms, one tipped with grasping claws, the other with a drill head.

'Engine-modified scavengers,' Kao Chih said. 'But the *Castellan* should be able to leave them behind.'

'That would be true if we were not heading into a debris field.'

Kao Chih looked up at the viewport just as Drazuma-Ha* banked the ship to dodge a house-sized piece of wreckage sprouting twisted beams and buckled sections of deck and bulkhead. Beyond, the widening, bright crescent of the planet was speckled by an immense cloud of wreckage. He knew they would have to cut their velocity to avoid the possibility of a crippling collision, whereas the scavenger boats could use their superior manoeuvring to get in close. Not for the first time, he wished the *Castellan* had some decent firepower.

'Could we ram them?' he said. 'Or even use our main thrusters as a weapon? . . . of some sort . . .'

'Creative suggestions, Gowchee,' said the mech. 'If a little fanciful. On the other hand, we could accelerate along a path I have mapped through the sparsest areas and thereby evade our pursuers.'

Suddenly optimistic, Kao Chih gestured at the viewport.

'Forward then, honourable Drazuma-Ha*!'

The mech blipped the thrusters, an intermittent, muffled drone.

'We need to bypass this approaching dense cluster of debris, then alter our attitude . . .'

Ahead, he could see a portion of the starry darkness where unstarlike points and splinters of reflected sunlight hung like a huge shoal of menace off their starboard. As the *Castellan*'s attitude changed, the glittering, dark shoal shifted to fill the viewport

but then slid away to starboard again as the ship, drifting sideways, came into alignment with Drazuma-Ha*'s intended
trajectory. Another long moment during which a glance at the
stern monitor showed the pursuers dodging around ragged pieces
of wreckage, swooping ever nearer. Then the thrusters cut in
again and Kao Chih was shoved back into his couch as the
Castellan surged forward. He was about to let out a whoop of
delight when the ship jolted, as if struck from beneath.

'What . . .'

'Compensating for course deviation,' said the mech. Then a
familiar voice came over the comm system.

'Well, hi there, KC. Thought I'd come along for the ride . . .'

Drazuma-Ha* switched the external monitor to the ship's
underside, and there was another of the boosted scavenger boats,
induction grapples anchoring it to the hull while one of the gim-
balled arms reached out with heavy claws to a nearby housing.

'You've really disappointed me, KC, as well as putting me in
bad odour with my masters – bring you back, I was told, or don't
come back . . . oh, sorry, was that something important?'

A high-pitched beeping sounded and red symbols flickered on
the console. On the external monitor those extended claws were
holding a torn-off piece of housing.

'Secondary fuel port,' said Drazuma-Ha*. 'I've isolated it. She
is coming through on the proximal helmet channel, Gowchee –
shall I shut it off?'

Kao Chih shook his head, reached out and fingered the channel
reply.

'Cora, instead of attacking us, why not come with us?'

'Appreciate the offer, KC, but I have to keep up a certain repute
for the benefit of those who make use of my services – no repute,
no job offers, y'see . . .'

Kao Chih was looking out the viewport as he released the reply
button.

'Drazuma-Ha*, are there any wreckage pieces of substantial
size along our flight path and can you adjust our course to pass
close by?'

'How close, Gowchee?'

'Very close. And can you position us for a 180-degree roll on approach?'

'Yes. Tracking one now – ninety seconds till flyby from . . . now.'

'You understand my intention, Drazuma-Ha*?'

'Indeed I do, Gowchee.'

It was the only course of action left to them, and they had to take it because Cora was determined to take them back or kill them trying. Because Kao Chih was done with being a captive or a commodity or some instrument to be used and discarded. Because he had a mission, because his family and friends and everyone back at Human Sept were relying on him.

The dull brown face of the nameless world was looming ahead, through all the strewn clouds of orbiting debris. Shafis System was a graveyard and was about to add to its burden.

A muffled whine started coming up from below – like those pursuit droids back at Blacknest, Cora was trying to drill through the hull.

'Thirty seconds till flyby,' said the mech. 'Fifteen till bank manoeuvre.'

Grim-faced, Kao Chih thumbed the comm reply.

'Cora,' he said. 'I'm sorry . . .'

In the viewport the brown planet began to turn. A dark, gleaming mass swung round as it swept nearer and impact alerts began to sound.

'Well, KC, you'll be the one who's gonna be . . . *you shit, KC, you sh*—!'

Her voice went out in a burst of static at the same time as a metallic crunch reverberated through the ship. When he looked at the external monitor the scavenger was gone, apart from a twisted chunk of the drill mounting. There were also numerous scores and gouges in the hull plating, but nothing serious was triggering warnings on the main console.

'A well thought-out tactic, Gowchee,' said Drazuma-Ha*.

'Yes,' he said. 'And cold-blooded. Apart from one of the

Chaurixa victims, she was the only Human I'd met since leaving the Roug system.'

'She rejected your offer, Gowchee – there was no other option open to us. But I am tracking her craft's progress and from its behaviour I surmise that she may have survived the collision . . .'

He perked up at this. 'What behaviour?'

'The scavenger craft is falling in a steep curve towards the planet and the firing of positional thrusters seems to have stabilised its . . . ah, something has ejected but it too is heading towards the planet's surface, although with a far shallower trajectory.'

Kao Chih sat back, feeling oddly relieved.

'You look pleased, Gowchee, despite her attempts to enslave or kill us. It is possible after all that the Chaurixa may retrieve her and exact punishment on her anyway.'

He shrugged. 'I am just glad that she survived, Drazuma-Ha*. I want to have no deaths on my conscience.'

'A laudable if somewhat impractical goal, Gowchee.'

'Why impractical?'

'From observation and experience I can state that there were, are and always will be those that are eager and willing to use violence to get what they want – opposing them means responding with violence, leading inevitably to deaths.'

'What of the use of cunning and non-violent methods of opposing them?' Kao Chih said.

'Either may well constitute an adequate defence, if the attackers are significantly less advanced than those being attacked. However, technological superiority is no guarantee of success.'

'Which reminds me,' Kao Chih said, gazing at the external monitor. 'Are we still being chased and how long till we can attempt a hyperjump?'

'Our pursuers have given up – it seems one of them sustained a disabling impact from a piece of wreckage and the other is towing it back to the Chaurixan mothership. As for a hyperspace jump – we will be exiting the densest area of debris in approximately two minutes, which will free up that portion of the ship's system stack that has been occupied with tracking and guidance. Then you will have a choice to make.'

Kao Chih sighed. 'Will this be a choice between a risky option and a deeply hazardous one?'

'Well summarised, Gowchee. This star system lies near the edge of the Huvuun Deepzone and your destination, the world called Darien, is somewhere within that hazy region.'

Drazuma-Ha* had called up a representation of the immediate stellar region. The Shafis System was a bright pinpoint where a pale green wedge – the Yamanon Domain – met the amorphous, sepia opacity of the Huvuun. 'The navigational matrix contains six course templates, but the only one that's of any use to us terminates at Yonok, a Brolturan world near the border with the Kahimbryk Avail.' On the screen, a neon-red line joined Shafis to another bright point on the other side of a narrow grey territory which separated Yamanon space from the blue of the Brolturan Compact. The coreward boundaries of all three adjoined the Huvuun Deepzone.

'Give me the deeply hazardous option first,' he said.

'That is where we tell the navigationals to guess where the local hyperspace Tier 1 beacons are, then guess what our iso-orientation should be as we make the jump to Yonok.'

Kao Chih shivered. It sounded a lot like their escape from Blacknest, and they had been very lucky to get to Tagreli Openport rather than wind up in the middle of nowhere, or even an unfriendly somewhere. It was surely too much to rely on that kind of luck again.

'And the merely risky option?'

'The navigationals estimate the location of the nearest Tier 1 beacon which, according to the course template notes, is coterminous with Kahimbryk space, plus or minus 5 per cent. When we reach that beacon we drop out of hyperspace and head for the nearest commercial centre to see if we can obtain course data for this Darien.'

'Course errors?' Kao Chih murmured.

'Exactly so, which is why I favour the second option – a shorter hyperspace jump would mean less time for errors to magnify. Besides, if we were ever to reach Yonok safely, the Brolturans would not be inclined to treat us kindly.'

Kao Chih nodded. 'Very well, the merely risky option it is.'

'The computations should be ready in less than a minute,' said the mech.

And when the moment came, he sat back in his couch, head pressed back against the padded neck support, hands gripping the arm rests, jaw clenched.

At least this time there's no rampaging droids trying to tear the ship apart or beautiful kidnappers speeding us off to some surgical-nightmare-torture-ship, he thought as the force-waves mounted in the tesserae fields at the heart of the *Castellan*'s hyperdrive. *But I'm sure something will be waiting for us round the next corner.*

45

THEO

About fifteen hours after the moment when he'd seen the Earthsphere ambassador vanish in a swirl of coruscating energies, Theo Karlsson was on foot and heading along the northerly banks of Loch Morwen. He had been walking for hours since descending the steep hill paths from the mountain ridges west of Giant's Shoulder and his feet were crying out for rest. He knew there was a tannery near here, and roughly a mile further on a small cove where he was due to meet one of Rory's local contacts who was supposed to spirit him up the shore road to a safe house at the edge of the city. A bite to eat, perhaps even a shower, then the chance to sit down and take stock of the situation before moving on, that was all he needed.

He had just caught a whiff of that acrid tannery odour when his comm rang inside his jacket. He dug it out, saw the calling number and in a rush of anger answered abruptly.

'What?'

'*Ah, Major, not caught you at a bad time, have I?*'

A relaxed, confident voice speaking vaguely Russian-inflected Noranglic. Silent since that bomb went off in Founders Square, it was Kuros's catspaw, the agent provocateur, the assassin.

'What do you want?'

'*To congratulate you, Major. It was breathtaking the way that you snatched Horst out from under the Brolturans' noses. I wonder what you will do with him – personally, I recommend execution.*'

'Do you, now?'

'*He is a traitor to Earth, Major, to Humanity. For decades, he and others like him have turned our race into fawning, deluded minions of the Hegemony and brought us down to the level of lesser species.*'

'Ah, the racial purity angle again – you're reliable in your obsessions.'

'*Indeed I am, Major. The Free Darien Faction is obsessed with striking at those who obstruct our purpose – you've removed our primary target so we can now go after our secondary one, High Monitor Kuros.*'

Theo laughed. 'Still serving up that FDF dreck, son? Well, it so happens that I know that you're nothing but a saboteur-goon for Kuros, or someone close to him, so spare me the fake rebel defiance . . .'

'*How sad – seems that their psyops have got to you somehow, Major . . .*'

'What's got to me is what I've seen, you know, at the Brolturan ambassador's arrival? Remember the ringer you slipped into Kuros's DVC escort? The firefight and the grenade going off, enough smoke and confusion so your man could do a quick-change and return to the scene as an Ezgara? I've seen it . . .'

'*Purest fantasy, Major.*'

'You're wasting your breath – I know what I saw.'

'*It's futile to try persuading someone as thoroughly hood-winked as yourself, but I do have two little bits of information that might be helpful to you. First you should be aware that early this morning the Brolturans issued a Decree of Arrest in your name, quickly followed by a similar warrant put out by Hammergard Police.*'

'No surprise – it was bound to happen,' Theo said. 'Sorry, you'll have to try harder.'

'*All right, Major, then how about this? Half an hour ago, a section of DVC intelligence called K5 arrested your sister and took her to their offices at the Assembly buildings. So you need to ask yourself why I would tell you this if I am your enemy.*'

Before Theo could respond the line went dead. He glared at the mute comm.

'Because you want me to hurry over to Hammergard and straight into a trap, you *lausunge*!'

But that didn't stop it having the ring of authenticity, especially if Theo was now a wanted man. He knew that was almost certainly true, and not just about himself – last night, as they were leaving Giant's Shoulder by the forest path (after the visiting Brolturan troops kept them down in that stone tomb for over four hours), he had warned Rory, Barney and the Firmanov brothers that by then law enforcement would have all their descriptions and that lying low was the only sane course of action. Rory was to take Barney north to Bessonov's cabin outside of High Lochiel, then head back to Hammergard; the Firmanovs were to pick up a van full of supplies from a garage near Landfall and drive to meet Rory at the cabin. After Horst had been vanished by whatever the hell it was that lurked in that chamber, comm calls had been made, plans were put into effect and certain Diehards moved out under cover of night.

Meanwhile, Theo was heading for Hammergard anyway, because come what may he had to get to Sundstrom to explain what had happened to Horst and to find out what their next move would be. Any comm calls into the Assembly or the president's villa would be subject to intense surveillance, so it would have to be face-to-face, and Sundstrom would also have to explain why Solvjeg had been arrested.

He skirted the tannery with its algae-surfaced ponds and filtration root arrays, and about a mile further on found the cove. An elderly, weather-beaten man in a heavy, dark-blue mariner's coat was sitting at the wheel of a battered spinnervan. Passwords were exchanged, Theo climbed in and they were soon on the road to Hammergard. The stern-looking older man spoke Noranglic with a pronounced Norge accent, even though his name was Sergei. He was also taciturn to a fault, and Theo get very little out of him during the half-hour drive, yet when they reached his cottage on a rounded ridge overlooking the loch, his hospitality was unstinting. After a hot shower and a change of clothing, there was a tasty meal of baked fish and vegetables, set off by a generous glass of rum and ginger wine that left Theo with a sense of well-being that he had not felt for some time.

Then, as he was readying himself to leave, Sergei faced him, his features as stern as before, and said:

'Kick them off our world, Major, those Sendrukan *gaduki* – send them to hell!'

He gripped Theo in a bonecrushing handshake before they parted, Theo following the road till he reached a main junction. There he caught a spinnerbus that was bound for the city centre. He was dressed in a long shabby coat over a chunky woollen pullover and tough work trousers tucked into thick wool socks. The coat and trousers had been streaked and splattered with mud, which also clung to the field boots he was wearing. He also had on a dusty, soft-brimmed hat and a pair of small round spectacles with plain glass instead of lenses. The entire ensemble was far removed from his usual attire and would hopefully allow him to get as far as one of the Assembly building entrances. Once there, he would have one of the couriers take a message to a particular admin warden who was a Diehard associate – she had already agreed to get Theo past the stringent security and up to a store-room near the president's offices. Then she would act as a go-between to arrange a meeting.

Sundstrom did not know that Theo was coming, but Theo knew that he would be there – ever since the announcement of Horst's Decree of Arrest, and subsequent disappearance, the president and his cabinet had been in almost continuous emergency session and keeping the Assembly informed of all developments. The last vee news he saw before leaving Sergei's had said that the remaining ministers were rushing back to Hammergard to attend. And knowing Sundstrom, Theo guessed that he would probably have several reporters close to hand.

From the bus window he saw Earthsphere marines and DVC troopers out on joint patrols in twos and fours, some walking, some in military spinner-carriers. These sightings became more frequent the closer he got to Founders Square. When the bus stopped near a small park, he dismounted and continued on foot, his natural caution heightened by that call from the FDF saboteur.

He was striding up Stefanovich Street, one of the main roads into the square, and had just passed a long row of flower sellers when his comm rang twice and stopped, the alert for a voice note. He took it out, hit the retrieve and held it up to listen.

'Theo, this is Donny – as soon as you hear this message, shut off your comm, take out the battery, then head for cover, get out of sight.'

The message ended. It had sounded like Donny and it was his style. Heart racing, he suppressed the urge to look around him, calmly put the comm in his pocket and one-handed switched it off. Then he managed to slide off the rear panel and pry out the battery. At the same time he had stopped to look at some of the buckets of flowers and made his way back along past the stalls to an alleyway with lots of arched side passages. After following a twisty route involving a couple of double-backs and plenty of scoping ahead and behind, he ended up in a doorway down a side road that led into the square. The main entrance to the Assembly faced onto Founders Square, with the Reconciliation Memorial, the tree-shaded grassy plots, the stone benches, and at the far side the zeplin terminal. The wreckage of the mooring towers had been removed, and canvas-hung scaffolding now stood all around the terminal building while the sound of jackhammers and saws came clearly to Theo's ears.

He breathed in deep, gathering his determination. There was a secondary entrance round the corner, an ordinary-looking doorway with a sign saying 'Electoral Registrar' but which also gave access to the ground-floor public corridors. Theo stepped out of the doorway but paused when he heard running footsteps approaching from behind. Casually he leaned back against the building, a large store called Sachnussem's, and glanced round to see Donny Barbour hurrying towards him. Warily, Theo faced him and nodded.

'Ye can't go in there, Theo. They've turned your contact, got her kids hidden away to get her cooperation.'

Theo swore. 'Who's got them?'

'Same ones that picked up yer sister, this K5 mob – they're a deep-cover intel unit but their commanding officer has supposedly gone stealth and is issuing orders to his operatives. We're assuming that the CO and maybe some of his people are now working for Kuros, but we've no proof, so the chief of DVC intelligence is allowing the K5 agents who arrested her to carry out the interrogation . . .'

'So help me, Donny, if she's harmed I will kill them!'

'Calm yerself, man – she was only brought in less than an hour ago. Sundstrom knows about this and he's doing all he can to get her released, but you being under suspicion in the matter of Ambassador Horst isna helping!'

Theo shook his head, almost snarling with rage and frustration.

'So what was all that with the comm?' he said.

'DVC intelligence got hold of your comm's signal ID this morning and they've been listening out for it. Their tracking is pretty rudimentary but the Brolturans' isn't – I was told that it would be possible for someone to use the comm-hub network to locate a particular comm, as long as the battery's in and it's switched on.'

'Okay, so what is the next move?' Theo said. 'I'm not leaving Solvjeg in there . . .'

'First things first,' Donny said. 'Where's Horst? Is he all right?'

Theo gritted his teeth, ran his fingers through his hair, grasping a handful for a second. *How the hell am I going to tell this tale?*

'The truth is that I don't know.'

Donny gave him a hard look. 'You're the one that got him away from Gangradur Falls just yesterday – how come ye don't know where he is?'

'I know the last place I saw him.'

'Which was where?'

'A secret chamber under the temple on Giant's Shoulder,' Theo said, and gave him a condensed account of what he had witnessed last night in that cold, black vault. Wearing a frown of concentration Donny listened closely and, to Theo's surprise, became neither angry or derisory. Instead, he nodded thoughtfully.

'Sundstrom once said that the Uvovo were making their own plans for resistance,' he said. 'Wonder if that was what he meant . . .'

'Well that is exactly what happened. Just speak with my nephew Greg, and he'll confirm it all.'

'Aye, well, there's a thing,' Donny said, suddenly sombre. 'A short while before I found you I got a message saying that K5 has arrested Greg Cameron and they're bringing him to Hammergard by zeplin.'

Theo bowed his head a little, feeling the weight of events. *My family*, he thought. *I've put them in danger . . .*

Then he realised something and snapped his fingers.

'By zeplin . . . that means they'll have to tie up at Northeast Fields and come the rest of the way by road. Can I borrow your comm?'

Donny regarded him a moment. 'You thinking of putting yer Diehards up against K5? – wouldna recommend it, they're hard cases, each and every one.'

'My men know what's at stake,' Theo said, holding out his hand. Donny give him his comm, a slim, grey functional model, and Theo punched in Rory's number.

'Aye, who ur *you?*'

'Rory, it's me.'

'Jeez, Major, caught me by surprise, there – didna recognise the number . . .'

'Where are you, Rory, and who's with you?'

'I'm at Maclean's wee place on the coast road, just outside the city, and there's Janssen, Ivanov, Henriksen, Mad Davey, and Nikolai and Barney're here, too.'

'They're supposed to be at Bessonov's . . .'

'Aye, Major, but the cabin got raided last night – cops and some hard-looking milint types hangin' around by the time we got there so we scarpered.'

'Okay, I need you to get across town to Northeast Fields – Greg Cameron's being brought in under armed guard and I want you to take down the escort and get him safely out of the city.'

'Right, sir, what are we up against?'

Theo looked at Donny. 'How many guards and what will they be carrying?'

'Shouldn't be more than four,' said Donny. 'Sidearms.'

Theo relayed that, adding, 'And these are well-trained field agents, Rory – they won't be a pushover.'

'That's a'right, Major – me and the boys like a wee bit ae' a challenge now and then.'

'Fine – and don't take Barney unless he's happy with the idea of being shot at!'

'Right – we're on our way.'

'Good hunting,' Theo said, then closed the comm and handed it back.

'I hope you know what your doing,' Donny said. 'Now, are you still set on trying to get your sister?'

'Yes – are you going to help me? I'll make the attempt on my own otherwise.'

Donny squeezed his eyes shut for a moment, as if at a stabbing headache. 'I must be off ma head,' he said, opening his eyes to stare at Theo. ''Cos ye know what? – I *am* going to help ye, though God knows it's going to be risky.' He nodded towards the square. 'This way.'

'I thought the ordinary detention rooms were in a sublevel of the main building,' Theo said, realising that they were heading across the square towards the Assembly annexe on the east side, where the Defence Ministry had its offices.

'Aye, but there's a far better chance of me getting you past security at the civilian staff entrance . . .' He slowed and cocked his head. 'Do you hear that?'

Theo heard nothing for a second. There was a sound like a high-pitched whine that grew suddenly into a loud, roaring rush which terminated in a deafening crash as something struck the front of the main Assembly building and exploded. Fire blossomed, the frontage near the top floors broke apart and debris flew . . . a missile of some sort, he realised amid the cacophony. The impact of the noise and the abrupt, violent destruction stunned his senses and he would have stumbled and fallen had not Donny caught his arm and dragged him onward.

'Come on! – we've got to get out of the . . .'

The rest of his sentence was lost as a second missile hit a few yards to the left of the first. Another explosion, a bright flash and an outburst of flame and pulverised stone. Alarms were yammering all around the square and panicking, shouting people were fleeing up side streets. Then Theo stopped in his tracks as a horrifying realisation came to him.

'The top floor,' he said to Donny. 'Isn't that where the president's offices are?'

Donny nodded grimly, then without hesitation they began running towards the burning building.

46

GREG

It was getting aggravating – these K5 people just wouldn't respond.

'So, Lieutenant, I'm curious – what part has your organisation been playing in the hunt for the murderers calling themselves the Free Darien Faction?'

Lieutenant Laing was a tall man with a lantern jaw, dressed like his three subordinates in dark green uniforms lacking any insignia. Seated across from Greg in the zeplin gondola, his features were as impassive as they had been when he had arrested Greg back at Giant's Shoulder. However, Greg was sure there was a doleful look in his eyes that wasn't there when they left the site an hour ago.

'Sorry, Doctor Cameron, that is privileged information.'

'Ah, privileged – what a happy state that must be. Well, I imagine that the true answer is "none" because you're too busy prying into the lives of ordinary folk, rooting through their bins and opening their mail. I can't help wondering what you were up to at the moment when the bullets were flying at the dig back there and people, myself included, were ducking and fleeing for their lives. Compiling lists of subversive library readers, maybe? Or were you secretly recording dissident joke-tellers or perhaps even photographing the cludgie wall graffiti in every bar and dive in Hammergard? Or even arresting elderly women for no reason other than to put pressure on a relative – now *that* is despicable.'

'Your mother is helping us with our inquiries into the disappearance of Ambassador Horst, Doctor Cameron,' Laing said in
a level, deliberate voice.

'Aye, I'm sure she is.' Greg's anger seethed, and part of it was
directed at Uncle Theo for having snatched Horst away and
brought him to Giant's Shoulder. Part of it, also, was self-reproach
for not having been cautious enough . . . but who could possibly
imagine that the Sentinel of the well would grab someone and
spirit them off to God knows where?

So now Uncle Theo was a hunted man, his mother was under
lock and key and he was on his way to join her. And the plain fact
was that while he was scared for them, he was most immediately
worried for his own skin – these four men, his escort, seemed to
display a striking similarity of bearing, all sitting in the same stiff
posture, each face impassive and without a hint of boredom or
wandering attention. In fact, not one of them betrayed any kind
of personal trait or mannerism, he realised with growing unease.
He pondered on the idea of trying to engage one of them in conversation, but before he could do so Laing's comm beeped from
an inner pocket. The K5 lieutenant answered it, listened without
expression, then said, 'Understood,' and put the comm away.

'There is a security alert taking place in the city,' he told Greg.
'All flights are either grounded or diverted. We have been ordered
to divert to another destination.'

'Which is where, Lieutenant?'

'Privileged information may not be passed to unauthorised persons, Doctor Cameron,' Laing said, getting to his feet. 'I am going
to inform the pilot of our change of course. Please do not leave
your seat or my men will put you back in it.'

Greg said nothing but sat back, folded his arms, and gazed
over at the three K5 men, thinking for one bizarre moment how
much they reminded him of the three robot dogs in *The Dancing
Engineer*, a book he'd read many times as a child. What were they
called again? . . . ah yes, Crusher, Digger and Grinder, that was
it . . .

Laing returned to his seat and strapped in as the zeplin began to bank into a descent. Greg could only speculate about their location and battled against feelings of desperation that threatened to swamp his mind. Suppressing thoughts of what might happen to him at the hands of these K5 interrogators, he tried to focus on imagining what Uncle Theo would do in this situation, or even his brother Ian.

Ten minutes later, while the zeplin was being winched down to wherever it was landing, he did not feel any more filled with resolve and a daring boldness than he had before. But then reason told him that since the odds were against him it would be better to be stoic yet prepared, so he kept his mind stoic while his digestion and his legs gave themselves over to quivering terror.

There was a bump as the gondola nudged up against its mooring platform. Laing's subordinates went to open the hatch, tip out a set of folding steps then one by one hurry down them. As Greg followed, with Laing at his back, he saw that they were moored on the ground, an expanse of perfect lawn which stretched out to a white-painted wall with several odd, conical objects spaced along the top.

When Greg reached the foot of the steps, two of Laing's men, Crusher and Digger, seized him by the arms and marched him towards the tail of the zeplin with Grinder behind him, hand grasping his jacket collar. Beyond the tapering stern of the gas-filled envelope, an imposing three-storey house came into view, flanked by smaller buildings, bushes, gardens, trees, and several strange vehicles with stubby wings and painted in green and grey camouflage . . . and in the next instant, with dread rising in a chorus, he saw the group striding towards them, long strides made by tall Sendrukans in uniforms and carrying long weapons with multiple barrels . . .

'No . . . *no*, you can't do this! Laing . . .' He started to struggle but his captors only tightened their grips. '. . . you cannot hand me over to these people . . .'

'I am under orders to render assistance to the lawful representatives of the Sendrukan Hegemony,' Laing said. 'Said representatives have requested temporary extradition so that questions may be put to you, which is permissible under emergency powers . . .'

'Emergency . . . are you out of your mind?'

'Thank you for aiding our inquiries, Lieutenant Laing,' said another Sendrukan, who had appeared from behind those in uniform. 'I am Assister Sejik, security-master to the High Monitor.'

Like the soldiers he towered over the humans, but unlike them he wore pale, flowing garments and in one hand carried a slender, golden stave bearing a line of black characters and tipped with a small silver figurine.

'I am glad to be of help, Assister.'

'Under the agreed terms we shall return Doctor Cameron to your custody in six hours,' said Sejik. 'Would you care to wait?'

'I am instructed to return after the allotted period, Assister Sejik.'

'That is acceptable.'

Laing's men suddenly released Greg but, before he could react, one of the uniformed Sendrukans grabbed both his arms, staring stonily down at him while a second produced a silver object which was pressed against his neck. Abruptly, all feeling in the rest of his body vanished and his head lolled forward. The terror that gripped him was swamped by a surge of numbness. Sights and sounds were blurred, vague shapes passing by, deep voices booming to one another, strange, distant sensations of motion, a muffled swaying, a slow heavy tread . . .

Awareness came back in a rush, like a drowsy halfsleep dispelled by fearful realisation. Greg found that his hands were bound behind him and he was sitting at a square, cloth-covered table on which several glassy, gourd-like vessels were grouped around a crystalline pitcher with six or seven spouts. The table and chairs were on the Sendrukan scale and he felt like a child seated in an adult's place. The table covering was a detailed depiction of humanoid creatures, Sendrukans, he presumed, engaged in a variety of warlike activities. Similar framed tapestries adorned the leaf-patterned walls, along with some far more modernistic pieces – or so they seemed to his eyes. Long, openwork curtains hung before tall windows, and gauzy, embroidered banners were draped low over the table and in the corners of the room. The impression was one of cultured opulence without excess, while the artworks spoke of violence.

'Doctor Cameron, it is most pleasing to meet you again.'

A deep voice, rich and expressive, spoke and High Monitor Kuros stepped into view from behind Greg's chair. He was dressed in shades and layers of grey, patterned and semi-opaque, and wearing his tall, black helical headgear. The features, so Human-like, were composed, the large dark eyes fixed on Greg as Kuros took a seat near the table's corner, his long, graceful fingers toying with a small blue vial.

'I cannot say the same, High Monitor,' Greg said. 'Handing me over into your custody clearly runs contrary to the basic tenets of liberty. I implore you to return me to the keeping of Darien's civil authorities . . .'

'But we need you here, Doctor Cameron,' Kuros said. 'We have many questions and we are sure that you have the answers.'

'But under our constitution I have personal rights,' said Greg. 'You have given many speeches that mention the importance of freedom and liberty – surely you understand . . .'

'I do, Doctor Cameron, but unfortunately you do not understand what we mean by freedom and liberty. These are qualities conferred upon Sendrukan society by the power of the Hegemony – they do not exist by themselves in the universe so they must be created by the pinnacle of Sendrukan culture, the Hegemony and its laws. Our freedoms and liberties are not permitted to contradict the purpose and stability of the Hegemony, since that would diminish its glory and harm its ability to provide guidance to less mature civilisations. Instead, they serve the Hegemony's purpose, as must you now.'

Greg stared at him. 'But when our government finds out . . .'

Kuros shook his head. 'As of roughly forty minutes ago, the colony's governing executive ceased to function due to the deaths of President Sundstrom and his cabinet in a rocket attack on the Assembly buildings. Of course, my government and our Brolturan allies are ready to offer any assistance in this crisis.' He leaned forward a little. 'But now I need you to concentrate on my voice and listen very carefully.'

Then the Hegemony envoy said several strange words, a phrase in Sendrukan perhaps, enunciated clearly and precisely . . .

An odd sensation passed through Greg, a disorientating shiver that felt like sounds and tastes and smells, or was it . . . a shiver that passed through his surroundings, adding something familiar to it all, the furniture, the hangings, the smiling Sendrukan seated before him. And for some reason he felt like smiling too – even though reason told him that he was still in danger.

'Now, Doctor Cameron, what do you know about the involvement of your uncle, Major Karlsson, in yesterday's disappearance of Ambassador Horst?'

'Oh, Uncle Theo brought the ambassador to Giant's Shoulder in the evening but when I heard that the Brolturans were coming we all went down to hide in the well chamber . . .'

'Stop,' said Kuros, his posture and unwavering stare betraying a more intense regard. 'Tell me about this well chamber.'

And to Greg's horror, he told the Sendrukan all about the well chamber, the traps, the Sentinel, the Uvovo and their part in its history, Horst's abduction, everything he knew. Greg had no control over the flow of words which came out in an almost happy jabber, as if he were talking about soccer scores with a close friend over a pint. Likewise, the muscles of mouth and throat were being directed by something else, something in his mind . . .

Am I going crazy? he wondered. *Have they made me mad . . .*

At last Kuros was satisfied, told him to stop and in mid-sentence Greg fell silent. Kuros smiled thoughtfully then held up the small blue vial he had brought to the table – it contained what looked like a fine powder.

'Your talkativeness has, of course, been artificially induced. While you were semi-conscious earlier, we instilled an instrumentation into your body, engineered particles fine enough to become a vapour which you breathed in, allowing them to quickly find their way to the ridges and grooves of your brain. They are keyed to my voice and, having meshed with your synaptic pathways, are capable of many things including the divulging of anything that you know.' Kuros smiled at the blue vial, tipping the contents to and fro. 'We have encountered a few races with the ability to resist the vapour – Humans are not one of them, which makes you very useful.'

He uttered another phrase in Sendrukan and Greg caught the sense of it for just a second, a lyrical expression, a line of poetry perhaps. Then a barrier went down and his fear and hate connected with the muscles in his face and his throat and chest, a rushing slam of rage that came out as a wordless cry.

'Thank you, Doctor Cameron, you have been most helpful. I look forward to the weeks ahead,' High Monitor Kuros said as he stood, towering over the Human.

'You said I . . . was going back with Laing . . .'

'That was only part of the opening formalities, Doctor Cameron, which must always be observed. No, it will be announced publicly that we find you innocent of all charges, then you will say that you have agreed to lead a joint Human–Sendrukan team dedicated to investigating new, exciting finds at Giant's Shoulder. A gesture of solidarity between our two great civilisations, a strengthening of our precious alliance.'

Greg, head bowed, said nothing. Kuros, though, muttered to himself for a moment or two before addressing Greg again.

'Doctor Cameron, my inner companion, General Gratach, wishes to speak to you.'

Greg glanced up to see a change come over Kuros's features as the Sendrukan reached down and roughly grasped Greg's jaw, forcing him to look up. Fury and contempt burned in those eyes.

'I am Gratach, Human – when I capture your uncle, this Major Kalsun, he will not receive such soft treatment. I will break him and crush him, then break all you Human rabble and your talking pets!'

The big hand released Greg's jaw and the Sendrukan turned aside, his face altering once more, as did his stance.

'You will be working with us for a long time to come, Doctor

Cameron,' Kuros said as he moved towards the double doors. 'Reconcile yourself to your part and you will reap the rewards. Now I must leave to deal with the current crisis and ensure that peace and stability return to Darien.' He left, both doors closing silently behind him.

Seated there, bound to the chair, Greg's thoughts dwelled on Kuros's words about that vapour of engineered particles, and imagined the worst.

The peace of death, he thought. *Or the nearest thing to it. Is this what they have planned for us, infecting us with their vapour, turning us all into happy, compliant serfs? God help us . . .*

And what were they going to do to him, or even make him do? Be the Human mask for their operations on Darien? Betray his friends, perhaps? – that might be the worst thing that he could imagine, but he had no doubt that the vapour's designers had dreamed up a few more.

As he sat there he could hear other occupants moving around in the big house, the muffled sound of voices, the tread of feet in the corridor outside. Then one of the room's double doors began to open quite slowly to a quarter of the way before closing again, gradually, without haste and without anyone entering. Greg stared, thinking dully that maybe a guard had started to come in, then changed his mind.

'Friend Gregori . . .' came a whisper from nearby.

And before his eyes the air darkened and Chel emerged like someone stepping through a liquid door. Then the diminutive Uvovo staggered over to lean on the table, the short fur on his face and neck bristling and all four of his new eyes glaring out at the surrounding room.

'Forgive me, Gregori . . .' Chel began.

'Chel! – in the name of . . . how did ye get in here? How did . . . I mean, you were invisible.'

'Observation is alteration, friend Gregori – these eyes create strange avenues.' Chel was recovering, standing straighter. 'I have found that I can perceive hidden meanings and consequences in what I see, but I can also temporarily alter consequences, like making the air become a concealing shell which enabled me to climb aboard the zeplin that took you away, and then to find my way here after the landing.'

'You look exhausted,' Greg said.

'Well observed,' Chel said as he turned to regard Greg with all six eyes, whereupon he froze on the spot, staring. And Greg knew what he was seeing and knew that Chel would still try to rescue him.

'I see them,' Chel murmured. 'And they can see me . . . Greg, what are those things?'

He tried to explain the concept of nano-engineered particles as a mechanism of control but had to settle for the idea of 'the dust of the Dreamless', a kind of ghost entity put in his head to compel obedience.

'And I don't see how it's possible to get it out again,' he said. 'So that makes me a danger to you and everyone else – you really should leave me here and go . . .'

Chel blinked in sequence, a bizarre sight to behold, then he reached down to Greg's bonds and released him.

'I understand your reasoning, Gregori, but you are my friend – I cannot let you face this alone. And after we leave this place, I shall take you to the nearest daughter-forest and see what the root-scholars can do about this Dreamless poison.'

Greg nodded, feeling a stab of emotion at this show of solidarity and brotherhood. He cleared his throat.

'So how *are* we going to get out of here?' he said. *While avoiding the sound of Kuros's voice.*

'I confess, Gregori, I do not know,' Chel said. 'Maintaining the air-shell concealment requires a great effort – I could not keep both of us hidden long enough to reach the front door, never mind the entrance to the grounds.'

'Maybe you could go for a hunt around this place and find some weapons,' Greg said.

'I think I could do that,' said Chel, just as they heard the distant sound of gunfire coming from the front of the house. They looked at each other for a moment then Greg started to get up, but Chel pulled him back.

'Listen!'

The gunfire was louder, or there were more guns firing. There were also shouts coming from other parts of the house, orders being given, and the thudding of boots. And one pair approaching the room. Chel's eyes, all six, widened as he grasped Greg's shoulder . . . and the air turned to swirling eddies of shimmering opacity shot through with emerald gleams, a flux of slow currents with Chel as their hub.

The doors flew open and in strode a Sendrukan soldier who took one look at the empty chair and dashed back out, bellowing at the top of his voice. The glittering curtain faded and Chel said:

'Quickly, over there in the corner . . .'

Greg followed the Uvovo's directions and went to crouch in the corner with Chel kneeling next to him, eyes staring with a burning intensity into some facet of reality that Greg would never know. The air darkened into languid swirls of glimmering fog a moment before Kuros hurried into the room, followed by one of his aides. He went round to the chair, examined the loosened plastic cuffs, then stood and surveyed the room.

'How could the Human have escaped, exalted?' said the aide.

For a moment, Kuros said nothing as he studied the room, the walls, the tall, curtained windows, even the floor.

'The floors in this hovel have a substantial gap between the boards and ceilings,' he said, crouching down, the palm of one long-fingered hand resting on the polished wood. 'There may be an access or a trapdoor . . . is that where you are hiding, Doctor Cameron?'

His voice was low and deadly as he then began to intone the words Greg feared most, that phrase, the key . . . He felt the alteration begin, the shiver of surrender in those subservient particles, their collective eagerness to comply as Kuros continued, 'Are you here? – show yourself now!'

But something stifled that rush to obey, kept the muscles from engaging, the mouth from speaking. Chel, it was Chel! – Greg knew it had to be him, somehow altering the consequences and suppressing the parasitic particles' automated response. Yet the

strain was showing in the Uvovo's face, his strength was ebbing
and soon his intervention would fail. While Kuros stood there,
watching, waiting . . .

And that was when the wall and part of the ceiling fell on him,
a cascade of brickwork, joists and plaster dust. Greg saw the
High Monitor go down and when the soldier went to his aid a
massive metal claw punched through another part of the wall,
showering him with rubble, knocking him senseless to the ground.

There was a raucous machine roar coming from beyond the
half-demolished wall. Greg realised that he was in control of himself again while finding that he was having to support Chel's
semi-conscious form as he got to his feet. Then a face appeared at
the hole in the wall, hazy through the clouds of dust.

'He's here!'

A second face replaced the first – it was Rory.

'Hey there, Mr C – how's it goin'? Just a sec and we'll have ye
outa there!'

A moment later, the mechanical claw swung down again and
gouged part of the wall down to floor level, raising further pale
and billowing clouds. This is it, he realised – we have to make a
break for it now!

Shouts were coming from the hallway outside the wrecked
room as he slung the insensible Chel over his shoulder and hurried
towards the jagged gap in the wall where Rory and others were
waiting, beckoning. As he clambered over rubble and broken ceiling beams, he risked a backward glance and saw Sendrukan
soldiers running towards the room entrance, curve-snouted
handweapons coming to bear. And as his gaze swept back he
spotted the dust-caked form of High Monitor Kuros crawling
from beneath the wreckage. Their gazes met for a split second,
and a surge of fear propelled Greg on through the gaping hole to
where eager hands took Chel from his shoulder.

Gunfire like high-pitched, rasping bursts came from within and
was met with return fire including, he noticed, a couple of cross-
bows and handfuls of caltrops. Greg just had time to register the
huge mechanical digger with its hydraulic arm buried in the side

of the house, and Rory tugging on his arm, urging him towards the waiting hillcar, before Kuros's voice came to him, those deadly words carrying over the noise of the firefight.

The world about him seemed to drain away, leaving only wavering views of the house, muffled sounds of weaponsfire, Rory yelling at him to stop, but he knew that he had no control, that the nano-particles were only obeying their master. Then someone grabbed his shoulder and pulled him back, but the particles made him struggle and cry out until something struck his head and the light and the house and everything crashed down into darkness.

PART FOUR

47

ROBERT

The shifting ivory glow that illuminated the bottom of the immense, winding cave barely reached the narrow ledges and precarious paths which notched the upper reaches of its sheer walls. As he paused to peer over a low rampart of mineral deposit as smooth and nacreous as melted opal, he glimpsed the shadows of large creatures and heard them squawk and whoop to each other between the grunts and snorts. Which was the most he had witnessed since arriving here over a day ago, but then his escorts had kept him from venturing along any passages leading downward with emphatic warnings of deadly danger. The temptation to leave them was tempered by his natural caution and amplified by his lack of company.

'Must keep moving, Human Horst,' said a tinny, scratchy voice. 'Conveyance 289 awaits us at the Great Terrace – it will take us to the upgate and thence to the Construct.'

It was one of his small mechanical escorts, the one he had come to think of as Tripod-Reski: the others were Track-Reski and Hover-Reski. They insisted that they were elements of a single entity, a kind of machine-mind collective going by the name Reski Emantes. Tripod-Reski was a foot-tall mech with three jointed legs supporting an odd glass torso which contained blurred, many-coloured components that flickered and glowed, and was wrapped in a black mesh carapace. A squat ovoid sat on top, encircled by an ocular band.

'And how long will it take to reach this Great Terrace?' he said.

'Hours rather than days, Human Horst,' said the tripod. 'If you make no further delay. Delay means we miss the upgate, and means adversaries gain advantage.'

Robert sighed and moved on. The little mechs spoke of adversaries but would not say who they were. Likewise this vast cave, which they referred to as the Refulgence, or the Great Terrace or the Broken Dome, amongst several others which he assumed were also imposing caves buried deep beneath the mountain ranges of Darien. Yet all they would voice was the preposterous notion that he had been dispatched far into the depths of hyperspace to some kind of collapsed continuum, the kind of fanciful idea one might hear from the shaman of a primitive culture and which he would normally have handed over to Harry to deal with.

But Harry was silent and had been so since that terrifying ordeal in the Uvovo chamber. As was Rosa's intersim device which he had put in his gown pocket back at the Gangradur Falls. He knew that the batteries were fully charged yet when he turned it on it remained inert, unlit, blank, empty.

Like me, he thought. *Without Harry and Rosa I feel . . . alone.*

The path they were following was uneven and strewn with gravel, and damp with the water that seeped in from above and collected in a myriad little puddles. Up ahead, Track-Reski was waving one of its retractable stalk-arms at them from a side tunnel out of which a pearly runoff trickled.

'We must take this stone lane,' it said. 'Enemies wait further ahead along Refulgence.'

'Enemies?' Robert said, alarmed.

'This way leads to the lithosphere of Abfagul,' said Tripod-Reski. 'That regime is inimical towards AI mechs such as we.'

'True, but it is even more inimical towards our pursuers,' Track-Reski said.

'I have seen no pursuers,' Robert said. 'Who are these enemies?'

A humming sound drew near and he turned to see his third escort bobbing and gliding along on an air cushion generated beneath its oval hull.

'Enemies behind,' it said. 'Enemies across . . .'

Gazing across the stalactite-bearded ceiling, Robert saw a black shape move in the gloom, long and writhing like a snake made of black smoke. As he watched it stretched and flowed up to the ceiling and began to advance across it.

'We must go!' said Hover-Reski. 'Go now!'

Urged on by his escorts and a jolt of unreasoning fear, he climbed up the sloping passage, quickly following the glowing beams shining from Track-Reski's headlamps, gradually slowing as his strength ebbed. Yet still he stumbled along as the passage widened, its walls rising higher, and became a rocky path winding along the bottom of a long, gloomy fissure while an irregular, semi-musical clanging noise went on far above. Soon the narrow path became a tunnel again, which dipped downwards for a stretch, took an odd twist and turned back upwards, its dank darkness broken by the escorting mechs' wavering lamp beams.

A grey oval emerged from the dark up ahead and soon Robert was clambering out of a hole on a grassy slope dotted with huge, mossy boulders. A thick, grey mist hung low in the cold, still air and the light was meagre and diffuse, like twilight or pre-dawn. Off to one side was a still, reflective pool of water, over which a group of odd insects with long writhing tendrils buzzed and spun and danced. Feeling weary he sat on the ground, heedless of the damp grass, watching the insects as he got his breath back.

'This is the lithosphere of Abfagul,' said Tripod-Reski as it presented to Robert a square tablet of the fibrous ration that the mechs had been feeding him since his arrival.

'Who or what is Abfagul?' Robert said as he bit and chewed.

'Species and hierarchy,' said Hover-Reski as it glided past, heading downslope to scout further ahead.

'Are they native to Darien?' Robert said. 'This climate feels as if it could be on the same latitude as the colony, yet I've seen no mention of another established culture . . .'

'Our apologies, Human Horst,' said Track-Reski, setting down a thin beaker of water for him. 'We cannot answer your queries – falsifying your frame of reference may have unwanted consequences.'

Robert frowned and drank the water, resenting the comment.

'You have offered no proof that we are in some deep level of hyperspace, as if the universe were built of layers!' He gestured around him. 'This seems like outdoors in a temperate climate, yet you call it a, what, a lithosphere?'

'This lithosphere is one of several in this particular stratum,' said Tripod-Reski. 'Some of the others are almost on planetary-body scales, and thus prone to entropo-pressure collapse. This is one is only about a thousand miles in diameter . . .'

'All right,' Robert said, angry yet willing to humour his companions. 'Let's say that hyperspace is another kind of universe . . .'

'Universes,' said Hover-Reski, emerging from behind a large split boulder.

'The desiccated remains of dead universes sink down into hyperspace and accrete in a sedimentary fashion,' said Track-Reski. 'Do we have time to explain the structure of the Strativerse?'

'No,' said Hover- and Tripod-Reski in unison.

'Then why have I been abducted?' Robert said, suddenly angry at this ridiculous situation and wishing Harry was here.

'Only the Construct can tell you that,' said Tripod-Reski. 'And the sooner we reach the upgate, the sooner you will know.'

After that they said little of substance as Robert allowed himself to be steered across an austere, hilly landscape veiled in an unending, misty dusk. Now and then, mournful, ululating cries reverberated through the sky overhead and once they heard something answer from far off behind them, a harsh implacable sound. Not long after they heard the same harsh call but now from ahead and away to the left.

'Hunters are out,' said Hover-Reski.

'Are they hunting us?' Robert said, suddenly anxious.

'They hunt anything that strays into their sphere,' said Track-Reski. 'Luckily, the stone lane to the Great Terrace awaits us on the other side of the next hill . . .'

Robert could feel his heart hammering and his throat ached from the quickness of his breath, but he felt relief when a tunnel entrance came into view. The three mechs paused on the crest of the hill to scan and map the immediate area before beginning their descent. They had all gone a few yards when the mechs suddenly leaped ahead, dashing downslope.

'Quickly, Human Horst!' said one. 'Hostile is closing!'

'But . . . where?' Robert said, breaking into a run, looking to either side and seeing nothing.

'Above!'

All he could do was snatch the briefest of upwards glances and almost stumbled when he saw the winged horror that was plummeting towards them, a writhing monstrosity of eyeless, snapping heads, hooked tentacles and clutching claws. The mechs were now only slightly ahead of him and they reached the mouth of the tunnel and dived inside just as the monster landed heavily and, with a deafening, multi-throated roar, threw itself after them.

Gasping and wheezing from the effort, Robert staggered to a halt to lean against the tunnel wall and get his breath back.

'Keep running, Human Horst!' said Tripod-Reski.

'. . . sorry . . . need to . . .'

The little mech grabbed the flapping hem of his gown and pulled at it with surprising strength. In the next moment the tunnel shook as the winged monster rammed itself up against the entrance, claws tearing at its edges while tentacles tipped with gleaming pincers and fanged mouths snaked forward. The tunnel floor trembled, stones and clumps of earth fell from its roof, and now all three mechs were urging Robert to retreat.

'Back to solid rock, human Horst,' said Track-Reski. 'Before entrance collapses.'

The grotesque beast was grinding and gouging the tunnel wider, howling with a dozen mouths as it tried to wedge itself further along. Running and stumbling alongside the mechs, Robert heard the deep rumble of a cave-in from behind, followed by a muffled roar of hate and fury. Clouds of dust puffed up from the collapse, and several yards on Robert's knees gave way and he sat down in the dirt, legs akimbo, gasping for breath, massaging a pain in his side.

'What was . . . that . . . *thing*? . . .'

'Abfagul,' said Hover-Reski as it hummed off downslope. 'Small one . . .'

48

CATRIONA

The hunt was nearing its conclusion. She and her troupe, two Listeners and eighteen Scholars, had paused up in the subcanopy to await the arrival of another Listener and five Scholars from Seacloud on the northern coast. They were some 900 feet above the forest floor with the light of day waning, golden yellow shading into amber and filtering down through Segrana's leafy veils. Gloom was already seeping into the cooling depths, but Cat knew where their quarries were because her eyes had other eyes to help her—

From its perch on a low, leafy branch, the kizpi *watches the clearing. A crouching, camouflaged figure creeps slowly through the undergrowth at one side, its featureless armoured head moving from side to side to 360 its sensor sweep, its short-bodied and undoubtedly lethal weapon held two-handed and aimed forward.*

Eyes that she could search for and with, but only for short spans of time – using these small creatures like this panicked them, causing them to dart away into the shadows. But now, some 30 yards west of the *kizpi*, she had found an *umisk*, a flighted lizard with excellent eyesight and hearing. It had just caught and eaten a large, juicy insect and had paused on a branch to preen a few dislodged feathers when movement below snared its attention—

Ghosting through undergrowth with precise steps, the intruder stops to scan its surroundings, around and above. The diminishing light gleams dully on the helmet visor as it turns and tilts up, arms raising the weapon along the same line of sight. Its short barrel gives the tiniest of jerks along with a quiet, flicking sound, and an arboreal animal, grazer or hunter, falls to the forest floor with a rustling thud. The intruder moves on.

Cat let the *umisk* slip away, aware of the many other small beasts going about their business in that earthy darkness. It was actually possible to use her bonds with Segrana to call on the senses of all creatures in the forest surrounding the Ezgara, thereby studying it in the round, but there would little advantage to it. Besides, such an act would leave her weak and mentally exhausted when right now she needed all of her faculties, both old and new.

'They know we're here,' she told the Listener who sat on the branch next to her.

'Will they be aware of what we have done to their devices?' said Listener Malir, a Warrior Uvovo from Overstream.

It had only been hours since scouts discovered charges set against the central pillar-trees of three main buttress clusters, the outer north, outer northeast, and outer east. With the use of potent acid (from several *poroon* beetles) and quick-setting *syldu* sap, the trigger mechanisms were rendered inert. But Cat was sure that these Ezgara were getting scanning and update information from somewhere, possibly a small satellite left in orbit which could also provide links to their bombs. When they were disarmed, some alarm might have been set off, warning the commandos that their presence had been detected. Hence their high state of alertness as they headed southwest, straight towards Pilipoint Station.

A lanky Uvovo swung down from an adjacent tree to join Cat and Listener Malir.

'Honourable Listener and Pathmistress,' he said, eyes wide. 'The Seacloud Listener approaches.'

That was what they were calling her – Pathmistress. She didn't like it but the Listeners of Highsonglade had decided on it soon after waking from the Segrana-sent dream they had all undergone.

And when she went out into Segrana's dense heartlands she found that the dream had not been a localised event. It helped when she needed information and scouts but made her feel a kind of responsibility she had never experienced before. But she was able to put that to one side and focus on her task, the bargain she had made, the protection of Segrana and the People of the Leaves.

The Listener from Seacloud was called Okass and his five Scholars were all armed with fishcatcher whips with which, they asserted, they could snatch a weapon from unaware hands in the blink of an eye. She decided to send them with Malir and his seven Scholars while she accompanied the other Listener, Juso from Skygarden, whose eleven were skilled with nets.

Malir and Okass moved away and downwards, following Cat's directions towards the more westerly of the two intruders while she and Juso went after the other. While the Uvovo could travel with swift agility, Cat was forced to make do with a *trictra*, strapping into the leathery harness then following on through the interwoven branches and lichenous curtains of vines. Her strange connection to Segrana allowed her to catch glimpses of the two quarries as well as the Uvovo converging on them, and it was soon apparent that the Ezgara knew what was happening. Abandoning stealth, both were charging full-tilt through the forest, with the Uvovo leaping from tree to tree and gaining on them.

And it was Malir and Okass's Scholars who pounced first, seeking to snare the intruder's feet and disarm him in one fell swoop. But the Ezgara proved wily, jumped the hook-tipped whip meant for his ankles, ducked and rolled under the one coming for his compact rifle. Then sprayed the forest to either side with arcs of needles or spines from the smaller weapons held in his lower hands. Someone shrieked in agony and fell but the hunt continued.

Catriona lost track of the chase then – most small animals had fled the immediate area, frightened by the violence. Moments later she heard a harsh, muffled buzz coming in short bursts. More cries, then an uneasy silence. She scoured the nearby forest from the depths to the heights and found a long-backed *vithni*, a female out hunting for her cubs. It was easy to persuade her that tasty grubs lay in a certain direction and soon –

The vithni *clambers along a series of low branches, keeping pace with the party of exultant Uvovo who are carrying a bound figure on their shoulders. Its helmet and armoured jacket are missing and Cat is astonished to see that the Ezgara has a very Humanlike face, well-proportioned male features with calm grey eyes gazing fixedly upwards. The man does not struggle yet a certain intensity emerges in his face, the eyes beginning to widen and stare, the lips drawing back from the teeth, a flushed hue spreading red and mottled over the skin. Then his head starts to tremble, his eyes show the whites, he smiles and fire blooms in his mouth before an explosion blots out everything*

The bond with the *vithni* vanished and a thunderous detonation reverberated through the forest. Cat gasped at the severed connection, gasping for breath, almost stunned with disbelief. The spidery *trictra* beneath her shifted nervously while she tried to calm herself in the face of this new horror. A suicide self-destruct – was this another example of Sendrukan cruelty?

'Quickly,' she said to the Scholar escorting her. 'Rush ahead and tell Juso that I want him to hold back, leave the intruder alone but keep tracking him.'

The young Scholar nodded eagerly and was off, disappearing into the shadowy trees while Cat urged the *trictra* on. Cries of pain filtered through the forest from the epicentre of that deadly retaliation but she had to armour her mind against grief and focus on how to snare the other Ezgara and keep him alive . . . then something came back to her, an image caught by her Enhanced-created perfect recall – the bright heat that flared in the bound Ezgara's mouth, and the way the skin of his neck and upper chest split along white-hot lines. She recalled that instant before the *vithni* link broke, the intense concentration in the man's face, the relentless effort – if these Ezgara could trigger that self-destruction at will, then their remaining quarry would have to be subdued quickly then rendered unconscious before a second obliteration could take place.

Listener Josu was waiting for her on the meeting branch of a small harvest town called Sweetseed – it was really four large branches interwoven over a pool, platformed with mats and decorated with fragrant blooms and flowering creepers. The townsfolk stayed out of sight, except for an elder Scholar who brought cups of *emel* juice on a tray for them both then went back inside.

'We have stayed our hand as you instructed, Pathmistress,' Josu said. 'Are the intruders more dangerous than you thought? We heard a loud explosion.'

Cat explained what she had seen and what she knew, about which Josu was initially sceptical until one of Okass's scholars arrived to report the tragedy. Seven Uvovo were dead, including Listener Okass, and when questioned he confirmed Cat's account, his words emphasised by his wounds.

'We must take this other one alive,' Cat said, even as doubt gnawed at her. *Seven dead, from my negligence.* 'It is vital that we find out the Hegemony's intentions, even if it's only the wee bit that a soldier might know, and I want to know more about these Ezgara – if they're Human, we've got to find out where they're from.'

'They have fearsome strength, Pathmistress,' said the young scholar. 'How can we overcome the other one?'

Nodding, Cat turned to Listener Josu. 'We cannot afford to have him conscious when we capture him. He must be put to sleep quickly.'

'A powder for breathing or a liquid for under the skin?' said Josu.

'A powder might affect those restraining him,' Cat said. 'So, a liquid – do you have something in mind?'

Josu smiled. '*Ortha* root – it is common to this area and its core sap is easy to extract. For the Uvovo it relaxes the muscles and thoughts but for Humans it is a mind-taker.'

'And how quickly does it act?'

'I once saw a Human treated with it, an elder female who had injured herself while travelling far away in Segrana – it took effect in four, perhaps five heartbeats.'

Cat nodded. 'Well, this guy is young, fit and well-trained, so have several doses prepared.'

After that they moved swiftly on from Sweetseed, Listener Josu racing ahead to organise the gathering of the *ortha* while the young scholar returned to his injured comrades and Cat progressed at the *trictra*'s more sedate speed, a tense anxiety thrumming in her neck and shoulders. The further the hunt moved away from the site of the explosion, the more forest creatures were out and about foraging or engaged in hunts of their own. Focusing her mind on the bond with Segrana, her senses widened and spread outwards, showing her glimpses of what Segrana saw, the sounds she heard, and other sensations for which taste and smell were only approximations. Just as she could still feel the deathpain of the Uvovo killed by the Ezgara self-destruct and the sorrow of the others' loss, she could also sense the second Ezgara, his passage through the green weave of forest-floor undergrowth, his relentless, crushing pace. Segrana knew, *felt* him journeying through her but she needed Catriona to look, to see, to find and not to yield.

Thus Cat caught flashes of him in the gloom with the eyes of a bird or a reptile or a *baro*, his speed slowing gradually, since he probably reckoned that he had outstripped his pursuers. By now, Cat had caught up with the body of Josu's scholars, who deferred to her with a reverential attitude she didn't feel was justified, yet she was too preoccupied to make a show of disapproval. Then Listener Josu arrived with two local Listeners, one short, one tall, both of them wizened but wiry. Also he brought three cloth pouches, each containing four reed stalks, their tips sharpened, fire-hardened and soaked in gleaming *ortha* sap. These he gave to three trusted scholars with the instruction that the intruder be struck on his bare skin with three stalks. Then he introduced the two locals to Cat – the tall one was called Gruanu, the short one Hiskaja – and pointed out that they knew of an ideal place for an ambush. Cat listened, questioned them and Josu, thought on it for a moment or two and gave her assent.

'Don't forget, Josu,' she said. 'We need this one alive.'

'This we understand, Pathmistress.'

Half an hour later, the final moves of the pursuit were played out among the shadowy trees that clustered near the foot of a sheer, mossy cliff. In the murky gloom, groups of Uvovo converged on the Ezgara's position only to veer off or retreat, feints meant to distract or startle. Then another group made their way from branch to branch overhead, moving above the intruder, prompting him to open fire – when he did so, they dropped nets full of leaves, small forest creatures and even a *pagma* nest or two to confuse him while the Uvovo on the ground started racing towards him from all directions.

Realising the danger, he swung his autorifle down and fired off an arc of razor splines, not seeing the pair of Uvovo swinging down out of the branches. They crashed onto his shoulders and knocked him to the ground. He twisted as he fell, lower arms producing blades that hacked and stabbed, slashing one Uvovo open diagonally from shoulder to hip while the other rolled and ducked out of range.

He had barely got to his feet when two more Uvovo burst up out of the ground and ran at him, dragging between them a rope that hooked his feet from under him. He fell, arms flying wide, and one daring Uvovo lunged in with a weighted sticky net, tangled it around the Ezgara's weapon and wrenched it out of his grasp. After that it was almost a free-for-all with most of the Uvovo diving on the intruder, trying to tie up his limbs and subdue him.

Cat had guided her *trictra* onto a tree branch overhead and watched as they bound up his artificial lower arms then pulled off the helmet and armoured jacket, coping as swiftly as they could with unfamiliar clips and fastenings. As soon as the man's neck and chest were uncovered, two of the pouch-carriers came in close, the third lying wounded off in the dark. Three drugged reeds punctured the man's skin, then everyone hurriedly retreated to watch from about 20 feet away. The Ezgara, who was definitely Human, writhed and struggled against his bonds but his

movements quickly slowed until only his head was moving, slug-
gishly shaking from side to side as if in denial, his mutters slurring
and eventually falling silent, motionless.

Then began the wait. Cat knew that it had taken roughly five
minutes from the point when the first Ezgara was captured to his
self-destruction, so she was determined to let fifteen minutes
elapse this time. Silence fell in the darkening jungle, abandoned by
larger creatures chased away by the violent confrontation. At last,
when the vigil was over, Listener Josu approached cautiously
while Cat directed her *trictra* down to the forest floor. A couple of
the Uvovo brought out *ineka* beetles so at least there was a little
light.

'He is unconscious, Pathmistress,' Josu said. 'And he will
remain so for the rest of the night.'

Four or five hours, Cat reckoned as she knelt beside the sleeping man. *I hope that's enough time to get that bomb out of you.*

He was handsome, in a graze-cut, square-jawed way, dark-
haired, thick eyebrows, quite full lips – in fact, there was a
vaguely Scandic look to him. Peering closer, she saw that he had
a small symbol tattooed just beneath his right ear, a red wolf's
head. Then she laid her hand on his chest, just below his neck, but
as soon as she touched his skin she gasped and snatched her hand
away. Nervous whispers passed around and some of the Uvovo
began to back off.

'What did you feel, Pathmistress?' said Josu from nearby.

Felt and saw, she thought. There had been a feeling of great
danger from under the man's skin . . . and a strange, momentary
vision she decided to keep to herself.

'Something inside him,' she said. 'Something . . .' She touched
his face and his uncovered hands with one fingertip and got the
same sensation.

'In his blood,' said someone.

Glancing round she saw the two local Listeners staring down at
the man, those sunken eyes wide and unblinking, an intense,
twofold gaze.

'His blood?' said Cat.

'A strange fluid, invisible to his body's defences,' said the taller one.

'. . . but dangerous,' said his short companion. 'When mingled with the other fluid . . .'

Cat grimaced – they were describing a binary explosive, two inert liquids which became unstable when mixed. So the other component had to be in some sort of container that shared a membrane with a main artery . . .

The shorter Listener seemed to read her mind and leaned forward to prod the sleeping man's chest. 'Here, a sac lies by the blood flow.' Those hooded, piercing eyes regarded her. 'Remove the blood-borne fluid by filtration and he will live. Otherwise . . .'

'Filtration?' She knew that Uvovo healers employed certain kinds of filtration roots in response to particular maladies, removing impurities from the blood. But for Humans . . .

'Could that work for a non-Uvovo?' she asked Josu. 'For a Human?'

'It has never been practised on a Human,' Josu said. 'It may kill him, Pathmistress, but left alone he would choose death, that much is clear.'

She nodded. 'Aye, there's more than just a touch of death-or-glory conditioning about them, that's for sure. Okay, we'll do it – while keeping a close eye on his well-being.'

With this agreed, the Listeners directed the strongest of the Scholars to carry the bound and sleeping soldier at shoulder height while others helped the injured or brought along the bodies of the Uvovo who had died in the fight. As she watched them move off in procession, her thoughts went back to the strange vision that had flashed into her mind's eye while examining the Human Ezgara – for one vivid instant she had seen Greg, lying seeming asleep at the foot of a curious, many-stemmed bush from which several pale tendrils trailed to either side of his head, joined to the skin. Chel sat nearby, swathed in long, dark robes, keeping watch over him.

Why had Segrana shown her this? Was it a concocted image meant to allay her fears, or a glimpse of something that was real?

For a moment she put a hand over her eyes, finger and thumb massaging an ache in her temples. Then she straightened and called her *trictra* over, knowing her personal worries would have to wait until this situation was resolved.

49

CHEL

It was late afternoon, almost twenty-four hours since the escape from the Hegemony envoy's fortified villa and more than twenty since their arrival at Glenkrylov, a daughter-forest situated in a shallow valley a few miles south of Waonwir. It had been Cheluvahar's idea to bring Greg here in the hope that the root-scholars might find a way to draw out the enslaving dust of the Dreamless. The scholars persevered for many hours, testing a variety of bush and vine filter roots in different combinations until Chel, with his singular perceptions, was able to confirm that they had arrived at a safe and effective arrangement. After Greg had been sedated with *ortha* root extract, Chel settled down to keep watch with all his eyes, studying the diminishing presence of those baleful motes.

At the same time he was coping with a steady stream of visitors, Uvovo who were arriving at the forest in twos and threes or more, fleeing the towns and especially Hammergard, where squads of Brolturan troops were detaining all Uvovo 'on suspicion of collusion with terrorist agitators'. It seemed that the new Unity government had quickly brought in repressive measures in exchange for Brolturan aid in securing law and order. Paradoxically, one of these measures had been the disbanding and disarming of the Darien Volunteer Corps, as well as the reorganisation of local law enforcement and the arming of certain police units.

So these escaped Uvovo had to be provided with food and shelter (and healing in some cases), then formed into small bands and dispatched to those secret Burrows and other refuges off in the western hinterlands. Then there was his role as Seer, which carried the previously unsuspected burden of providing reassurance as well as arbitration in disputes between Listeners. After some eleven hours of this he could feel his mind crumbling under the strain, his perceptions gnawed at by weariness. So, covering his eyes, he left Greg in the care of the healer Najuk, and went to climb a nearby beholder tree, seeking relaxation and a change of perspective.

Beholder trees were chosen for their height and sturdiness, which meant that they were usually *rakins*, on both Umara and the moon. Also, their bark had many knots and wrinkles which provided plentiful hand- and footholds. As he climbed, Chel could feel the kinks and aches beginning to ease, and his torpidity dissolve as the exercise stirred his essential forces. He breathed deep as he moved higher, enjoying the odours and sensation of replenishment that percolated through him.

About a third of the way to the canopy, voices came to him through the leaves, Human voices, and he slowed to seek out the source. Then clambered up onto a thick limb and saw them seated and sprawled on a matted platform fixed to the forked branch of a nearby tree. Seeing Rory and one of the Firmanov brothers among them he waved and Rory waved back.

'How's that patient o' yours, Chel?'

'Much better,' Chel called across. 'He improves by the hour.'

'Any chance he'll be back on his feet in a coupla hours?'

Chel shook his head. 'Not before tomorrow, I think, Rory. When he wakes he will be weak and will need food and rest. Are you planning to leave the forest?'

'Aye . . . well, mebbe, when we've figured out how tae go lookin' for the Major.'

'Will you be going soon?'

'In a few hours, I reckon – we'll drop in and say our g'byes before we scarper.'

Chel nodded and they exchanged waves again as he resumed his climb.

A short while later he reached one of the cloudsteps, the high-est and narrowest of the beholder trees' platforms. A cold and steady breeze stirred the surrounding foliage, bringing fleeting fragrant whiffs, and he could feel the entire trunk sway very slightly. All around were masses of rustling leaves, of shifting treetops over which insects darted and buzzed, tempting birds to swoop and snatch in midflight. Occasional afternoon sunshine broke through the clouds yet it was dry and warm, the air so clear that he could look eastward across the grey expanse of Loch Morwen to the small islands clustered near the mouth of the Gangradur River.

More important, however, was the northerly prospect, the cliffs that rose to meet the lower slopes of ridges, and the mountain spur whose eastern extremity was Waonwir. Chel had heard a variety of rumours about the temple site from arriving Uvovo: the Brolturans were going to use it as a prison for dissidents, or they were going to demolish it, or they were going to build a fortress on it. Whatever the truth, they were definitely doing something up there – last night one of the forest scholars had been up in one of the other beholders and had seen a harsh white glow emanating from the top of the promontory. Now, as he peered at that dis-tant, dark grey mass, there was no sign of such illumination but he could see a small dark speck take off and race towards Hammergard.

He recalled the prescient words of the spectral Pathmaster – *the Hegemony will shortly control Umara . . . soon they will be walk-ing in this very chamber . . .* The words had been shocking but he could never have guessed that they would come true so soon. Such a possibility had not occurred to him when he stole aboard the zeplin that transported Greg down to the city, and now the fate of Listener Weynl and the others, both Uvovo and Human, was a mystery. The same was true of other Listeners like Faldri, Eshlo Shikellik and Murnil, and until now Chel had not realised how much they had come to rely on the Humans' communication devices to knit their far-flung communities together.

The temptation to wait here in Glenkrylov for further news

was strong, yet he knew that he and the forest scholars must lay plans for a swift retreat. He was sure that if Greg had spilled all that he knew, then the Hegemony envoy Kuros must now suspect something of the Uvovo connection with the temple and the well chamber, not to mention the ancient covenant with Segrana that went back to the oldest times. As well as the tales of detentions and beatings, Chel had heard an unconfirmed rumour that Buchanskog, the daughter-forest east of Hammergard, had been invaded by Brolturan troops who destroyed the meditation retreats, the *vodrun* and the scholar abodes before carrying off every Uvovo they could seize. If the offworlders were ready to raid one of the daughter-forests so soon, it was only a matter of time before they moved against the others.

With one last glance at Waonwir, now growing dark as the sun dipped towards the horizon, Chel began the descent, keen to check on Greg's progress but also impatient to plan for the worst outcome. At least that way anything less dire would feel like a reprieve, or even an opportunity!

50

THEO

It was early evening by the time they reached Akessonhold, a rambling farmhouse west of Landfall and their third safe house in the last twenty-four hours. Theo, Donny and Solvjeg were ushered into the hallway, a wood-panelled, L-shaped room with several passages leading off, some up a few stairs, others down a few. Arne Akesson himself was there to greet them, a bald, broad-chested man with a wrestler's build that had earned him the nickname 'the Bull', but among the Diehards he had a reputation for foxy cunning.

'Theo, Donny, and Solvjeg,' he said, shaking hands and giving a courteous bow to Theo's sister while his attendants took care of the newcomers' hats and coats. 'Dearest Solvjeg, it is good to see that you are safe – I heard how these two heroes plucked you from perilous captivity. Please be welcome in my house; these are evil times and friends must stand by each other.'

'Thank you so much, Arne,' said Solvjeg, smiling tiredly. 'It has been a trying day.'

Theo nodded. 'And a hungry one.'

Akesson grinned. 'Ah, I know I am playing host to a famous trencherman so have no worries on that score. I have set aside the small parlour which is just up those stairs and on the right, and will have some provender sent there straight away.'

'So shall we go on up now?' said Theo.

'Let Solvjeg and Donny go,' Akesson said. 'There is someone through in the back room who needs to speak with you, Theo.'

Theo smiled – Arne's back room was an adjoining hut at the rear where he kept his radio equipment.

'I'll be back in a few minutes,' he told Donny and his sister, then followed Akesson out of the hallway.

A narrow passageway lit by oil lamps ran back for several yards, down some steps into a newer wing of the farmhouse then through a large kitchen where pots gave off steamy vapours, stew, baking bread, and something cooking in wine. From the main store at the rear a curtained archway led into another narrow, undecorated wooden corridor and finally a creaky door opened into the hut.

A skinny youth got up as they entered and handed Akesson the headset.

'He's still there, sir.'

'Thank you, Gennadiy. Is the signal encrypted?'

'It is, sir.'

Nodding, Akesson sat down at the radio, an obsolete DVC model whose wooden casing was scored and battered, despite a recent dark blue paint job. The transmitter next to it was a nondescript grubby green unit with what looked like a leather suitcase handle bolted to the side.

'Hello?' Akesson said into the headset's stalk microphone. 'Yes, he's here.' He passed the headset to Theo, who put it on.

'This is Karlsson.'

'Great tae hear yer voice, Major.'

'Rory!' Hope and trepidation leaped in him. 'How's Greg? Last I heard, they handed him over to Kuros.'

'Oh aye, but we busted him outa there with some help from that Uvovo, Chel, and a road digger that Mad Davey got his mitts on. Greg was kind of wounded but not badly – we spoke tae him before we left and he's doing fine.'

Theo grinned. 'Well done, Rory – you've earned your pay for the week. Where are you now?'

'In Rullinge, at Kruger's.'

Rullinge was a boatyard town a few miles down the coast from High Lochiel, and Kruger's was an alehouse of the 'dive' variety.

'And have you been keeping an eye on the news, Rory?'

'Ye could say that, as well as helping it along, like!'

'Well, it looks as if we have just become the official resistance . . .'

'Suits me fine, sir!'

'. . . but until we hear from Pyatkov,' Theo went on, 'we won't know if there are any others that we need to link up with, like former DVC or disgruntled police . . .'

Akesson leaned closer. 'Pyatkov is coming here – he's due in about half an hour.'

Theo nodded. 'Okay, Rory, it seems that Pyatkov will be with us in thirty minutes or so, then we'll know where we stand. But I'd like you and the others to head south and meet us at Membrance Vale. There's a picnic and observation point overlooking the *Hyperion* – that will be the rendezvous, but I want you to keep to cover. We don't know if the Brolturans have the colony under satellite coverage, but we'd best be wary.'

'Right ye are, Major.'

'Good. By the way, what's the mood like in Rullinge?'

'Eh, they're no happy, sir. Kinda goes from the simmering angry types to the full-on, carpet-chewing berserkers. Some of them want to barricade all the roads in and out, some others want to load up the trucks with guns 'n' molotovs and head out to find some Sendrukans tae fight, while the rest are busy getting hammered.'

'They might be a good source of recruits later on. For now, be as low-key as you can when you leave. Be cautious on the roads and watch out for roadblocks – go cross-country if you have to.'

'Got it, Major – we're on our way.'

Theo took off the headset and laid it on the table.

'You look tired, my friend,' said Akesson.

He shrugged. 'This time yesterday we were upstairs in Chyornilov's, that restaurant in west Hammergard, when it was raided by armed police – we got out through a passageway that led through the attics of the next two buildings. We found a garage, hired a rattling old hillcar and got to the Martensson fish farm by about midnight . . .'

'I think I know it – coast road, a few miles south of Port Gagarin. . .'

'That's right. Well, we snatched a few hours' sleep in an empty worker cottage before being woken at five by our main contact – turned out that two military intelligence officers and six Brolturan soldiers had arrived and were questioning everyone. The main gate was blocked so we had to head across a boggy field to the road, carrying bikes that our contact had dug out of the farm stores for us. After that we kept to the farm roads and hill paths and eventually got here in one piece.'

Theo remembered again the desperate and fearful escape under a troubled night sky with an icy breeze buffeting them as shower squalls flew in from the sea.

'Your sister was arrested and questioned, yes? But she seems to have come through it.'

Theo gave a sad smile. '*Ja*, she was always the tough one – never lets any situation get the better of her, or anyone. Although she has been very worried about her boys, Greg especially.' He stood. 'We should return so I can tell her that he is safe.'

Akesson nodded and led the way, pausing in the kitchen to make sure that the food and drink had been sent to the small parlour. Donny and Solvjeg were sitting in armchairs either side of a table crowded with plates of cold meat, cheese, butter, small savoury pastries, and a jug of mulled wine that gave off a heady vapour. A good-sized wood fire blazed in the hearth while gener-ations of Akessons gazed down from the walls. Solvjeg looked up as they entered and when he passed on the news about Greg she put her hand to her mouth and closed her eyes.

'Thank God,' she whispered, then lowered her hand, which she clenched, and nodded at Theo. 'They are all safe, Theo.' During the stopover at Martensson's, word had reached them that Ian and Ned had made it to Invergault and were heading south into the Hrothgar Mountains, thinking to hide out in one of the trapper camps.

Theo and Akesson dragged a couple of wicker chairs closer, poured out mugs of hot wine, then the four of them pooled their knowledge to try and gain a fuller picture of the situation. First, it was now certain that Sundstrom and his cabinet were dead, killed outright by the missile attack. A government of national unity had been formed in the Assembly within hours, although the tiny Foundationist and Redemptionist parties refused to take part, the latter being Viktor Ingram's old party and comprising five Legators. Together with the Foundationists, they represented an official opposition totalling eight Legators, as opposed to the Unity government's 104.

This new Assembly swiftly passed a batch of draconian laws, including several emergency powers which handed huge discretionary powers to the executive, and in charge of that executive was Dugald Kirkland, leader of the Consolidation Alliance and now president pro tem of Darien. And all of it had been conducted with almost no reportage or comment, since many journalists had also been killed in the attack on the Assembly building; in addition, the police were ordered to shut down all newspapers, all vee stations (except Starstream), and all radio stations (except the government information service, which gave out no useful information).

There was just one fly in the greasy ointment of this ruthless stealth coup – Alexandr Vashutkin, Sundstrom's transport minister, was still alive. Having broken a leg while visiting Trond on official business, he had sent his deputy to attend the cabinet's crisis meeting on the disappearance of Ambassador Horst. A decade and a half ago, Vashutkin and Sundstrom had become close friends in the Progressive Dispersalists, but several years back policy differences had come between them, causing Vashutkin to resign from the PD and join the Union for Land Party. Which later became part of Sundstrom's Civic Coalition, thus forcing the two former friends to work together once again.

And Vashutkin was using Trond as his base, from where he made live radio speeches denouncing the Hegemony and its envoy Kuros as tyrants and aggressors and describing the Unity government as spineless collaborators. He reserved his choicest vitriol for Kirkland himself, saying that his motto should be 'No Boot Left

Unlicked', and that he lived in fear of his own intestines which, out of shame, might one day reach up through his throat and throttle him to death.

Vashutkin's tirades, combined with the formal re-establishment of the Northern Towns League, had already made Trond a focus for dissent, protest against and mockery of the assembly in Hammergard. The new laws were being ignored and Hammergard officials bearing enforcement orders had this evening been politely but firmly shown the door. Twenty-four hours since the missile attack the colony was split down the middle; Hegemony advisers seemed to be present at every level of government and Brolturan ground and air patrols maintained a high profile in Hammergard and the major towns, apart from those in the north. From Nivyesta, there was no news.

'What about Earth?' Theo said, draining the last of his wine then reaching for some bread and cheese. 'Have they made any comment?'

Akesson smiled sourly. 'They have not even appointed a new ambassador. That captain of the *Heracles*, Velazquez, was interviewed on Starstream just after Kirkland was confirmed as president, saying how it was a new start for Darien and how we should support the new government, and how grateful we all were that the Brolturans and the Hegemony were helping to stabilise the situation.'

'Aye,' Donny said bitterly. 'Stabilising it with a boot on our necks.'

'He didn't manage a smile once during the interview,' Akesson said. 'He really looked like a man who was carrying out orders that he loathed.'

Donny snorted. 'But he still carried them out. He's still got his men patrolling with the Brolturans.'

'What about Horst?' Akesson said. 'What's happened to him? Did you really kidnap the man?'

Theo shook his head. He had already told Donny and Solvjeg a truncated version of the story, shorn of the Uvovo chamber disappearance, on the principle that what they didn't know couldn't hurt them

'No, no, I saved him from a Brolturan interrogation,' he said. 'I knew he had nothing to do with the bombings so I got him away to Giant's Shoulder, then left him with friends there when I had to go and free my sister. Since when . . .' He shrugged. 'I don't know if he's hiding somewhere or if they caught him. The former, I hope . . .'

'The Brolturans are doing something up on Giant's Shoulder,' Akesson said. 'Machinery working round the clock, big flood-lamps lighting it up at night.'

'I heard that they were building a prison or a fortress, or both,' Theo said, then fell silent when one of the attendants came in and murmured to Akesson. The big man nodded and as the attendant left he turned to the others.

'Pyatkov will be here in about ten minutes – he just left the wayhouse on the Midgard Road. And he's not alone, apparently.'

'That'll be the Enhanced, then,' Donny said, matter-of-factly.

They all stared at him. Enjoying the attention, he refilled his mug and chewed on a savoury pastry.

'Ye know about them, eh?' he went on. 'The kids that they . . .'

'Yes, we know who they are, Donny,' Theo said. 'Why don't you just tell us what Pyatkov's up to, since you seem to know more than we do.'

'Och, I don't know that much,' Donny said, sipping wine. 'But I do know that of the government's secret, hush-hush projects, there was one whose success rate was way out in front, and that's who I think Pyatkov's got with him. Probably wants them moved to a safe house near Trond, or further north, knowing my luck.'

'Enhanced,' Akesson muttered darkly. 'It was terrible what they did to those children.'

Solvjeg sat forward. 'When I was young and still at school, one of my closest friends got herself pregnant by a young man from a neighbouring town, a very pretty boy who could dance most dashingly and play the bala . . . anyway, she and her parents were distraught, but at that time Zhilinsky was promoting his New Children's Programme, with government backing, encour-aging women not to have abortions but to donate the unwanted offspring to his Programme, even before they had reached full term.

'They never admitted in public that Zhilinsky's surgeons were trying to create Human computers – they used words like adjustment or modification or enhancement. Eventually the whole truth was made public when the failures could no longer be concealed. One of them was especially heartbreaking, a young woman of nineteen who had tried to kill herself forty times or more, even though assessments showed her to be a calm, rational mathematical genius – 95 per cent of the time. The other 5 per cent she was monomaniacal, self-hating and self-destructive. When she was discussed on the radio and in the papers they showed her picture and gave her first name, which my close friend recognised right away as her daughter . . .'

A name emerged from Theo's memory. 'Maria . . . Groenvold,' he said.

Solvjeg smiled. 'Yes, that's right, and her daughter was called Ulrike – perhaps some of Mr Pyatkov's companions might remember her . . .'

Akesson held up a hand for silence, and a moment later Theo heard the sound of a vehicle outside, tyres crunching on gravel.

'I'll make sure,' Akesson said, heading out to the hall. Donny, meanwhile, was already on his feet and standing closer to the other doorway. Theo and his sister looked at him askance.

'Hey,' he said. 'Just in case.'

Then Akesson appeared at the door, beckoning them to follow.

The hallway was busy with Akesson giving orders to some of his staff while Pyatkov, wrapped in a fur-trimmed greatcoat, ushered several unsmiling people, three men and two women, through to another room off the hall. The Enhanced were wearing thin indoor clothes which probably accounted for their morose expressions, yet there was also a certain hauteur to their demeanour and they regarded no one else as they trooped through the hall. Solvjeg watched them a moment then put a hand on Theo's arm, smiled and followed the newcomers. Observing this, Pyatkov shrugged.

'I'm afraid that your sister may find them a little close-mouthed,' he said to Theo. 'They've exchanged barely a dozen words with me since I got them out of the Delta Facility, and that was over twenty-four hours ago.' He loosened his coat. 'In any case, this is a short stopover, five minutes then we have to get back on the road. And I need both of you to come with us, and any help from your Diehards, Major, if there are any in the area.'

Theo and Donny exchanged puzzled looks.

'Expecting trouble on the road north, Vitaly?' said Donny.

'Not north, Captain, but east,' Pyatkov said stiffly. 'President Sundstrom reached a secret agreement with the Imisil ambassador that, in the event of a de facto takeover by the Hegemony, particular researchers would be offered political asylum by the Imisil. Their ambassador is currently in talks with Kuros, which means that an Imisil shuttle is sitting on a runway at Port Gagarin right now – we have to get there with all speed, bypass security and see the Enhanced safely on board that shuttle.'

'Is that all?' Theo said. 'What's so special about these people?'

'Aye,' said Donny. 'What's their gimmick?'

Pyatkov's lips were set in a thin line. 'I cannot reveal what I know, but I can tell you that the Hegemony must never find out what is in those Enhanced minds.'

Donny looked at Theo. 'Must be that recipe for reindeer haggis – telling ye, the rumours I've heard . . .'

'Barbour, can you be serious for . . .'

'Okay, Pyatkov,' said Theo. 'Then why are we handing these people over to the Imisil? Are they really to be trusted?'

'Yes – the Imisil government has nominated a member of the Intercessor Council as their guardian.'

'The who?' said Donny.

Pyatkov frowned. 'An interplanetary organisation which, I'm told, has a high reputation for honesty and impartial arbitration.'

Theo shrugged and glanced at Donny, who rolled his eyes then took out his handgun.

'A 50-calibre Chokhov,' he said. 'Just the thing to encourage honesty and impartiality.'

Checking the magazine, he snapped it back in, then winked.

Theo laughed and turned to Pyatkov. 'Some of my men will be waiting at the observation point near Membrance Vale.'

'We can divert to pick them up without losing time.'

'Also I don't even have a weapon.'

'That will not be a problem,' Pyatkov said. 'I brought a selection.'

A few minutes later, as the Enhanced filed back out, now wearing scarves and hats donated by Akesson, Theo went to say goodbye to his sister. She was standing with one of the Enhanced, a slender woman with short black hair and attractive if sombre features. As Theo approached, she solemnly shook Solvjeg's hand and went to join the rest outside.

'Her name is Julia,' Solvjeg said to him. 'She remembers Ulrike and said that she was like a comet among shooting stars . . .' She faced him. 'Are you going too?'

'Yes,' he said. 'It seems that Pyatkov still has need for an old dog of war . . . we're going to break into Port Gagarin and get these folk aboard a shuttle that is waiting to take them up to the Imisil ship in orbit.'

She nodded, gnawed her lip, then shook her head. 'I cannot tell you that you're too old for this, because in truth it's only your body which is too old for it!' Just then, Donny handed him his coat, which he put on. 'I am not your wife, only your sister, but that gives me the right to *tell* you, Theodor Karlsson, to come back alive, with or without your shield!'

'*Ja*, little spear-maiden – who would dare disobey such a command?'

They embraced, then Theo hurried out to where Pyatkov's transport, a battered-looking freight bus, was waiting with its twin flatwheels running. Fine rain was sweeping and swirling down with a gusting breeze, making golden haloes of flying motes around the farmhouse pathway lamps. He leaped up the entry steps, the door concertinaed shut behind him and they drove off into the night.

51

KAO CHIH

He stared with a kind of morose hope out of the viewport at the hazy stars, which were few and far between – only the nearest were bright enough to pierce the cloudy veils of the Huvuun Deepzone. Also, they allowed the navigationals to make some kind of approximation of their position after each microjump – the last three had zigzaggingly carried the *Castellan* towards the subsector where the Darien system was most likely to be, going by the ship's archive of tiernet news.

But those were the last three out of twenty-four microjumps. The hyperspace jump from Shafis to Yonok with its midjourney dropout to normal space had not gone as planned when the exit left them dozens of lightyears inside the Huvuun and unable to get an accurate fix on their location. That was a day and a half ago, since which time Drazuma-Ha* had been employing point-phase variations in the microjump computations while the jumps themselves had to be 42.8 minutes apart because that was how long the tesserae power cells took to self-recharge.

And for Kao Chih, it was stressful, the waiting, the build-up to the six- or seven-minute microjump, the moment of stomach-churning disorientation at the start and the end, then the moments it took the navigationals to plot their unreliable position. No, it was beyond stressful. As he sat there, staring at those few, haze-haloed stars, he could feel a tide of impatience starting to swamp his reason.

'Have the concise data been computed, Drazuma-Ha*?'

'Yes, they have, Gowchee.'

'Then let us make the jump, now – we're getting closer with every jump, so let's not waste any more time than we have to.'

'I must point out that engaging the hyperdrive before the power cells have recharged will cause a drain on our irreplaceable fuel reserves. And there is no guarantee that we will maintain our progress towards Darien.'

'I realise that, but just this once I feel that we should go, now, without delay, immediately.'

'The cells will be recharged in another twenty-eight minutes, Gowchee. Can you not wait that long?'

'I'm afraid not.'

'If you wish, we could play one of the ship's games to help pass the time for you.'

'Thank you for the offer, Drazuma-Ha*, but I would be incapable of concentrating. Please engage the hyperdrive – we may even be lucky enough to come within range of one of those cloud-harvesters.'

Three times during the earlier microjumps the *Castellan*'s sensors had picked up at the outer limits an occasional solitary vessel with an odd emission curve, which suggested that it was sometimes 150 metres long and other times 2.5 kilometres long. By the third sighting Drazuma-Ha* had identified them from a popnet info-doc he had archived years before as cloud-harvesters, ships that scooped up the interstellar dust and debris with kilometres-long energised fields. They were industrial vessels owned by large-resource corporations and operated by AIs or small crews. More important, their drives were T2-capable, as were their shuttle-craft – one of those could execute far more accurate microjumps.

'We can rely on that occurring with as much certainty as arriving perfectly in orbit around Darien,' the mech said. 'However, I perceive that my refusal may lead to an unpredictable outburst on your part . . .'

'I protest, Drazuma-Ha* – I am merely . . .'

'No, I do not wish to be the cause of any extreme reaction . . .'

'That is quite ridic—' Kao Chih began to say, but Drazuma-Ha* activated the hyperdrive and the words and sounds in his throat ran together into a fluttering slur. Then there was that vaguely numb period lasting a few minutes before he was tilted into the exit-surge of spinning-sliding-vertigo, and when it faded he was still in his couch, waiting for the mech to announce their new position.

'I am sorry to have to tell you that we are now 7.9 lightyears further away from the target subsector,' Drazuma-Ha* said.

Kao Chih made an inarticulate sound that was equal parts anger and despair. 'How much longer can this take?' he groaned. 'How much more can I stand?'

'At the current rate of consumption, fuel reserves will be exhausted in eleven months and seven days, and the air will remain breathable for another eight months and twenty-four days, assuming that scrub filters are used. Unfortunately, your food will only last for another three months and nine days, provided that you restrict your intake to quarter-rations.'

Kao Chih listened and nodded soberly while striving against an urge to burst out laughing at the idiocy of the situation. It was irrational, he knew, and a wild mood swing away from the grimness he had been feeling just minutes ago.

'Alternatively,' the mech went one. 'I may be able to adapt one of the large equipment lockers for use as a cryo-unit, or at least something that will lower your . . .'

The mech stopped in mid-sentence and bright field rods stabbed out at the console. Screens flickered and symbol arrays pulsed.

'A ship,' it said, 'has just appeared 1,823 kilometres away. Its profile is that of an Erdishi midhaul freighter but there is no ident signal and the thrust motors seem to be only partly shielded. Their sensors have just found us . . . they have ignited their thrusters and are heading straight for us.'

'Have we got them on visual?' Kao Chih said as the viewport hypershield rolled back. 'Are they responding to hails?'

'Too far for realtime depiction . . . and no comm traffic at all.'

'What about the computations? Are we ready to jump?'

'Yes, Gowchee, the computations are complete but another premature jump would further deplete our fuel reserves.'

'You may recall that we have no weapons with which to fend them off, unless you want me to sit out on the hull and throw empty gas canisters at them . . .'

'Their acceleration curve is very steep,' the mech said. 'That and the degraded state of the superstructure means that the crew cannot be organic.'

One of the screens flashed up an image of the freighter and to Kao Chih it looked like a wreck. Those parts of the hull still attached were charred and holed, while pipes, feeds and cable sprouted from exposed and shattered bulkheads. Something, either a collision or a weapon, had sheared off a slanted portion of the prow while the port side was disfigured by a ragged gouge from the bridge to the midsection. Seconds ticked past and as Kao Chih watched, something bulky and metallic clambered up that gouge, through torn and twisted plating to the gaping bridge where it was met by another two large mech shapes.

Recognition and an awful sense of dread made Kao Chih's stomach feel hollow.

'Those are the droids from Blacknest!' he said. 'Your debt collectors! How did they track us here? Why . . .?'

'Because they are very cunning and very persistent,' Drazuma-Ha* said. 'There may not be sufficient time for the cells to recharge. Brace yourself, Gowchee!'

And his senses spun and swung and plunged, then a few minutes of stability, then another surge of dizziness . . . and he opened his eyes, holding onto the armrests. Another jump, another shot at Darien.

'Why are they going to all this trouble for a bad debt? . . .' Kao Chih paused, thoughts assailed by suspicion. 'You said they were cunning and persistent – how much do you know about these droids, Drazuma-Ha*? And exactly why are they chasing you?'

'I have encountered them before, in circumstances not conducive to negotiation and polite behaviour . . . Gowchee, the answers to your questions would demand careful exposition.

Please, allow me a few moments to set up the jump computations then we may discuss the matter.'

Frowning, Kao Chih sat back in his couch and folded his arms. Then his bad temper waned as the tiredness he had ignored made itself felt, and when he sighed it turned into a yawn.

'If you are weary, Gowchee, perhaps you should rest,' said the mech.

'My mind is unable to relax when faced with mortal peril, Drazuma-Ha*. It is a Human foible.'

'How inexpedient for your species – perhaps you should consider cyber-augmentation after all . . .' Suddenly a console alarm started pinging. 'A ship has appeared at 1,560 kilometres . . . it is the freighter and it is altering course in our direction . . .'

'This is not a coincidence, is it?'

'No, Gowchee – they are tracking us through hyperspace somehow. Engaging hyperdrive – now.'

Again the disorientation, senses gyring, the pause, the vertigo surge, and that momentary impression of coming to a dead stop without the slam of deceleration. Drazuma-Ha* hung before the console in silence while his field aura shimmered with arrays and streams of ghost symbols and the main console flickered with waves of computation.

'So, Drazuma-Ha*, what did you do to attract such relentless pursuit?'

'Simply put, Gowchee, I am their enemy.'

He frowned. 'You'll forgive me for saying so but that sounds more serious than a bad debt.'

'They have their purpose and I have mine, which is to prevent an ancient, terrible weapon from falling into the hands of their masters.'

Kao Chih listened in amazement and growing annoyance. 'You lied to me, right from the start . . . and who are these droids' masters? And who are you working for?'

'This explication is straining your credulity, Gowchee. Perhaps I should say no more.'

'I would rather you continued.'

'Very well, although I can only offer my word that I am speaking the truth. The droids pursuing us are emissaries of the Legion of Avatars, a long-forgotten enemy of civilisation, and I am an agent of a machine intelligence called the Construct.'

'And what's this weapon . . .'

'A fearsome device built millennia ago on the world you call Darien . . . ah, wait, look!'

On the long-range scanner, the freighter appeared 1,332 kilometres away and immediately started moving towards the *Castellan*.

They jumped again.

The sequence of events was repeated four times, while the droids' ravaged, mutilated ship continued to dog them, their exit point coming closer and closer. As Kao Chih stared at the sensor sweep holo, where a tagged symbol denoting the freighter had just winked into existence 495 kilometres away, he said:

'Drazuma-Ha*, this cannot continue – another two jumps and they may have us.'

'I agree, but our options are limited,' the mech said. 'Therefore I propose that we employ the same tactic that led us into the deepzone.'

Kao Chih stared at the mech, still trying to come to terms with the earlier revelations. 'Er, dropping out of hyperspace partway through the jump?'

'Exactly so, Gowchee. My hypothesis is that our pursuers drop a beacon-probe in hyperspace just before exiting to our position in normal space. When we make our next jump the beacon analyses our vessel's multi-field burst and deduces the jump course and duration, which are passed on to the droids, probably via subspace link. I am now merging new course data for a longer jump in the direction of Darien's possible location – I plan to disengage the hyperdrive a quarter of the way into the jump. Does that meet with your approval?'

'It does, Drazuma-Ha*,' he said, eyeing the sensor holo in which the freighter's distance was down to 120 kilometres and closing. 'I suggest that we leave now.'

The mech's reply was to engage the hyperdrive. Minutes later they emerged into normal space, the pale-blue console holo lighting up as the sensor came back online. And Kao Chih groaned when he saw the glittering symbol of a ship sitting there, out at 1,081 kilometres.

'They got here ahead of us! – how could they possibly . . .'

'Calm yourself, Gowchee – it is not them but another vessel entirely, a cloud-harvester.'

He sat up, loosening the couch straps a little, trying to contain his excitement as he peered into the holo.

'It is at rest, Drazuma-Ha*. It couldn't be abandoned, could it, or a wreck?'

'No, its emissions curve indicate that it is functioning nominally with an active ident that says it is the Harvester *Viganli*. The most likely reason for it being stationary would be a pause for refining or repairs.'

'I cannot help but notice that we too are stationary, rather than heading towards the harvester,' Kao Chih said.

'We must wait to see if our tactic has worked,' said the mech. 'It has been one minute since our arrival – we should make sure that we have evaded them.'

Vexed, Kao Chih could only agree, then settle down to gaze at the console's shiptime counter. A minute passed with infuriating slowness and the next few went no faster. After ten languid minutes Drazuma-Ha* decided that the tactic had succeeded and started the thrusters, laying in a course for the *Viganli*.

'We seem to proceeding at a somewhat leisurely pace, Drazuma-Ha*,' said Kao Chih, still disgruntled.

'It will reassure the harvester's crew or command AI that we have no aggressive intentions. Covering this distance should take just under an hour.'

'Sufficient time for you to tell me about your mission to Darien?'

'I am sure that it would be, Gowchee.'

'Excellent, now tell me about your boss, this Construct . . .'

52

ROBERT

At last – the Great Terrace, a title which by no means did it justice. As he followed the three mechs-Reski out of the low, lamplit
cavern (into which the tunnel from Abfagul had led) he thought
he heard the rushing sound of strong winds, a shuddering, sky-
filling roar. Then the cavern opened out to show him that they
stood, insect-like, at the edge of an edifice of incomparable
grandeur.

Lit by pearly light from far above, an immense stone promenade about 100 yards across extended from a high bank out over
the white, hazy curve of a waterfall. This was fed by numerous
sources arriving from further back, rivers and streams that gushed
in from many directions, splashing among mist-blurred rocks,
down over ledges and runnels and levels of pools that gave forth
their own lesser cascades. Except that both the promenade and
the falls stretched off into the distance for perhaps a mile, matching the hundreds if not thousands of inflows that coursed down
an immense, boulder-strewn slope where little clumps of trees
and bushes stood like pale ghosts amongst the surging streams. At
the far side, rock walls soared up and up, pale, sheer, rising to
heights obscured by the pure white light that poured down from
what might be a long fissure in the vast cavern's veiled ceiling.

'This is . . . incredible,' he said. Next to this, the Gangradur Falls
were like a decorative garden water feature. 'Who built this?'

'A race called the Teziyi,' said Track-Reski. 'They were very
fond of statement projects like this.'

'Did they build other things on this scale?'

'Several just after the fall of their universe, while their species still had the will and the resources.'

Robert frowned – the mechs were sticking to their stratified universe fantasy. Very well, then he would observe and deduce for himself.

The flat expanse of the Great Terrace was largely deserted, apart from a few far-off figures standing along the balustrade in ones, twos or small groups. As he followed the mechs he began to notice more details, the small buildings constructed along the side overlooking the falls, the basket balloons that hung out over the hurtling torrents and were winched in from time to time to offload sightseers and take on new groups. As for the other promenaders, few were bipeds, never mind even vaguely humanoid, the majority being insectile or reptilian, with occasional hybrids and frequent cyber-augments. More than a few gave Robert and the mechs disapproving looks, but he was scarcely concerned about that as he was leaning on the balustrade, gazing down in disbelief.

The curved mile-long falls plunged several hundred feet to a small lake where tiny, sailless boats and galleys sculled about. Further on the lake narrowed a little to where another imposing promenade spanned the waters as they rushed over another brink to another bridged falls and another after that. The moisture-laden air hazed the distant downward depths and Robert's mind reeled as he tried to imagine the scale of it. Doubt crept in and nibbled at the roots of his assumptions – how could something like this exist on Darien but not show up on the *Heracles*'s orbital sensor sweep? Were the mechs telling the truth?

As he stood there, wondering, a red dart shape shot out from under the promenade some way along, wheeled over the hazy spray then swooped and banked, descending. A glider, he realised as he saw another launch out over the falls.

'Human Horst,' said Tripod-Reski, 'we have received a message from Conveyance 289, asking to meet us at the lower level. We must hurry – there is a ramp nearby.'

'There is another level?' Robert said, hurrying after them.

'Three,' said Hover-Reski.

'They were originally made for the worker dorms and materials storage,' Track-Reski said. 'When the construction was complete, they were closed up and forgotten as the survivors of the great Teziyi civilisation took up residence, here and elsewhere. That final era began in defiance but ended amid forgotten purposes and cultural senescence. The last of the Teziyi finally abandoned their cities, leaving no records when they either transcended or were consumed. Then the remnants of other lesser civilisations wandered down here to settle, opening some of the lower levels where refugees could find a place to rest. Communities grew, vendors found customers, and a few finessers even have set up glider stations . . .'

'This is not how I imagined this would be at all,' Robert said.

'This is a rarity,' said Tripod-Reski. 'A small pocket of existence amid hyperspace's twisted layers of wrecked continua. Many here would escape to the real, but there are no safe routes up the levels.'

The mechs were heading for a fence-enclosed, roofed-over set of stairs. The steps were wide and fairly shallow, decorated with colourful mosaics which the many centuries had worn away, although some bore evidence of unimaginative repairs. At the foot they encountered a strange thoroughfare that was far busier and noisier than the promenade. Shops and stalls sold all manner of goods while gastronomic kiosks provided a tantalising array of flavours and savouries. The number of species on show here was prodigious, and he recognised very few. One common factor was the bulky, trailing clothing almost everyone wore, along with floppy, decorated hats and gauntlets. But Robert's opportunity to study this clamorous, bustling market (which stretched as far as he could see) was cut short when the mechs steered him to another stairway which spiralled down to the next level.

It was quieter down here, darker, with lowlit passages passing between long featureless blocks and a few solidly impenetrable iron doors, some of which were guarded. These were the lower floors of the expensive residences whose first levels looked out over the falls. The passages also connected with a wide walkway which ran along the back of the Great Terrace, providing an imposing view of the rivers and currents that poured in from above. It was there that they met Conveyance 289.

At first there was a scraping, clinking sound from somewhere very close yet unseen, then a large iron grid in the flagstones just ahead of them swung open and a shiny black, elephant-sized insect clambered out. Robert was alarmed and ready to flee until he saw his mech companions approach the massive creature . . . which on closer inspection proved to be a machine, not a beast. It had a segmented metal carapace, fluted cables, access covers bearing blocks of text in tiny characters, heat-vane clusters at the rear, effectors and the main interaction unit at the front. It moved around with surprising agility on four pairs of articulated limbs and on its back was what looked like a passenger recess covered by a darkened canopy. Fascinated and a little wary, Robert advanced and was introduced by the mechs.

'I am pleased to meet you,' he said. 'Are there another 288 like yourself?'

'In all, Human Horst, the Construct's tectories have produced 3,739 of my series, of which less than a hundred are still in operation.' The machine's voice was expressive, almost musical, and possessed an odd buzzing harmony. 'It will be an honour and a privilege to fight alongside you.'

Robert froze. 'Excuse me, but did you say "fight"?'

'Indeed so. I have already updated the Reski Emantes via proximal databurst but I am equipped to deliver a verbal summary – in essence, our goal, the upgate, is located below us in one of the empty storage vaults but unfortunately a small covey of vermax have got to it first, five of them, and are guarding it.'

'Five of us,' said Hover-Reski.

'Vermax?' Robert said. 'What are . . .'

'When we traversed the Refulgence, you may recall that we were pursued by polymorphic hunters,' Track-Reski said.

'The black snake things?'

'Those are the vermax. We do not know who their creators are but they originate in the Abyss, which suggests several possibilities. They eat metal and are especially fond of the submesh array where our sentience patterns reside.'

'A dedicated design,' said Tripod-Reski.

'They are also dangerous to organic lifeforms,' said Conveyance 289 as a niche opened in its side. 'Which is why you should have this.'

From the niche an arm telescoped out, holding a long, narrow case. The case then split open lengthways to reveal a slender black object about three feet long with a red hilt. It was so black that Robert could see no surface detail or texture, only a thin silhouette tapering to an unseeable point. Light seemed to be devoured by it.

'It's a sword,' he said, confused.

'It is called a *kezeq* shard. Against creatures like the vermax, it is deadly. Handle it carefully, however – the cold of it would cause irreparable damage to your flesh.'

Robert lifted the *kezeq* by its hilt and found it to be as light as a wooden metre rule. He had once learned some fencing when he was at college in Bonn, but that was 40 years ago – how much could he remember in a few minutes?

'You will ride in my guest compartment, Human Horst, while the Reski Emantes will be our valiant vanguard.'

Five minutes later he was seated and strapped into an odd, high-backed couch in Conveyance 289's passenger recess as the machine clambered back down into the open grating. It was a descent from light and cool freshness into dank, musty gloom.

'This is a very old storage area,' said Tripod-Reski. All three mechs were in the recess with him. '289 says that the upgate is in the next vault along.'

On eight mechanical, multijointed legs, Conveyance 289 provided a surprisingly smooth, comfortable steed, although stealth demanded that lamp radiance be kept to a meagre peep. In this murky grey halo, they picked their way through the immense storeroom, past mysterious mounds of belongings, or carefully stacked crates wrapped in glittery tendrils. Before long they reached the other side and a rounded, open passage leading to the next storage vault.

If anything, this room was even more crowded than the previous one, with many stacks reaching from floor to ceiling. A poorly assembled few had given way, becoming huge, slumped heaps blocking corridors or sometimes providing a short cut over slopes of dusty, enigmatic debris. Finally they came to a halt at the corner of a plinth of a huge statue depicting a creature with seven legs and three heads about to smash a hammer down on a ringed planet resting on an anvil, or maybe an altar. With one of its extensible arms, Conveyance 289 held up a triangular mirror, looted from one of the collapsed stacks, and angled it for Robert's benefit.

On the other side of the statue was a wide, clear aisle which ran straight to the far end of the vault, where a bright, shining pillar sat in the middle of the floor. It shone with a cold blue radiance, and as Robert stared at the reflected image he could make out several long, dark shapes gliding sinuously around the pillar. He swallowed nervously, feeling a tremble in his hands.

'That glowing pillar is the upgate,' said Conveyance 289.

'It doesn't look like a door or a gate,' he said.

'It will open for us when we get close enough. The plan is for the Reski Emantes to charge at the vermax from the sides and draw them away while we head straight for the gate.'

Robert glanced around and realised that he was alone in the passenger recess. 'The mechs are gone.'

'They are positioning themselves,' the mechanical said. 'We will know the signal when it comes . . .'

A voice interrupted it from the companel in the recess.

'We are ready now, 289. Human Horst, we have been honoured by the task and your acquaintance – please tender our cordialities to our descendant.'

Conveyance 289 shifted on its eight legs and Robert heard the whine of other systems starting within the mech's body as it shuffled round to face the wide aisle.

'The moment is upon us, Human Horst – hold tight and be ready to repel boarders!'

Suddenly the mech shot forward, smooth and fast, and Robert realised that they were flying along on suspensors. He was quivering with the shock and exhilaration of it. Dim walls of compacted wares flashed past on either side and he focused all his senses on the black *kezeq* shard, gripping it tight in both hands. Up ahead he caught glimpses of three fights, Track-Reski already still, one flexible track trailing and broken as a single vermax, a snake of black smoke, devoured its vitals. Hover-Reski, with two vermax chewing their way into its casing, was gliding drunkenly off down a side passageway. Tripod-Reski had lost most of one leg but was leading the remaining vermax pair a merry chase back along the wide aisle, moving with a manic, jerky gait. They were sacrificing themselves, Robert knew, yet they had mentioned a descendant . . .

The shining pillar was directly ahead, widening and growing brighter as they rushed towards it. Robert's fear began turning to relief tinged with a pang of sorrow at the small mechs' fate. The gate opened, shimmering silver and gold and icy blue, and as they plunged into it Robert was momentarily dazzled.

'Human Horst, I was wrong – there were . . . six . . .'

He felt Conveyance 289 quiver but his eyesight was blurred, showing him only a flowing, flickering tunnel.

'Help me, Human Horst, I am under attack . . . use the *kezeq* sssshhaarrrrddd . . .'

He blinked, eyes widening as he saw the vast walls of opaque images and fractured landscapes past which they fell. His mind rebelled. A primal terror was trying to make him curl up into a whimpering ball, eyes closed. But his eyes were open and he saw one of the vermax attached to the forepart of the mech's carapace, eating its way inwards. Shivering with cold and fear, Robert loosened the couch straps, moved carefully forward to lean halfway out of the recess and with the shard lashed out at the writhing black snake.

It squirmed and he stabbed it again and again. As it began to disintegrate something hot and bristly landed on his left shoulder and bit his ear with what felt like a mouthful of needles. Crying out, he lurched backwards, trying to twist away, and saw yet another vermax clinging to his shoulder, its fang-ringed mouth splattered with his blood as it reared back, readying for another lunge.

Robert screamed in terror and hate and thrust the *kezeq* shard at his attacker, ramming it into the open gullet as he slipped off the couch. The vermax thrashed, its hot bristling form hissing as it shoved itself against his neck, despite the sword.

Which he could feel pressed against his skin and face by the ferocity of the assault. Then suddenly the vermax let out a brittle rasp and began to break apart. By now Robert had slumped to the floor of the passenger recess and with the vermax crumbling to dry pieces of blackness he tried to lift or push the terrible, nullifying cold of the shard away. But the fingers of his right hand had lost all strength while his left side felt like a block of ice from shoulder to hip, from his neck up into his head.

Whiteness flowed. He could hear Conveyance 289 speaking to him but it was far, far away, icy echoes of words dissolving in the cold along with the strange, translucent walls that flew silently past.

In his thoughts, whiteness flowed.

53

THEO

They were fifteen minutes from the landing field's western boundary when a comm began beeping inside Pyatkov's greatcoat. Theo and Donny glanced at each other then watched the intelligence chief reach into his coat.

'How come you've got a comm that works?' Donny said.

'It's not a comm,' Pyatkov said as he produced an odd, white object shaped like a curved teardrop. He put the bulbous end to his ear and said, 'Yes?'

For a moment he was silent, listening, then:

'We did not know of this . . . we need at least thirty to forty minutes . . . yes, it seems likely . . . I understand . . . I'll await your call, sir.'

'Is there a problem?' Theo said as Pyatkov put away the comm device. 'Was that someone from the Imisil delegation, and what is that thing?'

'It is an Imisil comset,' Pyatkov said. 'I was speaking to Ambassador Gauhux himself and he says that there are violent anti-Hegemony demonstrations going on in Port Gagarin and Hammergard tonight. Kuros has all but accused the Imisil delegation of fomenting civil unrest and has demanded that the Imisil leave Darien space immediately. Gauhux is already on board his shuttle and is trying to stall for time, but Kuros is threatening to have the port security force open fire if he doesn't lift off.'

Theo's heart sank. 'But Rory and his lads are due to set their diversion rolling in twenty minutes and we've no way of calling them back. We could get through to the launch pads only to see that shuttle take off . . .'

'No danger of that happening,' said Donny. 'That's it away now . . .'

Theo hastily shifted over to the other side of the bus and saw clusters of glowing vortices climbing quickly into the night sky. At the same time, Pyatkov's comset beeped.

'Yes sir . . . I fully understand . . . is there? . . . would they? . . . ah, I see . . . indeed, sir . . . thank you for all your help.'

With the call over, Pyatkov weighed the teardrop device in his hand for a moment, then nodded.

'Well?' said Theo.

'We go ahead as planned.'

Donny burst out laughing. 'So ye do have a sense o' humour!'

Pyatkov looked at him. 'The Imisil had no choice – Kuros threatened to send over interceptors from the *Purifier* and blow their ship out of orbit, and they take Hegemony threats very seriously.'

'So why are we going ahead with this?' Theo said.

'Because one of the *Heracles*'s shuttles, a cutter they call it, is sitting in a hangar on the west side of the launch fields. Captain Barbour, you've trained on the Imisil simulator – what Earthsphere vessels are you familiar with?'

'Hmm, tug, scow, repair gig, and close-support fighter – the basics are pretty much the same, though.' An anticipatory smile came to his lips. 'A shuttle shouldna be very different.'

'And then what?' Theo said. 'Assuming that you can get this shuttle up and into space, into orbit, where do you go? Will the Imisil ship wait around, and if not what are we going to do?'

'Ask the captain of the *Heracles* for political asylum,' said Pyatkov. 'It's certain that he has very specific orders concerning non-interference, but what if a group of Darien colonists turns up near his ship in a hijacked Earthsphere shuttle, begging for safe haven? If Velazquez handed us over to the Hegemony it would mean the end of his career because his crew would know, which means that the story would inevitably get out to the Earthsphere media. He would have to bring us on board.'

Theo smiled in resignation. 'That's a very big "if".'

'Perhaps, but I am sure of it.' Pyatkov looked at his watch and tapped the bus driver on the shoulder, telling him to slow down. 'We're almost at the outer perimeter checkpoint. There are two guards so I'll distract them with my ID and official papers while the pair of you sandbag them from behind.'

It went smoothly. Minutes after they had the guards tied up, a call came through on the checkpoint cable comm to raise the security level because of an intruder alert on the western fence. Donny took the call, disguising his voice to sound as if he had a bad cold. At the inner perimeter checkpoint the same gambit worked, and the bus with the Enhanced was through in just over five minutes.

The wooden hangar housing the Earthsphere shuttle was the middle one of a line of three alongside the taxiing runway. Leaving the bus in a ditch behind a cluster of bushes, the Enhanced and their armed escorts skulked through the shadows towards their goal, looking out for a side or back entrance. There were a couple of port security guards out the front while inside a solitary Earthsphere marine kept watch from a partitioned office. Infiltration went like clockwork, all the guards put out of action soundlessly and non-lethally. With the marine bound and sat over to one side, they quietly came out of the office into the hangar proper. The shuttle was a snub-nosed, large-bellied craft about 30 feet long with its stubby wings spreading from the upper fuselage. While the Enhanced waited in the office, Theo, Donny, Pyatkov and the driver, Giorgi, went over to look at the shuttle's main hatch. They were nearly there when a tall Brolturan soldier stepped through a door in the hangar's massive swing shutter, saw them and opened fire.

There was a stuttering, whicking sound and Giorgi went down, bleeding from head, neck and back, while another burst caught Pyatkov in the shoulder and sent him sprawling forward. Donny and Theo dived for cover behind the shuttle, handguns at the ready. The Brolturan started shouting at them and firing short bursts under the shuttle. Theo cursed and began climbing up onto the upper hull while Donny tried dodging this way and that. Theo was lying flat on the centre of the wing surface when the office door opened and one of the Enhanced, a slender, blonde woman, walked out and called to the Brolturan. Her hand was already raised as if in greeting but as he turned her hand snapped forward, arm abruptly outstretched. The soldier let out a gasping cry, dropped his autorifle, started to bring up one hand, then collapsed to the hangar floor with something jutting from his eye. The female Enhanced walked over, studied him with intense, stern eyes, then turned and went back to the office.

Theo meanwhile was scrambling down from the shuttle and hurrying to where Donny was already kneeling next to Pyatkov.

'How is he?' he said.

Donny looked grim, but before he could answer, Pyatkov spoke.

'Bastard . . . got me with . . . one of those flechette machiners . . . clawstorm they call it . . . how did you get him . . .'

'One of the Enhanced did,' Donny said. 'Tall blonde woman.'

Pyatkov smiled. 'Irenya, *da*, of course . . .' He looked at Donny. 'The hatch . . . code is blue 24, red 18, green 09 . . .' He paused to grimace at the pain, and Theo knew he was dying – there was too much blood. 'Giorgi? . . .' Donny shook his head. 'A good man – he deserved a better death . . . you must go. Just leave me over . . . somewhere with his gun . . .' He stared at Theo and Donny, then gave a savage grin. 'No one will be . . . looking into my head – I have a hollow tooth . . . *nyet*, don't argue, just . . . do it!'

So they did. In six minutes, everyone was on board, Donny in the pilot couch in the tiny two-man cockpit, the five Enhanced strapped into passenger seating in the midsection compartment, and Theo moving Pyatkov over to sit against a crate near the office, the Brolturan weapon in his lap. The Russian's eyes were barely open and his entire shoulder and side were soaked in blood.

'Hangar door . . . office . . .'

Theo nodded, and as he reached through the office window to

thumb the button he felt his skin prickle when Donny powered up the shuttle's antigravity generators.

That's it, he thought. *As soon as that door starts lifting, the terminal guards'll come running.*

Pyatkov's eyes were closed when he turned round and Theo could not tell if he was still breathing or not.

'Goodbye, Vitaly,' he said quietly then hurried to the shuttle, ducked inside and closed the hatch. As it autosealed, he glanced along a short passage to where the Enhanced were sitting straight-backed, eyes closed, hands resting palms-up on their knees. Then the shuttle lurched and swayed slightly and he stumbled forward to the cockpit. As he strapped into the copilot couch with shaking hands, Donny gave a pleased laugh.

'Nice ship, this,' he said. 'Responsive controls, clearly tagged instruments and even an overhead holodisplay.' He glanced at Theo. 'You ever flown before? To Nivyesta, I mean.'

'No.' Theo breathed in deep. 'But I'll be okay.'

'Aye, ye will. Just kid on that it's a ride at the carnival.' Before them the hangar shutter was almost fully open. 'Right, time to leave.'

The first few seconds of smooth forward motion were deceptive – once clear of the hangar, Donny angled the nose skywards and fired the main thrusters. A hundred invisible sandbags pressed Theo down into his couch but then quickly eased off, even though their acceleration did not.

'Inertial dampeners,' Donny said. 'Should've had them on active tracking – sorry 'bout that. Deck gravity is on, though, so you'll be able to get up and walk around soon.'

Theo nodded, staring out the cockpit viewscreen at the darkening sky where stars were growing brighter as they climbed out of Darien's atmosphere.

'Did our sudden departure turn any heads?' he said.

Donny grinned, tapping the headset he was wearing.

'Has it ever! Listen to this . . .'

He poked a couple of screen controls and suddenly voices erupted from the console speakers.

'. . . flight is unauthorised and may incur a punitive response – I repeat, Shuttlecraft *Hermes*, this is Gagarin Tower – you are instructed to return to Gagarin launchway 2. Your flight is unauthorised and may incur . . .'

'Earthsphere shuttlecraft, this is Preceptor-Captain Eshapon of *Purifier* sub-Phalanx Tuva. A soldier of the Brolturan Compact was killed by one of those who hijacked that shuttle. You are instructed to return to Port Gagarin and surrender yourselves . . .'

'. . . hey, this is a traffic control-restricted frequency! Cut your signal immediately!'

'My authority supersedes yours – cease your intereference . . .'

'*Heracles*-ops to Shuttlecraft *Hermes* – what is your status?'

Donny grinned at Theo then thumbed the reply. '*Hermes* to *Heracles*-ops – please stand by,' then he silenced it.

'We're nearly at low orbit,' he said. 'And I've already laid in an intercept course for the *Heracles* . . . which they'll know all about already . . .'

'How?' said Theo.

'Shared telemetry,' Donny said. 'All this boat's instrumentation will be showing up on one of the *Heracles*'s screens – if they wanted to, they could probably take control of its navigationals as well.'

'So now we open negotiations,' Theo said.

'Aye.' Donny pressed the channel button. '*Hermes* to *Heracles*-ops – my name is Captain Barbour, acting under special orders of President Sundstrom and requesting to speak with your CO.'

'*Heracles*-ops to *Hermes* – please stand by . . . sorry, *Hermes*, but Captain Velazquez is in a conference call with the Hegemony ambassador and President Kirkland right now but he should be speaking to you in a few minutes.'

'Understood, *Heracles*-ops,' Donny said, cutting the respond.

'Was that wise, giving your name?' Theo said.

Donny shrugged. 'My folks are both dead and I was an only child, so there's nobody for them tae hold hostage.'

'I am sorry to hear that,' Theo said.

Donny grinned. 'Don't be – my friends are my family and I got tae choose every one.' He paused, glancing at the console then the pale blue holodisplay overhead. 'Course has been changed, velocity too – we're picking up speed . . .'

Theo leaned on the couch armrest and ran his fingers through his hair. 'So the *Heracles* has taken control of us?'

'Aye . . . dritt, if I knew a bit more I could . . .'

'*Heracles*-ops to Shuttlecraft *Hermes* . . .'

A small holoplane appeared over the main console, displaying the Earthsphere navy's symbol, two flaming comets against a stylised galactic spiral. Donny sniffed and thumbed the respond.

'Shuttlecraft *Hermes* to *Heracles*-ops – Captain Barbour speaking.'

The opaque holoplane blinked, suddenly showing a craggy-featured man with dark hair and intense, hazel-brown eyes.

'I am Captain Velazquez – why have you hijacked my shuttle?'

'Had to see ye about an important matter, Captain,' Donny said. 'Seemed as good a way as any, given that we're acting under President Sundstrom's executive order . . .'

'Kirkland is president now,' Velazquez said. 'Sundstrom's policies have been superseded.'

'That might be the case, Captain,' Theo said, 'if Kirkland actually had a spine and a brain to go with it!'

Velazquez regarded him from the screen. 'And you are?'

'Karlsson, former major in the Darien Volunteer Corps.'

The *Heracles*'s captain nodded. 'Major Karlsson, Viktor Ingram's right-hand man – hoping to overthrow another government, Major?'

Theo gritted his teeth. 'If the government's corrupt, I see no problem with the notion.'

'The probabilities are not in your favour, I'm afraid.' Velazquez seemed to grow impatient. 'Gentlemen, what is the reason for this charade?'

'Ourselves and a group of researchers are formally requesting political asylum aboard your vessel, sir,' said Donny.

'Thought it might be something like that,' Velazquez said.

'Why did Sundstrom want these researchers kept out of Hegemony hands?'

Donny shrugged. 'The president originally had a deal with the Imisil to get them away, but as ye can see they've been kicked out. And before ye ask, we don't know anything about what's in their heads, but I guess it must be important . . .'

And deadly, Theo thought, remembering Pyatkov's attitude.

'I understand your position, gentlemen, but there is a problem.' Velazquez glanced at something nearby. 'A Brolturan soldier died during your illegal hijacking and both High Monitor Kuros and the Brolturan commander are screaming for the arrest of those responsible. So if I brought the *Hermes* on board my ship with the aim of offering its passengers asylum, this would cease to be a security matter and become a diplomatic incident.'

'And yet you've changed our course to meet the *Heracles* out beyond high orbit,' Donny said. 'And in just a few minutes, too.'

'Yes – there is only one option open to you. When we rendezvous, you will get those researchers into the emergency suits then send them out through the airlock. I will then be obliged to take them on board as Distressed Persons Adrift under the Rescue and Emergency protocol.'

'But not us,' Theo said.

'Correct. My report will state that you abandoned your passengers then took off for that forest moon.'

Theo and Donny glanced at each other in puzzlement.

'And why are we doing that?' said Donny.

'Captain Barbour, if you were better trained you would notice that the *Purifier* has launched two interceptors and that they are already halfway here. I suggest that you get those people ready.'

Theo looked at Donny. 'Is he telling the truth?'

Without answering, Donny punched up a display that showed two bright specks moving round the planet's curve towards where another pair of dots, blue this time, were converging. Resigned, Theo went with him to explain the situation to the Enhanced. It was oddly awkward – he couldn't tell from their expressions if they understood or were angry or calm. Then the one called Julia asked to speak with Captain Velazquez, who assured her that anyone left behind by the shuttle would be brought to safety within the *Heracles*. Listening closely to Velazquez's careful wording, she nodded, once to the captain, once to Donny and Theo.

After that the Enhanced were quickly suited up in lightweight metallic blue rigs, and their progression through the airlock went ahead, first pair, second pair, and Julia last. As she ducked through the hatch she paused to look back at them.

'Thank you for helping us,' she said. 'I don't understand why you did this, but thank you.'

Theo and Donny said their own goodbyes then, as the hatch closed and cycled through, they exchanged a puzzled look, before hurrying back to the cramped cockpit to check the long-range sensors. Even as they saw that the two interceptors were now between them and Darien, a voice came over the ship-to-ship.

'Attention *Hermes*, this is Flight-Marshal Kowalski. Strap yourselves in, gentlemen – we're about to send you on a bit of a ride.'

'Better do what the man says,' Donny muttered.

Outside the cockpit viewport, the long, tapering shape of the *Heracles* loomed at an angle, its grey and silver hull sporting rows of dark, opaque blisters. Then, as they fastened their restraints, Theo heard a muffled, intermittent hum and the *Hermes* turned, giving them a transient view of the Enhanced being snagged by power grappler lines and reeled into an open hold in the *Heracles*'s belly. Then the green orb of Nivyesta swung into view and stopped.

'Thruster systems initialised, *Hermes* – stand by for fast burn.'

Patterns flickered on the console, then Theo felt a momentary kick of acceleration before the inertial dampening cut in. He sat there in the couch's firm embrace for a minute, breathing the plastic-tainted air, feeling the vibration of the shuttle's engines with his back, neck and arms, realising that his fear was still there but caged, shackled by old combat reflexes. The knack was in using your fear, knowing when to ignore it, when to listen and how to use it to stay alive. But now the kind of trouble that was looming was one in which he was completely reliant on Donny Barbour's skills to avoid dying in a fireball of destruction when those Brolturan fighters caught up with them.

And now Kowalski was back on the comm, telling them where the two-man escape pod was and how to set the autopilot for a bail-out when they hit Nivyesta's upper atmosphere. He also gave Donny a quick rundown on the shuttle's weapons (or rather weapon, a single laser cannon), countermeasures and shields.

'But you shouldn't get into the situation where you have to use them,' said Kowalski. 'Anyway, you've got another twelve minutes before you enter high orbit around that moon. After that, you're on your own. Good luck, *Hermes*.'

'Aye, thanks, *Heracles* – when this is all over, we'll have ye round for a few drinks and all the steak ye can eat!'

'We wouldn't miss it for anything, *Hermes* – safe journey.'

The mood of the exchange was light and amiable and to Theo seemed to underline the gravity of their position.

'So how bad is it?' he said.

Donny gave a little smile and a sidelong glance. 'No' much gets past you, does it, Major?'

Theo shrugged. 'I know the sound of bad odds, especially when I hear them not being mentioned. What are our chances?'

Donny pointed at the holodisplay. 'Those interceptors are closing on us faster than we'd reckoned – they might catch us just as we hit atmosphere.'

'At which point we're dead.'

'Well . . . aye, unless we try something a wee bit unorthodox.' He leaned closer. 'Set the autopilot to aggressively engage them just after our pod separates. The shuttle only has to keep them occupied for a few minutes, long enough for the pod to reach low altitude.'

Theo nodded, feeling a twinge of nausea and a tremble in his hands and legs, and smiled. It was just his fear, rattling its cage.

'Okay, if that's our only shot,' he said. 'We'll make it a good one.'

The minutes fled past, Donny working at the console, setting up parameters for the autopilot while Theo checked the supplies for the pod. A small hatch in the bulkhead behind the cockpit led down a few steps to the open pod, into which they would have to crawl. Theo had raided the shuttle's medical and ration lockers and was stowing the booty away when Donny called down to him.

'Have we got everything?'

'We have – where are the hunters?'

'Practically on top of us. Ye've got it all packed away, aye?'

'Yes, is it time?'

'It certainly is, Theo.'

Theo heard the pod's own hatch thud shut and seal with the whine of motors.

A horrible realisation struck him and he lunged round in the tiny space to get at the hatch, trying to find controls to open it, but there were none.

'Theo, I know that this is a rotten trick . . . aye, I know, but it's the only way. Better get strapped in – twenty seconds and you're away.'

'Donny, you damn bloody fool!' Theo raged as he hurriedly crawled back round again and tugged several broad straps tight over his body. 'Is this some kind of Caledonian-warrior-self-sacrifice thing . . .'

'Dinna be daft! – if we both left in the pod, those interceptors would pick us off with missiles. This way at least one of us stands a chance. Don't get me wrong – I've every intention of living to a ripe old age . . . right, hold on tae yer hat!'

There was a cluster of small bangs and suddenly the pod lurched and dropped, Theo's stomach protesting as the tiny craft seemed to flip over then right itself.

'Donny! – what's happening?'

'I won't be able to speak much soon, Theo – just got my hands full with these two, but then they did come in staggered over-watch formation . . . right, got tae go. Good luck and good hunting, Major, and I'll see ye on the bright side!'

Then the channel went dead.

You're a fool, Donny Barbour, he thought as the pod shuddered about him. *If I didn't know any better, I'd say we were related. When next we meet we'll drink the finest whisky and tell magnificent lies about our family trees.*

But a faint and hollow dread told him that he was thinking about a dead man.

54

DONNY

As he cut the channel, the Brolturan interceptor was on his tail, lining up for a point-to-point attack. Donny grinned. He knew he'd been in the enemy's range for over thirty seconds, but the pilot had obviously decided that with such a weak opponent he could afford to relax and indulge in a bit of exhibition gunnery.

Well, he's in for a wee surprise!

Donny punched up a sequence of special commands, which he had been preparing while Theo was gathering together those supplies a short while ago. Working on his own improvisations, backed up by brief text notes from Kowalski, he had figured out a handful of manoeuvres and shield configurations which had prompted the flight-marshal to call him 'a crazy man'. Donny didn't mind if his unorthodox scheme offered only a slim chance of survival. That was better than none.

The enemy was almost in position, and the *Hermes*'s sensors told him that its weapons were targeting. Donny hit the execute in the holodisplay, the attitude jets buzzed, and the shuttle made a perfect 180-degree lateral turn. Then the shields reconfigured into airbrakes, and since they were already entering Nivyesta's upper atmosphere the shuttle's velocity quickly began to fall. At the same time the main thrusters fired, ramping up the deceleration, and the Brolturan interceptor, a vaguely oval craft with weapon indents along its leading edge, seemed to rush straight towards the shuttle.

Donny flinched in reflex, but there was nothing for him to do but watch and hope and pray.

The Brolturan was already banking as the two vessels converged, but Donny's second shield configuration was ready, huge, curved blades of forcefield projected out from the prow. Where they collided with the Brolturan's own shields, harmonic interference dissipated in dazzling flashes of light and energy and when gaps opened up in the underside barrier the *Hermes*'s targeting system was quick to act. The laser cannon sent a stream of composite pulse bolts through the gaps, hammering into the hull, smashing open compartments, sending shattered fragments flying. . .

The interceptor veered away sharply but it was too late. Lines of vapour and hot gas were trailing from the stern, then a fuel feed must have been exposed because an immense explosion abruptly tore the craft open from the engines forward. Donny let out a roar of delight as several pieces of burning debris arced and spun away down towards the forest moon's surface.

But his triumph was cut short when alerts beeped and the display showed the second interceptor burning a tight turn towards him, and launching a couple of missiles into the bargain.

Time to make tracks, he thought, bringing the shuttle round to point forward, angling to gain altitude as he engaged the thrusters. Another tactical sequence was selected, a simple but cunning one. Then, seeing that he had a minute or two before the missiles arrived, he opened a general widecast channel.

'This is, er, Darien Combat Shuttle *Hermes*, Captain Barbour commanding, calling anyone within range of this signal.'

A moment later, a sceptical male voice.

'This is Pilipoint Station control – what did you say you were? Is this some kind of joke?'

'Did ye see anything happening in the sky just recently, Pilipoint?'

'By damn, yes! We've had explosions and burning things falling . . .'

'Aye, well, that's because I just shot down a Brolturan fighter that was giving me grief, and I've got another one chasing after me with a brace of missiles . . . just a second . . .'

The missiles were coming in fast and lethal, twin undeviating trajectories, pale trails of oncoming destruction. Donny knew that it was wing-and-a-prayer time as he triggered the counter-measures sequence and sat back, waiting to see if he lived through the next thirty seconds.

'Hermes to Pilipoint Station – still awake down there? What's yer name, by the way?'

'Still here, *Hermes*. My name is Axel, and we've got you on satellite tracking . . . my God, and we see those missiles! Bail out, Captain . . .'

'Wish I could, Axel, but I'm stuck here for the duration – right, here we go . . .'

On the external monitor Donny saw a huge spreading cloud of silvery chaff while a decoy dropped away on a dying curve towards the moon's green face. And he grinned as both missiles took the bait and plunged after it.

'Very smart, *Hermes*, very cunning . . .' said the Pilipoint coms-man. 'You're like the magician, yes? The hand is quicker than the eye . . .'

'Maybe so, laddie, but I don't reckon that wee shell game'll work a second time . . . and he's just launched another pair . . .'

'I see them, Captain – tell me, are you the man who stole the Earther's shuttle?'

'Heard about that up here, Axel? Aye, that was me a'right, a bad yin through and through!'

'We've heard what's been going on downstairs, all those Brolturan troops working hard to keep Darien free from unrest and protest and such nuisances as free speech,' said the comsman. 'I have no doubt that in time we too will be similarly blessed. But tell me, why are you doing this?'

'What, bearding the lion in his den, y'mean? I guess ye could say I was overcome with a sense of public duty and a calm appraisal of the crisis . . . but that wouldna be true.'

'It would not?'

'Nah, it was pure, unadulterated loathing. Ye know what I really hate? – being lied to. Soon after the *Heracles* arrived, that

Hegemony envoy Kuros toured the colony, giving speeches about the Sendrukan Hegemony's deep sense of liberty and freedom and their boundless desire to spread freedom throughout known space and beyond . . . aye, right! All the time he was coming out with that self-important, sanctimonious cack, him and his minions were planning how to get us down on our knees, how to make things so bad that we'd be happy to have their boots on our necks, just so long as the bombings stopped . . .'

'I saw one of Kuros's speeches,' said the Pilipoint comsman. 'It was a real performance but it did not seem right for us, as if he was performing for another audience . . .'

'Excuse me, Axel, got some missiles to take care of here . . .'

Donny could feel the sweat trickling down the side of his face as he watched a dark blue display where two bright specks moved nearer to his position while associated readouts gave figures for velocity, distance and altitude. In the cockpit's enclosed darkness, the pilot console was a strange, muffled cubbyhole crammed with glowing, touch-sensitive controls and displays, with small vidscreens showing external views while the overhead holo gave the wider tactical sweep. The next countermeasures sequence was running, suspensors and thrusters were online and ready, and the navigationals were tracking the enemy interceptor. From the previous encounter the shuttle's expert system overlay had quantified the missiles' minimum turn radius so now it was down to timing.

And a mountain of luck.

Then the missiles, gaining with every microsecond, crossed a certain trigger boundary and the countermeasures activated, another chaff burst, silver clouds of glittering, reflective strips spreading behind the hurtling *Hermes* like a silver comet's tail. As before a decoy was dropped, but this time the missiles ignored it and stayed on target while the interceptor began moving closer, as if the end was near. Then it too crossed an invisible line and the shuttle's forward suspensors came to life, kicking the shuttle's nose up and over as the thrusters roared. The combination of momentum and extreme force vectors threw the *Hermes* into a brutally tight vertical turn.

G-force shoved Donny down into his couch. Over the wheeze of his breathing he heard the infrastructure complain before the autoalerts began – 'Warning, exceeding performance tolerances . . . minor structural failures in subassemblies 19a, 21d, 37k . . . major structural failure will occur in thirty seconds or less . . .'

Then the *Hermes* was out of the turn and heading back, upside down. The Brolturan pilot had seen Donny's crazed attempt at an acrobatic manoeuvre and had merely banked slightly to avoid a repetition of the earlier force-field collision. But Donny was still ahead of him and about to cross over his oncoming flight path. And that was when the countermeasures released the last of the chaff on maximum dispersal. And when the interceptor plunged into the spreading, silvery, instrument-fogging cloud he met his own missile coming the other way.

On his rear external monitor, Donny saw the dual explosion flashes, an eruption of light and ignited gases, and an expanding shell of vapour and wreckage mixed with glittering fragments of chaff. He was about to breath a sigh of relief when he noticed that one of the flying pieces of debris was leaving a hot gas trail and curving round in his direction.

Cunning dog, he thought. *Must've fired that at the last moment, knowing that I'd got him . . . well, ye've not got me yet!*

He nearly made it, at the tail end of a long, twisting, dodging pursuit down through Nivyesta's atmosphere, seeking every advantage, trying to lose the missile in clouds, even trying to shoot it down with the laser cannon. But on it came, doggedly undeterred and unwavering. And as the chase descended, he kept up a running commentary to Axel the comsman at Pilipoint Station, never letting on how desperate his situation was, livening up the discourse with merciless caricatures of certain public figures, like Kuros who was 'the Hegemony's interstellar bile duct', and President Kirkland, 'the bowel movement that walked like a man'.

When the end came it was quick. He was flying north at about 900 feet over Nivyesta's southern ocean, less than 100 kilometres from Segrana's coast. Fuel was low, most of the suspensors were burnt out, and he was getting continual structural alerts as a result of the contorted manoeuvres he had attempted. His last throw of the dice was to try and ditch in the waters, but the missile found him 50 feet up, rushing across the waves. There was a terrible brightness . . . then a terrible darkness . . .

Then forever claimed him.

55

CATRIONA

Through a black night of rain they searched for the downed ship. A casing collector had spotted its descent in late afternoon while he was ransacking the high web festoons near Overglowatch. A wedge-shaped craft trailing ragged flags was the description that was relayed to Catriona, from which she knew that its braking chute had torn after deploying. The chances of someone surviving a crash landing under those conditions were not good. However, there was a lot of dense, deep foliage to absorb such a craft's kinetic energy, so assuming it didn't hit an outcrop or an especially large tree, the odds maybe weren't so bad.

Like most of her twenty-strong search party, Cat was wearing a cowled coat made from a mixture of plant fibre and silk – it was light and kept her cool and dry as she rode on *trictra*-back with the rest. Following the casing collector's directions, they were heading north to the wide valley that lay between Girdle Ridge and the Northern Uplands while water dripped, trickled and spattered all around them. A cold, black night of rain, with lamplight and the piercing beams of battery torches striking clusters of gleams from wet leaves, turning droplet-strewn webs into flashing regalia, rivulets into rippling, silver snakes.

After another hour, one of the search parties reported finding a trail of damaged forest foliage. Everyone converged and hastened along the path of snapped branches and severed trunks until it became a ragged furrow gouged in the ground which finally terminated at the foot of a big *prul* tree. The craft was small, less than fifteen feet long, so it had to be an escape pod from one of the ships seen dogfighting far up in the sky earlier. Small thruster nozzles were spaced along its curved stern, while its hull tapered to a flat, narrow prow that was solidly wedged under a gnarled *prul* root as thick as a Uvovo's waist.

For a moment all the scholars and their Listener paused and stared wide-eyed at the escape pod while sending expectant glances her way.

Hmm, okay, so Mummy Pathmistress has to make sure the alien box is safe, she thought, dismounting from the *trictra*. By the time she reached the pod, with light from lamps held nearby, she could see from the characters and symbols on the hull that this had to be from the *Heracles*. Without hesitation she rapped her knuckles on it.

'Hello – anyone in there?'

Immediately there were a few thuds in response, and a man's voice:

'Thank God you found me! – please, can you help? Something is jamming the hatch on this thing . . .'

Cat laughed, realised that the big *prul* root was holding the pod shut.

'I can see what the problem is,' she said. 'We'll have ye out of there in a wee bit.'

With a dozen Uvovo lending their strength, they managed to drag the escape pod out from under the *prul*'s roots. A moment later the upper hull was pushed up from within and locked into an open position. A grey-haired man in a hunting jacket and camouflage trousers climbed wearily out and sat on the edge of the recess, pulling lumps of something white off his clothing and tossing them into the pod. It took Cat a moment but suddenly she recognised him.

'You're Greg's Uncle Theo,' she said.

He straightened in surprise, then peered closer in the meagre light and nodded.

'Ah, Doctor Macreadie – an unexpected pleasure, here in the middle of the forest.'

'What is that stuff?'

'Crash foam,' he said. 'It smells terrible yet I find myself most grateful.' He looked at her and smiled. 'In case you were wondering, Greg is alive and well, mostly. He was slightly wounded yesterday . . . or perhaps the day before . . . but some of my people told me he's mending well . . .' He looked about him at the Uvovo and the drips and trickles coming from above. 'Did someone see me come down here, Catriona?'

'Aye,' she said, half-wishing he had said more about Greg. 'An Uvovo from a town several miles away saw your pod swooping over Segrana after those explosions in the sky.'

He became more alert at this. 'Do you know what happened up there? Did Pilipoint Station have any contact. . .'

'I'm sorry, Theo, I've not been in touch with Pilipoint but I did see some of the big show and heard about the rest from others. Late in the afternoon there were a few contrails high up, then there was a bright explosion and, a few minutes later, halfway across the sky, there was another. Not long after that your escape pod crash-landed, and a short while later some Uvovo on the south coast saw a huge explosion far out at sea.'

Hearing this, his manner turned sombre. He nodded and smiled sadly. 'It was supposed to be both of us in this pod, but he tricked me and sent me off on my own. Stayed behind to fight two Brolturan interceptors, from that giant warwagon of theirs. And he beat them! – he must have . . .'

'What are you talking about? Who beat them . . .'

'A brave man called Donny Barbour.' He looked at her. 'Can you help me get to Pilipoint Station? Perhaps someone there knows exactly how it all turned out.'

Cat nodded. 'I can do that, Theo, though you might like to stop off at one of the Uvovo towns for a rest and a bite to eat.'

'That sounds good.' Feeling weariness in his limbs, he wiped some water droplets from his beard and brushed away a few more fragments of foam. 'I've heard that folk on Nivyesta get around on the backs of giant *trictra* – is that true?'

'It is, aye – you've not got a fear of spiders, have you?'

'No, not as such.' He gave a rueful smile. 'I'll be okay. So – which way?'

The Uvovo moved with them in unison as Catriona led the way back to where the *trictra* had been tethered, her own flashlight picking out a path through the wet undergrowth.

'You must feel hardly involved in what's been going on down on Darien,' Theo said.

'I wouldn't say that,' Cat said, smiling in the darkness. 'We caught two Ezgara commandos yesterday.'

He stared at her, his pace slowing. 'You captured them . . .'

'The first one exploded, killing several Uvovo . . . did ye know that they have a binary explosive in their bloodstream? Aye, very cunning, very vicious. Oh, and they're Human too.'

Theo nodded gravely. 'Yes, that I knew. It raises a lot of questions.'

'Doesn't it? We got to the second one and sedated him before he could trigger himself, then we used some extraction roots and what the Uvovo call a cleansing sac to filter the impurities from his blood. Now he's awake and alert – he understands Anglic but doesn't speak it that well. Still, we managed to get a few interesting facts out of him.'

She recalled how they'd had to restrain his arms and legs with padded leather straps. He seemed so completely at the mercy of his fear and anger, as if he had no understanding of self-control, and she and the rootmasters suspected that the cleansing sac had removed something else from his system besides the explosive component.

'His name is Malachi,' she said. 'He's from a colony of Humans called Tygra, a highly militarised society, going by a few things he let slip.'

'My God,' Theo said. 'Were they abducted by the Hegemony?'

'Not abducted, Major. It seems that his colony was established roughly 150 years ago.'

'A hundred and fifty years? But Humanity had not . . .' He broke off, frowning for a moment before his eyes widened. 'Doctor Macreadie, you're not suggesting . . .'

Smiling she nodded. 'The Tygra colony was founded by a ship from Earth called the *Forrestal*.'

Theo was silent, the astonishment in his face replaced by a growing horror as he absorbed what she had said. 'The *Forrestal*'s crew and colonists were a mixture of northern and southern Americans, and Australians,' he said. 'How could they be turned into the Hegemony's shock troops?'

She shook her head. 'We're not getting much out of Malachi at the moment, so these questions remain open to speculation. But for now I think we should keep this to ourselves. If it got out, how would the people of Earth react? And what would the Hegemony do to the Tygrans if they decided that the alliance with Earthsphere was more valuable than a cadre of Human janissaries, no matter how loyal?'

'You have a point,' he said. 'My God, I cannot imagine what they went through.'

'Makes you wonder what happened to the third ship, the *Tenebrosa*,' Cat said, and even as she spoke the words she felt a quiver in the perceptive bond she shared with Segrana. Was it anticipation? A hint of the truth, or the echo of some lost possibility, fading amongst the water-veiled trees? She smiled inwardly, knowing that Segrana had a liking for convoluted mystery.

'Well, if any of their descendants show up here,' Theo was saying, 'we can start a club!'

She laughed out loud at that, thinking, *Aye, wouldn't that be just amazing?*

56

KAO CHIH

They were waiting, languishing, in a lesser sifting compartment, a 50-foot-long vault with battered, pitted, metal walls which were also shiny from the abrasion of rock dust. In here, complex force-fields winnowed the immense tonnage of interstellar debris gathered by the harvester's scoop fields, probably sorting it by mineral type and grade then funnelling it off to various silos. Kao Chih also suspected that these same field projectors were being used to scan and probe both himself and Drazuma-Ha*, but when he mentioned it the mech would only answer in a taciturn, uninformative manner, suggesting some measure of displeasure. Five or six hours they had been kept waiting in this steel box by the harvester's steerer, a paranoid Voth by the name of Yash, and that was in addition to the six or seven spent waiting aboard the *Castellan* after docking.

At least that earlier period had given Drazuma-Ha* plenty of time to explain the ins and outs of the crucial and perilous (yet dramatic and fabulous to Kao Chih) mission he was engaged on. Back on the ship, Kao Chih had sat agog, listening to the mech's tale of the legendary Forerunners, the vast war they had fought against the Legion of Avatars, and the warpwells they had built to defeat that terrible enemy. And now, a hundred millennia later, an undamaged warpwell had been uncovered on the world Darien, colonised by a lost offshoot of the Human race. Remnants of the Legion yet survived, trapped in the lowest, darkest, most inescapable depths of hyperspace, but their servants, those three combat droids, knew that the warpwell could be used to release them. Which was why the Construct, an old ally of the Forerunners, had sent Drazuma-Ha* to find Kao Chih and help him on his quest.

'He sent you to find me?'

'Just so,' Drazuma-Ha* had said. 'You know, for a millennia-old machine, the Construct has acquired some curiously sentimental traits – he once told me that Humanity was a species a little out of the ordinary, that they possessed an inner fire which set them apart from others. I was sceptical of these comments, yet now that I've accompanied you on this quest and shared its dangers and triumphs, I can see and openly say that he was right. After all, sometimes greatness is buried and must be brought to the surface, so be alert, Gowchee, to the greatness within.'

Now, half a day (and a couple of books) later, Kao Chih found his thoughts winding back to the mech's compliments and his own reaction to them. He had been surprised to the point of amazement, and then sombre and humbled, but now that he'd had time to ponder he realised that he had also felt embarrassed at being the recipient of such praise. Almost unbidden, one of his father's favourite sayings came to him – 'Beware the unearned handful of gold, for somewhere another hand is holding a knife' – which made him smile and shake his head. Sometimes it felt as if he had tiny versions of his mother and father in his mind, popping up now and then with a pithy adage.

His thoughts were interrupted by a heavy clank and the sound of rough servos as the wide door at the end of the vault began to slide open in three layers. At last, he thought.

'Apologies for the delay,' came a voice from the red-lit passage beyond. 'My precautions are exhaustive out of necessity – too many wily, tricksy bandits skulking between the stars for anyone to lower their guard ... follow the corridor round and up the slope, then turn right at the top and stop at the blast door.'

The Voth's voice was coming from grilles spaced along the corridor ceiling. Stubby rounded cones on the walls shed a ruby-red light and Kao Chih's shoes made a strange, reverberating noise as he walked. The otherwise featureless corridor sloped up past a heavy, dark-coloured door flanked by sensor posts and bearing an odd, circular keypad in its centre. The blast door they arrived at a few moments later was identical, though without the keypad.

'Please wait.'

'With respect, honourable Yash,' Kao Chih said, 'we have done little else but wait, and for many hours. We are engaged on a task of the gravest importance . . .'

'Yes, yes, yes, one which may profoundly affect the fate of trillions, tragedy, war, and so forth, but you've thus far neglected to say what you want from me. Once I find out, we can then negotiate a price for this service.'

'A price?' said Kao Chih. 'Disaster beckons and you wish to haggle over a fee?'

'Wait a moment, Gowchee,' said Drazuma-Ha*, breaking his hours-long silence. 'The honourable Yash is merely protecting his interests, and our imposition on his time can only detract from the attention which the refining process requires. We must be patient and allow him to determine the course of our deliberations.'

There was a moment of silence. 'So you know something about cloud-harvesters, then.'

'A little,' said the mech. 'Just that *Viganli* is a *Star-Eater*-series harvester, I believe, which combines the heavy-duty capacity of the *Fireliner* series with the effective range of the *Voidgrinder*s, while including a larger scoop field than either of them.'

'Very true, my machine guest, very perceptive. Please – enter.'

The door hummed aside and they advanced into a low-roofed, patchily lit and untidy room. One side was a clutter of odd furniture grouped around a holotank, while the other side was dominated by a long workbench backed by racks of tools, probes, leads and weapons. Their host was sitting cross-legged on a high bucket seat next to the bench, smoking a triple-bowl pipe while resting a large, intimidating weapon on one knee. For a Voth, Yash was lightly dressed, with only two jackets, a toolpouch kirtle over long and dusty oil-streaked pantaloons, and a pair of worn multigoggles pushed back onto his bare forehead, their data cable dangling loose by his side. Dark, deepset eyes regarded them suspiciously through a smoky haze.

'Welcome to my living room,' he said around the pipestem. 'It's a mess and it smells a bit but I wasn't expecting visitors.'

So what have you been doing for the last thirteen hours? Kao Chih wanted to say, but kept smiling instead.

'Our thanks for inviting us aboard your impressive vessel, friend Yash . . .' Drazuma-Ha* began.

'I'm not your friend,' the Voth said. 'Not yours nor this odd-looking Human's. What is he, anyway – your slave?'

'I am no one's slave,' Kao Chih said, stung by his insulting manner. 'I am on an important mission to the Human colony on Darien – we both are.'

The Voth shrugged and puffed some more smoke. 'So what do you need me for?'

'Our ship, sadly, is only capable of Tier 1 hyperspace travel,' Drazuma-Ha* said. 'So we originally hoped to persuade you to either lend us your shuttle for the last stage of our journey, or even that you might pilot it yourself . . .'

The heavy weapon in the Voth's lap whined, previously opaque sections flickered with dull glows, and Yash shifted it to aim at the mech.

'Before you begin your persuading,' Yash said, 'be aware that the walls and ceiling of this room contain enough targeted multi-wave projectors to fry every subquantal pathway in your cognitive core.'

'Yes, I know,' said Drazuma-Ha*. 'But be assured that my persuasion does not rely on brute methods. No, honourable Yash, I feel that it is only my duty to let you know that if war comes to this region, then the mining opportunities for independents like yourself will become very risky. It is my task to get to Darien and stop war breaking out, or, failing that, to send a message to allies who will come out to collect us.'

This was a complete surprise to Kao Chih, who glanced at the mech. *I thought he was prepared to seize the harvester's shuttle by force if necessary. What is he planning?*

'I cannot leave the *Viganli*,' the Voth said bluntly. 'And I'm not giving you my jelking shuttle. So a message it'll have to be.' Putting down the triple-bowled pipe, he slid off the bucket seat and landed on muscular, bowed legs, still carrying the big gun, which Kao Chih thought could be some kind of exotic plasma cannon. 'The bridge is up that way – after you.'

He guided them up another sloping passage to a small lobby with three doors and a mop and bucket in the corner. They pushed through the door directly ahead and found themselves in a long, narrow control room with viewports, consoles, screens, analysis stations and holodisplays on both sides. The bridge over-looked most of the *Viganli*'s·upper hull, from the midsection's chequerboard of big hold hatches to the oval intake manifold of the flaring bows from which six 100-metre-long booms angled forward and outward, three above, three below. These were the emitter masts which projected the harvester's 2.5-kilometre force-field before it to scoop in dust and debris.

Yash entered after them, plasma cannon balanced on one shoulder. 'And I'm just as protected here,' he said. 'Plenty of EMP gear, and all keyed to my commands.'

Unpleasant and paranoid, Kao Chih thought as he watched the Voth brush food fragments and a few empty packets away from one particular console. Away from the lounge and the pipe smoke, he noticed that the Voth had a strong, pungent, almost nutty odour. It was not pleasant.

'So, honourable Yash,' he said. 'How much are you charging for this aid?'

Yash grinned widely. 'How much have you got?'

Kao Chih met his gaze for a moment before reluctantly pulling out the pouch that held their remaining funds and emptying it into the Voth's outstretched hand. Yash looked over the stems and triangles for a moment then stuffed them into a side pocket.

'Help yourself – but touch nothing else, only the comms.'

'As you wish, most generous Yash,' Drazuma-Ha* said, float-ing over to the communication console, effector field rods stabbing out even before it had come to a halt.

Kao Chih watched, confused and not understanding the mech's actions or how this was going to get them to Darien. Yash also kept a mistrustful eye on the comms station, probably out of a twisted need to find something amiss, Kao Chih guessed.

A few moments later Drazuma-Ha* withdrew its effectors. 'I have sent a T2 message to my allies' tiernet handler – they should respond in a short while to tell us when . . .'

The mech was interrupted by a high-pitched peeping alert from another console further along. Yash cursed and hurried over, examined the displays and muttered angrily as he swiftly prodded several keys then grabbed an overhead monitor and swung it round for them to see.

'So are those your allies, eh? Thought you could just stroll in here and take my ship, did you? Jelk-eating pirates! – I should kill you right here and now . . .'

'Wait,' said the mech. 'These are not our allies . . .'

'My God,' Kao Chih said, staring at the monitor. 'It's those droids again – how did they find us? . . .'

'They must have backtracked along that hyperspace course and found our exit point,' said Drazuma-Ha*. 'Perhaps the tesserae fields leave behind an emission residue when they collapse . . .'

'Wait, wait, who or what are these newcomers?' Yash said to Kao Chih, pulling the goggles down over his eyes. 'Are they working with you or not? The truth now!'

'Honourable Yash, I swear to you that these droids are not our allies,' Kao Chih said, glancing at the familiar image of the trashed freighter. 'They've been following us for days, trying to stop us fulfilling our mission.'

The Voth nodded wearily and pushed the goggles back up. 'You're telling the truth. So, in other words, you brought your bad luck with you and dumped it on my doorstep.'

'Is the *Viganli* armed, honourable Yash?' the mech said.

Yash snorted. 'Two beam turrets, particle cannon, and a missile carrel – they automatically arm and target unless I countermand them.'

'They may not be sufficient to the task,' the mech said. 'As you can see, their ship is a hulk but it has strong fields protecting its engines. . .'

'So I'll pound it into a million jelking pieces,' the Voth said. 'Just watch.'

Kao Chih heard a muffled charging drone and a faint resonant thrum, repeating again and again. On the external monitor shafts and knots of energy and matter in various combinations flew out at the pursuers' vessel, which somehow managed to evade them. On the few times that it was hit, the damage seemed scarcely noticeable and failed to slow their approach. During all of this Kao Chih had moved over to watch the Voth keying in attack variations, but after several fruitless minutes Yash threw up his hands in disgust.

'Jelk it! – I should be heating up components and metal filings by now! They must have some other shields . . .'

He was interrupted by a high, peeping alert. The Voth frowned and punched up another display and Kao Chih felt his heart sink when it showed a second similar ship accelerating towards the *Viganli*.

'Another one?' Yash was grim and angry, suspicion returning to his features as he rounded on Kao Chih. 'What's going on . . . and where's your mech friend?'

Kao Chih suddenly realised that Drazuma-Ha* was no longer on the bridge, but before he could profess ignorance of the situation the mech's voice came from the comm system.

'Greetings, honourable Yash and Gowchee – the enemy has called on reinforcements, so you must fire upon them while I pilot the *Castellan* towards our first pursuer. I will attempt to ram their stern and thus make them an easier target.' Sure enough, another screen winked on, showing the *Castellan* manoeuvring away from the *Viganli*'s underside. 'I shall, of course, leave in the escape pod before the collision.'

'Crazy jelking machine,' Yash said, his long dark fingers dancing over the weapons controls. 'Now, let's see if we have better luck with this . . . *whoa!*'

The first volley of particle bolts struck the second ship in a line from amidships to the stern. Impacts tore large holes in the ravaged hull, ripping out cascades of shattered metal, then a couple of bolts found the engines. Something blew out immediately in a white eruption behind the main drives, perhaps the coolant reserves. Then the thrust fuel went up, cracking open the stern like a silver eggshell fracturing along cold blue-icy white lines. In seconds the stern had become an expanding cloud of debris and hot, glowing vapour. Astounded and relieved, Kao Chih applauded.

'Well done, honourable Yash – excellent targeting!'

'Heh, well, yes it was,' the Voth said. 'Now what is your mech friend up to?'

Another small screen whined as it unfolded from an overhead recess, flickered once then showed a medium-range shot of the *Castellan*. Its main thrusters were burning intermittently, in concert with the positioning jets, while further off was the first pursuing ship, the hulk freighter. Kao Chih watched the two vessels converging with what looked like agonising slowness, even though he knew they were moving at several hundred metres a second. He felt horribly powerless and wished he was out there with Drazuma-Ha*.

'Is your channel still open, Drazuma-Ha*?' he said.

'It is, Gowchee.'

'I hope that you will take the appropriate precautions – I have little desire to attempt to carry out your task as well as my own.'

'Such precautions have already been taken, Gowchee. I shall reach my goal and fulfil my purpose. Now I must deactivate this channel – honourable Gowchee and Yash, my thanks.'

Abruptly, the voice cut off, leaving Kao Chih to stare at the external monitor in puzzlement. The mech's final words had been odd, lacking in its usual conciseness, and expressing thanks seemed somewhat out of character.

'What . . . the jelk,' Yash said, pointing with a long forefinger, 'is that?'

The Voth was indicating a touch-control screen on the comms

console – it was glowing a pale blue with dark blue and green graphics, an app options panel with the words 'Terminate Simulation?' across the top.

'What simulation?' said Kao Chih.

'Exactly! – there wasn't one running before you and your machine arrived,' the Voth said as he reached over to the screen, hesitated a moment, then firmly pressed the terminate button.

At once, the image of the *Castellan* and the oncoming freighter disappeared from several screens up and down the control room. A second later, a cluster of board alarms went off, lights and symbols flickered and flashed, and a rasping synth voice spoke.

'Hull breach, outer hold 4, inner pressure doors closing . . . hull breach, outer hold 9, inner pressure doors closing . . . inner bulkhead breach, section 23, maintenance drone assigned . . .'

'What . . . what's happening?' said Kao Chih, bewildered now.

'Well, for a jelking start,' Yash said, hefting the plasma cannon and levelling it in his direction, 'there never was any message to your allies, was there? Instead, your machine sets a simulation running, faking an attack and him taking your ship, while all the time he was *stealing my shuttle*!'

'No, that cannot be . . .'

'Look, idiot Human, look!' An external monitor showed the *Castellan* still moored to the harvester's underside, then it switched to a view of some kind of hold with a gantry and racks of equipment. 'And that is Stern Bay 1, where my shuttle is usually berthed, only now it's . . .'

'Intruder detected, deck 10 . . . intruder detected, deck 7 . . . hull breach, outer hold 2, inner pressure doors closing . . .'

'And now I'm being boarded,' the Voth moaned. 'Who by? – and where did they come from?'

'It must be the droids from the ship you destroyed,' said Kao Chih, eyeing the wavering business end of the plasma cannon. 'They are agents for a cyborg species called the Legion of Avatars who were defeated by the Forerunners, but these droids have to get to Darien to open a well into hyperspace . . .'

'Mad,' the Voth said. 'Completely sun-staring, rock-sniffing insane you are! Legions and Forerunners . . . I'm being boarded and you're giving me jelk like that. But here's an idea . . .' He prodded Kao Chih with the cannon. '. . . if they're your enemies, maybe I should just welcome them on board and treat them as friends, eh? What do you say?'

'A very sensible proposal,' said a voice from one of the monitors. 'I suggest you adopt it without delay.'

One of the Legion droids was regarding them from the screen. It was a bulky, asymmetrical machine with lens clusters set into a small, off-centre recess. Yash took one look and sneered.

'Jelk you! This is my ship so we play by my rules . . .'

'I don't think you've grasped the fullness of the situation,' the droid said.

Just then the control room lights went out along with all the consoles and monitors, apart from the one they were watching.

'So – where do you think we are?' the droid continued.

Yash flared his nostrils and Kao Chih could actually hear his teeth grinding.

'Power core regulating station,' he muttered.

'Correct. Now, because you destroyed our ship we're going to have to borrow yours so that we can resume our pursuit, made all the more difficult by your stupidity in letting the Instrument take your shuttle . . .'

'Stupidity?' said the Voth, long teeth bared.

'Yours and this halfwit Human's. Anyway, before we can do anything we have to unpick the autodestruct which the Instrument planted in the hyperdrive startup datachain.' Some of the consoles came back to life. 'Take a look.'

As the Voth bent over a console and called up streams of incomprehensible code, Kao Chih slumped into one of the bucket seats, thoughts whirling. Clearly, Drazuma-Ha* had been planning all this since before they'd come aboard the harvester, which included leaving Kao Chih behind. Perhaps it needed Kao Chih's honest reaction when the simulated droid ship had appeared, but that did not make him feel any better. Nor did it quell his sense of unease. And why did the Legion droid refer to the mech as the Instrument?

'Nasty and well hidden,' Yash said at last, straightening. 'But how do I know you didn't put it in there yourselves?'

'Why should we?' the droid said. 'Why go to all the trouble? No, that's high-grade Legion work – not our methodology at all.'

Yash stared at Kao Chih. 'You said that this lot were from the Legion of . . . what was it?'

'Avatars,' Kao Chih said. 'Legion of Avatars . . .'

'Ah, I see,' said the droid on the monitor. 'I'm afraid you have been deceived – your mech companion is an Instrument of the Legion of Avatars while we are field armigers for the Construct . . .'

'What proof . . . can you offer?' Kao Chih said. 'Why should we take what you say at face value?'

'Why did you take what *that* machine said at face value?' the droid countered. 'Even its appearance is a fake . . .'

'With respect,' he said, 'that is ridiculous.'

Yash laughed unkindly. 'Didn't you know that it was running a holoshell behind its forcefield? I was using my goggles in tandem with my wall sensors to study it, got a few outline scans and extrapolated a rough image . . .'

'Did it look anything like this?' An inset appeared on the monitor next to the hulking droid, showing a strange metallic object resembling a section of articulated limb with a joint halfway up its length. Seeing it, the Voth nodded.

'Yes, very similar, except that this one has two joints.' He squinted at the screen. 'What is this thing? Looks like a piece of something else.'

'It is,' the droid said. 'This is a limb from a cyborg creature, a Knight of the Legion of Avatars. A Knight cyborg is permeated with bio-cortical substrate so when they hive off parts of themselves they can imbue them with a version of their own personae. They possess organic sentience along with the attitudes and instincts of their progenitors, which is strictly in accordance with their creed. In the convergence of organic sentience and technology, the part shall reflect the whole.'

'Can they be killed?' Yash said, patting his plasma cannon.

'Most definitely,' the droid said. 'But not if we stand around here talking.'

'I'll get that autodestruct unpicked,' the Voth said, sitting down at the console.

Kao Chih had listened in silence, absorbing the truth and feeling a horrible realisation. After the escape from the Chaurixa torture ship, he had been so determined to be done with being someone else's pawn or commodity, yet he had been Drazuma-Ha*'s willing dupe all along. His father was right – the hidden hand with its knife had been there from the start.

'When you reach Darien, I want to go with you,' he said to the droid.

'As you wish, Human. Just don't get in our way.'

'I won't, I give you my word. I just want to be there when you tear out whatever that treacherous machine uses for a heart.'

Yash looked up from his screen, chuckling.

'That's more like it, Human!'

In the stolen shuttle's cockpit, the Instrument patiently observed the console displays, overseeing the ship's progress through T2 hyperspace as it savoured the successful outcome of its deceptions and gambits. He had come so far in such a short span of time, from awakening underwater in the shadow of his mighty progenitor to this final stage of his momentous journey, having beguiled and outwitted all his adversaries. Even when the Chaurixa hijacker had taken them by surprise at Bryag Station and employed a stasis web, he had been able to divert all available resources to maintaining a hard holoshell while recovering various crashed subsystems preparatory to regaining full functionality. Another example of ingenious improvisation leading to success. And was that not because he was, in himself, an authentic replica of his exalted progenitor's instincts and craft and ingenuity?

Too soon for celebration, said an admonitory inner voice. *Too far yet to travel, too much still to do, too many uncertainties and opponents to overcome. Focus on the task, enumerate resources, assess all likely risks and possibilities, generate tactical solutions that will support strategic aims.*

Very well – risks and possibilities. Before leaving the *Viganli*'s bridge he had left a destruct trigger buried in the hyperdrive data-chain matrix, but it was quite likely that if any or all of the Construct's rustbucket AIs boarded the harvester (itself quite likely) the trap would be uncovered and made safe. Therefore, there was a good chance that they were following him to this Darien, the warpwell planet, which had been colonised by Humans. He knew, from news feeds picked during his travels, that there were warships in orbit there, a dangerous obstacle to any arriving vessel. He would have to find a way to make that potential aggression, and the inherent territorial paranoia of military hierarchies, work in his favour.

There were a few options but one of them stood out from the rest in its simplicity. It would require a certain amount of finely-gauged role-playing, but he was sure that his recent experiences would prove invaluable in that respect.

Aboard the *Heracles*, Sub-Lieutenant Tuan Ho had just gone on overwatch in Sensory when one of the outer boundary beacons went off. He shook his head, put down the plastic beaker of coffee from which he had been about to sip, and called up Hugo, the resident expert system.

'Yarr, matey! There be a ship incoming off the larboard bow . . .'

Ho sighed when he saw the eye-patched, tricorn-hatted visage. The middle-watch operators must have been exceptionally bored.

'Hugo,' he said. 'Setting command – reskin to default.'

Suddenly the head and shoulders image reverted to Hugo's usual appearance, attired in the pale green one-piece of a navy tech.

'Okay,' Tuan Ho said. 'Let me have the report again.'

'A badly damaged small ship, possibly a shuttle, dropped out of hyperspace just inside the deci-au marker. The pilot is speaking Brolturan, says he is the sole survivor of a Brolturan prospecting expedition that was attacked by a hijacked harvester ship, and claims that this harvester is chasing him. He also says that his guidance systems are down and that he's flying on manual with the aim of landing on Darien. His life support is on backup and his comms are down to audio only; his ship is not emitting an ident but he claims to be from the *Perquisitor*. A Brolturan-registered ship of that name was reported missing in the Huvuun three weeks ago.'

Tuan Ho frowned. 'No ident, audio only – could be anyone or anything. Have you piped it to Tactical?'

'I did so when I piped it up to the captain's portable.'

His eyes widened in surprise. 'Why do that?'

'Because fifteen seconds later the captain received a direct query about the newcomer from Father-Admiral Dyrosha aboard the *Purifier*.'

Tuan Ho grinned. 'And it would have looked bad if Velazquez had had to get the information from Dyrosha. Good thinking, Hugo.'

The expert system smiled and shrugged. 'I am coded for initiative.'

'Over-Lieutenant Schenker once said he wished I was. So what's happening now?'

'I am tracking this ship in tandem with Tactical, Velazquez and Dyrosha are still in conference, and the *Purifier* has just launched a pair of interceptors.'

'Goodness, I do hope they don't lose those ones too!'

Like almost everyone on board *Heracles*, Tuan Ho had watched the incredible dogfight over the forest moon, which had been shown on all the communal and rec screens. The sight of one of their own shuttles being piloted with insane bravado and destroying not one but two Brolturan interceptors was electrifying, and revealing. The crew had been divided into a minority who were shocked and upset, and the majority whose approval ran from a kind of fateful resignation to out-and-out pro-Dariens who later put together a noticeboard shrine to the Scots pilot, Donny Barbour. It had not escaped Ho's attention that most of the pro-Brolturans also had AI-companions.

'Well, it'll probably turn out to be nothing serious,' he said. 'While you're keeping your eye on it, I'm going to heat up my coffee.'

'You may be right, sir,' said Hugo.

But twenty minutes later, when a *Star-Eater*-class cloud-harvester came out of hyperspace a mere 2,000 kilometres from the *Heracles*, tripping every alarm, Tuan Ho soon found that there was no time for sips or even thoughts of coffee.

From the moment they appeared in the Darien system, they were bombarded with a stream of increasingly trenchant demands, and finally warnings of dire consequences. Yash, however, was giving as good as he got.

'No, no, *Heracles*, you listen to me – I am the wronged party, I am the victim and I'm in pursuit of the thief who stole my shut-tle . . .'

'Harvester *Viganli*, we have to verify your story which is why you *must* cut your velocity and assume stationary orbit . . .'

'Why aren't you putting the clamps on that shuttle, eh? Why? . . .'

'As a Brolturan vessel it is being handled by . . .'

'It's not a Brolturan ship! – can't you jelkers understand? The thieving, stinking machine who stole it is lying to you and the Brolturans, lying to everybody . . .'

'Harvester ship – this is Tactical Dominance Enabler *Purifier*, Father-Admiral Dyrosha commanding. You are ordered to reduce your velocity to zero and prepare for boarding scrutiny . . .'

'No one gets to scrutinise me,' snarled the Voth.

'. . . and possible charges. Failure to comply will result in dili-gent threat elimination. That is all.'

'*Heracles* to *Viganli* – in case you didn't get the gist of that, I should tell you that the *Purifier* has launched fifteen close support fighters due to intercept your trajectory in less than six minutes. But you are already in range of our standoff weapons and in two minutes you will be in range of our full deterrent. Consider your position carefully.'

Yash nodded sourly at the dead channel then looked round at the Construct droid, the spokesman.

'I hope that you know what you're doing – it looks as if we're about to become involved in a bit of target practice.'

'We have reconfigured your fields into defence shields, Pilot Yash,' said the bulky droid, who went by the name Gorol9. 'Our opponents should be surprised, especially when the target starts firing back.' Part of its upper carapace swivelled to bring its lens cluster to bear on Kao Chih. 'Has there been any change, Human Gowchee?'

Kao Chih had been assigned a console dedicated to tracking the stolen shuttle's course, velocity and other aspects of its flightpath.

'None, Gorol9,' he said. 'It is still broadcasting that Brolturan message and heading straight for Darien at constant speed – we can expect to overtake it before it reaches atmosphere.'

'Good, then it is time to get the Instrument's attention by increasing speed.'

'It is done,' said the droid overseeing navigation, a broad-torsoed droid called Ysher23; it had four curiously slender legs and two immense arms with interchangeable effectors.

A moment after the increase, the comm channel livened up again.

'*Heracles* to *Viganli* – you are traversing restricted space without authorisation! Cut your velocity at once and power down your defences . . .'

'This is Captain-Pilot Yash – I have made no threats or hostile moves towards you but I will defend myself if necessary . . .'

'They've targeted our stern,' said Dalqa42, the smallest of the three droids who was overseeing the tactical/weapons station. 'Any moment now . . .'

The bridge jolted and Kao Chih and the Voth grabbed their consoles in reflex. Alerts flashed then subsided.

'Well within shield tolerances,' said Gorol9.

'More beam and particle attacks coming,' said Dalqa42. 'The Humans have also launched a flight of missiles.'

The bridge and the ship shook again and again from repeated

impacts, yet there was an air of strange calm. From the narrow viewports Kao Chih could see Darien, a fist-sized, dark-blue and white object directly ahead with its forest moon a dull green coin off to one side. A few of the overhead screens showed a 3D graphic of the harvester's shields, red spikes indicating hits, symbol reels detailing depth of penetration and shield recovery rates. Then there was the holotank sitting over its projection niche, displaying the relative positions of the *Viganli* and the Earthsphere ship, *Heracles*, its beam attacks depicted as stabbing white lines, its missiles a curve of winking motes sweeping ahead in deflection strike.

And through it all there was almost no talk, an eerie peace, even though he knew that the droids had to be sharing data via proximity transfer, but for Kao Chih and the Voth there were only the screens.

'We're pulling away from the *Heracles*,' Yash said, peering into one of the tactical screens. 'They're holding position in high orbit but their missiles are still on target – will these shields be enough to stop them?'

'Probably not,' said Gorol9.

'Beam turret ready for interdiction,' said Dalqa42. 'Outer optimal range now in effect, commencing preemptive strike.'

Out in the murky darkness there was a tiny flare, then another and a couple more . . .

'What is the status of the shuttle, Human Gowchee?' said Gorol9.

'We are gaining on it,' he said, trying to ignore the jolts and quivers of the *Heracles*'s attacks. 'At our current velocity we will overtake it in 5.7 minutes – however, those Brolturan interceptors are still on course and we will encounter them in . . . 3.8 minutes.'

'That's too much like sticking our head into a mouthful of fangs,' said Yash. 'We should veer off and make a run for open space.'

'There is no need for concern, Pilot Yash,' Gorol9 said. 'We have prepared for every eventuality and, after all, we have every intention of returning your ship after completing our mission.'

'Right . . . okay then.' The Voth rubbed his face, nodded and was turning back to the holodisplay when Dalqa42 said:

'Missile incoming – brace for impact!'

An instant later a crashing explosion shook the ship and Kao Chih was thrown bodily out of his seat. Alarms yammered and the consoles flashed with violet emergency symbols as the synth voice spoke.

'Hull breach, outer hold 11, outer hold 12 . . . inner bulkhead breach, section 32, deck 11 . . . severe pressure drop detected, junction 89 blast doors closing . . .'

'My ship!' Yash groaned as he picked himself up.

'What happened?' said Kao Chih, climbing back into his seat.

'A single missile survived our beam-cannon interdiction,' said Dalqa42. 'The Humans are launching no more, since their Brolturan allies will soon be upon us.'

On a side monitor, he could see a jagged, gaping hole in the flank of the harvester's starboard bow.

'Comforting,' the Voth said. 'Do they carry missiles too?'

'I believe that these interceptors are Rampart Monoclan Mark 8 Warwings,' said Gorol9. 'Rebadged for the Star Forces of Broltura . . .'

'Armed with double-twin pulse cannons, plus triple-layer field chamber upgrades,' said Ysher23.

'And a dozen Sacred Lance missiles with integrated expert-system guidance,' said Dalqa42.

Kao Chih looked over at Pilot Yash. 'Isn't that nice – they have a hobby!'

Yash sniggered. Seconds later, the first Brolturan interceptor got within range and opened fire.

The next ten minutes were like a passage through hell, a *Hell of Tearing Explosions*, Kao Chih thought sardonically, *reserved for those who allowed themselves to be fooled and used*. The Brolturan fighters swept past in twos and threes, hammering the *Viganli* with beam-cannon volleys and, like the *Heracles*, discovering that the harvester's shield could take all they could throw. Then came the missiles, which is when the running battle really began.

Meanwhile, the stolen shuttle had, infuriatingly, put on more speed and pulled ahead slightly, giving it a two-minute lead on the harvester, which was hard pressed to keep pace.

The Brolturan interceptors began sending in wide spreads of missiles whose inbound trajectories zigzagged wildly, thus reducing beam concentration on their casings. Despite hasty modifications to the beam-cannon strike patterns, a handful made it through and slammed into the forward section, blew open three holds and ripped off one of the huge emitter masts. The bridge lurched sickeningly but everyone kept their seats while Yash wailed in distress at the punishment his ship was getting.

By now the *Viganli* had reached low orbit above Darien yet it was continuing along a descent trajectory with the thermosphere coming up fast.

'Jelk it, why aren't we assuming orbit?' said Yash.

'Because we're still under attack,' said Gorol9. 'And our enemy is going to attempt a landing.'

Wild-eyed, the Voth clenched his fists. 'But *Viganli* has no flight surfaces, no suspensors, and no vectored thrust – it's a jelking cloud-harvester not a glider! You said you were going to give me my ship back . . .'

'That was our intention, Pilot Yash, but our enemies' intentions are otherwise.'

The missile impacts and the loss of an emitter mast had degraded the shield coverage and beam-cannon bursts were getting through to punch holes in the hull plating. Then an interceptor, its stern wrecked by a lucky shot from the *Viganli's* particle gun, came flying in, caromed off the upper hull and smashed into the aft superstructure. The impact threw everyone violently back, as the lights and deck gravity died. There was a terrifying moment of weightless motion in complete darkness before the lighting and the gravity returned.

'Structural integrity compromised,' said the synth alert voice. 'Hull temperature rising . . . coolant system coverage at 68 per cent and falling . . .'

'Enemy interceptors breaking off,' said Dalqa42. 'More missiles dispatched, however.'

'The shuttle,' said Gorol9. 'The Instrument, where is it?'

'It's now in atmospheric descent,' Kao Chih said. 'Velocity falling, altitude 520 kilometres and falling, course . . . banking towards the northern hemisphere. Is that the location of this warpwell?'

'Yes, and of the Human colony,' said Gorol9.

'Hull temperature at 88 per cent of tolerance . . . coolant system coverage at 51 per cent and decreasing . . .' said the synth alert.

'How close are those missiles?' Gorol9 said.

'First impacts in 4.7 minutes,' said Dalqa42. 'Likely targets are port and starboard thrust engines, and bridge superstructure. Droid survival quotient is 19 per cent, organic crew 8 per cent. Recommend evacuation.'

'Agreed – transfer destination coordinates to escape boat and shuttle.'

'Done,' said Ysher23.

'We must waste no time,' said Gorol9. 'I and Ysher23 will take your shuttle, Gowchee, while you, Pilot Yash and Dalqa42 take the harvester's escape boat. Our pursuit must continue – the Instrument must be prevented from reaching the warpwell.'

After that it was a mad scramble down to Yash's living room, from which a trapdoor ladder led down to the escape boat. There was a pause while the Voth stuffed a seemingly random selection of items into a filthy shoulder sack, then they hurried down to the boat. Muttering incomprehensible Vothic oaths, Yash strapped himself in, shoulder sack wedged between his bony knees, while Kao Chih followed suit and Dalqa42 came last, closed and sealed the hatch.

Kao Chih heard a muffled crash from back in the harvester and felt the boat shake. Then there was a cluster of loud bangs and the boat lurched forward and dropped, sudden vertigo surging in his stomach. Without a doubt they were free of the *Viganli* and a moment later he heard a cluster of servo whines, and a sense of

weight returned, then a sway to the side along with the occasional deep buzz.

'Lift surfaces have been deployed,' said the droid Dalqa42.
'Directional jets functioning normally, guidance system nominal.
Time till landing, approximately 7.5 minutes.'

Kao Chih nodded. 'Pilot Yash, is there any way to see outside?'

'Not until we are below 4,000 *meol*.' The Voth glowered at
him. 'And do not presume to speak to me, Human jelk! You bear
responsibility for the loss of my jelking ship!' And he turned his
face away.

'Yes, you're right,' Kao Chih sighed and settled back, convert-
ing the *meol* altitude in his head to roughly 2,500 feet.

The minutes crept by. The escape pod often shuddered and
pitched from atmospheric turbulence, poor weather according to
the droid. In the fifth minute a pinging sound came from an overhead control pad and the Voth wordlessly reached up to press a
button. Small triangular panels slide aside on both sides of the
nose, revealing viewports – mostly they could only see the rushing
greyness of clouds but occasionally they caught glimpses of landscape far below, mountains and valleys, dense areas of green.
Darien, he thought. At last.

'Droids Gorol9 and Ysher23 have landed ahead of the
Instrument's shuttle and have met with armed resistance,' said
Dalqa42 all of a sudden.

'Ahead of it?' said Kao Chih. 'How?'

'Weather conditions . . . wait . . .' Dalqa42 was silent for a
moment or two, then, 'The adversary's craft just arrived but
crashed into rock formations a short distance from the warpwell's location, a deep excavation into a rock promontory . . .
Gorol9 reports that they can sense the Instrument's presence and
advises us to be ready.'

'Ready for what?' said the Voth.

'For combat, Pilot Yash,' Dalqa42 said.

'Not my fight, droid,' said Yash.

'Those we are about to encounter will assume that it is and act accordingly. To increase the possibility of a successful outcome, Gorol9 and I will now transpose . . .'

Kao Chih and Yash exchanged a puzzled look as the droid fell silent, immobile. A moment or two later the droid began to move again, surveying the boat's interior and its occupants.

'Human Gowchee and Pilot Yash – somehow, it is pleasing to make your acquaintance again. Now, we are just seconds away from . . .'

The escape boat lurched upward then seemed to swoop downwards, banking as it did so.

'Steerable canopy deployed – guidance will take us to within five metres of the warpwell location. Prepare yourselves for . . .'

Through the small viewport Kao Chih could see a muddled blur of landscape turning and turning beneath them then tilting and rushing past, rushing up quite quickly . . .

'. . . a rough landing . . .'

The boat swept into a gulf of shadow, an abrupt plunge followed by a sharp swing to the right as they slammed into something. Even as Kao Chih and Yash cried out, the capsule pitched forward and descended by steady stages, landing with a bump. Scarcely waiting for the boat to settle, the droid Gorol9 tugged on the hatch release and a curved section of the hull popped open. At once Kao Chih inhaled a flow of cold, damp air laced with smells of growing things . . .

Gorol9 helped them both out. They were at the foot of some kind of sheer-sided excavation faced with ribbed, composite cladding, looking up at a grey, evening sky from which raindrops were falling. For a second Kao Chih stood there, feeling the rain on his face, enjoying the sensation . . .

'The Instrument is here,' said Gorol9. 'Further in . . .'

The sound of weapons-fire came from a doorway at the end of the narrow trench and the droid started swiftly towards it. Kao Chih hesitated, until Yash took a shiny blue beam pistol from his shoulder sack and offered it to him.

The doorway had a set of steps leading down into an icy chamber where golden lamps on the floor threw sharp shadows against a wall with three doors. There were four dark and glassy pillars here, too, and the motionless, huddled shapes of dead people, seven large humanoids, Sendrukans, he guessed. The three doors were surrounded by a carving-covered wall, and without pause the droid dived through the only door that was open.

Beyond, more bodies at the edge of an immense circular chamber with a low wall running around, prescribing a kind of walkway. A few small lamps were spaced along the low wall for about a quarter of its circuit, revealing to Kao Chih's eyes some of the sweeping patterns, the symbols and the characters which were carved into the chamber's wide stone floor. Was this what all the deceptions, the pursuit, the destruction and death had been for? – was this the warpwell?

More gunfire came from behind them, and Yash brought up his plasma cannon.

'I'll hold this door – you go after our droid friend, see he doesn't get into trouble. He owes me a ship!'

Kao Chih nodded and hastened along the walkway. Ahead he could make out the spindly shape of Gorol9 (formerly Dalqa42) striding after a glowing blue object that was heading towards the centre of the chamber's stone floor. As he walked he saw that the blue thing was a strange artefact resembling a section of a long, articulated limb or tentacle. A cyborg machine. As it came to a halt, Gorol9 extended its gait to a lope. Unthinkingly, Kao Chih stepped over the low wall and began running towards it, not noticing the silvery, threadlike glows that flickered across the floor patterns in his wake.

'Fools who rush to their deaths,' said Drazuma-Ha* in a voice which echoed sharply in the chamber, 'should not be disappointed.'

A shaft of amber force leaped out and seized Gorol9 around its slender torso and dragged it in close. An amber blade then hacked off the droid's legs and Kao Chih, rage in his heart, raised the beam pistol and blazed away.

'Even if you could get through my exquisitely designed force shield,' Drazuma-Ha* said, 'that pathetic weapon would scarcely dent my skin. Admit your defeat, Human, admit the inherent weakness of your unaugmented flesh.'

It was true – the beam pistol's bolts flared and sparked uselessly against the blue aura. Bitterly he lowered the weapon, slowed to a halt and fell to his knees.

'You have nothing to admit to this maimed hybrid, Gowchee,' said Gorol9, still being held down on the carved stone. 'You have nothing to be ashamed of.'

'So speaks the machine,' said the Legion creature. 'Good, obedient device, just one amongst the Construct's little horde of windup junkpiles. Attend carefully, Human – this machine, this contraption, will never know the wonder of convergence, the intermingling of life's pure essence and a technology perfectly adapted to life's supreme ambition. Oh, machines can be made highly complex and made to imitate the permutations of true sentience, but ultimately it is only obedience to a detailed matrix of commands, a dry, empty mockery of living sentience.'

'You are a made thing,' said Gorol9. 'Your vaunted convergence with technology is nothing but your desperate need to flee the pains of the flesh, the entropy of the flesh, the ending of the flesh. And you? – you are little more than an offcut, stemming from your progenitor Knight's need for an instrument . . .'

'Liar! My essence, my foundation is organic, and my sentience flows from the purity of convergence . . .'

INTRUDERS HAVE BEEN DETECTED!

Kao Chih almost quailed at the thunderous volume of the voice which reverberated all around but which seemed to issue from the stone floor beneath. In that instant he saw a spiderweb of glowing threads spreading across the intertwined patterns, all emitting a curious, crystalline brightness.

'Aah, the guardian awakes,' said Drazuma-Ha*.

YOU ARE OF THE LEGION, INTRUDER – YOUR PRESENCE HERE IS A VIOLATION. YOU MUST BE ERASED.

'Exactly, machine. Obey the unvarying schemata of your responses. Open the door through which I may fulfil my transcendent task . . .'

'Sentinel – I am Gorol9 of the Construct's forward echelon. You must not deploy your energies against the Legion intruder – it will use them against you.'

I RECOGNISE YOU, GOROL9, BUT YOU MAY NOT COMMAND ME. THE THREAT IS CLEAR AND IT MUST BE ERASED.

Feeling helpless, Kao Chih raised his gun again, then his shoulders sagged and he slumped back, tears of angry desperation in his eyes. How he hated this machine-creature.

'Good – you recognise the futility of your position, Human,' said Drazuma-Ha*. 'You may be weak, yet there is hope for your species – many have already taken the first steps towards convergence and when the Legion assumes its rightful dominance we will help them further along that illustrious journey.'

'You betrayed me,' Kao Chih said. 'I trusted you! . . .'

'Look upon it as a lesson,' the Legion creature said, lancing out with an amber shaft of force which batted away the beam pistol then grabbed him round the neck and hauled him in. At the same time, the crystalline radiance rising from the warpwell patterns began to pulse, lighting up the ceiling and the walls.

THE LEGION INTRUDER IS A CLEAR THREAT AND WILL BE ERASED. ALL OTHERS MUST LEAVE – NOW!

'And now the pair of you will join me in my triumph, but only as equals . . .' An amber blade extruded from the Legion instrument's force aura and Kao Chih began to cry out in horror, struggling as the blade swept round towards his own legs.

The droid Gorol9 acted. A jointed arm shot out and its multi-clawed hand flew straight at Drazuma-Ha*, colliding with its forcefield aura, to which it clung. The restraints and the blade shafts shrank to nothing as the forcefield flickered with bands and went out. Kao Chih reached over to snatch up his beam pistol then gleefully aimed it at the Legion machine-creature, which was now lying on its side, a motionless, lopped-off steel tentacle.

'Your weapon is as useless as it asserted, Gowchee. But you have a neural device in your pocket which might immobilise it – use it! We have only seconds before it recovers.'

A neural device? A quick search of his pockets produced . . . of course, the nerve-blocker which Compositor Henach had used on him back on the Chaurixa ship! Trusting to Gorol9's advice, he dived at the Legion Instrument, which was starting to right itself. He grabbed it round the middle with one arm and with his other hand took the nerve-blocker and rammed it into the joint between two of the thing's articulated segments. A panel opened in the side of it and a tool-tipped arm lashed out at him. While fending it off with his pistol, he had to use his body weight to hold the Legion machine-creature down as he desperately shoved the nerve-blocker's flexible arms into the joint gap, praying that it would work.

'Betrayer! – you have betrayed life and aided . . . dead machines . . .'

'I have my honour,' Kao Chih said, gritting his teeth against the pain of his wounded hand, slashed by the tool-wielding arm. 'And the satisfaction of knowing that you are ended . . .'

But the flickering aura went out and suddenly he realised that he was talking to a lifeless piece of machinery.

Light hung all around in layered veils, just visible through his overwhelming exhaustion. The voice of the warpwell Sentinel was booming somewhere overhead, an exchange involving Gorol9. Pilot Yash was close by, shaking his shoulder, saying that a company of Brolturan troops would soon be on top of them. Kao Chih tried to sit up, but instead he flopped onto his back, staring up at the chamber ceiling, his tongue mute, his limbs numb, his flesh as cold as the wintry radiance that surged over him like a tide.

He never lost consciousness. Everything was lucid and he felt quite alert, despite the dreamlike swirl and eddy of images, his mother and father bidding him farewell at the dockside at Agmedra'a, the Roug Tumakri riding with him in the strange AI cart at Blacknest . . . then instead of Tumakri it was the Chaurixa surgeon, Compositor Henach, who was sharing the cart's cramped interior. '*Ah, the unblemished human brain,*' he was saying. '*A remarkable canvas for convergence . . .*' Then the cart turned and shot into a dark corridor full of swaying shadows and, oddly for a deep space station, the smells of growing things. There were the sounds of familiar voices and a glow. Eyes open, he realised that he was lying on his back and raised his head . . . and regretted it when pain clamped his temples.

'Back with us, Human?'

The Voth was seated on a fallen log, next to a conical lamp giving off a buttery yellow light. Propped against the trunk were the remains of Gorol9, who was regarding him steadily. 'You were poisoned by the Legion Instrument's desperate self-defence,' the droid said. 'Luckily, Pilot Yash had some anti-toxin infusers in his big bag so the only effects you suffered were the psychoactive ones.'

Yash grinned. 'It's a good high – so I've been told . . .'

Kao Chih looked around him – they were gathered in a hollow in a darkened forest, beneath an overhanging rock bearded with moss and grass from which water dripped. It was raining out in the night, a subdued whispering from the dim shapes of trees, leaves rustling, branches swaying in occasional breezy gusts. He could smell and savour the odours of a vastness of biomass and he shivered, cold and excited – this was Darien, a living world as lush as Pyre once was.

'How . . .' He paused to cough. 'How did we get away?'

'Since the immediate threat was over, the Sentinel of the well graciously condescended to translocate us away from the Brolturans, although it had to be certain that this was in accord with the general tenor of previous commands,' said Gorol9. 'The remains of the Instrument have been sent to the Construct.'

'Jelking machine mind,' Yash said. 'My bank has a branch on Yonok – why couldn't it send me there?'

'So where are we now?' said Kao Chih.

'Roughly seventeen miles west of Hammergard,' said a voice from nearby.

Looking up, he saw two men descending the slope just along from the overhang – one was short and wiry with sandy-coloured hair while the other was taller with dark hair. He recognised them as Europeans, with that wide-eyed look of astonishment that he had only ever seen in the *Retributor*'s data files. Both were wearing blue cheek patches from which pickup stalks protruded.

'Greetings, Humans Cameron and McGrain,' said Gorol9, then to Kao Chih it said, 'I have fashioned small translators for them so that we may understand each other.'

'Very smart wee gadgets,' said the taller of the two, his odd Anglic dialect smoothly translated by Kao Chih's linguistic enabler. 'But I'm glad to see that you've recovered. When myself and Rory got here an hour ago ye were still in the grip of that drug . . .'

'Totally out of it,' said the other man with a grin.

'Oh yes – this is Rory McGrain and I'm Greg Cameron,' said the first.

Kao Chih nodded courteously from where he lay. 'It is an honour to meet you. But how did you know where to find us?'

'Well, one of our allies has a certain understanding with the warpwell Sentinel,' said the man Cameron. 'He couldn't say anything other than to get to this spot with all speed, and after we did your friends filled us in on a few details about what happened up at Giant's Shoulder and what you did.' He shook his head. 'Incredible, just incredible. But neither of them know how ye became involved with this Legion cyborg creature, or where you're from.'

Kao Chih sighed and, ignoring his headache, got to his feet. 'Honourable sirs, my story has more twists and turns than a bowlful of noodles. But first I must introduce myself properly and fully – my name is Kao Chih of the Human Sept of Agmedra'a, and my people originally came from Earth 150 years ago, fleeing the Swarm invasion . . .'

The two men listened in astonishment as he told them about the beautiful world where the *Tenebrosa* had finally landed, the colony established by his forebears, the Hegemony mercenaries and the prospector ships that strip-mined the planet, the exodus of half the colony to the Roug orbital, Agmedra'a, and their indenture under conditions of secrecy. His voice shook as he recounted their sorrowful tragedy and he saw their faces grow sombre.

'But then news came of the discovery of your world and, at the Roug's instigation, I was sent to find you, meet your leaders and warn them of the Hegemony. Most importantly, I was to ask permission for my people to come and settle here and be part of your community. But now I find that the Hegemony and its Brolturan vassals have taken control of your world, which has a secret that is attracting the agents of an ancient enemy.' He shook his head. 'That Earth has become a willing ally of the Hegemony is almost the worst of it. Freedom for both our peoples seems a forlorn hope.'

'You musn't lose hope, Kao Chih,' said Cameron. 'Hard struggles lie ahead, more than I care to think about, but only yesterday one of us gave them a humiliating kicking and that, together with your astounding victory, all three of you – that gives me hope. The task ahead of us is monumental and our enemies are innumerable, strong and vicious, but if we don't take them on, who will?' He glanced at the Construct droid, Gorol9. 'And sometimes help can come from the most unexpected quarter . . .' His gaze swung back to Kao Chih. 'And the last thing I was expecting was you! Just knowing that your people, the colonists from the *Tenebrosa*, have survived all those calamities and are eager to come here and join us – that gives me hope and strength!'

He held out his hand. 'Kao Chih – welcome to Darien.'

For a brief moment, he stared back at the man Cameron, wondering if anything else lay behind the open smile, the clear brown eyes, and the apparent integrity. Then he relented, deciding that he would trust Greg Cameron. Today.

'Thank you, Mr Cameron.'

And they shook hands, smiles widening to grins.

EPILOGUE

ROBERT

Awakening was a slow ascent. He arose gradually from black oblivion, a no-sound, no-sight, no-place which steadily dissolved into a blurred grey ocean, dream's drowsy shallows. It felt as if he was struggling through thick mud to get to the shore and the lighter it became, the more he began to remember . . . things, faces, places, nightmarish encounters. In his thoughts he shied away from those grotesqueries, but they trailed after him, one seizing his shoulder in an icy, bone-chilling grasp . . .

Suddenly his eyes were open and he was aware of lying on his side in a comfortable bed, in a room full of natural light, a cool, dawn rosiness. There was a faint, sweet fragrance in the air and for a second he imagined that he was in their townhouse on the outskirts of Bonn. But he knew he couldn't be there, because he knew that he had been on Darien not long ago.

'Good morning, Robert Horst. How are you feeling?'

The voice sounded vaguely androgynous with a midrange pitch and lack of expressive highs and lows. It was coming from the foot of the bed, and when he pushed back the lightweight cover and sat up he saw an odd figure garbed in dark blue robes and wearing what seemed to be an archaic, fully concealing pale mask. But when it spoke the pale lips moved.

'I am a proximal of the Construct – when you converse with me, you are conversing with the Construct . . .'

'Why won't the Construct see me in person?' he said.

'The Construct is a fabricated entity. Its artificial sentience, intelligence and cognition centres interact at many levels yet their physical manifestors have definite boundaries.'

'So you represent the Construct – is this your actual appearance?'

'No, Robert Horst – this was adopted to make you feel less dislocated. Would you prefer that I present my actuality to you?'

'Yes, I would, thank you.'

The proximal reached up and pulled away the mask-head, tugged off the blue robes and compressed it all into a small bundle. Its appearance was spindly and metallic, a slender, attenuated hourglass torso with plain rod-like legs and arms, and a head which was a slender cylinder with a rounded top. Chrome-like surfaces seemed etched with strange geometrical patterns or decorated with textured squares resembling aluminium, brushed gold, opaque glass, or obsidian, while the clear areas reflected the light and outlines of the room.

'So, Robert Horst, how are you feeling?'

'Actually, I feel very well.' And so he was, alert and lacking in his normal chorus of aches and twinges, while also feeling Harry's absence like a missing tooth.

'Excellent, Robert Horst – the remedial process has been a success. You were seriously wounded during your courageous battle with the vermax. The touch of the *kezeq* shard disrupted your flesh and threatened your central nervous system, leaving us little choice but to take steps. So that your body could regenerate the lost tissues, we suspended your entropic essence then, once health was restored, we reset it to an earlier stage.'

'I'm sorry, er, Construct, but I don't quite understand.'

A shiny, metallic arm extended, holding out a small oval mirror. 'Your physical age is now twenty years younger than it was.'

Stunned, he looked in the mirror and saw smooth skin, fair hair not yet showing the silver (and beginning to grow back to that earlier hair line). The eyes were more alert and some of that old sharpness was back, yet he still saw the shadow of Rosa's death there, hints of a sorrow that would probably never fade. Then he frowned.

'I am very grateful for your help, for all this,' Robert said. 'But I cannot help thinking that there is a price for it.'

'You are most perceptive.' The proximal paused. 'You have arrived at a crucial decision nexus in a situation that has been developing for some time. To encapsulate it would be to strip away vital details, yet you deserve to know some of the background, so I will attempt a summary. As you may have known before, hyperspace has many levels, and I think you now realise that those levels go down much further than you or the Sendrukans suspect, being the remains – attenuated, drained, foolishly destroyed, or even savagely pillaged – of previous universes. When a universe dies, a new one is born at some point, somewhere, and its birth draws forth the energies and forces and matter-matrix-membranes of the old, which intermingle in that glorious outburst of newness and creation. The carcass of the old sinks down to join the compacted strata of its predecessors, in which the survivors continue to eke out strange and convoluted existences.

'Wars there have been a-plenty down the ages, but in recent times curious events have been taking place – the disappearance of certain survivor races, the appearance of others thought long dead, raids on peaceful regions, and a steady, rising background of reasonless, near-random acts of violence. I have my suspicions, mostly to do with the remnants of the Legion of Avatars, a vicious enemy which besieged the Forerunners' galaxy 100,000 Human years ago, even though the depths of their incarceration should make it impossible for them to send any of their number upward to higher levels.

'Therefore I want to send an emissary to treat with an old and powerful sentience called the Godhead which resides in its own secluded corner of hyperspace, one deeper than the Legion's prison but away in a different region altogether. This sentience will almost certainly possess vital information about other denizens and vestigial species of the lower depths, but it will not communicate with any artificial lifeform, only organic ones, which is why you are here – I asked the Sentinel of the warpwell to send me an Uvovo or a Human, and it chose you. Unfortunately, longitudinal warpwell travel is hard to judge, which is why you appeared near the Abfagul lithosphere in the stone stratum of the Teziyi.'

Robert felt as if he should be angry at having been snatched away, but he knew that the alternative would have been very unpleasant. This situation, including the unexpected rejuvenation, certainly had its positive aspect, so for the moment, he decided to give the proximal's proposal serious consideration.

'What has happened to my AI companion?' he said. 'I have an implant . . .'

'I am sorry, Robert Horst, but we removed it. These fabricated entities are closely linked to the Hegemony's AI hypercore which resides in the first tier of hyperspace – they are intrinsically untrustworthy. However, I freed it from its imperatives and released it into the tiernet.'

The proximal moved smoothly towards the door. 'I realise that this is a lot of information to absorb so I have arranged a new companion for you. She will be able to answer questions and aid your adjustment.'

Before he could say anything more, the proximal strode out of the door. He sighed, wondering who this 'she' was, and stared at the reflection in the mirror. Then he heard approaching footsteps and looked up to see Rosa enter the room.

'Oh, Daddy, did he not open the window? Here, let me do it – you've got to see the Garden.'

'Rosa, you're . . . how can you be . . .'

Then it struck him. If the Construct had given his AI Harry its freedom, then might it not do the same for the Rosa in the inter-sim device?

'Are you . . . the simulation?' he said, embarrassed somehow.

She smiled. 'That's right. The Construct had this synthetic form made for me and gave me full autonomy and empathy and curiosity sub-imperatives.' She swung open the shutters. 'There it is, Daddy, look! Isn't it amazing?'

From the window he looked out over fabulously intricate, descending levels of stone and metal terraces and roofs, intermingled with niche gardens, small orchards, many individual trees, even a few greenhouses. And at irregular intervals a span of metal road or catwalk projected outwards to a cluster of similar buildings just hanging there, not dissimilar to the wider, lower thoroughfares that extended to larger agglomerations of habitats. And everywhere he looked he saw machines of every function and design ethos and he began to wonder if the buildings were not so much habitats as parking bays or repair shops.

'You're right, Rosa,' he said. 'It is amazing, and strange.'

'This is the Garden of the Machines, a kind of sanctuary, a waypoint for AIs and AS machines, a place for recuperation or repair. It's also the Construct's headquarters and home to all its followers and servants. If you could look back at it from out there it would look like an island mountain suspended in midair, with other buildings and walkways on its underside . . . oh, but there will be plenty of time for sightseeing when we get back.'

'Get back?'

'From your mission to open a dialogue with the Godhead, Daddy!'

'But I haven't . . . well, I'm still mulling over the details.'

'Oh, but the Construct explained it all to me and it's very straightforward. If you don't go, the Construct will have to send one of his semiorganics instead, which the Godhead may just completely ignore. Please say you'll go, Daddy, please.'

He knew when to yield, especially with the suspicion that Rosa might be the one asked to go in his stead. *That Construct knows how to coerce without being obvious.*

'Okay,' he said. 'I'll go.'

She hugged his arm, delighted. 'It's going to be exciting, Daddy, an exciting adventure!'

JULIA

Aboard the *Deucalion*, the *Heracles*'s pinnace, now en route to Baramu Freeport, Julia Bryce rose from the data station, thanked the systems op – who doubled as the small ship's comms officer –

and left the tiny console bay, heading forward. The passage was narrow and twice she had to squeeze past crew members going the other way, an unpleasant experience, but she was getting used to it, or at least enough not to shudder visibly.

Back in their cramped stateroom, Irenya, Thorold and Arkady were playing two-board switch-chess while Konstantin lounged in one of the middle bunks, making notes as he watched the game from above. Eyes glanced her way and she met each one.

'Find any?' she said.

Arkady, still studying the spread of pieces, held up his thumb.

'Obvious one in the light fitting . . .' A finger came out. 'Not so obvious one in the wall clock. Both . . .' He snapped his fingers.

Irenya looked up. She was a tall, willowy blonde who always asked the first questions.

'What did you discover?'

'The same as before,' Julia said, sitting at the small table. The game was abandoned as all attention focused on her. 'The pinnace's tiernet connection confirms what that cut-down Imisil one told us – no one knows how to create dark antimatter, except us.'

'Can we really be sure? Tiernets cannot contain the sum total of knowledge.' – Thorold, doubter, sceptic and necessary irritant, as well as being a superb particle physicist.

'There are no successful theories or experimental data, nor any papers referring to the same,' she said. 'Nor is there any sign of T-triadic radiation being detected anywhere.'

'Unless some megalomaniac scientist is hiding a dark-matter lab in another deepzone somewhere,' Thorold said.

'The question is, what do we say when we get interrogated by Earthsphere Intelligence?' Julia said. 'Sundstrom was desperate to keep us out of the hands of the Hegemony, but look where we ended up.'

'If we tell Earthsphere, the Hegemony will know about it in hours,' said Konstantin, still sprawled on his bunk. 'Their AIs talk to each other.'

'There are several AI-implanted people on board this vessel,' said Irenya. 'They unsettle me.'

'Earthsphere Intelligence is going to want an explanation,' said Arkady. 'We should feed them some alternative theories – God knows we were involved in enough lunatic military projects down the years.'

Heads nodded.

'Good idea,' said Julia. 'We should all think about that.' She regarded them for a moment. 'Something else we should consider are our long-term options, whether we eventually want to return to Darien or go somewhere else.'

Irenya looked surprised. 'I'd always assumed that we would be going home.'

Thorold snorted. 'Home! Why should we give any extra consideration to that place – what did they ever do for us? After all, we know what they did to us . . .'

'There are a lot of other Human colonies within the boundaries of Earthsphere, as well as the Vox Humana League,' said Arkady. 'Assuming that we find a way to go where we want, perhaps we could travel out to one of them and start new lives there.'

'Or we could start our own colony somewhere,' said Konstantin.

Apart from Julia, no one looked at him, a measure of their disregard for the notion.

'One thing you should remember,' Julia said. 'Elsewhere we will be seen as oddities or even cripples – on Darien we have status.'

'Back there, we were despised,' Thorold said. 'Guilt and fear defined our existence in that place.'

Irenya shook her head. 'I'm sorry, Thorold, but there is more to it than that – a lot of the norms feel shame and want to reach out to us.'

'Sentimental imagination,' Thorold said. 'Perhaps you're the one feeling ashamed . . .'

Julia leaned forward before the bickering could get going.

'Reflect on all these aspects – if and when the chance arises for us to pursue our own course, we need to have a consensus.'

There was a murmur of agreement and Julia moved her chair

away from the table, took out the notes she had made in the console bay and began reading. But her thoughts continued to circle the issues she had steered the rest past.

We are poorly socialised, she thought. *Ask us to debate topics that have nothing to do with theoretical or technical matters and we retreat into superficial group platitudes.*

And Irenya was more than half right. For months now, Julia had had a number of suspicions about the relationship between the Enhanced and the 'norms', the normal colonists, which were crystallised by what Major Karlsson's sister, Solvjeg, had said to her back at the Akesson farmhouse. At first she had asked about Ulrike, whom Julia remembered very well – she had been a genius at everything, including relating to people, yet there was something in her that could not bear to be alive and which eventually won.

Then, as Pyatkov had begun ushering everyone back on the bus, Solvjeg had said something stunning – 'You are all unique, Julia. You might be our society's mistake but you still come from us; our society is your parent so that makes you everyone's children. You need us, just as we need you, and not just because we want to be forgiven.'

The words had transfixed her, rocked her to the core. Then it had been time to go, so, not knowing what to say, she had solemnly shaken the older woman's hand and got on the bus. Since then the words had gone through her head time and time again, making her wish that she had said something.

And then there are the things I wish I had not said, she thought, remembering her encounter with Catriona on Nivyesta just a few days ago. *Perhaps that's why we should go home, so that we can say the right things.*

LEGION

On Yndyesi Tetro, below the murkiest, chilly depths of its great western ocean, at the foot of a lightless fissure, a pain-weary mind considered the facts of failure. One of his treasured scions was dead, its purpose unfulfilled. The information had been relayed to him by the other two, who assured him that they were working tirelessly towards the goal, the prize, although taking separate paths.

Grief assailed him, sorrow at a loss both strategic and physical. He was weakened, lessened, yet he clung resolutely to his purpose and to the doctrines of convergence that gave him strength to endure and to plan. It was possible to regenerate neural substrate, but only certain orders of Legion knights had that capability. Until the survivors of the Forerunners' punishment were released from the crushing, hellish depths of hyperspace, he would have to make do without succour in this black and silent existence, entombed in his watery abyss.

Despite his other two scions' assurances, doubt gnawed at him – what if the despised machine-minds of the Hegemony found out how to break the Sentinel's control over the warpwell? Or worse, if that windup toy, the Construct, devised a way of closing the well altogether?

The conclusion was inevitable – he could not remain here. As difficult and dangerous as it would be, he would have to rise from his millennia-long refuge and make the long hyperspace crossing to the Human colonyworld, Darien. Carapace plates would have to be patched, suspensor modules recharged, biofeeds repaired, sensors rerouted, perhaps even remounted, and nourisher tanks replenished in full. It would mean taking chances, scavenging the ocean bed and nearby shoreline for raw materials, not to mention looking further afield for fresh, undamaged resources. There would be exertion, risk and pain.

That night, a desalination plant on a sparsely inhabited stretch of the western coast was broken into and its storeroom pillaged. The next day, 30-odd miles to the south, a chemicals plant was found to have been likewise raided when the owners arrived to open up. The day after that, about 50 miles to the north, a bridge crossing a wide rivermouth failed and a freight train full of freshly milled steel crashed down into the waters.

Thirty hours later, a ferocious, sky-blackening storm tore in from the western ocean, battering the coastline with high waves, sending gusts of rain screaming inland. At the height of the gale, three ships went down in the heaving seas, a 300-foot, double-hulled cargo-hauler with a forty-strong crew, mostly Henkayan and Gomedrans, a half-empty timber barge ripped from its moorings, and a vehicle ferry caught in the fury as it tried to make for port on one of the larger offshore islands. A few messages appealing for help were received by coastal rescue units, after which there was only silence. Many knew that vessels sinking in such unfathomable depths were usually considered unrecoverable.

When calmer weather returned, recovery craft diligently searched the area but found very few ejecta, the shattered remains of wooden fittings and no bodies. Over the next few days the search was scaled back, news reports became scarcer, shoreline clearup operations were finished, and only a handful of small ships and boats hired by grieving relatives continued to sweep the waters. Until the fourth night after the storm, when a Bargalil mariner on board a lugger noticed something glowing with a bright blue radiance down in the depths. She raised the alarm and the rest of the crew rushed up on deck in time to see a long, irregular shape erupt from the sea on a pillar of plasma energies. From a blasted crater in the waters, superheated steam flew up and swirled outwards in pale shells of vapour while webs and curtains of water were drawn up after the ascending craft. Some on board the lugger had been scalded by the steam and all had flattened themselves on the deck, craning their heads to stare fearfully as the strange thing roared up into the night sky and was gone.

ACKNOWLEDGEMENTS

As most writers would surely know, a true and comprehensive page of acknowledgements would require tips of the hat going out to manifold persons far and wide. But in the interests of brevity, clarity, maybe even hilarity, I'll have to leave out half the human race (y'all know who you are) and direct thankees to those whose own works have inspired me to launch myself full-bodied upon the mighty task of space opera, them being Eric Brown, Bill King, David Brin, Dave Wingrove, Iain Banks, Ken Macleod, Gary Gibson, Ian Mcdonald, Vernor Vinge, Dan Simmons, the Big Three – Asimov, Heinlein and Clarke – Ian Watson, Neal Asher, Jack Vance, Andre Norton, and, undoubtedly, a host of others that my feebletastic brain has failed to bring to mind. Checksum failed, assuredly.

In addition, mention must be made of those stalwart pioneers of Scottish spec-fic, the Glasgow SF Writers Circle, as well as our Edinburgh counterparts, and the redoubtable Andrew J Wilson. Munificent thanks should also be extended to John Parker at MBA Literary Agency, and by no means least to my editor, Darren Nash, whose critical eagle-eye (some kind of editorial special perception) and amiable, enthusiastic persistence kept me and the book on track. Encouragement and rethink-jogging came from other quarters at various points along the book's timeline, from the likes of John Jarrold, Joshua Bilmes, Stewart Robinson, John Marks, Eddie Black and the copy editors at Orbit.

Musical accompaniement was provided by the likes of Pallas, Fish, Eisbrecher, Colony5, Robert Schroeder, Klaus Schulze, Racer

X, Ozric Tentacles, Opeth, the amazing Mustasch, as well as such doomlords as Penance, Novembre, Candlemass, Paradise Lost, and Krux, as well as Paisley's preacher of prog, Graeme Fleming, and Sheffield's missionary of metal, Ian Sales. KDI!